Amelia's Tears

Sara Powter

Bible Quotes from King James Version

ISBN: 9780645110739
Paperback

Pacific Wanderland Publications
ABN 99 768 734 831

Kincumber NSW 2251

saragpowter@gmail.com
sarapowter.com.au

1st edition 2022 printed by Kindle, an Amazon Company;

Australian Historical Novels
(All stand-alone books)

A First Fleet Story (1788)
Gentle Annie Soames *(2024)*

The Hunter to Macquarie Collection (1795-1822)
When Upon Life's Billows (2025)
Saddler's Song (2025)
Tuppence to Pass (2025)
His Majesty's Pageboy (2025
Far From the Whispering Sheoaks (2026)
Bound Down in Iron Chains (2026)

Unlikely Convict Ladies Trilogy (1792-1840s)
Dancing to her Own Tune
(co-authored by Sheila Hunter & Sara Powter)
Amelia's Tears
A Lady in Irons

The Lockleys of Parramatta (1800-1900)
Hands Upon the Anvil
Out Where the Brolgas Dance
Diamonds in the Dirt
The Earl's Shadow
Once a Jolly Swagman
Jonty's Journey

The Convict Birthstain Collection (1830s-1840s)
No More, My Love
The Vine Weaver
Scotch at The Rocks
Waiting at the Sliprails
Convict Shadows of the Past
In Defence of Her Honour
I Can't Stop Tomorrow *(2024)*
Madeline's Boy *(2024)*
Jam or Marmalade for Tea *(2025)*

Shelia Hunter's
Australian Colonial Trilogy (1840s-1850s)
Mattie
Ricky
The Heather to the Hawkesbury

Acknowledgement of Country:

In the spirit of reconciliation, I acknowledge the Traditional Custodians of country throughout Australia and their connections to land, sea and community. We pay our respect to their Elders, past and present and extend that respect to all Aboriginal and Torres Strait Islander peoples today.

Dedication
In Memory of
our female convicts who spent months in the
Parramatta Female Gaols
Thank You.

Sarah Watkins, who was assigned and had a child to her 'owner'
Mary **'Amelia'** Harlow was baptised on board the *Wanstead* in 1814
Catherine Lattimore, nee Hines, arrived with Amelia on the *Wanstead* in 1814
and
Susanna Nairn (Riley) had a child en route, 2nd fleet 1792

Mary Amelia and Catherine
were transported on the Wanstead 1814 and kept in the
Parramatta Female Gaol.

The new Female Factory opened in Parramatta on 1st Feb 1821.

May your stories never be forgotten,
Life was tough, but for them and others like them,
our lives would be vastly different.

To my wonderful husband Steve, the discovery that our gg grandmothers, Amelia and Catherine, went through much of this together was truly amazing. They were assigned to men two doors apart in Windsor.

And thanks to Roby Aiken, my grammar angel
and to Dasha Brandt, who did the final check-through.

Character list at the back.

Table of Contents

The grammar and language in this book are
Australian English spelling.

Chapter 1   Torment and Anguish
1827

The clanging of the big door slamming shut for the night made Amelia jump. She sat on the side of the sleeping pallet, rocking with her eyes closed. A tear fell unnoticed onto the thin blanket covering her knees. It was her last night in the Female Factory in Parramatta.

Memories of the past year came flooding back. These made more tears slide unchecked down her cheeks. It was as though she was back in London. She had thought the gaol in London was terrible enough until she was sent to the Hulks in the Thames River. The memory of the smell was enough to make her dry retch.

She had known back then that they would have to spend the following months, if not years, below decks and locked up with the filthy creatures she had walked alongside. With her eyes closed, she imagined that she could still hear the sound of the tramping feet and the jangle of chains as the women were marched down from the gaol to the river. The memory of the sheer and absolute horror of what had befallen her overwhelmed her as she finally viewed their temporary destination.

Each woman had their eyes focused on the stinking, rotting ship hulk that was moored in the middle of the river.

The stench could be detected from the riverbank.

She remembered thinking that getting out to the ship would be difficult; she saw a row of longboats tied up to the rickety jetty and realised that this would be the means of entry to hell. A dead cat floated by, rats swimming to get to its swollen, distorted carcass.

The women in chains jangled along the river's edge, and the soldiers escorting them herded them roughly, shoving them down the narrow walkway.

Two by two, they had shuffled carefully.

None could swim, so they had no wish to fall into the fetid water. Each had carried the chains that were attached to both their feet and wrists. All were manacled.

Whoever thought she would be arrested for such a petty thing? She'd had no idea how long she'd been in prison already. Months, a year? One night had been too long, and she'd been there for many, many nights. Her clothing was filthy; she had no money. She had missed the handout pack by a group of ladies. They had run out, and the others didn't like to share. She had nothing but what she wore. Now, this!

She thought back to the last day she saw her big brother. A sob caught her; she thought she saw a vision; even the sailors looked like him. No! Wait – it *was* him. The sailor on the dock was her brother, Jimmy. What was he doing there? How did he get the uniform? One day, she'd get to ask him. One day…

The line of thirty women had made it onto the jetty safely. Jimmy sidled up to her. Under the guise of berating her for something, he handed her a leather coin purse.

She pretended to trip and shoved it down her exposed cleavage. She checked that the strings were tucked in and not visible.

Jimmy had reached out to stabilise her and slipped a note into her hand. As it looked as though he was assisting her in regaining her balance, it went unnoticed.

"Are you all right, miss?" he asked.

She had nodded, knowing that she would not be allowed to speak. She turned her back on the other soldiers and mouthed "Thank you" to her brother.

He whispered back, "I love you. Don't give up. I'll find you."

She would lie in the dark on the wooden pallet. Tears were sliding down her cheeks at the memory of his words to her. She remembered she had shaken her head. "Too dangerous," she whispered so only he would hear.

"Trust me," he whispered back.

"No, don't try anything." She shook him off, knowing that if anything happened to her, he could be injured. "Just get me on the next ship."

Jimmy had an idea. He slid his arm along her shoulders and pretended to kiss her. He whispered that he cared and never to stop praying. Another soldier came up to her and growled at Jimmy for "fraternising with the whores".

"Leave off, gov. They are covered in lice. Or you'll get the crabs if you touch 'em that way."

While they were talking, she shoved the note down her front with the purse. Hopefully, she'd get a chance to read it later.

The soldier walked to the end of the jetty to start loading the first women on the longboats.

Jimmy slipped another thing into her hand; it was a small leather-bound parcel and obviously a book.

She swung around and looked at him. She knew from the size what it was. It joined the purse down her front. She grinned as he winked at her, her Bible.

Now, she was in Parramatta for her last night before the assignment. She had been here for some six months. They had frozen in the unheated rooms through the cold of the winter. She lay on the hard pallet and stared into the darkness. Her nose had become used to the stench of the unwashed bodies. She closed her eyes to sleep, but the memories kept flooding back.

She had sat in that ship's hulk for months. She could read her tiny Bible only at noon when a sliver of light entered the hatch and gave her some light. For most of the time, they sat in the gloom and existed as best as they could. They were locked below decks most of the time. The river rats were their constant companions. Some even caught them and ate them. The thought of that again made her dry retch with disgust.

Amelia had made friends with one woman who did not belittle her for reading.

Mary Adams wanted to read too, so in the dim light, the two women sat, and, letter by letter and word by word, Mary grasped the idea of reading. She was excited that there was at least one woman with whom she could talk.

Mary moved into the other half of Amelia's wooden bunk. It was near the back of the section of the ship and out of view of the soldiers. They often came to claim a woman for a bit of mild relief from their boredom.

Many were ready to volunteer their services for extra food rations, and the two friends were not worried by such demands. It had been winter when they were taken to the hulks.

As the days were now getting hot, it must be near summer.

One day, another ship came alongside and took the women on board.

"Welcome aboard the *Morley,* my dears." The well-dressed gentleman was serious. He watched the bedraggled line of women pass him by. His eyes kept glancing towards the shore.

The line of filthy women seemed endless.

The doctor spoke again, welcoming them with superficial enthusiasm. "I am Doctor Reid, and I shall be sailing with you."

The doctor kept up his banter as they boarded across the gangplank from the hulk to the ship. He changed the greetings as they walked past, but he was trying to raise the morale of such women was difficult.

Master Arthur Brown frowned at the cheerfulness of the surgeon. "Sheesh! Cheerful brute, isn't he?" He said to his first mate.

The first mate nodded in reply.

The pair moved some distance away.

The doctor gave a sign of relief. His words had been for show.

Doctor Reid again looked to the riverbank. He saw what he was writing for. He pulled Amelia and Mary aside. "Hey, you two, you're quite clean; you can help me with the medicals. I don't suppose either of you can read?"

Amelia very politely admitted that both did. "Sir, we both read well."

The Doctor grinned. "Good, assist me; I need you clean too. So you'll both have to wash." The doctor wondered what their reaction would be; he had to get them aside somehow, and this was the easiest way to do so. He was pleasantly surprised by the speaker's well-modulated answer.

Amelia was delighted. "Sir, we would both relish the opportunity to clean ourselves up properly. We have not had the required facilities to do so in our previous accommodation." Her cultured accent was vastly out of place in the squalid conditions they were in.

Yes, he had the correct girl, phew. The doctor raised his bushy eyebrows. "You, girl, name and where are you from?"

"Amelia, um, West, from the South," she said with some hesitation.

"An' I be Mary Adams, sir," Mary added in her cockney accent.

"West, eh? Are you from Kent? Sound like it," the doctor asked.

"Yes, sir," Amelia replied gently.

"Good!" He saw Master Arthur Brown walk away and leave them chatting.

"Miss West, Jimmy sent me," he whispered, "Trust me."

He saw her eyes fly open, and he nodded.

She gasped.

He motioned for her to look at the foreshore. "Look."

Jimmy was there waving madly. No longer in the uniform, he had come to say farewell. She turned to surreptitiously wave back.

Jimmy blew her a kiss and put his hands together to tell her to keep praying.

She could only nod in reply and lift a hand in farewell while it was hidden by her body.

The doctor turned to the Captain, who was now on the deck above him, "Captain Brown, I'll claim these two as assistants. They seem to be the cleanest of them all."

The doctor had his back to Amelia but heard her gasp.

"I'll have them in that tiny room next to my cabin. Chain them together if you must, but I don't wish to waste time scrubbing them every time I need their help."

Master Mariner Arthur Brown scowled but nodded. "Fine, but they'll be your responsibility. Is that clear?"

Both the doctor and Amelia sighed with relief. Once all the rest of the women were on board, some one-hundred and twenty of them, the doctor escorted the two chosen women to the tiny cabin. He ushered them inside and closed the door.

"Miss West, Miss Adams, we must keep our voices down. Your brother Jimmy has asked me to assist you if I can. I'll need you both to play along, but it will keep you both safe. Is this understood? You'll earn your keep and really will assist me. The harder you work, the better the privileges I'll be able to get you."

Both girls nodded, Amelia weeping with relief.

"Anything, sir; thank you so much," she said quietly.

"Right, the first thing is we have to do a medical check of everyone on board. Miss West, you can be a scribe and Miss Adams, you will be assistant and hand me things. Can you do that?"

Again, both girls nodded.

He left them to wash and change into the nondescript calico gown on the bunks. So, the five-month trip started. Their cabin was breathless but clean; even the rats didn't enter the stuffy room. The doctor kept them all clean and healthy. The crew made themselves free with the women below decks. As his assistants, they were protected from their attention. They often heard squeals of bawdy laughter coming from below decks. By the time they reached Sydney in September, nearly half the women were with child.

~

On arrival in Sydney, the doctor said his farewells to Amelia and said he'd pray for her. He had taken Amelia aside the day before they arrived and handed her £10 that Jimmy had given him for her. She thanked him, carefully placed it in her Bible, and tucked it down her bodice into her corset.

He stood sadly, watching the two women rejoin the others. They were all to be taken to the Female Factory in Parramatta. None had died on this trip, and he thanked the assistance of the two girls for this, for they showed the others that cleanliness brought reward.

Over the months on the Hulks, the coins in the purse had saved her from many, many situations. She still had six coins left. The £10 note she still had safely in her Bible. She'd sewn the remaining coins into the bodice of her gown and eked them out. The note Jimmy sent had been an assurance of his love and continued care for her, and the last parcel from him had been her tiny Bible. It had been small enough to stuff down her corset and sit flat on her ribs. The feel of it was comforting. The leather wrap had protected it all this time. She slept with it and took it with her everywhere.

She drew a deep breath, knowing that she must sleep, unaware of what tomorrow would bring. For tomorrow, they would be assigned farmed out to some person to work for the next five or so years. She prayed that someone would be kind to her. She had managed to find some water and wash, including her face. Oh, she wished to be clean again, like on the ship.

Sadly, she'd become used to the stench and filth of the others at the Factory.

Jimmy had said, "Trust him." She did, but for how long? He'd sent the doctor, but even he was long gone. She heard a warder coming in for a nightly liaison with some willing woman. She had managed to belay that final humiliation. There were others always more than willing to oblige them. Finally, she slept.

Chapter 2   Assignment to Hell

*T*he August day dawned with a biting chill in the air. They were woken at sunrise by a bell clanging outside. They each had to rise immediately and fold their single thin blanket. She'd not been able to have a full wash since her arrival, as the water was in very short supply. Washing was not something the others often did; a single bucket of water was provided for those who wished to attempt some form of ablution. Amelia dressed by pulling her outer drill gown over the shift she wore to sleep in. She tucked her precious items back down her bodice and went to wash the sleep out of her eyes. They had run out of dresses when she arrived, and she'd been allowed to keep her own gown. Her six remaining sovereigns were still safely sewn into the bodice of her gown. As she already had a petticoat and dress, the remaining garb of a mob cap, apron, and bonnet was given to her. All were calico. Her shoes were better than the ones offered, so she rejected those. Her lace-up half-boots were of much better quality than what even the matron wore. If they had not been so small, she was sure they would have been stolen from her months before. She was only allowed to wear a calico apron for work, as she was told that there were not enough to go around. Fear was useless. She could do nothing to change her situation, but she still had not given up hope or praying.

Breakfast was served; no waking to hot chocolate and triangles of toast and marmalade here. They were given a slice of stale hard bread and a bowl of lumpy, warm porridge. At least it was filling. The lady serving the food was Matron Findlay; she liked Amelia, so she was always given a big ladle full. She sat minding her own business and ate her meal. Mary often joined her. There would be enough stress later in the day for them to add to it now, so they sat quietly. Back in the dormitory, she said farewell to the expectant women who were staying. Mary followed her out the door to the waiting soldier. Each stood with their small personal bundles under their arms. Amelia and Mary were taken along with the other women into the yard, some thirty in all. They were released from their shackles and told to line up against the wall. The two girls stood holding hands and praying.

A soldier walked along the line and jabbed her in the stomach. "Head up, girl. Inspection time again; stop snivelling, woman. Today, you get out of here," he said to Mary.

Amelia met his eyes. They were brutal and non-sympathetic.

Mary was crying softly. She sniffed but managed to lift her head. Both knew that they would be parted today. They had been together for over eight months. Longer if you count the three months in gaol, but they had not been isolated there. They were now good friends. Mary could read fluently as they still found time to sit quietly and both pray and read. Others had initially sneered at them, but Amelia offered to teach them to read, too, and some took up her offer.

One guard had brought them a few slates and some chalk. She encouraged the women staying to keep practising once she'd gone.

A line of men again perused the women. Some looked familiar; they had come before. The first one passed and checked the teeth of each woman. She felt like she was a horse. Thankfully, he found what he was looking for before he reached her. The red-headed woman was dragged out of line and told to follow her new master.

Another fat man in what looked like a minister's robe walked along the line and asked each woman if they were already married and, if not, they would like to be.

She was surprised by the questions, "Are you married?" and the next, "Are you prepared to be married?" She answered "No" and "Yes" to both, not thinking of the consequences.

More men came, and each chose from the line-up. Standing behind her, Mary had been selected too, and she took Amelia's hand and gave it a squeeze; both were tearful. A fat, unkempt sloth ambled along the line of the women and stopped in front of her. She'd seen him before. She remembered his smell. His breath was so bad that she nearly passed out from the stench. His stinking body was obese, and his clothing reeked with body odour, urine, and vomit.

"No, please God, no," she prayed he'd not chosen her, but he had. She remembered him from a month before and was revolted then.

Horrified, he then grinned. His teeth were black and rotting, and his gums were red and bleeding, making his breath stink. Again, Amelia smelt him before he even made it to her. She watched as he spat out a stream of stinking black liquid; it was filthy chewing tobacco. The little fat minister asked her a question. She didn't hear him as she was so horrified at the man before her. He asked her again; she heard him, "Did you hear me?"

She hadn't, but answered "Yes," not knowing what she'd agreed to. She dry-retched with disgust; this filthy man owned her for the next five years.

She had no voice and no choice but to follow him. He grabbed her arm and dragged her after him to the table to fill in the paperwork. She signed her life away, quite literally. Not reading the paperwork, she just wrote "Amelia West," where the warder pointed. Amelia's owner was Cyrus Ephraim Black; she read that on one of the sheets she'd signed. Mary's was James McTavish, a red-headed Scotsman. The fat minister was sitting, signing papers and handing them to the new owners.

Amelia glanced at the man who'd taken Mary. At least he was clean. She prayed that she'd be happy. Each woman was questioned and paperwork completed; they hoped that they could see each other. The two women were told to follow their new masters. Both would be heading to the Castlereagh area. Hopefully, they would be close.

Cyrus loaded Amelia into a filled vehicle. He whipped up his gig and took off at a pace. James stood chatting to another farmer and left Mary sitting on his cart waiting for him. They waved to each other and wiped away tears.

They were some distance out of town when Cyrus pulled up and told her, "Come, wifey, you can get down and find a tree if you wish. Don't bother running, as the snakes will get you."

She walked to the back of a fallen tree and relieved herself. On return to the gig, Cyrus stood waiting. "Drop them, luv. You're mine, and I'll use you how I wish."

She looked puzzled. She had absolutely no idea of what he meant.

He grabbed her and threw her on the ground; she fought until he punched her hard; she was dizzy and dazed. Dragging off her drawers, he brutally raped her. No gentleness, and with no knowledge of what a man could do to a woman, she was horrified when she felt him enter her. She screamed. She continued to fight him ineffectually, making him enjoy it all the more. Having never been with a man, his action was excruciatingly painful. He pumped himself vigorously into her, then hauled himself off her and told her to get dressed. She made it to her hands and knees before she got violently ill.

"Leave off, wifey. Anyone would think you have never been wiv a bloke before," he said.

"I haven't," she whispered, wiping away the vomit with the back of her hand.

"Well, youse has now. I thought you was tight. Anyway, get used to it 'cos it'll happen often," he grinned evilly.

Somehow, she dragged herself up onto the gig seat, and they set off again. Every bounce on the unpadded seat was painful. She sat silently weeping.

"Leave orf, wifey," he said cruelly.

They stopped an hour or so later, and he produced a half-cob loaf of bread and a lump of cheese. He also had a stone flagon of beer. "Luncheon, girly, you'll be earning your keep, and that means you have to start looking after me, cooking me tucker and wot."

"I can't, sir; I don't know how to cook," she said.

"Wot 'cha mean ya carnt cook? How can youse be a female and carnt cook?" He looked stunned.

"Well, I can't, sir. I've never had to. We had a cook when I was young. I was a teacher and worked at a school. They cooked for us," she explained.

"Bloody hell! I choose me a woman who carnt bloody well cook. Well, you're gonna have ta learn, aren't cha?"

"Is there someone to teach me?" she asked gingerly.

"No, there bloody well isn't. Wot ya think I got me a woman for?" he said, exasperated. "I might see if I can swap you wiv someone. At least you're a good lay; the last one weren't much good."

She fell silent. The land around here was sparse scrubland. There were strange hopping furry animals and some gigantic long-legged birds that stood taller than a man. She was still in shock at what had already happened to her at the hands of this creep. To stay with him, she knew, would be soul-destroying, but she had no choice. He sat his hand on her leg and squeezed her thigh. She tried to pull away, but there was not enough room. By late afternoon, they could see the line of trees that signalled a river. They drove through a town named Penrith and turned right onto another narrow track.

"See that place there; that be ours," he pointed to a dilapidated shack.

"Oh," was all she could bring herself to say. It was horrible.

"That over there is McTavish's farm, and over there is Collett's. It's on the ford. But don't get no idea of running as there's not much across the river but snakes, bush, and blacks."

At least Mary would be close, she thought. They pulled into the driveway, and he told her to go inside. She took her small bundle and gingerly walked to the door. After his more than rough handling of her earlier, she knew she was bleeding. She could still feel the pain as she walked. Amelia opened the door carefully and saw a scantly furnished cabin with one single straw-stuffed mattress on the floor. There was a table and two chairs, a single old kettle-belly stove with one hob. She stood weeping at what she saw. How was she reduced to this? Surveying the interior, she realised there was a lamp. She went to light this but could not find a tinderbox, so she couldn't light either the lamp or the fire. She stood waiting for him to come in. She heard a noise behind her; it was him. She jumped.

"Who'd ya expect it ta be, luv, the Gov'nor? The tinder box is on the shelf there, and we'll need more straw for the mattress. That's not big enough for two, an' we be sharin'. As for that, I'll have you again now, for I've not had a woman for a long time, and you're a tasty morsel. Get yourself here."

She didn't move.

He grabbed her arm and dragged her to the mattress. She fought like a cat again; another violent punch to her face stopped her struggling. He gathered her to him, and with his foul-smelling mouth bearing down upon hers, she screamed again. He laughed and then silenced her with a kiss. His breath was nowhere near as bad as his taste; it was simply disgusting. Like rotting fish. "Cummon wifey, that's not a nice way to treat yer man."

She pulled away dry retching.

"Chuck up, and youse gotta clean it yourself," he cackled and threw her on the mattress and divested himself of his trousers. Lifting her skirts, he not very gently drew off her drawers and took his time degrading her by fingering her private parts; then, he violated her savagely again.

Sobbing silently, she kept her head turned, knowing now that it would be less painful to submit than fight. He was too strong for her to escape, and no one would come to her aid as he now owned her. She lay still until he finished pumping her full of his seed again. As he rolled off her, she pulled down her skirts, curled into a ball and wept. Was this her lot in life? To be used like a whore? How long must she endure this? How long until release? Five long years?

~

For the next three months, most mornings and evenings, he raped her. She could not call it anything other than that. For it was not consensual; it was taken violently, and she had no choice. She refused to submit and would always have to be forced to do so. If she stood her ground, he'd hit her, then throw her on the ground wherever they were and just take her. He refused to allow her privacy unless it was to use the privy. Then he told her she stank and to stay away from him. She so wished she could say the same to him. She knew that would not be advisable. She wept when she realised that he was right when Cyrus said he could take her when he wished. He did, everywhere, in the yard, by the road, even once while she'd been out milking the cow. He could not get his fill of her. It never got better, each time more degrading than the last. He'd say, "Wifie, drop 'em," or something equally crass each time. Once, she tried to say no, and again, he struck her; she only realised he'd again violated her when she awoke with her skirts over her head. He would knock her out; she almost even preferred him to do this. He enjoyed making her distressed, and almost suffocating her with her own skirts was one of his pleasures. It was even worse if he wished to take his time. For then, he'd touch her with his filthy hands, with a lamp sitting near him so he could see her intimate areas clearly. His touch was not gentle nor caring. This was usually when he was drunk, so he reeked with rum, too. His hands were not only filthy but rough and relentless. Thankfully, this didn't often happen; if he came in early from the fields and found her bathing and in a state of undress, she knew what would follow, "a tumble," as he now called it.

In the weeks they had been together, she'd not yet seen him wash either his hands or himself. He said it was a waste of water. If she objected to his touch, then he'd extend the abuse.

In the mornings, he'd wake and reach for her, use her, then tell her to feed him. She'd then rise to make their porridge. The daily chores of milking the cow, making morning porridge, and basic cooking became her daily grind. He'd shown her how to light the fire, even how to milk a cow, having never done that before. She watched him make the porridge the first morning and followed his example. She only burned it twice. Each time, she received a hard slap. Cyrus would get water from the river and split the wood, but everything else she had to do. He drank rum and beer and chewed tobacco, which he spat in a black stream where he wished, even indoors, which she then had to clean up. She found that it was this that made his teeth black.

In the evenings, he would peel off her clothing and then ravage her again. That's when he'd often get violent, as he'd been drinking heavily by then. If she didn't fight, he'd just roll off her and go to sleep. If she fought, she'd get punched in either the face or the stomach. She refused to ever fully undress when he was around as she knew what would happen. He took her at his pleasure over and over and over.

After two months, she realised she had not had her monthly flow. Horrified at her discovery, she stayed silent until she was sure of her condition. That came one morning; some weeks later, she woke and needed to exit the cabin quickly to be violently ill. She was still dressed in just her shift.

He followed her and saw her vomit. "You increasing?" he asked.

She nodded. "I think so."

"Well, wouldn't that slay ya?" He cackled wickedly. "Sure, it's mine?"

Again, she nodded. "I told you I'd not been with a man before you."

"Good! Can ya still work?" he asked with little sympathy in his voice for her illness or condition.

"Yes, I can for the moment, but I don't know how long for. I know nothing about babies," she replied morosely.

He heard the fear in her voice. "There's a lady out along the road called Mrs Walker; we'll go see her. She lost her hubby last year in a flash flood but got three kiddies herself, in the meantime, I want's ya. You look real nice in that thing; better out of it, though. Get it orf now."

She stood still, knowing that it would irritate him, but she would not strip naked outside, even knowing what he'd do to her. It may be November and not so cold, but she just wouldn't strip in public as the cabin was visible from the road.

He slapped her face, grabbed her arm and forced her to the ground; he took her on the grass outside the cabin, but at least he didn't strip her.

Disgusted and degraded after he'd finished, she went inside and made tea and porridge. The sweet black tea settled her stomach. She felt like death warmed up. She was sure his slap was still visible on her cheek.

"How far along are ya?" He asked when he came inside.

"Well, I've not had my monthly flow since I came to you, so I'd say three months."

He nodded. "Fine, we'll get along and see Mrs Walker and see what she says." With that, he walked outside again. She'd wash as soon as he left to work the fields. She sank to the floor and sobbed. Distraught that she had come to this.

At home, she knew that she'd be cast off from her family for being with child and not married. Not that she hadn't been abandoned already. As a convict, Jimmy alone had stood by her. Her parents had not even shown up at her trial. "Oh, Jimmy, I'm so afraid. God, you alone can help me now." She muttered to herself in a half prayer. If only someone else was there to listen. This was not her choice. None of this was. Mary may have been close, but Amelia wasn't allowed off the property to see her. All they could do was wave to each other from their doorways. No one visited them at the cabin, and Cyrus didn't encourage fraternising with passing travellers.

She was by herself. As she'd dressed that morning, for some reason, she had tucked her Bible down her bodice. She didn't know why, but she wanted it close. It gave her comfort. Her coins were still sewn into her bodice edging. She only had one dress, so she always had them on her. Her blanket and shawl were the only other possessions she had. He'd taken the blanket from her and put it on their bed.

Later that afternoon, he harnessed the roan horse and loaded her into the gig. He threw her shawl to her. Here, wifey, you'd better take this; it could get cold on the way back. An' hurry up, the hoss don't like waitin'."

They headed north along the road to Windsor to Mrs Walker's farm. She sat on the gig seat in the late spring air as they drove. She was numb with shock. Would it never end? He'd taken his pleasure with her again just after lunchtime. She received another slap on the other cheek, "Just to even things up." Her black eye from last week's punch had stopped hurting. It was still evident and yellowing around the edges, not that she knew what she looked like. His violation of her no longer physically hurt, but the shame she felt was simply awful: used, abused and demeaned. She had resigned herself to the years ahead, long, horrific years of physical degradations. Being regularly abused and degraded by the man's filthy, unwashed body. Now to be carrying his child. The thought of that alone made her dry-retch again. She asked to pause the gig while she vomited. Surprisingly, he did; she went and found a tree to lean upon and vomited again and again, tears of sadness falling as she did so.

He took the opportunity of the break and relieved himself as he held the reins. Something must have frightened the horse as it reared and must have caught Cyrus on the head with its hoof.

She had not seen it happen as she had been occupied but had heard the commotion. When she turned, Cyrus was lying on the road. The horse and gig were just taking off; she saw the wheel run over his throat. She went to him but, without even touching him, knew he was dead. His head was oozing from various orifices. Gore was dribbling onto the ground; flies were quickly buzzing around him. She stood and watched for a few moments.

She was now alone in the scrub with a dead body.

She moved some distance away, sank to the ground and wept. What more could go wrong? As she sat, she felt her Bible dig into her ribs. She sat with her hands resting one on her stomach and the other on her Bible. "God help me! I don't know what to do," she murmured, almost to herself.

Chapter 3   Death and Despair

She had no idea how long she sat beside his body. The shadows lengthened, but no one came near. She could hear the whinny of a horse and thought it would be their roan and gig returning. She looked up when she realised it was coming from the opposite direction. A man and woman were coming towards her in an uncovered dray. Horrified, she realised that on the back were children. Panicking, she thought, "They must not see this." So she raised herself to her feet and went to stand in front of Cyrus's body, so she cut off the sight of him from the children. She waved them down but motioned for them to stay back.

The driver pulled up about fifty yards from her and handed the reins to his woman. He jumped down and came to her.

When she moved aside slightly, he could see why she'd motioned for him to stay back. The sight he beheld was gruesome. The eyes protruded, and the head was unrecognisable as a human and was now covered in flies. The hoof print and the wheel's imprint on his throat were still clearly visible. His blackened teeth protruded. The view alone made her sick again.

"Hey, lassie, I'm Jack Turner. That's my missus, Martha, and our brood. We're heading out Windsor way for a drive. At least we were. Are you all right?" He offered her something that had been lacking for the past year: compassion.

She shook her head. Unable to trust her voice. The look of horror on her face needed no words.

He turned and beckoned Martha to him.

She heard the woman say, "Marc, come hold the horse. Children, turn your backs. Do not look."

A boy about eight or nine came to the head of the horses and held them.

The woman came to her and enfolded her in loving arms. Only then did Amelia sob, not with sadness, but with relief. A simple act of kindness from one human to another was her undoing. The woman, Martha, led her towards the dray.

Amelia felt ill again, but she was too weak to move far. She turned and once again vomited.

"Oh dearie, such an awful thing to happen to your man," she said kindly.

A flash of anger darted over her face. "He wasn't 'my man,' he was my owner, and he raped me, over and over again, and now I'm with child, and he's gone and… and…" Finally, it hit Amelia that he was dead. She stood sobbing and was again enfolded into the kindly woman's arms until she sobbed.

Martha waited. "You're assigned, dear? So were we, but we'll look after you."

Amelia met her eyes and saw more than compassion; she saw love, and even more, she saw trust. "You'll help me? Really? I have no idea what to do."

"We will, dear. We might even be able to get you assigned to us. How long do you have left?" Martha asked kindly.

"Um, something over four years; I was with him for only three months, three months of daily hell," Amelia said almost under her breath, but Martha heard her. Amelia felt like kicking his body.

They were still far enough away from the dray not to be heard by the children. She met Martha's eyes, "He raped me for the first time just out of Parramatta the hour he got me. He couldn't even wait until we got to the cabin. There was nothing gentle about him. I'd never been with a man before, and for the last three months, I was his chattel. He'd take his pleasure when he wished, and he wished often. Usually twice a day, sometimes more. Do not fear that I will grieve for him, for I won't. He was a sadist, a beast, and filthy too."

Martha nodded. She could see the remnants of a black eye, and the two slap marks from the morning and afternoon abuse were still red on both of her cheeks. Both ladies were now watching Jack cover the body with a canvas he'd taken from the dray. "We'll have to return to Emu Plains and send out the soldiers."

"Dear, do you have something here?" She touched Amelia's bodice.

"Yes, ma'am, my Bible, I carry it with me everywhere. I'm sorry, did it dig in?" Amelia spoke apologetically.

"Yes, dear, but does that mean you believe? I was hoping that it might be that. I know how precious they are. Does it mean that much to you?" Martha inquired.

"Oh yes, Martha, it's been my only source of comfort." She rested her hand on it as she spoke. "When things got really bad, and I couldn't even bring myself to read it, I'd just hold it. Even that brought me comfort." Her eyes misted as she spoke; she pursed her lips as if to hold back the tears.

"Come, dear. You're safe now. I think we shall get along well, for we both believe in God. Our faith is strong, too. I think we'll take you home, and I'll send Jack in to report the death. Ten minutes won't matter in the grand scheme of things. So up you get, lass." Martha assisted her onto the back with the small children. There was another boy and three little girls.

"Hello, I is Jenna, and I is nearly six, and that's Alex, 'n' he's nearly eight," she said, pointing to the quiet boy beside her. Then pointing to the lad holding the horses, "That's Marc, he's just nine, and this is Vicky, she's only free, and the baby is Cafhy 'n' she's nearly two. Maa has another one growing too." The bubbly little girl stood with her hands on her hips. "So, who's you?" she asked.

"I am Amelia," was all she could bring herself to say.

Jenna tipped her head sideways and looked long and deeply at her. Then gave her a beaming grin. "Well, I likes you. But youse looks like youse needs a hug. Cun, I gives you one? They is good ones."

Amelia put her arms out and was given a big two-armed hug from the little girl. Within moments, two more sets of arms were around her. Vicky and Cathy were also hugging her.

"I've had a bad day, girls. I needed that so much," Amelia said to the sweet children.

"Our Maa and Pa will look after youse. So youse stick wiv us. Okay?" Jenna said. She was obviously the spokesman of the tribe of adorable light brown-haired, honey-eyed children.

"Amelia, are you all right, dear? Don't let the children bother you," Martha said.

"No, Martha, they are a delight." She released a huge sigh. "They are adorable." For the first time in a long, long time, she gave a smile. "Thank you, Martha, you too, Mister Jack."

Jack had now turned the dray and was heading back to Emu Plains.

They crossed the ford to Emu Plains at Birds Eye Corner ten minutes later. "Amelia, I'll drop off Martha and the children before we double back to the prison. Sorry, but you will have to come with me. There are no other officials around. They are really only just up the road from us, so we won't take long. I'll tell them you'll stay with us until you get yourself sorted."

Amelia nodded, barely believing the kindness this couple had shown her. "Thank you, Mister Turner."

"None of this 'Mr Turner' stuff, I'm just Jack. Never you mind, lass," he said. He pulled up the dray in front of a nearly completed building. Martha and the boys hopped off. Each turned around and lifted off a small girl.

"Smile, Milla; we'll get our bed ready for tonight," Jenna said as she waved them farewell. "But you're gonna have to wash." She smiled innocently at the backhanded compliment.

Amelia gasped as "Milla" was the pet name her brother Jimmy called her. Amelia and Jack trundled back down the road and over to the Prison Farm.

An hour later, Amelia had been released into Turner's custody. A team of soldiers were dispatched to collect Cyrus's body, a messenger was sent to Parramatta to the barracks, and a rider had also been sent along Windsor Road to see if he could find the horse and gig. All there was to do was return to the inn and wait.

Jack knew that one more thing needed to be done: write to Major Edward Grace personally. Only then could he feel he could relax. The mail coach was due through in an hour. He'd pen a letter, tell Major Edward the story, and send it in.

On return to the inn, Amelia was met with a warm welcome.

"She's ours, for the time being, Martha dear. We'll see what the major says, but I'm sure he'll listen to me," Jack said breezily.

Over nine years before, Jack and his friend Charles had reported a proposed mutiny on the convict ship out. Major Edward Grace had arranged Tickets of Leave for both men on their arrival as a thanks. Jack knew that he would understand once Amelia's story was fully explained. He and Marc put the dray away, and Marc led the horse away into the stables. Jack went inside and wrote a long letter to the major.

Martha welcomed them warmly. "Come inside, luv. Do you mind having to share with the little girls? If you do mind, then there's always a spot on the floor in front of the fireplace."

"Oh, Martha, really, I can stay here?" she asked very tearfully.

"Yes, dear, at least until we hear from Major Grace. Jack is writing him a letter now. We should hear back by this time tomorrow. Thankfully, it's a full moon, so the mail coach will drive through the night. They stop in here for a horse change; then they are off again. He'll appear in a bit," Martha explained. "Now, lovey, would you like to help in the kitchen or look after the children."

"Oh Martha, the children, please. I'm a teacher, and I miss children so much," Amelia begged, then added with a smile, "Trust me. You don't want me in the kitchen; I've learned I can even burn porridge." She gave a wry smile. "At least I hope you won't punch me in the face if I do."

Martha swallowed, shocked at the blandness in her voice. The poor girl was crushed. "Then the children it is. We all eat together, but Alex and Jenna will tell you what needs to be done. Marcus is doing the outside chores tonight. They need to set the table and also wash up the children. Jenna, you help Amelia."

"Yes, Maa. Milla, you come wiv me. The pump is out here, and it's too big for me to pump. I can hold the jug to prime it, but you can pump."

Amelia took the hands of the two littlest girls and went through the kitchen to the outdoor pump. The joyful giggles of the five children were a delight. She'd not heard the joyous laughs of children for nearly three years, possibly longer. She had been a teacher at an exclusive ladies' school in Kent. She loved teaching the girls the grooming and deportment they each would need for their future lives as Peeresses of the Realm. There she was, Miss Westaweller, and the daughter of the Headmistress. Her parents had started the school in an unused wing of the family Manor house on their Kent Estate at Aylesford. At twenty, her mother had allowed her to teach some of the younger girls. That was nearly five years ago. All this had occurred before an incident with a duke's daughter. The child had stolen some items; Amelia had confiscated them, intending to return them to the rightful owner later. She shook off the memories. One item had disappeared: a gold bracelet.

Amelia watched as Jenna picked up a jug of water and held it under the pump's nozzle. "Now youse pump six times, and that's called 'priming'. Once you do this, then the water comes out good."

Amelia pumped the handle, and sure enough, by the fifth pump, she could feel resistance. On the sixth pump, water gushed out of the nozzle. Amelia was amazed. In Kent, she only had to ring a bell, and a maid brought in water. At the cottage, Cyrus collected it from the river, storing it in barrels. She would try not to think of him again. She may be carrying his child, but never would he be part of her life again. She knew the life in front of her would be challenging, but she'd cope. She had to.

The little girls made wash-up time great fun. By the time they were finished and the table set, dinner was nearly ready.

She sadly had nothing she could change into, and she dearly would have loved to have a complete wash. She had, however, managed to wash her face and hands thoroughly. Martha saw her eyeing off the children's hip bath.

"Amelia, can you come here, please, dear?" Martha ushered the children inside and set them preparing for dinner.

Amelia stayed with Martha in the kitchen. "Yes, Martha, can I assist with anything?"

"Yes, dear, I have a favour to ask. I know you have nothing other than what you stand up in, and I was wondering if you would be happy to borrow an old gown of mine while you wash your own. If you were anything like I was, I could never scrub myself clean enough. Especially after, well ... you know." She met Amelia's eyes and saw both shock and sympathy. "I, too, had a horrible time on the ship out. Thankfully, I never conceived a child. But I was so skinny back then I wasn't regular. I rarely had my menses. I was only eighteen when I was sent out, and well, I am thankful it never happened." She paused and looked at Amelia. "I took some food for my family, who were starving." She shivered. "I saw other girls abominably used and know what you went through. I think a nice warm bath and clean clothes would do you wonders. What do you think?"

Amelia looked at the lovely lady in front of her with a lump in her throat. Two tears escaped the confines of her eyes. "You too? But ... ?" Amelia looked towards Jack in the backyard.

"We both know how most women are treated in the hulks. I was no different. I went to Mrs Walker for the first few months, then went to Camden and met my Jack. So, Amelia, I know. Talk to me if you wish." Martha was so caring. She knew what it was like, and it hurt like hell. "I had a friend I opened up to."

"Thank you, Martha. I would love to scrub myself clean. I wish I could scrub this away too," holding her stomach. "But this child is innocent. I just don't know how I will cope. Will they send me back to the Factory?"

"Over my dead body, lass! The major will see you, right. Trust me. There will have to be an enquiry, but we'll stand with you."

Amelia was astounded that Martha was so sure that this elusive major would be able to sort things out that she almost began to feel confident.

"I'll put on a big pot of water, and you can have a big bath in the cellar. It's cool down there, but it's private. It's where I have mine. There is a big hip bath there, too. Jack bought it for me."

"Oh, could I? Really?" Amelia cooed with delight.

"Yes, really, and as to the child, if you stay with us, we're due about the same time, I'm guessing. Are you over the sickness yet?" Martha asked.

"No, I hid it from him for over two months but couldn't this morning. As soon as I threw up, he realised why. So, he only found out today. We were heading to see a lady named Mrs Walker along Windsor Road. He said she'd know what to do and give us some advice. We never got there," Amelia said in a matter-of-fact tone. Her voice was devoid of emotion.

"Well, at least he was on the right track. Mrs Walker is a wonder with those sorts of things. She had three of her own children, and she's an excellent midwife." Martha chattered on while she finished preparing their evening meal. "Interested in cooking?"

"Um, I have no idea. It's food, and I eat it. I've never really taken much note of how to prepare it. I've never had to before, Cyrus. Even then, was the same thing every night: salted beef and dried beans. I never ever want to see them or eat them again. So as to learning to cook them," she smiled, "no thanks."

"How about kangaroo tail stew? It's what we have tonight." Martha grinned at her.

"Fresh meat? What does it taste like? I've not had fresh meat for years, not since home," Amelia said in awe.

"It's a cross between beef and venison. Rich and lean. You can't overeat, or it will upset your stomach, but in a stew, it's fine."

Amelia met her eyes. "Real meat. Oh yes, please!" She met Martha's smile with a smile.

"Careful, dear, because the smell can turn your stomach. Any cooking meat can do that. Or even seeing soft eggs," Martha laughed.

"Well, I wouldn't know – I haven't had either." Amelia smiled, then burst into tears.

Moments later, she was gathered in Martha's arms. Sobbing with relief, she sank to the kindly shoulder of the lady. She felt the small arms of a child wrap around her skirt. Jenna had heard her crying and come to offer her comfort, too. Surprisingly, this helped. Amelia dropped an arm and stroked the child's hair. "Sorry, Martha, I'm somewhat of a blubber pot at the moment," Amelia apologised.

"That's the bubba, dear. Your emotions will be all over the place. It should settle in the next few weeks." Martha got back to the cooking. "Now, this won't cook itself."

Amelia wiped her face and took Jenna's hand. "I find I'm in great need of a cubble, Milla," the little girl said. Amelia was led into the sitting room and pushed her into a shabby armchair. Jenna then climbed into her lap and gave Amelia a big cuddle. Within moments, Cathy and Vicky arrived. They joined her, climbing up on her lap and hugging her.

Amelia got the giggles. Who would have thought that her day would finish like this? She remembered her plea to God when Cyrus died. She had cried, "God help me", and He had. She was safe, and she'd found godly people to help her. Now, if this Major Grace was as good as they say, things would look survivable.

The evening passed with laughter; once the meal had been eaten and the kitchen cleaned up, Martha handed Amelia a large towel, and she was taken to the cellar. "Now, dear, no one will disturb you down here. You just take your time and wash yourself clean. There's even a cake of rose-scented soap. I made it myself. So you go and have a lovely scrub, dear." Martha turned to walk off when she remembered. "Oh, here's a nightgown for you for tonight; scrub your own gown, dear; leave it soaking, but hang your smalls and petticoat. I don't have spares of those. Tomorrow, we'll sort something else for you to wear."

As the evening was warm, Amelia sat in the hip bath and scrubbed herself long and hard. The cellar was cool; however, it had been so long since she had been able to do so that she was not inclined to hurry. Once her body was scrubbed, Amelia washed her hair with Martha's rose-scented soap. She placed her gown in the water to soak while she dried herself and put on the calico nightgown. The luxury of having clean apparel was a delight. She tidied up as best she could and decided to leave her gown to soak overnight as Martha suggested. Its filth and grime would not come out too easily, nor would the coins. She washed her drawers, camisole and petticoat and hung them outside as she left the cellar.

Martha met her as she emerged. "I sent Jack to bed. So it's just us. Here, let me dry your hair while we talk, dearie."

Amelia sat in front of the stove with the towel around her shoulders like a shawl, and Martha brushed her long, wet hair until it was dry. They talked, and each unburdened to the other. Martha had known the abuse of many violations as well. Her time in the hulks was long. "I came out in 1819, dear. Jack came the year later, and I was working where he was employed, and we got married very quickly. Considering the abuse I had on board, I fell with Marcus only two months after we married." Martha gently stroked her cheek. "You will get over this, Amelia. Life will go on, and you will survive. I spent six months healing with a lady down the river. Hetty Walker is now a friend. Come and talk to me when things get too tough to cope with." Both shed healing tears. Finally, Amelia's hair was dry enough for her to sleep. They parted with a hug. Amelia finally sank into the big bed, cuddled by three warm little sleeping bodies. "What will tomorrow bring?" She thought to herself, and for the first time in nearly a year, she relaxed.

The morning brought giggles and lots of noise. Five children were soon up and buzzing around the house. Each had their own chores to do in the mornings, but first, they raced out to the pump and washed their faces. The two boys had dressed and gone to milk the cow. Jenna, too, had dressed and ducked out to collect any eggs she could find. Vicky and Cathy tried to tidy the room, but being only nearly two and three didn't manage to do more than collect their sister's discarded nightgown and shove it under a pillow.

Amelia finished what they had started. She was wondering what to dress in when Martha arrived with a blue drill gown. "Here, dearie, this should suffice for today. I meant to ask you if there was anything you needed to collect from the cabin?"

Amelia turned to Martha and looked in fear. "No, thank you, Martha. I never wish to see that place again. I only had a blanket, and that was thin and from Government stores. If you wish to help yourself, feel free. I think I can claim it as mine. Cyrus had no friends or family here. Well, there is a brother he mentioned once, but he didn't know where he was. So anything left in the cottage will be fair game for thieves." Amelia slipped the clean drawers and petticoat on, then drew on the blue gown. "There's the horse and gig somewhere. I don't want it, but you may as well keep them. It's the one that ran over him, so I don't know where it is. If you want the cow, you can take her too. Oh, and there are chickens, but there is nothing else alive on the farm. Jack and the boys can go and collect them. Lamps and everything else is yours if you want it. Help yourself."

She had known these people for less than a day. Did she trust them enough to hand over all her money? Yes, she did. "Martha, I have a favour to ask. As I left London, my brother got some money for me. It's in my Bible. I was wondering if there is somewhere I can hide it? I also have some coins sewn into my gown."

"Yes, dear, there is. Being an inn, we have a secret hiding place for valuables. I can store them for you until you need them," Martha said. "As I hung your gown, I felt them, dear. But I'm glad you trust us enough to say this. You know you can… trust us, that is."

"I do, Martha." Amelia went to her Bible and drew out the £10 note from the back. "Martha, this is all I have to do me for the next four years or more, this and the six coins."

"Then we'd better take good care of it, hadn't we? Come, and I'll show you the secret spot." Amelia was so surprised that she was being trusted with this information.

"Well, dearie, if you can trust us with your worldly goods, then we should be able to trust you with our secret spot. What's more, you might need to get to it when we're not here."

Amelia followed her new friend into their tiny bedroom.

Martha flipped back the carpet and opened a trap door. Under the floorboards, she drew out a metal box, and she placed the precious money carefully inside. "I'll get Jack to pin a note on it saying it's yours, dearie. Just so everyone will know." The day passed in a flurry of activity. Amelia was so absorbed with all the children's activities that she forgot the turmoils of yesterday. For the first time in years, she laughed at the children's antics. She knew that there still had to be an inquest. The Captain at the Prison had told her that, but for the moment, she was safe. For the first time in a long time, she had carefree fun with children. The afternoon brought the mail coach back with a letter from Major Grace.

> *The Barracks*
> *Parramatta*
> *13th Nov 1829*

Jack Turner
Arms of Australia Inn
Emu Plains
Hello Jack,

Good to hear from you. Thank you for your prompt letter. I will sort out her situation from here. Sad that this situation has arisen. I have reported Cyrus Black's death. Please inform Miss West that the cabin contents are hers if she wishes, as he has no next of kin other than a brother, Erastus, but no one knows where he is. They both came as free settlers.

I have had notification from the Captain at Emu Plains and agree that Amelia West is to be transferred into your keeping until the Inquest at least. I shall see if I can make this permanent. She has four years and three months to serve.

You say that she was poorly used and is now with child. This is a sad situation and, unfortunately, one I have seen often. There is little I can do for her, but leave her in your keeping. She should go to the Factory by right, but she will be far better off with you two.

The Captain also reported that the roan horse and gig turned up along the Windsor Roadway. It had blood on its front foreleg and on the carriage wheel, so I do not see any problems with the Inquest. It will be a mere formality.

Yours in His service

Major Edward Grace

Jack smiled. He knew Major Grace believed in God, too. The capital H on "His" could easily be overlooked as a reference to the King. He envied his friend Charles Lockley as he'd got to stay close to him. Jack had taken a job down at Camden soon after his release, but he met Martha there, so in all, he would not complain.

The beautifully written letter was handed to Amelia to read. The nightmare was now virtually over. She could breathe again.

She met Jack's eyes with hers that were tear-filled and overflowing. "How can I ever say thank you? You have no idea what this means, sir."

"We do, Amelia. We know exactly what this means. It means that we can repay a kindness that was once shown to each of us. We call it paying it forward. We were not supposed to be on the road at that time, but Martha wished to go for a drive. We were heading out to see her friend Hetty Walker. She's never done that before, you know. She just said we needed to go 'now, dear', so we did."

Amelia listened to him in awe. "God sent you, Mr Jack. I know He did."

"Yes, lass, I believe He did. And as such, we know you are meant to be here. So you can now relax." Jack patted her hand.

The following days were bliss. Amelia luxuriated in the joyful family life; only this one was so much more loving than her own. When she told Martha that she could read and write and was a teacher, Martha asked her if she'd teach the children. Amelia readily agreed, and in a short space of time, the three older children could write their own names. And the two little ones could copy some of the letters.

Martha joined in as she rarely had a chance to practise.

Jack could already write beautifully, and he was keen for his family to be able to as well.

When anyone came to the inn, Amelia was introduced as their Governess. She smiled but did not contradict them.

The Inquest had been held, and she was exonerated. Her transfer to Jack Turner's care was formally filed, and she settled into life with the Turners.

One morning, about a month after she arrived, Amelia was working in the kitchen with Martha, and she'd been feeling funny butterflies in her stomach. She placed her hand on her tummy and said, "Oh Martha, I do think I have wind or some such. I'm feeling the most strange things."

"Like little flutters or butterflies? That be the babe moving," Martha smiled. "I've been feeling this one for nearly a month, so you're a bit behind me, I'm thinking," Martha explained a bit more to Amelia.

"You mean this is the baby?" Amelia said, stunned. "I'm still as flat as I was before."

"Well, you won't be for long. From next month, we'll have to get you into some loose-fitting gowns for the final months. I'll order some fabric from stores, and we can get down to teaching the girls to sew and making some more clothes for you. Now you go write a note, and we'll send it in with the mail coach when it comes." Martha found some paper and dictated what Amelia should write.

When the mail coach arrived, she handed over the letter simply addressed to "Major Grace, Government Stores, Parramatta." The mail coach changed horses, loaded up three other passengers, and mail and took off.

The next afternoon, on the return trip, the driver on the mail coach handed Martha a large parcel wrapped in string and a letter. Martha took both and thanked him. She placed the large parcel on the kitchen table and cleared off the table before they opened it.

The parcel contained two extra blankets, a selection of long fabric lengths in both drill and twill and two shorter lengths of poplin. There was also a long length of print fabric that the children loved. Martha also found a long twenty-yard length of calico. The poplin and calico fabrics were both stained but certainly useable for undergarments. The ladies enthusiastically opened the long lengths of coloured cloth, one in a blue, one brown, and an olive green length. Martha had never thought to ask for more fabric. There would be plenty left over to make some children's clothing and also give some to her friend Maureen Murphy.

Maureen already had four children and was expecting her fifth. Most in the small village helped them where they could. The Murphys were a very hard-working Irish family who eked out a living growing potatoes. Six-year-old Eion helped his father in the fields, as did Colleen, aged nearly five. She was a fabulous worker, and nothing was ever too much for her, but all of them were skinny and underweight.

Colleen chuckled, "Pa calls me scrawny."

Finn, their father, had made a wattle and daub hut, and they all slept on the earthen floor. They were Irish Protestants, and Martha loved them dearly. They each helped the other, birthing their children, and also both assisted others in the same condition. They were the closest thing Martha and Jack had to family.

Jack smiled when he heard of the bounteous supply of fabric, realising that this would be the major's doing. His way to assist them, having taken on another mouth to feed.

Chapter 4   Bounteous Gifts

With the arrival of the fabric, the letter had been overlooked. Martha had placed it on the mantlepiece, where it sat for three days. Amelia was dusting when she came across a letter in writing she recognised. The letter itself was dirty from passing through many hands in the months since it was written. She was stunned to see it was addressed to her and even more so to recognise the writing.

Jimmy had found her.

For years now, she'd had no contact with her family. Jimmy's final words to her were, "Trust me." She did then, and she did now. He'd sent her money, he'd arranged for Dr Reid to look after her on the ship, and now he'd found her in Australia. She looked at the date. It had taken over a year to get to her.

She took it in her hands and sank to the floor, just holding it. She put it to her cheek, kissed it and just sat holding it,

Finally, she could put off opening it no longer. She sat, wiping away her tears; the two-page letter was all she could hope for and more. It was filled with love, encouragement, and, more than that, hope. It had been written more than eighteen months before.

Pittford Manor
Aylesford, Kent.
8th January 1828

Miss Amelia Westaweller
Female Factory

Parramatta

My Dearest Milla,

It's taken me so long to find where I can write to you. I asked and asked, and eventually, I found a man who said most women prisoners were taken to the Female Factory at Parramatta until Assignment. So I am writing to you there in the hope you will receive this.

Well, my dearest sister, Mother and Father explained your absence by saying that you are travelling overseas. So, no one asked for more details. My beloved sister, please stay strong. I am still working hard to get things sorted this end. I hope that soon, the child's obnoxious father will withdraw his complaint against you. The confiscation of an item in class surely cannot be classed as theft. I dare not write names, but you know whom I refer to. How this was ever allowed to get this far is totally beyond reason.

Doctor Reid told me on his return that he was able to assist you on board the ship. Sadly, once you arrived, you had to go into the system. He had no control of things then. Dearest Milla, please keep remembering that I love you and will never cease striving for your release. Keep praying. If you can write to me, send it to Robert Styles, c/- Broome-Hall Manor, West Sussex. He will pass the letter on to me as, at the moment, it's best not to send mail to me here. It also gives me an excuse to see him.

Please let me know your direction and situation as soon as you can. Do not hold back on details, as I have heard how bad things are for others. Robert has been accompanying me and is petitioning all those he can. He knows the situation, so trust him, my dearest sister. I will now write of happier things at home ...

She continued reading the screed. Oh, how wonderful life sounded for them all. She wept joyfully to know she was still remembered with love, even if only by her brother. Even the signature was loving.

All my love to my beloved, innocent sister.
Jimmy.

She was able to obtain some writing paper from Jack and reply to his letter. She wasn't sure about how much to write but decided she had nothing to lose. She told him all, even to the assignment, rape, and her consequent condition. Then, when she got to Cyrus's death, the tears started to fall. Some fell on the letter and smudged the ink. Once he read this, he would wipe her from his life, but he had to know. Someone had to know what life as a convict woman was like. Surely, he could do something if he knew the truth. More than that, she wanted her parents to know what they had been responsible for.

Their neglect of her had brought her to this. She had done nothing wrong, and if they had stood up for her, she would not have been brought down to this degree. No, she knew she had to write it all down.

She unpicked a coin from the bodice of her gown and paid for the postage. The change from one of her remaining sovereigns she again eked out, but she treated herself to a few personal items, like a new hairbrush, a means of cleaning her teeth, and a comb. The jangle of shillings in her new purse gave her some confidence.

Over the following weeks, gowns were cut and made, as were underclothing. Oh, to have some new clothes, what a delight. Martha knew how to adapt patterns for maternity use. Seams were left un-sewn and cords inserted to tie around the waist. Martha showed Amelia how to use every skerrick of fabric.

Maureen and her children also came, and together, the three women cut and sewed new clothes for them all. The new underclothing was the most incredible treat for the ladies. The soft poplin was so lovely on her skin compared to the stiff calico. As they had no thread, Maureen showed them how to unravel some of the calico and use that to sew the new items.

Two weeks later, another parcel arrived. This time, it was more fabric, some thread, sewing needles, and ten slates with chalk. Inside was a second package with three books and a children's book called Mother Goose Nursery Rhymes. The note merely said,

"Happy Christmas, E"

Martha and Amelia gasped. They had not ordered these. Martha asked Jack when he came in if he'd ordered them.

He said no, then laughed. "The major," was his only comment.

Sure enough, every month for the following months, something else would arrive, occasionally with a note, more often than not, none.

The last package contained some small gardening tools, a box of nails for Jack, a white baby's shawl and two dozen new flannel napkins. The note with this one said,

"Not sure if it's a boy or girl. E."

Each parcel made them giggle with the randomness of the contents. Inside this parcel was a special small parcel marked for Amelia.

"Just something to assist in the months ahead. I'm sorry you have had to suffer as you have. I hope these help. E"

When she unwrapped the bundle, there was an exquisite handmade baby gown. Pinned inside the gown was a small handwritten note.

"NB, I know Jimmy. I should have said it before, sorry."

E"

Amelia gasped.

Martha watched her as she held up the gown; their eyes met. She showed Martha the tiny note.

"Oh, Martha, now I know why he's been sending things. Jimmy is my brother. He must have written to him." Amelia's eyes watered. "How old is this major?"

"Um, he'd be thirty-ish, I'd say. Jack said he was about the same age as them."

"Jimmy is, too. I wonder if they knew each other in England," Amelia queried. "I dare say I'll never find out."

By now, both Martha and Amelia were nearly at full term. Both ladies were waddling around the house.

Jack laughed. "I should open a birthing room. Maureen is not far behind you two."

"Well, my Jackie boy, I was going to tell you that you'd better trot along and get her. I've had back pain most of the day, and contractions have now started in earnest." She gasped and doubled over. She stood, taking deep breaths until the pain passed. "You'll probably be a papa again by tonight." Martha went in to prepare her bedroom for a delivery. "Amelia dear, come and assist so you know what's ahead. First, we need lots of hot water. This is so that everything is clean and also for hot towels to assist with the pain. You'll discover that heated towels onto the lower back really helps and how good back rubs are. Remember the deep breathing, too, and when your time comes, I'll be with you."

Amelia listened hard, knowing this would be her very soon.

Sure enough, Nicholas John Turner was born at four o'clock that afternoon on 26 April 1830.

The three little girls slept in one room; Martha and Jack had moved the two boys into the lounge room the month before Nicky was born. Amelia found sleeping with the little girls when eight months with child was difficult. She was now sleeping in what had been the boys' room. The boys were happy to sleep on the floor as it meant they were near the fire. May was cold, and their room was furthest from the only fireplace, so neither complained.

On May 9, Esther Martha Ruth West arrived less than two weeks later. "I'm naming her after you, Martha, and Ruth means 'friend', and Martha means 'lady'. 'Esther' means 'star' as she will be a guiding star for me. As it's what you are to me." She'd been born in the boys' bedroom. It was nighttime when she arrived, and Amelia had stood at the window of the room looking up at the stars. She'd prayed that the Lord would give her strength to see her through the birth. He had. She was born with only a few hours of hard labour. Jack had to hold her in a squatting position as the contractions had stalled. Amelia had watched how Martha fed Nicky. However, when it came to her turn, things were not quite as simple. "She won't feed Martha. What am I doing wrong?" Amelia pleaded.

Martha showed her how to help the baby latch on and feed properly. Once shown, Amelia was able to feed without any trouble. She then slept the rest of the night and the next morning was ready to help with the milking and her daily chores – Amelia, like Martha just weeks before, bounced back quickly.

The changing of Essie was another eye-opening experience. Amelia had never had anything to do with babies. Changing a baby's dirty or wet napkin was another skill she had to learn. Thankfully, with Martha's assistance, she coped brilliantly.

Amelia was thrilled that she was not going through this alone. Knowing how differently all this could have been had Amelia still been at the cabin. Esther was adorable, and she had fallen in love with her tiny daughter. Another parcel arrived the week she was born: a pink-knitted blanket and a rag doll with dark, curly, woollen hair and sewn blue eyes. She chuckled as it reminded her of what she looked like as a child. The note attached to it merely said…

A W

Praying for you. Never give up!

from E & J

Amelia was still puzzled as she had no recollection of an Edward Grace.

Within weeks, Esther's big blue eyes followed her as she moved around the room. By the time she was a month old, she had a tooth. She bit once, and Amelia yelped.

Martha giggled. "Pull her off and tap her cheek. She'll learn fast enough not to do this."

Essie, as Amelia was calling her, was growing fast. As she fed, their eyes would lock, and the baby would place her open hand on Amelia's breast. Each time Amelia thought her the most beautiful baby ever, she often wept with love for the child. Cyrus may have forced himself on her, but this child was born innocent and would now be loved with every emotion she could muster.

Maureen had her fifth child, Brodie, in June. Both Amelia and Martha had assisted in the birth. Five-year-old Colleen knew what to do and handed the right things to Martha at the correct times. Finn held Maureen in a squatting position, as Jack had done for both Martha and her. Amelia stood in awe, watching the miracle of birth.

They settled into life and months ahead. By the time Essie was sitting up, Amelia was wondering how life would work itself out. She had set up a day school in the barn.

Jack had requested more slates, and the major had sent more than that. He'd sent educational books that the children could read from. He'd obviously hunted high and low and sent everything he could find that a teacher could use. The supplies arrived in a large wooden crate. The note attached just said,

Keep up the good work

E

Letters from Jimmy had arrived every few months since her arrival at the Turners. Each was filled with news from 'home' but little to no mention of their parents. Amelia was so contented now in Emu Plains that she wondered where home now was.

Towards the end of August, a letter arrived for Amelia. This was again in the beautiful calligraphy of Major Grace.

The Barracks

Parramatta

18th August 1830

Arms Of Australia Inn

Emu Plains

Dear Miss West,

I am writing with an offer for you. I am not sure if you wish to take up this position, but I feel it could assist your case. I have recommended you as a Governess for the Governor and Mrs Darling. I know your background and am assured that you would be welcome. Be assured that they know of your daughter, and she, too, could accompany you.

Please do not feel pressured. You are free to stay with the Turners if you wish, but I think this is too good an opportunity to refuse. I need your answer within a week, though.

Major Edward Grace

Amelia sat looking at the letter in her hand. She knew she had to go. She had outstayed her time at Emu. She had been with them for nearly a year. It's not that she was no longer welcome but that the business was growing so fast that they needed the room.

Martha walked in as she sat holding the letter. Amelia could do no more than hand it to her. Martha perused the message and said, "You're going, aren't you, love?"

"You need the room here, Martha, and this would be good for Essie. As the major said, it could help my case, so I have to go." She gave a sob. The last year had been wonderful. She still had three years to serve, and if she could do that in Government House ... "Yes, Martha, I will take the offer. I have to." Amelia took the letter back and watched the tears drop onto the paper. "I'm beginning to hate change."

They discussed the letter with Jack over tea at the kitchen table. He, too, advised that this would be too good an opportunity not to take. "Amelia, you will always have a home here, should you need it. I hope you know that. But this is something you need to do. The major knows that, too."

By the end of the week, she had packed her clothes in a homemade bag and was nearly ready to leave. Amelia was about to leave when she said, "Oh, Martha, my money! I totally forgot about it."

Jack quickly extracted her £15 from the safe spot. She tucked the note once again into her Bible. Then wrapped the coins into a fold of paper and into her Bible, too, then slid it down her corset.

"How can I ever thank you for everything you have done for me? You gave me hope. You gave me love, and more than that; you taught me to trust God again." She hugged Martha, "For that alone, I can never thank you enough."

"Amelia, you are a delight to our hearts, too, my dear. And so is Essie. We will keep you in our prayers. I can never thank you enough for teaching us to read. This, too, will change our children's life. With the knowledge you have given me, I will continue your lessons. Jack can correct me." She turned to her husband. "Won't you, love?"

"Yes, dear!" he said with a chuckle.

The mail coach arrived and did its change of horses before loading her in. Amelia's bag was about to be thrown up onto the roof when she realised all Essie's napkins were in it. So she asked for it to be placed in the cabin with her. She was glad she did as, by the time they had travelled a few hours, it was raining. As her bag was not waterproof, everything would have been drenched.

The major had arranged for her to alight in Parramatta at an inn and travel the trip's final leg via ferry the next day. That was a trip she'd always wanted to do. However, more than that, she wanted to meet the major.

Major Grace met her in Parramatta as the coach arrived at the Rear Admiral Duncan Inn. As she alighted, he greeted her warmly. "Miss West and Miss Essie, I presume?" His smile was heart-melting.

What a handsome man he was. "Yes, sir, I mean major." She was as nervous as a schoolgirl. He looked vaguely familiar. Shaking her head, no, it couldn't be the same person; his name wasn't Grace. She looked again surreptitiously.

He said, "I'll come to see you safely checked in at Bill and Molly Miller's Inn. Molly will look after you. I'll come up and meet with you after I finish my shift and fill you in on a few things. I must return to work." He gave her a smile that would have melted the hardest heart, then bowed to her as would befit her original status. He tickled the chin of the little girl, then took his farewells.

Molly Miller ushered her into a room at the back, just off the wide verandah. "Your little one is about the same age as our youngest dear. What's her name?"

"Essie, well, Esther, actually, but I call her Essie. Thank you, Mrs Miller; this is delightful." Amelia looked at the beautiful big bed. The view of the river was also a delight. She could hear the burbling of the water as it ran past towards the sea.

"Forget the Mrs Miller bit; I'm Molly. Nothing more, nothing fancy." The joyful lady made Amelia relax. "Now, as to your darling little girl, our Ellen, as I said, is the same age and feel free to leave them together when the major comes. I'll look after them both."

"Thank you, Molly; I may do that. May I meet Ellen?" Amelia placed her bag on the bed and changed Essie. "May I also wash her napkins? I have a few dirty ones from today's trip."

"Yes, dearie, come with me, and I'll show you the washroom. If they are not dry by the time you leave, we can swap."

They walked out of the room, and in an hour, Amelia had not only done the washing and met Ellen but sat relaxing with Molly in her kitchen as she prepared the meal for the inn. Amelia entertained the two little girls and Ellen's older brother Sammy, who was three.

Molly's two other children were Timmy and Gracie. Tim, aged nine, was at school in Sydney; Gracie, six, was stacking firewood for the kitchen. There was a gentle knock at the door, and Major Grace entered. Molly offered to take all the children. Molly saw the fear sweep over Amelia's face. "Dear, you can trust the major; he really is a true gentleman. I've known him for many years."

Amelia then looked at him and back to Molly; she nodded. "Thank you, Molly."

Molly showed them into the sitting room.

Major Grace sat on the far side of the room so that Amelia was closest to the door. She relaxed, knowing that she could run if needs be.

When Molly departed, they sat alone in the sitting room. "Miss Westaweller, may I call you that?"

"You probably shouldn't, sir. Here I am, just Amelia West. My family, other than Jimmy, have disowned me. If Mother had appeared at my trial or spoken up before that, I would not be here. I must have been a great disappointment to her. Jimmy is all I have left." Her eyes had filled, but she blinked the tears away. "So please, just Amelia."

"Jimmy and I knew each other from our youth in Kent. I spent some time at Christ's Hospital School, and my youngest brother, Douglas, was a friend of Jimmy's. We four brothers often visited your house when we were young. It was only about fifteen minutes away by shortcuts. A couple of other friends, Gerry and Rob, would meet there as your folks didn't seem to mind lots of children around. I had the story from him, Amelia. All of it, and more, I have had from Jack Turner. I do wish I'd known you were here as I could have taken you from the Factory and placed you with friends if not assigned you to myself. I had no idea, and I am so sorry. Sorry for what you have had to endure, too. Before you got to Sydney, I just wanted to meet you and let you know what I have arranged."

She fixed her eyes on his face, peering back into her memory; she was sure it was the blonde boy she remembered from so many years ago. Amelia sat listening to his beautiful modulated voice. Yes, he was a man she could trust. It had not taken her long to realise that. Jack had said he, too, believed in Jesus. "Sir, I'm away from the life that Cyrus made me live. I will not go into details, but it was undesirable, to say the least. He died the day he found out I was expecting. I'm sure you have read the report. I won't go into more detail than Jack told you, but he took great pleasure in all forms of abuse. Nothing can be as bad as that." She met his eyes again and saw great compassion.

"It's why I have arranged this for you. The Darlings will take care of you. Eliza is compassionate, and I have filled her in on a bit of your story. I do hope you won't mind, but she wanted to know something about you, as I personally recommended you."

Amelia shook her head, "No, sir, I don't mind. I'd almost rather they know beforehand, as then there will be no surprises. But do they know Essie's history?"

She read compassion in the major's face. "Yes, Amelia, Eliza does. I'm not sure if she told her husband." He paused in his discussions. He, too, remembered the adorable little girl he used to look after with Jimmy. "Amelia, I am 'Neddie'. Do you remember me?"

She nodded. A smile settled on her lips, "I do, sir. I wondered if it was you. You've, um, grown, and I was sure we called you something…." She looked at the door, "…Something different. You weren't known as Grace."

She saw him glance quickly to the door. "No, but I can't tell you here," he said softly in case anyone was listening near the open door.

They spent some time conversing about Kent. Then, the major took his leave. "I won't see you tomorrow as I have a morning parade. I'm due to see the Governor next week, and I have a friend I try to catch up with while in Sydney; he's from not too far from home in England. So I'll stay the evening with him and will try to see how you've settled in."

"Thank you, sir; I do appreciate everything you have done for me." Then she gave him a beaming smile. "You really have no idea how your parcels brightened our lives. Jack would just chuckle every time they came."

His reply was to return her smile. "It was a delight!" He gave her a grin. "Molly and another friend, Sal, chose some of the items. I hope you get to meet her as her husband, Charles, is a friend. I wish you could have met her now, but Charles is currently ill, well not exactly ill, but he's injured, so she can't leave him alone. They run another inn in town as well as Government Stores. He and Jack were the two who reported the mutiny on our ship out. It is how they got their tickets."

She had heard the story of that from Jack and Martha. "Oh! Well, thank you anyway," Amelia said.

"Amelia, I have also recommended that you get an Absolute Pardon on your release so you can return home. Governor Darling will talk to you about that." The major stood to leave.

"Thank you, major, but do you think that's wise? I now have an illegitimate child, and I'll not leave her in an orphanage. Other than Jimmy, my family have already disowned me, and I'm a social outcast," Amelia said in a very matter-of-fact way. She and Martha had talked long and hard about her situation. "My options are limited, sir, even here, where many are in the same situation. I possibly could find a man to marry, but I doubt that returning home would benefit me in any way." Her voice was flat and emotionless.

"Amelia, sometimes when things look at their bleakest, that's when God shines brightest. Trust Him, my dear. There are people and places you can go on return home. When that time comes, I will be in contact with you again, if not sooner. You have three years to serve. Use that time and absorb the goodness of the Darlings." He took her hand and patted it like a child. "Amelia, trust God. He, and He alone, can sort this all out." His kindness and empathy were her undoing. As he departed, she sat and wept.

Molly came in and enfolded her in loving arms. "Oh, my dear, are you all right? It's not like the major to leave a lady in distress."

Amelia gave a soggy chuckle, "Oh, it wasn't that. It was his kindness. He's done so much for me already. He truly is a friend of my brother from Kent. No, Molly, he is all things good and proper. Where I'd be if it were not for him, I do not know. He moved mountains to let me stay at the Turners after Cyrus Black was killed." She heard Molly gasp, then saw a look of horror pass across her face.

"I don't know the Turners, but Cyrus Black took you? Essie is his?" Molly had fallen back and was sitting on the floor, aghast. "He is, no was, disgusting. Bill threw him out often and eventually banned him from our inn. Oh, Amelia!" Molly had tears pouring down her cheeks. "I could smell him before I even knew he was there."

"Yes, Molly, he was everything evil. If you think he was bad from a distance, he was a thousand times worse close up," Amelia said simply. "His depravity did not stop with his lack of cleanliness either."

"Oh, my dear, oh, Amelia! He is horrible," Molly replied sadly.

"He was, and he's dead. On the day I told him about the child, he was killed by his horse." Amelia's look of pain made Molly once again embrace her. Amelia added softly, "It was three months of hell, Molly."

"We've all got horror stories, Amelia. Most of us won't talk about them much, but sometimes it helps to unload to understanding ears."

"Thanks, Molly. I did, to Martha Turner. They found me a short time after he was killed. Jack wrote to the major, and he had me transferred to them. I've been teaching their children and a few others to read, as I'm a teacher. Anyway, because the major knew my brother, he has recommended me to the Darlings." Amelia sniffed. "Cyrus was a brute. A sadistic brute, he raped me the first time by the side of the road less than an hour after I was assigned to him. I'd never been with a man before, and he was everything that was horrible. After that, it was… it was… shall I just say a regular occurrence. I must have fallen with Essie soon after, as she was born a little over nine months after my assignment. I suppose one day I'll let her know about him, but not until she's fully grown. She'll have to know, won't she?"

Molly wiped the back of her hand across her own cheeks, "I know him, well, at least I knew him, Amelia. You're right. He was a sadist, but you're alive, and he's not. You're starting a new life, and it can't be any worse than what you've already coped with now, can it?" Molly gave Amelia a wan smile. "Amelia, the worst bed at Government House will be better than any we have here, and we're the best inn in town."

Amelia smirked. "Yes, but after a canvas-covered pile of dead grass, you can't get much worse. He called it a mattress." The fact that she could even laugh about that amazed her.

"Now, how about tea? I find it is very soothing. Not to mention, it warms you from the inside out." Molly told her that she believed tea was the panacea for many ills.

Amelia nodded, wiping away an errant tear as it escaped. Kindness was still hard to cope with. She'd still get angry with herself for crying. She still thought of it as a weakness.

Bill knocked. "May I bring the children, dear? I have to return to the counter." He had the two little girls in his arms and Sammy at his heels.

Essie held her arms out to her mother as Ellen did to Molly. Essie was dark like her father. But with the most adorable big blue eyes. She was now nearly five months old. Amelia's heart melted whenever she saw her. She often thought of how something so beautiful could come from one so evil. She scooped the child up in her arms and gave her a kiss and a hug.

"Hello, poppet, I missed you. Did you have a nice play?" Amelia knew she'd receive no reply. She would do whatever she could to protect this innocent child from the evil repercussions of her father.

Chapter 5   A Darling Start

*T*he ferry left the wharf at 9.10 am. The high tide carried the little vessel

out into the river and then out of sight. Amelia had briefly met Sal Lockley as Molly stopped in to see if she needed any assistance with her patient. She nodded a greeting to the fair-haired lady and waited on the verandah with Essie. Essie needed a change, so Amelia took the opportunity to do so. The baby needed some fresh air, and Amelia thought that she'd start slowly walking down to the wharf to await the ferry. She knocked gently, and Sal came to the door. Amelia told her that she was going to head off to the wharf.

The mist had lifted from the water, but the August morning was still cold.

They had just arrived when Molly joined her, with Ellen in her arms and Sammy at her heel.

"Oh my dear, I'm so sorry. I do get carried away when talking to Sal. We rarely get to see each other. She was wondering if you'd give this to the Captain for their son, Eddie. He's living in Sydney for school. He's at Cape's Academy with our Timmy. Captain Roberts acts as a courier. He's a bit late today so that I won't get time for a chat. If you can give him these two parcels for the boys, that would be wonderful. Charles normally comes down for a chat, but with a sprained ankle, he'd been told not to put his foot to the ground. Sal has five other children, and her youngest is only three, so she's flat out. I'll take Luke and Wills home with me when I return. They are the two littlest boys, and Sammy and Ellen love playing with them. Sal often takes

Gracie as she loves Anna and Lisa. Anyway, that's all beside the point; Sal's tuckered out poor love. I'll go along and give her a hand on the way back. So I'll just book you in and head back if that's all right?"

Amelia giggled. "Oh, Molly, you don't have to stay. Give me the parcels, and I'll make sure they are safely delivered. What was the Captain's name again? Robbins?"

"No, Captain Stephen Roberts, dear, he's really nice." Molly was puffing as she hurried to join Amelia. "Are you sure, dearie?"

"Yes, go, Molly, but before you do, thank you so much for being so kind and caring. You have really put me at my ease." She bent and kissed the loving lady.

Molly handed Amelia the two parcels and, swapping farewells, she waved and then departed.

Amelia and Essie watched them leave.

Essie's adorable chuckles caught the attention of other passengers heading down to the ferry. Essie sat on Amelia's hip, waving, then uttered what sounded like "Bye-bye-bye."

Amelia was stunned, shaking her head in disbelief, "Yes, poppet, bye-bye." She giggled. Martha said that it would be about ten months before she would start talking. "Now we're going in a boat, and you must hold me tightly. Do you understand?"

Essie snuggled to Amelia's neck and stuck her slightly muddy thumb in her mouth. She spat out some dirt and a bit of grass and poked it back in again.

Captain Roberts saw her struggling with the baby, her bag and two packages. He came to her rescue. "Here, ma'am, can I assist?"

"Oh, thank you, sir; you must be Captain Roberts. I have two parcels for you for Eddie and Timmy. Do you know them?"

"Yes, ma'am, I do. I regularly take things to them and bring letters home. I shall stow these and deliver them to the Evans' household tonight." He assisted her up the gangplank and kept hold of her until she reached the tiny cabin. Essie was now asleep. Amelia sat in the cabin and relaxed on the padded seat.

Within minutes, the little paddle-wheeled steam ferry, the *Surprise*, pulled away from the wharf, headed down river and chuffed merrily towards Sydney. It gave a small belch of black smoke from the funnel occasionally.

As they sailed down the Parramatta River, Amelia watched the myriad of birds they passed. She moved seats so she could see where they were going rather than where they had been. Essie was dribbling down her neck, so she moved her to lie in her arms. Amelia, too, lay back and relaxed. Something she'd not done for years. She sat watching the scenery pass by. The slosh of the little paddle wheels from the steam ferry was lulling her to sleep; she must have dozed a few times as the scenery had changed. They called into several jetties on the trip and collected and deposited various other passengers. None joined her inside until the last stop.

At North Sydney, they collected a lady who sat in the cabin, too. Amelia did not feel like talking to a stranger, so she nodded and motioned the lady not to wake the sleeping baby.

The lady nodded and sat quietly, watching Amelia. Occasionally, she'd smile, but she did not attempt to converse.

They had crossed the Harbour and pulled into the Phoenix Wharf at the Circular Quay about fifteen minutes after the last stop.

Amelia was hoping Essie would stay asleep at least until she could alight. Captain Roberts accompanied her down the gangplank carrying her bag; he then carefully placed it on her shoulder. Essie was just stirring and woke to cry. Amelia sat in the shade and hunted in her bag for something for the child to eat. Amelia had just settled the baby on her lap when the lady passenger sat beside her.

The unknown lady spoke. "Poor poppet, they hate waking in strange places. I'm Mrs Hill. I've been visiting a friend in North Sydney while my husband is looking after the children, not ours. We have none, but he's teaching some of the orphans to read."

The kind lady gave Amelia the confidence she needed.

Amelia dared to converse with the bold lady. "She wants a drink, but I've only got water. I can't exactly give her a feed here, can I?" Amelia said, very worried.

"Give me the water. She'll probably take it from me if she's really thirsty," Mrs Hill said.

Amelia nodded. "Her father is dead. It's hard bringing up a child alone. I have no knowledge of what is to come and no support. I'm off to a new placement, ma'am."

The kind lady said without judgment, "Service time? How long to go?"

"Yes, ma'am, three years left. Major Grace has arranged a new placement for me." Amelia wasn't sure how much to tell the lady.

"If Ned Grace says you can travel alone and has taken care of your placement, then that's good enough for me. If I can do anything for you, let me know. How about I call a lift, and we get dropped off? Where are you heading, love?"

Amelia was astounded by the lady's reply.

The lady assured her she would be safe if the major had her under his protection.

Amelia gave a slight gasp at the use of his nickname but said nothing about that. "I have to go to Government House. My new position is Mrs Darling's governess-cum-teacher for their children. My name is Amelia West." Amelia saw the lady look at her hands, "Yes, ma'am, Miss Amelia West. My darling babe is the product of my first placement. I was abused from an hour after my assignment to when he was killed by his horse three months later. I was with the Turners at Emu Plains for nearly a year. Major Grace has kindly now had me transferred here." Amelia sighed. "Oh well, she was nice. Now she'll ignore me, she thought."

"My dear, I learned early on in my time in the Colony never to be hasty in judgment. My husband is Reverend Richard Hill, and I'm Phoebe; we have lots of calls for compassion and not much time for condemnation. You are worthy of every skerrick of it. Hold your head high, dear, for you *are* worthy in God's eyes. You could have abandoned your child in the orphanage, but you chose to keep her and love her. I can see that you do. You will get no condemnation from me." Phoebe looked at the poor girl. She quietly said as she gave the little girl a drink of water, "Men are beasts. Slaking their lusts on our poor innocent girls." She handed the child a small cup of water again and held it to her mouth.

The baby drank thirstily and went, "Ahhh," when she finished. Then she grinned at the stranger and gurgled with laughter.

Phoebe smirked. "I do love them from this age until about ten. They start getting their own minds, then. She's adorable, Miss West, absolutely adorable." Phoebe dropped a kiss on the child's head. "Now, about this cab, we'd better get moving. What's her name?"

"It's Esther, but I call her Essie." Amelia collected her bag and went to pick up Essie. "Her name means 'star' for that is what she is, my guiding star. My life decisions from now on will be for her."

"Well, Miss Essie, may I carry you for a little while?" Phoebe asked.

They walked the short distance to the roadway and intended to wait for a hackney. A town carriage was already waiting. Phoebe saw a crest on the door. "Excuse me, are you waiting for someone?" she asked the driver.

"Yes, ma'am, a passenger named West. I'm here to take her to Government House. Are you her, ma'am?"

"No, I'm Mrs Hill; this young lady is named West. Would you drop me in Pitt Street at the church on the way, please?" Phoebe asked.

"By all means, Mrs Hill, we'll go past your door. Sorry, I didn't recognise you, ma'am," the driver said apologetically. He assisted Amelia into the vehicle.

The driver handed in Essie, and then Phoebe followed her in. Once they were seated, he climbed up onto the driver's seat, released the brake and eased off gently up the roadway. Phoebe gave Amelia more encouragement and said that she'd see Amelia at church on Sunday. "We're at St James Church, and the Governor and Mrs Darling usually worship with us, so I'll see you there." Phoebe bent and kissed Amelia's cheek. "Take care, my dear, and don't hesitate to call on me if you need me. And, Miss West, fear not; they too believe and are a delight."

"Thank you, Mrs Hill, I shall remember." Amelia watched her get out, and she turned and waved.

Essie smiled and said, "Bye-bye," and waved.

Amelia giggled again. Not the usual first words, but then she'd never heard *dad* in her life.

The carriage continued past a gatehouse and up a sweeping roadway. Through the trees, Amelia caught a glimpse of a beautiful slate-roofed building. It reminded her of the Dower House at Pittford Manor. Home. Ha! It was no longer home, was it? She released a great sigh. Well, this was home for a while. The driver pulled up at the front of the building. She gasped. She thought she'd be taken to the staff entrance.

The driver opened the carriage door and assisted her down.

"Mum, mum, mum," the child giggled joyously.

The driver passed her bag to the waiting footman, and Amelia followed him inside. He led her to a door off the foyer.

The footman said, "Her Excellency is waiting for you, ma'am, in Red Drawing Room, ma'am. Please follow me." He knocked and entered.

The large room was red, very red. "Aptly named," Amelia thought as she looked around the red room; she saw a lady standing near a window.

"Come in, Miss West; please be seated." She walked to the settee near Amelia and sat down. "What an adorable baby! What's her name?"

"Thank you, ma'am. It's Esther, ma'am. However, I call her Essie," Amelia said politely as she curtsied.

"Star, a beautiful name," Mrs Darling said.

"She is, ma'am," Amelia answered nervously.

"Miss West, or should I call you Miss Westaweller? Amelia, relax; I won't bite, you know. My name is Eliza."

Amelia's eyes flew to hers, stunned at her familiarity.

"Oh, I know your story and even who accused you. I've had my own run-ins with that man myself. I also know it's trumped-up rubbish. Confiscating an item in class, my foot! There's more to this story, but we may never find out the whole. For you to get seven years and transportation is not appropriate recompense, is it? It's ridiculous, actually. I have read your file. Major Ned Grace filled me in about you. He said he's friends with your brother, James?" Mrs Darling looked questioningly at Amelia.

"Yes, ma'am, he is," Amelia spoke softly. She was still puzzled at the use of his nickname again.

"I'm so sorry it's put you in the situation you now find yourself in. So while I'm here, you shall be my children's Governess and, in private, my friend. I have few enough of them and could do with a sympathetic ear. Your upbringing is far better than mine. Even now, you really should have higher precedence than me, bar one slip of paper. I shall have to call you West, though."

Amelia was reeling with the change in her welcome from what she'd expected. She was being treated like a guest, not an assigned convict with an illegitimate baby.

Amelia replied, "Thank you, Mrs Darling. I appreciate that. I have shamed my family enough, even though, as you say, I did nothing wrong. I was convicted, and that was enough." Amelia was almost in tears.

Eliza Darling smiled at the young mother.

Amelia was told by the major to trust this lady and to trust God. She had doubted. She leaned her cheek on Essie's hair. "And this cherub, how do I explain her?" Amelia met her eyes. Her own were full of unshed tears.

Mrs Darling smiled. "Ahh, yes, well, I have an idea with that too, if you're prepared for a little more subterfuge. You are already using the name of West; how about we change the Miss to Mrs? Her father is dead, so it's not as if he'll appear." She raised her eyebrows and waited for Amelia to think over her suggestion. "It's not like you'll be challenged. If I introduce you as such, so it will be."

"You'd let me do that? Really?" Was this woman really giving her a way to regain her dignity? Her tears, unable to be held back, rolled down her cheeks; she merely nodded before she was able to add, "Yes, please."

"Good, then all we need is a ring. I'll arrange for you to get one. I believe the new jeweller, Richard Lamb, can supply that. In the meantime, slip this on. It was my mother's, so I'd like it back." She pulled off a plain gold band from her right hand and held it out to Amelia.

Amelia slipped on the ring and looked at her hand. She raised her water-filled eyes to this loving lady. "Why, ma'am? Why are you doing this? I'm not worth you getting into trouble," Amelia whispered.

"Are you not a child of God?" Eliza asked simply.

Amelia nodded.

"Ned Grace said you are. Then you are worthy, and this is one way I can assist you. Your situation is not of your making. So, I intend to do what I can to assist you. Let's just say it's what I do." Mrs Darling smiled, "I try to fix things and try to make lives better for the unfortunate people here."

"Thank you! Thank you so much. So I'm a widow after a three-month 'marriage'?" Amelia queried. This is not how she expected this interview to go. She would be given respect; she would not be ostracised. She could hold her head high as Phoebe Hill had told her to.

"Yes, let's stick as closely to the truth as possible. You're a common-law wife; in reality, it was just not by choice. Now, let's get you settled. Come, we'll go to your rooms. Remember you are my friend from England. No one is to know differently. Hence, your entry via the front door and not the servant's quarters. Major Ned suggested that to Ralph. Also, did you note that the coachman asked for a passenger named West, no Missus or Miss?" Eliza explained. She rose, as did Amelia. Essie was now asleep again, and they followed her to the door.

Eliza Darling walked to the door and called for the housekeeper. "Amelia dear, this is Mrs Christopher; ask her for anything you need." The housekeeper led the two new friends to the suite prepared for Amelia.

They chatted happily as they walked.

To all listening, this was Eliza Darling showing a friend to a special room. She was paving the way for her as a path back to respectability.

Mrs Christopher opened the door to a ground floor room at the back of Government House. Amelia gasped. The room was magnificent. She spied a bassinet of almost royal proportions, a cot and a basket of toys for Essie. Her bag was empty and on her bed.

A maid stood waiting for her and unobtrusively curtsied and offered to take Essie. "My name is Janey, ma'am. I'm here to assist with your little one."

Amelia turned to Mrs Darling. "Use her, dear; it will free you up to assist with our baby Darlings. Frederick is at school in England; I miss him dreadfully," she chortled at her play on words.

Amelia felt as though she'd been caught up in a whirlwind. Eliza kept talking and sweeping Amelia on in her wake.

Eliza was still prattling on; Amelia was finding her chatter very relaxing. "It will be a win, win situation dear. With the loss of your entire wardrobe, we need to get you some new gowns. Mrs Henderson, my seamstress, will arrange for you to be fitted out, but you can borrow a few of my gowns until they are ready, and Miss Essie will have her clothes replaced. So sad that you lost everything, but we will get you fixed up, dear. It's just over a year since you lost your man, my dear, so we will not get black this time, dear. Would you be happy wearing colours again? That blue does suit you; however, I know you can't be choosy when borrowing clothing."

Would this lady's kindness never stop? "Yes, please!" Amelia teared up again. She couldn't say much in front of the staff. "She needs a change," Amelia said as she passed Essie to Janey.

Essie wasn't sure about this new person. She looked to her mother, who nodded.

Amelia knew not to force her.

Essie soon held her arms out to the new person.

"We'll get her sorted, ma'am. Miss Caroline is about the same age, and if you're not to mind, I can find her something to wear of hers. Would that be suitable, ma'am?"

Again, Amelia turned to Eliza.

Essie was in a homemade gown.

Her look was greeted with a nod. "They can share until we get everything of hers replaced, my dear. Your brother, via your friend, has supplied funds for that. Now you settle down, and I'll introduce you to my four later. Edward, Augustus, and Cornelia will be your students. Janey can look after both little girls while you're teaching the other three."

Again, Amelia said, "Thank you so much. You are so kind."

~

Within a week, Amelia had a brand new wardrobe of clothes, as did Essie. Everything was supplied, from new half boots to a parasol. They were nothing luxurious, but they were fresh, clean and new, right down to the lace-edged lawn drawers. Eliza Darling insisted on being called by her first name when in private. "Amelia, you are a Viscount's daughter; I am only a Governor's wife. This is one way I can assist you. We can't, of course, introduce you as who you really are."

Amelia fell back into the lifestyle in which she had grown up. Her official duties were teaching the three older children.

As Augustus and Edward were only three and four, Amelia could only start them on how to hold a stick of chalk and to practise copying letters and shapes. Cornelia was well advanced for eleven, and she took great pleasure in progressing her education. She discovered that the reading material provided for the young lady was well advanced for her age group.

Eliza encouraged Amelia to join her and some of her colonial lady friends to visit some of the less fortunate women in the Colony. Her inclusion in visits to the various meetings of the Female Friendly Society was an eye-opening and joyful experience. Mrs Darling was truly 'practising what she preached'.

~

Amelia was not the only recipient of her benevolence, for she discovered that a Female School of Industry had also been set up at Parramatta, where female convicts were assisted in having a better life. The women were taught moral and religious education but showed Jesus's love and forgiveness in such a way. Eliza and Amelia were often accompanied by five other ladies, two of whom were the Misses Macleay.

The seven women would be seen visiting various of the charities set up to assist the unfortunate women.

Amelia realised that Eliza's care for her was simply righting one more wrong, so she accepted gracefully. Her life at Government House was interjected with the involvement of the many good works undertaken to assist the plight of the unfortunates. When in prison in England, Amelia was visited by Elizabeth Fry, a lady she initially thought was an angel. Many women were handed care packages by Mrs Fry and her team of friends, one of whom Amelia found was Ann Dumaresq, Eliza's mother. Sadly, they had not taken enough care parcels with them that day, and Amelia had missed out; the other women were not inclined to share. The visit was enough to keep her spirits and beliefs going. However, many of the women benefited from Mrs Fry's kindness.

In Amelia's dejected state, the vision of a caring soul in the squalor of gaol brought hope. Amelia had also missed out on the sewing packages distributed on the ships, but as Dr Reid had assisted both her and Mary, she felt she was better off anyway. Now, here she was, working with one of the organisers. She threw herself into the work as well as her teaching duties. Miss Barclay and the Misses Macleay were keen to assist. Mrs Phoebe Hill, Mrs Sadie Landon, Mrs Roberts and other parishioners from St James often accompanied them. Meetings were regularly held, and ideas were put forward for ways to assist. Eliza would often seek Amelia's input in private; then, these ideas would be submitted for consideration.

The domestic cooking school was enlarged, sewing materials supplied, and teachers employed to instruct how to draft and cut out dresses and underclothing.

The now-familiar water-damaged fabrics seemed to be never-ending. She wondered where it came from but dared not to ask. Amelia suggested other skills, and these, too, were taught. She also recommended that the supply of both washing and bathing facilities at the Female Factory be installed and a new water pump for access to clean water.

When in private, she described the conditions at the Factory, and Eliza was aghast. The Governor hastily arranged a trip to this venue.

Once the inspection was done, without warning the warders, changes were made, and the health of the female inmates was improved somewhat. Many were still falling with child in unexpected circumstances as they were not supposed to fraternise with the guards.

Eliza reported to Amelia that her husband would be arranging further regular inspections. The Local Board of Officials were to oversee these. Ralph Darling accompanied them on some of these visits. He insisted that all the female prisoners be treated with respect where possible.

A classification system of grading the female convicts was instigated, and rewards or punishments were changing their grades. The women were not permitted to fraternise immorally with the warders, nor vice versa. Hopefully, their conditions will improve. They certainly could not be much worse.

After one of their return trips, Amelia was told that washing facilities were now completed and were being regularly used. But having spent time there, she knew that many women had no idea how to keep clean. They needed to be taught how to bathe. Washing of their bodies was foreign to them. Many had never had a bath in their entire lives. Lice were something that one just learned to live with at the Female Factory.

Amelia shivered with the memory.

Typhus was also common in this situation. Thankfully, she had escaped an epidemic, but others had not been so lucky.

Eliza and Amelia worked tirelessly toward the improvement of the women. It was only when alone that they could talk freely.

Amelia was still subdued, never overstepping her place in the household. Knowing that she still had nearly two years yet to serve, Amelia was still overawed by the way the Darlings treated her.

Chapter 6   Sent Home

When Amelia had been with the Darlings for nearly a year, Eliza confided that she was expecting again. However, Amelia could see there was more to tell. Eliza had twice opened her mouth to speak and shut it again. Finally, she spoke, "Amelia, we are being sent home. Ralph has to face an enquiry, and we're basically going home in disgrace." Eliza dissolved into tears.

Amelia went to her and comforted her friend; she was horrified. Not only did she feel for her friends, but what would happen to her?

"The timing is not good, Amelia, for I will be due to give birth on board. I do not have the choice to stay." Eliza looked forlorn. "I will not be able to take you with me, as your time here is not done. We have hidden it from many, but it can't continue. My dear Amelia, you have been succour to my soul. A friend in my hour of need, as hopefully, I have been to you."

Amelia held a weeping Eliza in her arms. She was stunned. Cast adrift again for two more years. "Eliza, the 'succour to the soul' has been you to me. You gave me hope when I had none. You have given me a reason to believe again. I have had my faith renewed and my dignity."

"We have eight weeks, Amelia; in that time, I have to find a new placement for you. Somewhere you can still keep working, somewhere you can still have your self-respect," Eliza stated. "I also need to make sure that the various committees will continue and that the Benevolent Society has ample funds, and also with the Female Orphans School moving to Parramatta. There is so much now to finish in a short space of time. I so wanted to see it completed, and now I will not have the chance. Oh, I am so undone. Why do men have to fight over trivial, power-hungry things? Can they not see the greed in these positions they so lust after? All we wished to do was help. You must write to me and tell me how it all goes. Write care of my mother, Ann Dumaresq, in Cheltenham. Promise me, Amelia, please?"

Amelia promised she would write. Eliza withdrew from Amelia's arms. She sniffed in a very undignified way. "Not a good look for the Governor's wife, is it?" She gave Amelia a wan smile. She had just mopped her eyes on a fine lawn handkerchief when there was a knock at the door. She took a deep breath, catching Amelia's eyes; she smiled and did her magic swipe and called, "Enter."

"Ma'am, Mrs Hill and Mrs Landon have called. Are you 'at home'?" the butler inquired.

Eliza saw Amelia's smile. "Yes, I am Johnson. Please bring them in and tea for four, please." She turned to Amelia. "God's timing? I was hoping that one of these two could take you." She heard Amelia's tiny gasp, then saw her smile and nod.

"Phoebe, Sadie, please come in," Eliza welcomed her friends. "I have asked Amelia to stay. Do you mind?"

"Absolutely not, as it's about Amelia that we have come," Sadie said. "Ralph spoke to John and Richard yesterday at church, and knowing the situation, we thought we'd come and visit."

"Do you wish me to leave Mrs Landon?" Amelia said to the kind lady.

Sadie Landon smiled encouragingly at Amelia. "No, my dear, we three are some who know how your situation sits. We also know that your work with us has been invaluable, and as much as Phoebe would love to have you stay with her, I would have an excuse as our little Amabel is at the stage where she needs a Governess." She saw the amazed look at the child's name. "We couldn't decide if we should name her Amelia or Isabel, so we made up a name." She smiled and then continued. "This is so we could continue the pretence. John and I would love to offer you and Essie a room until your term finishes. It will mean that you can stay on and not have to explain your situation to anyone else."

"You would do that for me, Mrs Landon?" She couldn't see her very well, as the tears welling in her eyes blurred her vision. "Why are you all so kind?"

Eliza touched her arm. "Have you heard the saying, '*There but for the grace of God, go I*'?"

Amelia nodded. Eliza continued. "My dear, any of us could have been convicted for the petty things. Do you remember I said when you came that I looked into your case? I know you are innocent, and your case should have been thrown out of court. If it had not been a duke bringing forward the case, it would have been. You were merely a scapegoat. I think it was to spite your father. Did you know of the animosity between them? I can't understand how the duke sent his daughter to your parents' school in the first place unless it was his intention all along to slight the family. It just doesn't gel.

Some information is missing from the story." Eliza held Amelia's hand and patted it. "Amelia, your work with us this last year has given us so much insight into the needs of the women in the Factory. We would never have thought about bathing facilities. We all presumed that water would always be made available; it's just so fundamental. Even teaching some of the basic things like sewing, cooking, and bathing. These things would not have occurred to us either. I just wish I had some way of undoing what was done to you."

Phoebe Hill picked up the conversation. "Amelia, do you remember the day I met you?" she asked. "It was the day you arrived. You were sitting cuddling your sleeping cherub. The look of adoration on your face when you looked at her tore at my heart. I saw then that there was no ring on your hand. I wondered. I knew Eliza was expecting 'help' and that she was apparently 'special'. Amelia, I saw in your love and compassion. I saw someone who the world of men had hurt. You have never held Essie's birth against her. You love her as you should; she is innocent. But in this world, society is not so forgiving. We three know your story and love you and accept you, but not everyone will." Phoebe paused, letting her words sink in. "Amelia, in two years, you will have to decide what you will do with the rest of your life, but until then, you will come under our care."

Eliza gently squeezed her hand. "Amelia and I were just discussing our departure before you came in. I was going to ask if either of you would take her. Sadie, if she were to go with you, no questions would be asked. So, can I leave her in your care? Amelia, will you go to my friend?"

Sadie Landon was a dear lady. Amelia nodded. "I'd love to Mrs Landon, and I'd love to look after Amabel. She and Essie love each other already, or I'll even be a laundry maid. Anything rather than go back in there." She gave her a beaming smile and released a nervous sigh. Under her breath, she was thanking God.

The following weeks passed in a flurry of activity. Eliza needed to hand over the running of things in her various committees to other ladies. Packing and sorting everything from the past six years took time. Only days before they left, Amelia and Essie were moved to Landon's house, this time accompanied by cases of possessions. The room there was lovely. She could again have Essie with her in her room and was to be a governess again. Eliza gave Amelia many of her unwanted warm climate clothes as she knew she'd not need them in London. There were also shawls, bonnets, gloves, and numerous other items, also no longer required. Amelia shared the bountiful gifts with other staff members. One beautiful deep blue velvet evening cloak Amelia could not bear to give away. It had a small mud mark on the hem, which Amelia was able to remove. Even at home, she'd not had one so nice and warm. It had a matching muff, and both were edged with swansdown. There were also two fabulous lightweight ball gowns: one light blue and one in soft mint green. Eliza also gave Amelia all the children's old clothing she'd decided not to take. "You won't need all these, but take what you want and give the rest away." Caroline, at three, had outgrown her baby gowns, but with Eliza increasing, she knew she'd need some clothing on board.

The week before departure on the *Hooghly*, the Governor called into the sitting room while the two ladies were talking. "My dear, I have some interesting news for you. I'm not sure what you will think, but I can see God has chosen our travelling companions. They are a couple who will need our assistance."

"Oh, who, Ralph dearest?" Eliza asked.

"Do you remember I told you there was a reluctant Earl in the Colony? Pennecuick, that solicitor from London, came and saw me last year, and I pointed him to *Rock Cottage* up on the hill. The name of the man was Samuel Corbett." The Governor sat and relaxed. "Well, it turns out Sam didn't want the role and tried to fob it off to his son Daniel, who's now Viscount Clarestow." He waved his hand as if brushing aside the information. "Anyway, I knew all that. It seems that Daniel's wife died in childbirth earlier this year, and he now has a son and heir. They are returning to England with us, my dear." He had heard Amelia gasp.

"Are you all right, Amelia?" Eliza asked, surprised at her reaction.

She nodded, then said, "Viscount Clarestow, Nigel, was one of my father's friends."

"Does the name Garney mean anything to you?" the Governor asked.

"Yes, that was Mr Nigel's name. He used to visit Father. I vaguely remember a younger brother, but I overheard Mr Nigel telling my father his brother was a black sheep." Amelia's heart was racing at the mention of the family.

Ralph continued. "Well, that would be right. I looked into his case. He was accused of attempting to steal from the poor box at their church. He's served his time, again, for a trumped-up charge of nothing. The poor man was given seven years for *not* stealing, for he didn't even get the thing open. Anyway, he's been living here under the name of Samuel Corbett, but his name is really Garney. The Corbett was his mother's name, I believe. I looked into his file yesterday when I realised whom we were travelling with." Ralph looked at his wife. "Well, my dear. This will be an interesting trip. Lord Sam's wife, Lady Anne, will travel with them and Lord Daniel and his four small children. We're the only cabin passengers, so I have booked the rest of the vacant cabins for us. Lady Anne came as a convict, but I read that her case was quashed some years ago. I wonder if anyone actually notified her of that?" He sat grinning, looking lovingly at his wife. They sat discussing the trip, and then Ralph turned to his wife. "I wonder if Lord Samuel had permission to return. I think his release was only Conditional. Lady Anne, of course, has no problem, as I said." He fell silent, thinking deeply. "I'll take some paperwork with me just in case. I'll also add an Absolute Pardon form as I'll still be officially Governor until I land; I'll date it before I leave, though, just to make sure. This will be an interesting trip." They smiled at each other. "I may as well give the rules one last poke before I have to answer to the powers that be." He gave a huge grin, then excused himself.

Eliza's brown eyes twinkled gleefully. "I think God has been busy, dear. Have you wondered where you'll go after your release? I told you Ralph is leaving instructions that you are to get an Absolute Pardon, too, when your time is up. This means you can return home should you wish. Amelia, I shall write to you once we are settled. By the time we get over there and then write, nearly a year will have passed, but I shall let you know where we are living. You are welcome to make your home with us if you so wish."

"Oh, Eliza, are you sure? I'm not sure I'll even return yet. I have not heard from Jimmy for some months now and am wondering why. I just hope he's well." Amelia had not thought about what would happen to her after her time was up. Places open to her as an unpaid servant would close once she needed payment. "I'm sure that when the time is right, I'll know what decision to make. I still have the £10 Jimmy gave me, and that will pay for a ticket home, and I have five of the ten sovereigns, too. I do not know what the next two years will bring. I shall do what is required, and I shall strive to assist Sadie and Phoebe where I can."

"Thank you, Amelia. Please know that I will keep you in my prayers." Eliza patted her arm.

The day finally arrived for their departure. Amelia and Essie travelled down to the docks with the younger children. She would settle them in their cabins and say their goodbyes once on board. It was mid-October, and a chill wind blew off the water. Once she had settled the two boys in their cabin with Cornelia, she left them and took Caroline and Essie to find Eliza. As she left the cabin, she bumped into a man whom she presumed was the Earl.

He looked at her as though he'd seen a ghost but said nothing. She, too, remained silent, just nodding to him. In shock, she realised this was the Sam Garney from her father's youth. She turned and watched him as he walked into his cabin. She knocked and entered Eliza's cabin. "I think I just bumped into the Earl. He's nothing like his brother Nigel."

"Oh, this will be interesting." Eliza chuckled. "Oh, how I wish I could get you to come home with us."

"Don't tempt me. I've travelled with less." Amelia laughed. "At least this time, I'd be a little more comfortable. Thankfully, I wasn't below deck on the way out. Mary and I were the ship's surgeon's assistants, thanks to Jimmy. I think the doctor was another of my brother's friends. Either that or well bribed. I think the latter may have been correct, but he was kind. Talking of which, have you met the ship's doctor yet? I believe his name is Surgeon James Ellis. I have no idea if he's any good or if he's just the ship's butcher."

"Oh, Amelia, I should meet him, shouldn't I? Leave the girls with me, and can you see if you can send someone for him, please? You know what will happen if I appear on deck," Eliza asked.

"Thank you, okay." Amelia left Essie with her and went to find either the doctor or someone who could find him for Eliza. As she left the cabin, she bumped into Sam again. This time, she didn't move out of the way. "Sam, you won't remember me as we've never met, but I'm Horace Westaweller's daughter, Amelia. I believe you and Nigel used to come and stay at our place in Aylesford. Do you remember? Not that you'd remember me as I wasn't born, but I remember Nigel; he used to come often."

Sam was stunned, but he nodded.

She continued. "I'm serving out my sentence. I believe you did, too. Sam, I can't talk now, but you can trust Ralph and Eliza Darling. I've been working as their Governess. I have two years to go on my term. Ask Eliza my story. I'll let her know she can tell both of you everything. I think you will understand."

He took her hand. "I will, Amelia. I remember your father well. I enjoyed my various stays at Pittford Manor. Thank you for stopping. It means a lot."

"Make friends with them, Sam; trust them. They can help you. Ralph has something for you already, but I'll let him tell you about that." Amelia knew she had to find the doctor for Eliza. "I must go, Sam. It's been nice meeting you, though. I'll pray for you." As she left, she smiled to herself. 'So, not how one is supposed to speak to an Earl.' With that thought, she left.

Sam was now standing alone in the narrow corridor. Her family home was one of his few happy memories from his youth. Horace was one of Nigel's friends, so they were not banned from visiting them. Why was she out here as a convict? He stood looking down the empty corridor, stunned by the recent revelation. A smile slowly spread over his face. He felt as though he'd just spoken to a messenger from God. He and Anne had nearly cancelled their trip when they heard who they would be travelling with. Now, he was sure they were where they were meant to be. Amelia was the image of her father. No wonder she looked familiar, even though he had never met her. He knocked gently on his cabin door and walked in to tell Anne of the strange meeting and stranger conversation.

Amelia found a ship's maid who went and found the doctor for her. She waited on deck until he arrived, and she led him to the cabin to meet Eliza. She took Caroline and Essie into the adjoining sitting room and left the doctor in the cabin with the door ajar. Five minutes later, the doctor departed. "Thank you, Amelia; I think he'll do nicely. Well, I don't have much choice, do I?" She smiled. "I suppose travelling expectant is easier than with a tiny babe."

"Eliza, I saw Sam again, only this time I stopped him and had a quick chat. I told him he could trust you. I also said I'd give you my permission to fill him in on me. Everything you think is necessary. I don't know why, but I think he should know." The two women sat playing with the two little two-year-old girls. "Eliza, he's absolutely nothing like his brother. Nigel had the most beautiful blue eyes. Sam's are the most delicious chocolate browns. I shouldn't say that about a strange man, should I? Let alone an Earl." She giggled girlishly and blushed.

Eliza giggled. "Don't let Ralph hear you."

There was a tap on the door. "Half an hour, madam," a steward announced.

"Oh, Eliza!" The two knew the time had come for Amelia to go onshore. Up until now, they had both held their tears, but now neither could. "I hate goodbyes, but this time, I insist that you return and live with us. You are a sister to me, Amelia. Promise at least you will visit?" Eliza enfolded her in her arms. "Come. We will gather the other children and watch our departure from on deck. We shall brave the crowds. Ralph will need to be on duty until then." She turned and collected her wrap and a letter. "Amelia, I have a letter for you. Please do not open it until you get back to Landon's. I have enjoyed this last year so much. Thank you, my dear." With that, she gave her another hug. Now, to put on my fake face for the last time for a while. "Pray for us, Amelia, for we will need them. Read your Bible daily, and do not ever give up. God is already using you and your experiences to assist others."

Then she did as Amelia had often seen Eliza do before. She saw Eliza pass her hand over her face and put on her official face. Amelia had giggled when she first saw her do this. Now she understood its meaning. It was a facade. The official persona that Eliza detested. She called it her *fake* face. She would miss the fun they had, the verbal dissections after the functions when they arrived home. That, too, had now finished, at least for some months. They left the cabin together, each with a small girl in their arms. Amelia saw Sadie and Phoebe waiting on the dock; their husbands accompanied both. Many others were there, too, though they looked like trouble. She frowned, and Amelia squeezed Eliza's hand in farewell, and she headed down the gangplank with Essie in her arms. Once on the dock, she walked to Sadie and stood beside her.

She saw Sam and a younger version, which Amelia presumed was Daniel and a lovely-looking older lady. The three were standing alone. She waved and received a wave from Sam and the lady in reply. Also, a nod of acknowledgement from the younger man. She noted a small baby in the lady's arms and could see the fair heads of the three little girls they were travelling with. The young man lifted the shortest child; Sam then picked up the next youngest so that now all could see over the railing. Everyone stood waiting; one by one, the ropes were readied to be cast off. The sailors were waiting up the masts, ready to unfurl the sails as soon as they reached the channel. Amelia and Sadie were drawn back from the rest of the crowd by Sadie's husband, John. Phoebe and Richard Hill moved with them. Soon, the five of them were crushed and decided to leave the dock and move onto the grassed area on the hill east of the quay. They waved and pointed to the other side of the ship. From there, they watched in horror as the angry mob began to get rowdy. Some eggs were thrown, and they started jeering and then as the ship was pulled away from the dock. The cheering and booing of the Darlings started from the rabble. Ralph and Eliza had moved out of sight of the rabble and came to wave a final salute to their few friends.

Amelia turned to Sadie. "Why are they being so mean? What have they done? How cruel are these mean-spirited people?" Amelia stood aghast at the rudeness of the crowd. She saw Sam and his family also move to their side of the ship. It was only then that she noticed Major Grace and another older man standing near them.

"Major," Reverend Richard called. Both men turned and walked to join them.

Major Grace laughed. "Tom, come and meet my friends."

Richard Hill made the introductions, "Major Tom Turner, you know my lovely Phoebe, of course, and this is John and Sadie Landon from church, and Mrs Amelia West, who will be making her home with them."

Tom bowed to them. "Greetings! This is a sad day for the Colony, totally undeserved. We'll need to pray hard for them all," Major Tom said, and all agreed.

Amelia realised that the Landons didn't know Major Edward Grace, so she did the introductions as a friend of her brother Jim. Tom stood chatting to Reverend Richard and Phoebe.

The younger, very tall, fair-haired major walked to Amelia's side. "How are you coping? I noted the new moniker?" He chuckled.

"It was Eliza's idea. I've never been asked, so I have neither confirmed nor denied it. These friends all know the truth," she motioned to the group around her, "but we don't discuss it." Amelia smiled shyly at the handsome soldier. "Have you heard from Jimmy lately? He's been silent, but I have not heard for over six months now. That's not like him."

"No, I'm sorry. I have heard nothing since you left. That's a bit of a worry, though; I'm sure he has a good reason. Maybe he has a new lady-love." Ned chuckled, trying hard to lighten her anxiety.

"I've not had a chance to thank you for your referral to work with the Darlings. They have been wonderful, and I shall miss them. Eliza became a good friend, and I have enjoyed working with her and her team of friends from the Benevolent Society. Eliza insisted on first names the day I started. It was her idea that she introduced me as Mrs West. I didn't contradict her." Amelia stole a glance at his profile. She had not admired a man for many, many years. Pity she was still a convict and he a soldier. "She's invited me to make my home with them in England on my release."

"Will you go?" He glanced at her and met her admiring gaze. "You only have two years left. You will have to start thinking of what you will do."

"I know, I'm torn. If it were not for Essie, I'd jump at going home. But 'home' will not be welcoming that much, I know. I've not heard from either parent since the day of the accusation. Neither came to the trial, and both probably sided with the duke." She had a hint of sadness in her voice. "If I have a place with Eliza, I may go, as I can be useful while there. I'm determined not to sit and twiddle my fingers as I'm no longer a lady of leisure." She saw the sails drop from the top of the crossbars on the masts as the ship reached the centre of the channel. First, one, then another filled, and the ship jumped forward as all nine sails filled with the strengthening breeze. "I shall continue Eliza's work with the Benevolent Society while I'm with Sadie and working for the improvement of facilities for the convict women and orphans. I know what it's like; I know what I would have wanted while I was in there. The last thing we started was supplying women with fabric and thread. That parcel you sent to Martha Turner inspired that. Her friend Maureen even showed us how to make buttons from river pebbles. Even how to unravel the calico and make a thread. I learned so much in that year. Your monthly parcels were, dare I say it, my 'sanity savers'."

Ned brushed off her thanks by saying, "Jimmy sent some money, but I had to work out how to stretch it for you. When I found the load of water-damaged fabric, my friends Charles and Sal were over the moon. So I got Sal to select some for you, and well, you know the rest of that story." His smile sent her heart spiralling.

"Essie still has the dolly you gave her when she was born. She won't sleep without it," she whispered.

"I bought that from a church stall. I knew you were due soon. Funny, but I thought you'd have a girl. She's very like you were when not much older," he smiled at Amelia. "I had bought it months before, soon after I heard you were expecting. I kept it until I heard you'd safely delivered and sent it that next month." He looked at the dark-haired child sitting quietly in Amelia's arms. The child's huge blue eyes caught his, and she smiled. "She really is adorable. You have done well with her." He bent and stroked her cheek.

"She's my life, major. I find that she's more and more affectionate as she gets older." As she spoke, Essie gently rubbed her mother's cheek with her hand, then snuggled to her neck and, with one chubby arm wrapped around her neck, closed her big blue eyes. "See? It melts my heart every time; she's totally innocent of her father's evil. I'll never hold it against her. My life is now for her alone."

"You're a wonderful mother, Amelia. I've been honoured to assist you in a small way." He smiled that devastating smile of his. "Martha and Jack send their regards, by the way. I was out that way last month, and they are well. Martha asked me to let you know that baby number seven is due early next year. She wishes you were back to assist her. At least Jack has now finished building the inn and the stables. They have a loft with hammocks for overnighters now, and many are using the service."

"Oh, that's wonderful! I'll write and congratulate her. Thank you for letting me know." Amelia was delighted. "I find one a handful. I'm not sure I'd cope with seven. I dare say it's easier with someone to assist."

Ned couldn't answer that. He had no idea. As they spoke, the ship slipped around the headland and went from view. Essie had her thumb in her mouth and was asleep on her mother's neck.

Chapter 7   Another Start

*A*s John and Sadie turned to leave, Sadie bent to whisper to him, and then John turned and invited everyone to join them for afternoon tea. The handsome young major caught Major Tom's eye and nodded. Reverend Richard asked Phoebe a silent question with a single eyebrow raised. She, too, nodded. Amelia was trying to juggle the sleeping child; her shawl had fallen from one shoulder. The major saw her struggle. "May I?" Ned asked. He took the child from Amelia and had her lying in his strong arms. "I'm used to cuddling my friend Charles and Sal's children. They have six, so I've had lots of practice."

Amelia smiled. It finally dawned on her whom he was talking about. "Molly told me it's Eddie; he's Edward too, isn't it? He's the one named after you, isn't he? I had to bring a parcel to him when I came. He and Timmy are at school here, aren't they?"

Ned nodded. "Yes, I have another parcel for him. They named their second son after me; only they didn't realise how exactly the same his name was. It was a bit embarrassing, but he was born on my twenty-second birthday, and I love him dearly. Charles and I could be brothers; we are so alike," he explained, but Amelia saw a flash of anxiety cross his face. "And no, Eddie is not my child. I can guarantee that. But he looks like I did as a lad, and so does his brother Charlie, although he's a little more like my brother, Douglas." With Major Ned now holding the sleeping little girl, Amelia meandered up the hill with the group of new friends. What a difference twelve months makes! "She really is adorable, Amelia, but you know that. Don't you?" Ned said quietly.

"Yes, and if my life is problematic because of her, she'll never know it. I now know of a mother's love; it makes me understand better Jesus's love for us. I'd give my life for her, and she'll never know it. I may yet have to do just that," Amelia spoke softly. "It's also why I'm so confused about my own parent's abandonment of me. I just do not understand it."

Ned looked at her in a glance of both compassion and sorrow. "Don't let it bury you, Amelia. Remember you told me Jimmy said, 'Trust Him.' Well, I know you do, but trust Jesus even more. Even if something has happened to Jimmy, your faith will keep you strong. Jesus will make a path for you that you can follow without having to compromise that choice." Ned said softly, "Just trust him."

Amelia could not believe that she was having this conversation with one of the most handsome men she'd ever seen. He was carrying her illegitimate child cradled in his arms, and he was telling her to trust God. Her eyes misted, and she brushed the errant tears away. "Major Ned, I doubt, all the time. Mostly, I can't see where He's leading me, so I just keep walking in faith. If a door opens and feels right, I go that way, like staying with the Darlings and now the Landons. It wasn't so hard with Eliza here as I could see a glimmer of light, but now she's gone, I'm floundering again."

They had fallen slightly behind the others so they could continue chatting privately. Ned checked where the others were, "I'm going to issue you a challenge. I want you now to start thinking about your return home. Jimmy wants you there, and I think you should go." He snuck a glance at her to see what her reaction would be.

"Really? But wouldn't it be better for her here?" she asked shyly.

"No, if you keep the 'Mrs' moniker, you won't need to explain anything. Mrs Darling was wise as it gets rid of most of the most obvious problems." He paused, thinking. She saw the look of puzzlement cross his face. "I might check the paperwork and see if Cyrus filled in the paperwork correctly. He may have mentioned an intention to marry. Either way, it's a common-law marriage." Ned again took a glance at her.

Amelia didn't know how to answer. "But is that legal?"

"Probably not, but out here, things get blurred, you know that. You can even marry here if you have a spouse at home. Back home, no one will ask. We both know you did not choose your life. If you settle with the Darlings in England, it will just be presumed it will be above board. You have nothing to hide from them. If you wish to marry, then I'd advise you to tell your future husband before you agree to anything."

"Oh!" She had so much to think about.

"Something to think about," he said quietly. "I think we are here." He saw the group in front of him open a gate and walk into a lovely home. "Nice place. I'm sure you'll be happy here."

"I am, thanks, Major Ned. I've been here a few days already. They are as lovely as Eliza." She gave a deep sigh. "Do you want me to take her?"

"No, she's quite comfortable and no weight at all. If you could hold the gate, then I won't need to move her. She's so different from the other six. Luke is Charles' youngest, and he's a year older than this poppet. They are all fair."

Oh, if only she'd met this man when she was just Miss Westaweller, he would make the most wonderful father. "I appreciate you carrying her. She's a deadweight for me when she's asleep." She held the door open, and they walked inside. He gave her another heart-melting smile but said nothing.

Sadie Landon saw the major with the sleeping child. "If you follow me, major, we'll take you in, and you can put her straight into her bed." Sadie was already protecting her. Ned smiled at them both but followed silently. Thus getting rid of any impropriety by going into Amelia's bedroom. The three of them walked to Amelia's new rooms, and the major gently placed the sleeping child in the cot. As he did so, he stroked her cheek, placed her doll in her arms and then departed. Amelia slipped off her little shoes and covered her with a blanket. Essie slipped her thumb back into her mouth and settled comfortably back into dreamland.

In the front room, the two majors settled down for tea with Reverend Richard and Phoebe Hill. John Landon was talking about importing goods for the colony. Amelia caught the words 'damaged fabrics', and her eyes lit up. She'd ask more about that later. She knew that Eliza always had a good supply of fabric to use for the Female Factory, and she had wondered where it came from. Amelia did not get a chance to pass more than a word or two with him before they departed. She learned that Major Tom had just retired and moved into Sam and Anne Corbett's house 'Rock Cottage' up next to the Glebe.

Ned, being much the same age as their son, Danny, used to visit him while Tom visited Sam. They had all become friends. Tom lived alone and hoped that Ned would use the cottage as a base while in town. The house gave Ned a bed in Sydney rather than at the Hyde Park Barracks. He'd come into town to see off his friend Danny. Ned also had to see the Evans family and check in on the two boys. He told Tom he'd meet him at the cottage later as he had an errand to do. Amelia knew he would see Eddie and Timmy as he looked at her and smiled. Yes, he loved children. She knew that now. The stroke of Essie's cheek had shown that he really cared. She decided to pray for him that one day he'd find his own happiness. Their conversation had achieved something, though. She was now sure she would return home. Essie would be five by then, and she'd be easier to travel with. She had a lot to think about.

"Major Ned is nice, isn't he?" Sadie said after all the visitors had gone.

"Yes, he sent me parcels when I was at Emu Plains for the year. My brother had given him the money, and Major Ned bought the things we needed. One was a huge parcel of water-damaged fabrics." She glanced at Sadie. "I heard Mr John say that he imports fabrics. Is that where they came from?"

"Probably Amelia, nicely avoided topic," Sadie chuckled.

"I can wish to the end of the earth. Major Ned is Jimmy's friend, and that's all. He's like a big brother. And even if I wanted more, he's not interested. What's more, he knows everything, and I mean everything. I also told him of Eliza's suggestion of the 'moniker' as he called it, of 'Mrs'. No one has ever asked, and I have never been in a situation where I've had to confirm or deny it. Eliza bought my ring, and she gifted it to me. So I say it was given in love. Major Ned said it was a common-law marriage. Sadie, I'm so confused. I had no choice. He took me by force, but as I said to Major Ned, I would do anything for Essie now. She is totally innocent, and I'll never tell her about him. Imagine knowing what he was like?" She was sad but looked up at Sadie and grinned almost wickedly, "Having said that, Ned is so handsome, isn't he? I wish I weren't a convict. I can but dream," she smiled and sighed.

"He's the sort of man that gives a uniform a good name," Sadie chuckled. "Many don't, my dear."

Amelia met her twinkling eyes with a smile and a nod. "I can but wish." She giggled in a mischievous manner. "Did you see him when he put her down? He stroked her cheek and tucked the doll he bought her in her arms."

"Oh, he bought that, did he?" She raised her eyebrows in wonderment.

"Yes, it was in the parcel after she was born. It arrived with a beautiful child's gown, her pink blanket, and more napkins. Somehow, I think that Jimmy didn't supply money for those sorts of things. I had not even met him then." She met Sadie's surprised look. "I have only met him a few times before today, well as grown-ups, and the first time was the night before I came to the Darlings. He arranged for me to come by the morning ferry, and he'd arranged accommodation with Molly and Bill Miller at the Rear Admiral Duncan Inn with money Jimmy had sent. He came to the inn, and we sat and talked. He filled me in on a lot, as did I for him. I remember when I was a child, at least I'm pretty sure it was him, a boy of ten who had nearly white hair and was always kind to me. I would have been five when we first met. He knew most of my story as Jimmy had filled him in, so I told him the rest in detail. I probably shouldn't have, but I did. He knows exactly what I went through. I didn't think he'd believe me if he heard it from another woman, but from me, I knew he would." She wiped a tear away angrily; just thinking of Cyrus made her shudder. "Some of those men should be banned from allowing women to be assigned to them. Cyrus was one. Molly and Bill knew him and were horrified." Amelia had a wave of sadness cross her face. Sadie saw it. "Ned told me I was not Cyrus's first assignee; the last woman died. Now I wonder how that happened. It probably would have been my lot if he'd lived." She shuddered again.

Sadie came and placed a loving arm around her. "Tell me if you wish, dear." Her care and compassion broke Amelia.

In between sobs, Amelia once more poured out her story. From the initial punch and rape while she was groggy, the first time by the road and the continual abuse for the next three months, to the incident where the horse killed him on the day. Then she told of how she told Cyrus she was expecting a child. The shame washed over her afresh; she sat rocking on her seat. Lifting her water-filled eyes to Sadie, she said, "How can I go back to a normal life after that? How can I even think of a man like Major Ned when he knows what happened to me? I'm used and abused. Soiled goods." Her teary eyes met Sadie's. "I'm surprised that Jimmy has not wiped me, too. I poured out everything to him in detail."

"God has a man for you somewhere, dear. Someone special, I'm not saying Major Ned isn't, but, no, he's not for you. Treat him like a handsome brother, and he will keep caring for you." Sadie glanced at her. "Mind you, I wouldn't tell John, but he is drop-dead gorgeous, isn't he?"

The two ladies' eyes met, and they giggled, and both nodded in agreement. "Yes, he is," Amelia agreed with her wholeheartedly with a soggy chortle. "And he's kind, and all that is good too. He also encourages me in my faith. And no, I'm not in love with him, although I do love him, and I do love what he's done for us." She gave a deep sigh.

"Enough of the daydreams; we have work to do, my dear. Come, it's time you saw my Aladdin's Cave." Sadie led her into the workroom at the back of the house. This had initially been a winter sitting room and was now used for damaged fabric storage. John Landon would bring in the most damaged bolts of fabric for use by the convict women. These were so damaged that he could not on-sell. Sadie opened the door, and Amelia gasped. Sadie had not shown her to this room before.

"Oh, Sadie! I'm in seventh heaven. All this fabric and oh…." Amelia was lost for words. She stood gazing at more than fifty bolts of water-damaged bolts of fabrics. They sat cutting the drill into ten-yard lengths for dresses and the lawn and poplins into three-yard lengths. Other fabrics were measured out and packaged. After measuring and cutting three flat bolts of drill, Amelia said, "Sadie, do these need to be perfect ten-yard lengths, or can I do approximate yardages? Will an inch or two matter?"

"Um, no, I don't suppose it will. Why?" Sadie looked puzzled.

"I've measured much fabric over the years. This is a yard if you hold it to your nose tip with your head turned away, to clenched fingers with your arm outstretched. See…" She measured the length of the fabric and then asked Sadie to check it.

"Less than half an inch out. Oh my, that will save hours, Amelia." Sadie stood looking at the bolts of fabric. "Hours and hours of time." She plopped herself on a chair and giggled.

"How about I measure one and see how much I'm out over the ten yards?" She measured the length of the blue drill. Then, she marked the length with a pin. Sadie then measured it again, and there was an inch out.

"I can live with that, Amelia. Let's tear it?" The two started measuring and tearing the lengths and piling up the ten-yard lengths. As they measured and ripped, the pile grew quickly. Together, they then folded the torn lengths into neat piles. Thus stacked, they were then able to sort the extras. Ribbons, cords, buttons, small packets of pins and needles, and a small stick of chalk and thread were added to various baskets on the table. Each bundle would have one item from each basket added to it.

Amelia had just placed the last length of cord. "Mama called these 'notions,' I have no idea why. Or should I say, I have no notion why." They laughed heartily. The packing of the actual charity bundles would wait until others arrived.

Some of the more delicate fabrics were not torn but cut into smaller sizes and would be used for other projects like bags, buttons, trim, and even hats. With each packet, some matching thread and a small package of needles were added. The needles themselves had to be packed as they arrived loose in a bundle of one thousand. Each had to be pinned into papers and folded over to prevent rusting. Pins, too, came in bulk and had to be sorted into small bundles. They put three needles and about twenty pins in each pack.

"Sadie, I've not said thank you for taking me in. I hate secrets, and I hate lies, but I know that to continue under the guise of 'Mrs West' is wise." Amelia had obviously been deep in thought while she worked. "Mrs Hill knows all, but I am still a 'Ticket of Leave' convict. Nothing will ever change that."

Sadie asked Amelia about the conditions of the Factory. She looked at Sadie. A wave of sadness passed over her face. "Do you want the truth or the watered-down version?"

"The truth, unadulterated too, starts with when you first went in. It will help me to understand the needs of the girls."

Amelia nodded. What she could tell them would help others. "I'll tell you, Sadie, as you need to know what that first day was like. We were taken off the ship and herded like cattle into the Factory. The soldiers were rough and loved man-handling us, a squeeze here and a pinch there. They'd press themselves against us whenever possible. Even then, I think some women may have been *had at* while in the queue. The men seem to think that all women want to have close personal relations with them. We could hear screams coming from the back of the group. Mary and I wondered if that's what was happening. Many of our shiploads were poor Irish girls. Some were only fourteen. They were far too young to have been with a man, and yet they were pack-raped, sometimes up to ten of the guards, one after the other."

Sadie's eyes filled with unshed tears as she listened.

"Sadie, when I look at all this fabric, I think of what is officially supposed to be given to each convict woman. All of us were required to bathe upon admission. It's the only full wash we were allowed to have. We were allocated one bucket of washing water per dormitory for up to fifty women. That first one was the only bath I got for the more than six months I was there. While we were washing, we were inspected by the Matron. She then searched the discarded clothing, took any money that was found, and confiscated it. She missed the money in my Bible. As soon as she realised it was a Bible, she threw it down without checking it. Thankfully, it didn't fall out. We were then supposed to be issued with clothing or 'slops' in blue or brown serge, a white apron and a straw bonnet for Sunday with a jacket and coarse apron for weekdays. First-class women were supposed to be issued special Sunday clothes: one white cap, a long dress with muslin frill, one red calico jacket, two cotton check handkerchiefs, one blue petticoat, one under petticoat or factory flannel, one white calico apron, two shifts, one pair of grey stockings, one pair of shoes, one straw bonnet, and a clothes bag to hold all. You know that list. For work, we were supposed to have two calico work caps, a drab serge petticoat, a drab serge jacket and one apron; only there were so many of us on my ship that we had to split the bundles. I only got a work apron, a mob cap and a clothes bag. As I had shoes, stockings, a dress and petticoats that were far better than what was on offer and being small, none of the other clothing fitted, so I could keep my own clothing. Matron missed my six sovereigns that were sewn into my bodice. She'd be livid if she realised she missed £16."

Sadie didn't interrupt her but was stunned that the *Female Friendly Society of the Town of Sydney* efforts supplied all these things. Now, the Benevolent Society was assisting, too. They should have had ample supplies. She frowned and shook her head. "Go on, dear. What are the facilities like?"

"The beds in the Factory are, in essence, wooden pallets. We were allocated a blanket, but more often than not, they were old and riddled with holes and sometimes fleas, too. We'd see piles of new ones delivered, but none ever made their way to us. There was little heating other than the brazier outside. It was little better than a drum with a fire in it. But it was often colder around the brazier than it was inside and out of the wind. I kept my Bible down my bodice; it was enclosed in a leather wrap, as our possessions were rifled with every new group of arrivals." Amelia wiped away tears. "After we were graded, the first class were all the newly arrived women. Particularly from England, some of the Irish girls are mistreated, particularly the really young ones. Just because they were Irish. I knew of one poor girl who was raped over forty times by one group of soldiers. She was ill for a very long time." Amelia fell silent, again wiping away angry tears. She fell to thinking of the young girl. "She was nearly unconscious when found naked and bleeding badly. Sadie, second-class women are those on probation. Some of the Irish women are also placed in this category. If they have been caught in a compromising situation, regardless of whether it's their fault or not. In other words, they were being raped, yet they got punished. They are put in this group. Others are also placed in this group if they are returned after assignment or are expectant women. The third class were supposed to be the rough ones. Convicted of crimes here after they have been sent out. Sadly, if you get on Matron's bad books, it's enough to get you demoted into third class for no reason. It's all at her whim. She was only reasonably new when I arrived in 1828, but she was no better than the one before her after six months. Her husband is a bad egg, though. He and his soldier friends would come in after we were asleep and have their way with the women. Hand over their mouths and a punch to the face if they yelled. If they reported it, they received no rations the next day and were demoted a grade. I took the furthermost pallet from the door, and he never bothered coming into Mary and me. There were younger ones closer." Amelia paused. "Are you really sure you want me to go on?"

Sadie wiped the tears from her face with the back of her hands; she stifled a few sobs. "If you feel you can, dear. It makes me understand you so much better."

Amelia shrugged and continued. "We were allocated various jobs, from smashing rocks for the third-class women to working the looms for the first-class ones. Some were set to card the fleeces, but there were many other chores, too. They make linen there, too, so the flax needed processing. One of the best jobs in winter was doing the washing. The boilers were so nice to work near. The soldiers' red woollen coats were never sent; the soldiers sponged them clean themselves, but the shirts and smalls were sent in. The ironing was also a good job as it, too, was warm, but I was really only there during the colder months. I'd hate to be in either of those areas during the summer. Sadie, I think that's enough if that's all right?" Amelia stood with her head bowed, leaning on a table. Silent sobs shook her shoulders.

Sadie went to her and took her in her arms. "Oh, my dear Amelia, I didn't want you so upset. To have gone through what you have, I feel terrible making you relive it. However, now I have an idea of how we can assist them all." Amelia relished the hug. They were very rare in her life.

Chapter 8   The Dream Continues

Sadie and Amelia were joined the next day by Phoebe Hill and three other

ladies. One was Caroline Evans from church, another was Mrs Roberts, the ferry captain's wife, and Mrs Iles, the bookmaker's wife. During the conversation, Caroline discussed her three boys and the two Parramatta lads who had made their home with her. She saw the look on Amelia's face and asked, "Do you know them, dear?"

"No, Mrs Evans, but I brought two parcels from Eddie and Timmy's mothers last year on my way to Mrs Darling. And I know Major Ned Grace. He's a friend of my brother. He mentioned recently that he had to call in to see them."

"Ah, yes! Major Grace. One of God's true gentlemen, isn't he?" Caroline smiled. "He's easy on the eyes, too," she snickered naughtily.

The six ladies had all met the handsome major, and all agreed. Conversations centred around him for some time before returning to the Female Factory. "Did you hear there was another riot there recently? For some unknown reason, the Matron withdrew privileges and sent some of the second-class women to third-class, and they rebelled. There was a mass breakout. Some two hundred escaped, but only half were recaptured."

Again, the conversation concentrated on the Female Factory for some time. Amelia had got along okay with the Matron. Having said that, she still didn't like her.

Amelia stayed silent, knowing that if she started talking, they would soon realise her own status, that of Ticket of Leave convict. Sadie caught her eye, and she dropped her head and retreated into herself. Sadie supplied luncheon for them all, and they sat in the garden enjoying a picnic while Essie and Amabel played together on the lawn.

On return to the workroom, they found three more bolts of material had been delivered. These were exquisite and far too fantastic to be used for prison clothing, one of dark green velvet and two of shot satin. There was no way convicts of any class would wear fabrics fit for a queen. The ladies gushed over the sadness of such a loss of such lovely fabric.

Amelia made a suggestion. "These are far too good for the Factory, but if we made things ourselves and sold them, then we could use the money to cover costs." As they had already completed nearly one hundred parcels that morning, they decided to become more industrious and make some items for sale.

The un-watermarked sections of the green velvet could be made into short capes, bonnets and plain reticules. Also, once the damaged area had been cut off, Amelia realised that they could make small cushions from it, and the damaged sections could be enhanced with embroidery. The others weren't quite sure what she meant, so with one eight-inch square of very damaged velvet, she proceeded to embroider a lovely floral scene using the watermarks as a background. Very shortly, she finished the beautiful landscape scene, and the outcome was delightful.

"Oh, Amelia, that is exquisite. It's too good for a pillow; you could even frame it," Caroline said. "However, I can see what you mean."

The worse the fabric damage was, the easier it was to use as a background for a sewn painting. The sixty-inch wide bolt of velvet had only about a foot width of damage the entire length of it; however, that was nearly forty yards of fabric. However, as they unrolled it, they found the water had syphoned up the central cardboard insert and spread wider the further they unrolled. This would usually have been thrown away. With Amelia's idea, they could now turn this waste into artwork that could make money. Sadie and Amelia unrolled the entire bolt on the table, and foot by foot, they cut off the damage. The edge was uneven, but they were left with over 80% of the bolt in perfect usable fabric. They cut some into neat squares, and they divided them so each could take some home to sew pictures or pillows and even make up some other ideas. One section Sadie decided to make into a table runner. There were still some twenty yards of the damaged fabric. But they had no need to use it all at once. They would start with some small pictures and see how they sold.

"Amelia, you are so clever. We can sew these at home; then we can turn them into pictures, pillows and the like," Phoebe said.

"Actually, I was thinking we can also make some into reticules, sewing a long section together. And we can use some of the worst damaged bits as the bottoms of the bags. Heavily embroidered, of course." Amelia grinned, knowing that the society ladies would look lustfully over these. If only they knew they were made from damaged offcuts. "I'll make one so you can see what you think. But I'm sure they would sell well. Each would be unique. We can do the same with satins and other fancy fabrics. It will be like a reward for us after the packs are done. It's also something we can each do at home."

They continued their good work as a group. Amelia realised it was also a fabulous excuse for a chat and a meet-up, meeting most weeks, sometimes even twice a week. Often, others joined them. They made soaps with lye, and Amelia showed them how to make the essences to add to them. Rose was her favourite, and they could obtain the flowers from various gardens to distil the essences, and it was easy to make. Once added to the soaps, it smelled divine. This was another thing taught to her by Martha.

Sadie and Amelia had sat discussing some of the things she'd learned at home, and the more Sadie knew of Amelia's upbringing, the more she wondered about her. Amelia had not yet confided in her about who she really was.

She'd been with Sadie for nearly six months when an excursion was planned. The Benevolent Society had decided to make a personal visit to the Female Factory. Normally, the Sydney women sent their goods to Parramatta by ferry, and they would be delivered by one of the soldiers from the military barracks in Parramatta. On this April day, they had been asked to 'do' an inspection with the new Governor and his wife. Major-General Sir Richard Bourke had arrived in December after the Darlings had departed, and it was his first visit to the Female Factory.

Amelia did not wish ever to darken the door of the place again. Sadie persuaded her to come on the excursion; it was more that she wouldn't take no for an answer. She felt more like she'd been press-ganged.

Essie and Amabel would stay with the nanny, and she would be freed up to accompany them. To say she was fearful was a vast understatement.

The night before, Amelia woke with a nightmare. Dreaming about the last time she saw the place. It had been the day she was assigned to Cyrus Black. The night before they went, she was sleepless and tearful. "I don't really wish to see it again, Sadie."

"I think you need to, Amelia. I have a feeling something will come of this, but I don't know what." Again, Sadie would not take her no for an answer.

The day dawned bright and sunny. The Governor had sent a town carriage to collect the various ladies who were accompanying them. Phoebe Hill, Caroline Evans, Sadie and Amelia were taken to the waiting ferry. There, they were all introduced to the new Governor and his wife, Elizabeth.

Amelia tried to distance herself from the Vice-Regal couple as much as possible. Eventually, she found herself standing alone on the windy side of the cabin.

Captain Roberts was concerned and tried to get her to move into the cabin. She was so slight that he felt a puff of wind would blow her overboard. He could see her tears; she'd angrily wipe them away.

"Please, ma'am, come into the cabin at least," he pleaded.

She shook her head and stayed where she was. The fear on her face was almost tangible. She was looking back at Sydney as it faded into the distance. She did not hear the footsteps approach.

"I'm glad I find you by yourself, Mrs West, for I wish to confide that Eliza Darling left a private letter for me hinting of your story."

Amelia swung around and met the Governor's wife's eyes with her own teary ones, "No," she said softly.

"Yes, dear, and as such, you will be of great assistance to us. We are here to keep the work going. We have seen far too much cruelty to the convicts and know there is much reform needed. I will need to consult you as to the needs of the women, for I feel you can contribute much to their rehabilitation. Would you assist me in this?"

Amelia was stunned. "How much did Mrs Darling tell you?"

"Well, firstly, she told me you were a friend and on first-name terms. That speaks volumes. Then she wrote that it was at her suggestion that you use 'Mrs' for your name and that your daughter is the most adorable child she's ever met. I also know you have less than two years before you can return home, and yes, I will make sure you receive an Absolute Pardon, too. So I think I know enough. Trust me, my dear, as you did her. I shall keep your confidences." She took Amelia's hand and drew her out of the brisk wind. "Sit with me in the cabin, dear; I'm not well enough to stand here."

Amelia followed her into the cabin. She was finally able to get a good look at the lady. As she sat down, Lady Bourke gave an over-exaggerated shiver.

Amelia stifled a giggle.

"Good, now, Mrs West, I wish also to tell you that Mrs Darling said that you are, in reality, a Viscount's daughter and, therefore, outrank even us. Due to your situation, I am going to request that you call me by my first name in private. It's Betsy to my friends. So may I call you Amelia?" The Governor's wife's riotous brown curls had been blown about in the wind. Her brown-gold eyes were soft and caring. Amelia could see she was not in good health.

Amelia nodded, "Yes, ma'am, to both questions." She dropped her head, thinking, why were people so lovely when she felt so undeserving?

"Amelia, I read your file. I know your story. I am so sorry for what has befallen you, but together, we can bring about change for others and need your assistance. This may be why God has allowed you to be put in this situation. Not that I am putting words into God's mouth, but I can see His hand in it."

Amelia lifted her face to the kindly older lady. Her eyes were filled with tears. She whispered a "yes," she paused before adding, "I don't want to go back in there. I don't want to be recognised by any who may know me. It could destroy you all. Don't you see that? You are all in now on my secret, and therefore, you could be cut by society just by being a friend to me and what I am."

"You are thinking of us? Are you more concerned for our welfare than your own? Oh, Amelia, I knew I was right to befriend you," Betsy stated. In awe that at a time like this, she was concerned for the new friends.

Amelia looked startled. "Yes and no. Don't get me wrong; I have no desire to return."

"Only a true believer would care so much. Have you no concern for yourself? I have no doubts that the experience you had there was bad and that you have no wish to return but that your concern for us is, shall I say, overwhelming."

"Lady Bourke... Betsy, I'd rather work from behind the scenes. I can achieve much and be an advisor without harming anyone. This work needs doing, and I'm willing to assist. But please don't make me go with you today. Please, I'm just not ready. I just can't do it." She finally sobbed. "I'm terrified."

Betsy Bourke drew her into her arms, and Amelia wept.

Amelia continued, "By rights, I should be still in there as I fell with child when assigned. I should have been sent back and (*sob*) ...and...I should still be there (*sob*). Major Grace had me reassigned to the Turners at Emu Plains. He's a friend of my brother. And he's so nice (*sob*). I just can't do it, not yet." Amelia lifted her swollen, reddened eyes and pleaded with Betsy.

"Then you shall not. You can wait for us near the wharf." She pulled a clean handkerchief from her reticule. "Now wipe your eyes, dear, as we are pulling into the river, and Major Grace will be escorting us. You don't want such a handsome man to see you looking so sad."

Amelia hung her head. "He knows all, and I mean all. He is like a brother to me, no more, no less. However, you are correct; I would not like him to see me in such distress." Amelia wiped her eyes.

Sadie had been watching as she'd been in view of the pair inside.

Betsy motioned for her to come inside, and she did with all speed. "Mrs Landon, I feel it will be better for Mrs West to stay near the ferry today; she is not feeling well."

Amelia gave her a wry smile. That's an understatement, she thought.

"I'll see if I can lie down at the Rear Admiral Duncan Inn for a while, Mrs Landon." Amelia saw the sadness pass across Sadie's face. "They have a nice quiet room I should be able to rest in," Amelia said, with a meekness belying her true feelings. As she was still bordering on panic, even being back in Parramatta, she just wished to lock herself in a small dark room and become invisible.

Sadie looked concerned and sat down beside Amelia.

Seeing Amelia was in loving hands, Betsy left them together to find her husband.

Before the cabin door fully closed, Amelia spurted out, "She knows all, Sadie, Eliza Darling told her, yet she wants me to work with her as I did with Eliza, but I just can't go with you today. The closer I get, the more I'm panicking. You have no idea what it was like. I'm still supposed to be there, Sadie. I should have gone there when Cyrus died; only Major Ned pulled some strings. I don't want to stay in there again. I just can't, Sadie." She gave a deep sob. "They can't take my baby. They would if they knew. They would take her and put her in the orphanage, and I'd never see her again." A heart-breaking sob escaped her again. "I won't let anyone take her from me." She angrily wiped away the tears. "No one, never ever, will take her from me, ever."

"Oh, Amelia, I forced you to come; I had no idea." Sadie slid an arm around her. "Stay at the inn, dear, and we'll collect you on our return. We'll talk more about Essie later. No one will take her from you while I have anything to say about it. And as you are officially assigned to me, that won't happen, so cheer up. That handsome young soldier of yours is on Government duty, so wipe those eyes."

Amelia did and then gave a very undignified sniff followed by an embarrassed giggle. "He's not 'my' anything. No more than a friend, remember. Please don't make more of it than it is." But she giggled again. "Oh, but he is handsome. I'll give you that. Divertingly so!"

The *Surprise* was a little paddlewheel steam ferry, and it drew closer to the wharf at Parramatta. As it pulled in, the bottom dragged on the muddy river's edge.

"Darn. The tide is too low. We'll have to wait a bit until it comes in," Captain Roberts muttered. "Sorry folks, we will have to wait until we can dock. The tide needs to come in some more. We should only need ten minutes, and I'll be able to bring her along to the end of the jetty."

The Governor questioned the Captain. "How often does this occur, Captain?"

"Sadly, I must admit far too often. The draft of this boat is just too deep for this run," Captain Roberts admitted.

"Are any of the others suitable?" the Governor enquired.

"Not really, sir, as the *Sophia Jane* is even larger than this one. I try to time the trips, but I often have to stop on the other side of the river. Sometimes, I get Charles Lockley to unload goods with his rowboat. The situation is not too good, though, sir," Captain Roberts explained.

"Hmmm, leave it with me, and I'll see if anything can be done. We may even just be able to work out a way to shuttle from the last jetty to Parramatta. I'll sort out something, Roberts." He was about to walk off. "I'm actually glad this happened. I like to know of these sorts of problems, then they can be addressed."

Captain Roberts looked astounded. That wasn't the comment he was expecting. He thought he'd be blasted.

The Governor and Lady Bourke sat in the cabin waiting. The ladies stayed in a group on the far side of the boat, and Amelia pointed out the Female Factory and the Orphanage to the ladies. She then shivered.

Sadie took the opportunity of this to say in front of the others, "Amelia dear, you don't look well; why don't you stay at the inn, and we'll collect you on the way back?"

Amelia gave her a weak smile. "I think I shall do that, Mrs Landon."

Sadie gave her hand a gentle squeeze. "I think a lie down will do you a world of good, my dear; you're looking peaky."

After a few minutes, the ferry was able to be pulled to the wharf by ropes. It was tied up, and the gangplank finally lowered. Amelia saw Ned, and they smiled at each other.

Ned stood at attention, saluted and announced himself, "Major Grace of the 48th Battalion, sir." He was there to officially greet the Governor, Major General Sir Richard and Lady Bourke. He ushered off all the guests, with Amelia intentionally alighting last.

Ned sidled up to her and said, "Amelia, I need to speak to you; it's important, life-changingly so," he whispered. He had held her hand as she came down the walkway.

"I'm not going up there; I can't, Ned. I'm staying with Molly," she explained quietly.

"Okay, I'll catch you up later. I'll make some excuse to see you; if not, I'll come to Sydney. Trust me; it's worth the effort. Now chin up." He now, by all rights, should have released her hand, yet he hadn't. He gave her fingers a slight squeeze. "Rest, and I'll catch you later."

Amelia smiled, her heart singing. What was it about Ned that brought her so much comfort? It was not romantic, although she wished it were. She still occasionally dreamed of the handsome dark-haired man at her debut ball, but as she did not know who he was and would, in likelihood, never see him again, it was no use dreaming of him. She loved the care, compassion and, yes, even being cherished by Ned. Singled out amongst many others, he always showed her special attention. Unfortunately, that meant many eyes were always upon them. He was just too good-looking for her comfort.

Sadie, too, noticed his little chat and made her way to Amelia's side. "Is everything all right, dear?"

"Yes, Sadie, he's found out something that he needs to show me. I wonder if it's some paperwork from Cyrus. He said he'd look into it." Amelia looked puzzled. "Sadie, he said it's life-changing."

"Then we're going to have to make time for him, aren't we?" She smiled while tucking Amelia's hand in her arm. "You go on up to the inn, and I'll get him to accompany me after we have completed everything and then make myself scarce."

"Oh, Sadie, would you? If I can't find out today, I'll be unable to sleep. I'm sure of it." She bent and kissed the lovely lady's cheek, so much for a relationship of convict and owner.

The Government town coach collected the group at the top of the path on Phillip Street.

Amelia then walked to the top of the road, escorted by two soldiers from the 48th. They left her at the inn on Church Street, where she was greeted by Bill. He thanked the soldiers and then turned to Amelia. "Go inside, dear, and have some tea with Molly."

Bill returned to the taproom and left the ladies with two-year-old Ellen.

Molly greeted her with a big hug, then handed Ellen to Amelia and pointed to a seat at her kitchen table. "Now, dear, let me get a nice cup of tea while we chat."

Molly placed the tea in front of Amelia.

Amelia sat looking into the depths of the swirling black liquid, thinking of the two vastly different men as well as the Factory. She was completely lost in thoughts too unpleasant ever to voice.

"Dear?" Molly voiced gently.

"Sorry, Molly, I couldn't face going back in there, even for a visit. I just couldn't do it. As I said to Betsy and Sadie on the boat, but for Major Ned, I'd still be there. He got me reassigned to the Turner's when, by rights, I should have been sent back. I only found that out last month, and I just couldn't face today's visit. When I was met by him, he said he needed to have 'another little chat' when he gets back. Oh, Molly, I'm so worried." She angrily wiped away a few falling tears. "Do you know, before the last few years, I never cried? Now, I'm a veritable fountain. Jimmy used to tease me because no matter what I did, I'd never cry. Even when I dislocated my collarbone and broke my arm. I did a jump too high on a hunt once. My horse clipped the hedge, and I went over her head: bruises and breaks and still no tears. Now I'm in tears so often. I could water a farm in a drought; there have been so many tears shed."

Molly's eyebrows raised. "Well, carrying a child and motherhood change things, dear. Put it down to just that."

The two sat talking over the doings of the family. Timmy had been home for Christmas and was due back again at Easter. He was doing very well at school.

Molly admitted to her that Tim had earned a scholarship to Cape's Academy. He was a bright boy. "Bright or not, whenever he's home, he's down at Lockley's and hanging around their youngest daughter, Anna. She's just nine, and he's now ten, but he'd do anything for her. Being Eddie's younger sister doesn't hurt her either, as they are all off on some excursion or other.

They all pitch in and get the chores done as a group and then head off on some childish adventure. She often tags along with the group: Eddie, Anna, Tim, Bertie Ellis, Charlie, and Liza. Our Sammy goes when I let him, but he's a bit younger than the others."

Amelia talked of Essie and her stages. She could hold chalk and was scribbling on a slate; she could even trace some letters.

~

The two hours passed in a flash, and soon, they heard the sound of boots on the verandah.

Molly welcomed the major and then showed them both into the sitting room. She then went to sit with Mrs Landon and little Ellen on the verandah.

Amelia greeted him and sat on the edge of her seat, anxiously waiting for him to speak.

She looked as though she was going to melt into tears at any moment. He wasn't sure how to really cope with crying females as he'd not had much experience with them. Ned thought he would dive in boots and all. "Amelia, do you remember I said I would check what paperwork Cyrus filled in? Do you remember signing a sheaf of paperwork when you were assigned? Did you read any of them?" he asked gently.

She shook her head and looked amazed at his question but answered firmly. "Yes, I remember signing them, and no, I didn't read them." She didn't ask what, as she knew he'd explain. "The day is a blur, Major Ned. There were so many people, and I was so horrified that this filthy human had claimed me that I couldn't think. I was so covered in tears, so I couldn't read anyway." Her eyes welled with tears at the horrible memories.

Ned continued, hopefully getting her mind off the unfortunate event. "Well, one of the functions of the Female Factory is not just to assign convicts but to provide wives. About a month before he came, were you all viewed?" He probed gently. It was a polite way of inspecting the poor women from the Female Factory. He considered it totally degrading. They were lined up to be examined and later claimed by the needy and sometimes greedy men. It disgusted him, but it was his duty to see that things didn't get out of hand. However, he'd been off duty at the time, seeing off his friend Danny and his wife and three girls back to England.

She nodded. Not trusting her voice to reply. She'd felt so humiliated.

"Well, rather than be assigned, he had actually claimed you as his wife because he got a double ration of supplies from the Government Stores by doing that. Amelia, the Banns were read the month before you were released, and he had legally married you."

She could not believe what she was hearing. Her eyes were wide open in shock; again, tears welled. "Married? ...To him?"

"Do you remember a round-faced, fat man who looked like a

minister? Did he speak to you?" Ned asked.

"Um, yes, but I don't remember what he said. He asked me a question, but I didn't hear what he asked. He asked again if I could hear him. I replied, 'Yes.' Why?" For some reason, she remembered that bit clearly. As it was seared into her memory and she had seen the scene over and over in her nightmares, she'd not be likely to forget it too quickly.

Ned smiled reassuringly at her. "Amelia, that rotund man was Reverend Samuel Marsden. He would have asked you if you were willing to be married. Your reply of 'yes' to him was your vows of marriage. I've seen him do these mass weddings myself. Sadly, they were very quick but perfectly legal."

She gasped. "No!"

"Yes, I hoped to have a chance to see you alone today, and when the Governor said who was in his party, I volunteered, well, I assigned myself to this detail, actually. I wanted you to have something that you will need, so I included this when I dressed." He unbuttoned his uniform coat, and he pulled something from inside his red jacket. "Amelia, she's legitimate. You were legally married on the day of your release. That's one of the sheets you signed. I have since altered the documentation to your real name, and it's official." He handed her the certificate. "This is your signature?"

"Yes," she said breathlessly.

"Well, that is Reverend Marsden's signature," he smiled ",...And Cyrus's too."

She took it and, laying it on her lap, read the words 'Marriage Certificate' Cyrus Ephraim Black and Amelia Mary Westaweller, 25th August 1829. Her shocked eyes met Ned's.

Ned said softly, "Amelia, you can go home and resume your life. For once, Cyrus Black did the right thing by you."

Amelia was so stunned that she sat gazing at the paperwork in her hands. Eventually, she murmured, "He used to call me 'wifey'. I presumed it to be just a term. I suppose I am thankful but not really sure how I feel about it." She felt ill; that's how she felt. She lifted her glistening eyes to his and smiled a beaming grin. "Thank you so much. Oh, Major Neddie, thank you!" It was just too much to take in. That man had married her, and she'd not even known.

The paper fluttered to the ground as she wept. Her head in her hands, her shoulders shook as she rocked back and forth. Wracked with shock, grief, pain, and sadness. The entire episode washed over her afresh.

Ned called for Molly but was back beside her in an instant, enfolding her in his arms. She was sobbing uncontrollably on his shoulder when Molly and Sadie entered.

Seeing the situation, they both stopped.

Ned saw her look. "No, don't worry, she's just had some, I suppose you can say, good news." He nodded his head to the abandoned sheet of paper.

Sadie picked it up and read it. "He married you?" Sadie said, looking from Ned to Amelia

Molly looked shocked, "Major, you married her?"

Ned's eyes flew to Molly's. "No, Molly, not to me!" He grinned at Molly. "To Cyrus Ephraim Black, Essie's father. He married her when he took her on. He just never told her. Essie is legitimate; her marriage was legal. I have changed her name to her real name, but it's fully legal. I have made sure it was registered with Harry Moffatt at the courthouse."

Both ladies read the "Westaweller," and finally, it gelled; this was Amelia's real name. The major really did know who she really was.

Amelia drew from his comforting arms, staring up into his face. "But Essie is registered under West."

Ned knew she needed comforting, "I had that fixed too, Milla. Essie now has that as another middle name of West, and I just added Black as her surname. Oh, and that reminds me, has she been Baptised? For I think I'd like to be a godfather," he grinned. It broke the ice.

Amelia was astounded. She giggled at the ridiculousness of the situation. "No, there was no church at Emu, and well, I never got around to it in Sydney. Sadie, do you think Phoebe would arrange it?"

"Yes, dear, and I'd like to be a godmother too; who else?" Sadie gave a chuckle.

"I think we'll do it privately and under all our real names; what do you think, Amelia?" Major Ned said.

Amelia nodded, knowing his secret. She was the only one here who knew his true identity. He was who she had first thought. She did remember him from when she was little.

"Yes, please, Major Neddie," she smiled a beaming smile. Her tears now dried. "Yes, but do I really have to be known as Mrs Black?"

Ned thought a while. "Ahh, I think we'll keep up the deception until your term has expired. There is already a subterfuge, only it wasn't the 'Missus' as we thought. The ticket home will be under your legally married name." Ned said.

"My married name!" she whispered. Suddenly, a thought occurred. "I'm a widow." Her beaming smile was like the sun coming out. She giggled, then laughed a deep, joyous belly laugh.

"See, I told you I had good news for you." He stood to take his leave. "Mind you, informing someone they were a widow has never been so pleasant. We really must all be going; the tide will catch the ferry again. Are you up to walking down, Amelia? I could carry you, but it might raise some eyebrows." His look to her was a slightly naughty smile.

"Walk! I could fly! Major Neddie, I'm going to hug you, you know, because I can do it here. I just need to hug you." She did and then kissed his cheek. As she pulled from his arms, she held him at arm's length. "Thank you, Major Neddie. Thank you from the bottom of my heart. I'm so pleased I didn't know while he was alive. I may have gone for a long, deep swim in the river with lots of rocks in my pockets."

He chuckled. "Then I'm pleased you didn't know because I would not have had a goddaughter. Oh, that reminds me. I have had a letter from Jimmy; he said he'd broken his leg. I'm not sure why that stopped him from writing unless he was sick with that, too. He could have had a servant post it, but you know Jimmy. Here, take it." He handed her the letter, still warm from being tucked close to his chest.

"Thank you. I'll give it back when I see you next time." She gave his hand a squeeze in thanks.

"No, keep it, Milla," Ned said softly.

They said their farewells to Molly, and then the three exited the inn and walked back down to rejoin the Vice-Regal group waiting at the wharf. Ned was in the centre with the ladies on each arm.

Amelia looked back and waved to Molly, who was standing on the verandah, grinning.

Bill came and slipped his arm around her waist, "All good, love?"

"Yes, Bill, all is good. The major found she had been married, and she didn't even know. One of those 'Factory Marriages' that Marsden presided over. No one even told her, the poor dear." They stood watching until their guests were out of view.

As the three departing people left, they chatted. Ned said, "I think you can drop the 'Major' now, Amelia; you were like a sister to me back then. You always have been. I used to call you 'Milla' when you were little. I doubt you even remember my visits as you were very small, but I remember you. Essie is the image of you; it's why I bought that doll. It reminded me of you. You would have been about five when I first came from school. Jimmy would have been eight, and I would have been ten or eleven. Jimmy was in class with my youngest brother, Douglas. I came each school holiday for the next five years. On the first visit, I came with all three brothers, David, Paul, and Douglas."

Sadie had excused herself, walked ahead of them, and rejoined the others, leaving Ned and Amelia within permissible distance to the group but able to talk quietly in private.

"I do remember you, Neddie. Although your hair used to be so fair, it was almost white, like sunshine. And you were always nice to me, unlike some of the other boys Jimmy brought. You and Jim's friend Robbie were a sort of barrier to stop the others from teasing me. Our neighbour, Jack, also looked after me." She thought back to those carefree days. "I wondered if you were that boy, but you were Neddie Lockley back then, weren't you? I thought it must have been you when I first saw you, but I wasn't sure. Mama used to make me stay away from you all. You're, um, different, now." She smiled. Knowing that he'd not been known as Grace. She did, however, know that his father was indeed Gracemere, the Duke of Gracemere. His name was the same as the little boy he now visited in Sydney.

A wave of sadness crossed his face. They had arrived down at the wharf. "One day, I'll tell you everything. Maybe when I come in for her Baptism."

"Thank you, Neddie. For that's what I think of you as. Little Neddie, not that you're little anymore, and no, I won't let on your secret, Neddie Lockley." At over six feet, he was no longer little Neddie anything. She wished to hug and kiss him again, but she would not. She met his eyes and smiled. "Till the Baptism then, if not before."

He kissed her hand in farewell as was polite. "Deal," he murmured. Then resumed his escort duties to the Vice-Regal party.

A wan-looking Betsy Bourke could see Amelia was now more than just happy back on the ferry. Sadie was never far from Amelia's side, and even the way she waved to the handsome soldier was joyful.

Amelia's reticule was bulging, and she couldn't wait to read Jimmy's letter. She was puzzled that he'd not written to her.

Betsy was sitting in the cabin, and she beckoned Amelia to her. Sadie saw and followed. In the small cabin, Amelia slowly opened her reticule and drew out a sheet of paper. She handed it to Betsy without saying anything.

"I didn't know. I had no idea." Amelia met her smiling face with a grin. "It doesn't change what he did to me, but it does change Essie's future. So I can live with that, especially really being a widow. I'll serve my time under the name of West and then change it to Black for my return trip home. Now, none can take Essie from me." She flopped back on the cabin seat, grinning broadly.

"Oh, my dear and the major found this out for you?" Betsy asked. "He's the one from the 48th?"

"Yes, ma'am, he's my brother Jimmy's friend from childhood. He used to holiday at our place as a boy. So we knew each other quite well back when we were children. I had not seen him for years." Amelia looked at both ladies. "My real name is ..." she smiled, "Or was Westaweller, it's now Black." She looked from one face to the other. "My father is Viscount Horace Pittford of Pittford Manor, Kent. Ned's place is in the next town; it's only a few miles away." Amelia admitted that much but would keep his confidences. He would have his own reasons. That story was not hers to tell.

"So, this changes a lot of things. May I tell Phoebe? We have to ask her something else, don't we?" Sadie asked

"Oh yes, please, I'll go and ask if she could join us." Amelia was up and out before they had even thought about the comment.

Phoebe bustled in, wondering about the summons. She noticed the change in Amelia's appearance and how she was almost bubbly. She'd learned to love this young woman over the past eighteen months. Her honesty and bravery were inspiring to her. "Amelia, what's happened? I can tell by your face something has." Her question was answered by a nod and a grin.

Amelia handed her a sheet of paper. "Major Ned gave this to me. I had absolutely no idea, Phoebe. None at all!"

"No, really? Oh wow! Amelia, this changes everything for you." Phoebe read the document in front of her. She'd filled out many of these for Richard over the years. "I can vouch that this is legal. I have written many of these myself over the years. Westaweller eh? I did wonder."

"Yes," she said quietly. "Please don't say anything. West will still do. But I'll go home under my legally married name, Black." Amelia sat looking at the names on the paper. "At least no one can ever know how horrible he was from this." She shivered, still holding it and amazed that again, Ned had done so much for her.

Chapter 9   Final Years of Servitude

Their trip to the Female Factory signalled a regular inspection of the facility. For the next two months, Governor Bourke would send a private message to Major Grace, and the two of them would spring a snap inspection. Then they stopped as Lady Elizabeth Bourke died unexpectedly. She'd been constantly ill, but her passing was still a surprise. Ned and some of the Board of Directors still made unexpected visits. The Matron, Anne Findlay and her husband Robert were not impressed with these, Robert especially. It seemed he had assumed the responsibility of various administrative duties at the Factory, including the bookwork. The new water pump in the yard gave the women an unlimited supply of water, and the cleanliness of the women had undoubtedly improved from when they first visited six months before. Rations were still a work in progress, and this still had to improve. Some of the Benevolent Society benefactors had started a charity shop as part of the outreach at St James church. The money was recycled to assist the less fortunate. The damaged fabric was supplied by Sadie and John Landon and converted into either charity packages or used to make items for sale.

Amelia's embroidered bags were bringing in a good amount of money. So much so that the embroiderers, sewers, and seamstresses were finding it hard to keep up with demand. The turnover from them was financing much more assistance. Some women used the velvet to embroider sewn 'pictures', which were then framed and sold. Others used paints to paint scenes on the discarded fabrics, especially some of the dark velvets. Samples were made of each idea and put up for sale. If they sold quickly, these ideas would be put into production. Embroidered bookmarks were another quick seller. These were much quicker to make. Even the children were taught to sew them. Sewn needle covers, handkerchiefs, embroidered felt balls, even Christmas decorations; if anyone thought of something, each submitted a sample to vary the ideas. From the poplins and lawns, some embroidered around the hems to cover the water-staining. But some fabric was so badly stained that Amelia dip-dyed the selvedge edge in gum-leaf tea solution and covered it completely. It turned into a fabulous, greenish colour, so they made a child's dress from it, and then they embroidered the dyeline with blowing leaves. It looked marvellous and sold for £3 the same week it was placed for sale.

With Amelia's change of marital status, her attitude changed, as now there was no way anyone could take Essie from her. She was legitimate, so they no longer had to hide. Never would Amelia have replied *yes* to the minister's question all those years ago, yet because of Essie, her world had changed. She would not have been on the road that day, and Cyrus would probably not have been killed. She, however, may have been by him and his ongoing abuse. She had just under a year to now serve. Her time was to expire in October 1834.

It had taken over twelve months to arrange the Baptism on a date that would suit everyone. Sadly, this was because of the passing of Lady Bourke on May 7, 1832, just six months after their arrival and eight weeks after the trip to the Factory. It was now more than a year since Ned had given Amelia the Marriage Certificate. He had come to visit a month after that to talk to Reverend Richard and Phoebe. Ned now visited Amelia briefly every time he was in town. Amelia thought it was mainly to see Essie. She adored him.

As Ned suggested and Amelia wanted, Reverend Richard held a private Baptism for Essie after church one Sunday in June. With Lady Betsy's death, Amelia was saddened that she would not have her as godmother, as she'd offered. She asked Phoebe to fill that role instead. She was thrilled. Richard, Phoebe, Ned, and the Landons were the only ones other than Amelia in attendance. They had stayed back after church to meet with the Rector for some private discussions; the church doors were shut, and the group gathered around the font for the Baptism.

The three godparents were asked to make the promises on behalf of the child. Ned, Phoebe and Sadie all agreed. Amelia then handed Essie over to Ned. As godfather, Ned held her as she was Baptised. Essie's absolute trust in him was beautiful to see. Each time Ned had come into Sydney over the past year when he visited them, he brought Essie a book, a tiny toy, or a flower. She laid back in his arms, and he tickled her cheek as Amelia had seen him do before. Her large blue eyes held his. "Lie still, poppet, and we're going to pour a bit of water on your head. If you wiggle, it will go everywhere. It's warm."

She nodded. "Okay, Uncle Neddie," She lay still for the first slosh and for the second, but the third, she looked sideways and tried to reach the water with her hand. She, therefore, became somewhat wetter than she should have done. Ned chuckled, saying, "I told you."

She blew out her cheeks and made a 'raspberry' to him.

Amelia bit her lips to stifle a giggle. Ned met her eyes, and she could see him smile.

Reverend Richard mopped her brow and then blessed her with the sign of the cross.

Ned then sat her up. "All finished, poppet."

"All wet!" she muttered. She screwed her face and wiped away a drip from her hair.

"You'll dry. I did tell you not to wiggle," he chuckled again. "Now you are my little girl too. My special goddaughter, my only one, actually! I have something for you later, but you have to be quiet for now. Shhh!" He put his finger on her lips. She nodded and went shhh, too. She snuggled to his neck. Amelia met his eyes and smiled; it was returned again.

Reverend Richard finished the service with prayers. They decided not to have a hymn as it could be heard by any who had stayed outside. Then gave the dismal prayers, and they turned and chatted with each other.

"So I've now Bap-til-ised?" she asked innocently

"Yes, but the word is Baptised," Ned explained.

"An' I don't need to have it done again?" she questioned.

"No, never again, but as you grow up, you have to make decisions for yourself. Today, Aunty Sadie, Aunty Phoebe and I made them for you, but when you're grown up, you have to make the decision to follow Jesus yourself. You don't need to worry about that until you are much older."

"Okay, Uncle Neddie," she again wrapped her arms around his neck and snuggled close, her wet hair against his neck. He smiled as she snuggled to him. The absolute adoration of the child warmed his heart. They had a celebratory luncheon at Landon's house. Mrs Endean, their cook, had concocted a sumptuous feast.

Phoebe and Richard Hill arrived with their five little recently fostered girls. Amabel Landon was already playing with Essie, so the house was filled with the joyous giggles of seven small girls. Margaret, the oldest, even joined in. The Hills had fostered the girls after their parents had died of Typhus. They had gone from having no children to an instant, ready-made family and were having difficulty with them. The oldest, Margaret, had not settled and, therefore, neither had the others. Phoebe was exhausted, and Richard always looked tired. The girls ranged from seven to one. All were missing their parents, and the older one had taken a dislike to Phoebe.

Earlier in the week, Phoebe had said to Amelia. "Oh, Amelia, I don't know how you coped alone. I have all of you to assist me, plus we've had to get in two of the latest Irish girls, and I'm still exhausted. I wonder if they will ever sleep through on the same night?" She put her head in her hands and sighed.

Caroline Evans said, "I can't believe I've taken on two more boys either. Mind you, my John would sleep through an earthquake. He slept through the most amazing storm the night after Eddie and Tim arrived. My problem had been getting the five boys up and out of bed. Eddie seems to motivate them more than I ever can. He's an amazing child. Getting Timmy to school is also no effort. So, I suppose I am blessed. But eat! My goodness, the five boys can devour an entire shop. Our maid-cum-cook, Effy, finds it hard to cook enough to fill them."

Amelia had told Ned about that conversation. She was worried about Phoebe.

After the Baptism, Ned watched the behaviour of the oldest girl, Phoebe. She was moody and sulky. Pulling away when Phoebe touched her, and she was generally disobedient. The four younger girls mimicked her. Ned happened to be talking to Richard at the time and asked if he may have a word with the oldest girl, Margaret.

"Good luck if you can even get her to even talk to you politely. She's a moody one, that one. We've tried everything. We may have no choice but to surrender them to the orphanage after all." Ned saw a look of sadness pass across his face. "We have no wish for that to occur, but Phoebe isn't coping; she has to be my priority."

Ned looked saddened. "I'll have a chat with her."

Subtly, the two men moved closer to the older child. Richard introduced Ned officially. "Margaret, this is Major Edward Grace; this, sir, is our oldest foster daughter, Miss Margaret Blenheim."

Although a flash of anger initially crossed her face, when she saw Ned, the young girl did a perfect curtsey to Ned and gave him a beaming smile. "Pleased to meet you, Mademoiselle Blenheim." He bowed low over her hand, as one would for royalty, and she giggled.

"I'm not a queen, sir; you do not need to do that," she replied.

"Ahh, Miss Blenheim, we are each worthy to God. Surely you know that. Ooh, my back," Ned feigned injury. "Would you care to sit and converse with me for a while so I can rest my back?" Ned put his arm out as he should have done for any lady.

"Surely, sir," Ignoring his arm, she not so gracefully heaved herself up onto a settee beside him.

Ned kept up his pretence of a bad back.

Sadie and Phoebe were watching his performance from the other end of the room. "What do you think he's up to?" Phoebe asked.

"I'm not sure, but if I know the major, he'll deal with her sulks'. Let's watch." They sidled a little closer so they could hear what he was saying. "I've seen many times he's intervened in a family situation where a parent had died. He assists them in many different ways. Much as he's done for Amelia."

Ned and Margaret had already been chatting for a while. Phoebe heard him ask, "Miss Blenheim, do you like flowers?"

"Why yes, sir, I do; I love violets, especially because when you crush them, they smell beautiful." She beamed up at him.

"Hmm, yes, they do smell nice, but only when they die. Did you know that? If you smell them while they are growing, there is virtually no perfume. You have to kill them before they release their nice smell. That's sad, isn't it? Why do you think that is?" he asked gently.

"I suppose they have the smell inside them," she said.

"Yes, do you know we all have a 'smell' inside of us? Some are good smells or behaviours, and some are bad smells, like naughtiness and meanness. Love is a good smell, and so are manners. A bad temper is a bad smell, and so is naughtiness, but so is sickness, and some sicknesses can kill quickly. In some people, it comes out in our actions that can be either nice or mean. Miss Blenheim, when your Papa became ill, who came to help?"

Tears started to fill her eyes. "No one, sir, no one at all." She folded her arms. "But Mama didn't tell anyone he was sick, so no one helped. He died, and the Reverend came and took him away." She gave Richard a foul look. "Then Mama had to look after us all by herself. She cried a lot."

"And then what happened?" he prompted

"Then Mama got sick too and told me to keep the others away from her. I didn't know what to do for her. Mrs Hill came when she saw me crying outside one day. She had come to visit earlier after Papa died. But now she came daily and brought food, and then she took us away with her. I didn't get to see Mama again." By now, the child was glaring at Phoebe.

"Miss Blenheim, Margaret, when Mrs Hill came, do you know why she wouldn't let you see your Mama?"

"It's 'cos she's mean," Margaret snapped.

"No, it was for two reasons, firstly and most importantly, to keep you safe. Your Mama died that last afternoon Mrs Hill came. Your Mama had a 'bad smell' or bad sickness inside her, the same one that took your father. She caught it from your Papa just by being near him. Mrs Hill should have taken you all to the orphanage and left you all there, and you wouldn't have seen your sisters again. Is that what you wanted?"

"No," she said, absolutely horrified. "I love my sisters." She ignored the tears running down her cheeks but held his eyes solidly.

"Could you have looked after them all by yourself?" he inquired gently. She shook her head. He heard a sob. "Well, the other reason Mrs Hill didn't let you see your Mama is that just before she died, she didn't look as pretty as normal. Mrs Hill wished for you to remember how pretty she always looked. It was because she loved you; even then, she didn't want you hurt. That's why she wants to keep you all herself. Margaret, you have not grown in her tummy as you did with your own Mama, but you have grown in her heart. Other people have no choice in what child God sends them, but Mrs Hill chose to have you all. She wants to give you a home, and you have not made it easy for her."

Margaret looked to Phoebe. She saw the lady smile at her. "You mean she wants to keep us together, for always? As their own children?" Margaret asked Ned.

"Yes," Ned said simply. He let that sink in.

"I've been like a bad smell, haven't I? I thought she was mean, taking me from Mama. I didn't want to stay with her, but I know we can't go home. I want to stay with my sisters." She looked from Ned to Phoebe and back to Ned. Without saying anything, she ran across the room and into Phoebe's arms, sobbing her little heart out.

Phoebe just hugged her until she crawled up into her lap and wrapped her arms around her neck. "I'm sorry, Mama Phoebe. Can we stay, please? I'll try to be a nice-smelling violet now."

"You are our girls now, Margaret, and you will all stay together with us forever," Phoebe said. She saw Richard come and stand next to her.

Margaret reached up to his hand. "Sorry, Papa Richard; please, keep us together?" she pleaded.

"Of course, sweeting. You are all our girls now, but we'll need your help with the others. Can you do that?" he asked gently. The child nodded while clutching Richard's hand and smiled at Ned through her tears.

Ned lay back on the settee and grinned his devastatingly good-looking smile at Phoebe. Richard caught his eye and mouthed, "Thanks" to him. Amelia walked over and seated herself next to him. "Thank you, Ned, that was wonderful. Margaret would not let any of us near her. We could all see she was hurting but didn't know what to do or say." Over the past year, their friendship had reached a stage where they had become easy in each other's company.

"I've sadly seen children go through this before. I've been the bearer of bad news too many times and have seen children like this too often. We forget they understand far more than we give them credit for. Margaret just needed to have the bare facts laid out for her. She only had one choice to make: either the orphanage or a loving home. I just had to put it in words she could understand." Ned looked at his new goddaughter, who'd just come in with Amabel. "She really is like you. You would have been only two years older when I first met you. I'd not had anything to do with girls before, having only brothers. I thought you were the most adorable cherub. Back then, I was so protective of you."

Amelia blushed. "Thank you, Neddie. She certainly has character. I wonder what will become of her now. Thanks to you, the world is now her oyster."

"Not thanks to me. I just found the paperwork. You're the one who had made a brilliant job of her upbringing… mind you, she's only three; she has a bit more growing before we help guide her to a worthy husband." He smiled that heart-melting smile.

Sadie was watching them from across the room. She leaned to Phoebe. "Pity, you know. They would have made a great couple. But they really are more like brother and sister. He takes no liberties, and she expects none. She is just appreciative of everything he's done for her."

"If I were her, his attention certainly would have gone to my head," Phoebe giggled softly. All the girls were now playing together.

"Trust me; we've all thought the same thing." Sadie smiled at them. "It has not. She adores him, but as I said, like a brother."

Across the room, Ned saw they were being watched. "I think we're being talked about again," Ned whispered, "But lovingly so!"

Amelia threw her head back and laughed lightly. "No, they are just jealous of me, Neddie."

His eyes flew to her. "Why?"

"Oh, come off it, Ned, you've seen yourself in a mirror. I'm just like a sister, though. No strings attached, oh, except for a goddaughter now. But, may I also say you are my best friend?" She grinned mischievously. "Seriously, you are, though. I value every moment with you. Dare I say that?"

"Yes, to me, you can. The others may misconstrue the relationship… or lack of one." He nodded to the others, that he acknowledged their scrutiny. "We must still be circumspect. I do admit that it's nice to be able to really be myself with you." Ned dropped his voice and quietly said to her, "You know who and what I am, and it's reciprocated." He paused for a while, watching the children play.

She could tell he wanted to say something but was struggling to find the words. Eventually, he said, "Milla, I wrote to Sam Corbett some time ago, and I heard back from him this week. They have a position for a teacher at their place. I think you should consider taking it. It's not long until your time is up, and if you make preparations now, you will find it easier to sort yourself out here. With up to five months each way, then turn around with mails, you will need to let him know if you're willing to come when you can. You can make yourself a home there, and no one will be any wiser, but you will be close to Jimmy. I presume you know Sam's history?"

Her eyes were almost dancing, "Yes, I met Sam on the day the Darlings left. I sort of introduced myself, but I told him to trust them." She looked somewhat embarrassed, "His brother, Nigel, was a friend of Papa's."

"Sam would have liked that. Did you tell him who you were?"

"Yes, sort of; I thought it best not to give him too much information. Ned, could I truly fit in at his place?" she asked pensively.

"Yes, but I think you should know who you'd be teaching. They are illegitimate children of the peerage. It's what they are doing with their inheritance. Like an exclusive orphanage. Giving these children the love and attention they deserve and would not otherwise get." He wondered what her reaction would be. He was not disappointed.

"Are you kidding? I'd love to do that. Misfits, all together!" She gave him a beaming smile. "Absolutely, yes, please. Can you write to him? If I give you a letter, can you include it with yours?"

He was surprised at her joy. "Yes, delighted to." Ned smiled. His plan to get her home was now sorted. She'd be safe with Sam and Danny, as well as useful. He had liked having someone near who knew about him, but Sydney was no place for a single woman. He wanted to see her safe back in Jimmy's care.

At that moment, Mrs Christopher came and announced luncheon.

"Get your letter to me as soon as you can, Milla. The position is open for you whenever you return. They can use whatever teachers they can get," Ned said to her as he rose and assisted her up.

Amelia nodded but had no time to reply. She loved it when he used her childhood name. Jimmy was the only other person to call her so.

The staff had prepared a children's table, and little Margaret came and asked Phoebe if she could round up the children and help settle them. She turned to look at Ned and gave him a loving smile.

He met her look with a smile and a nod. Margaret then said, "Come and see, Mama Phoebe." She took Phoebe's hand and pulled her up.

Phoebe was stunned at the change in the previously sulky little girl. In less than half an hour, Margaret had obviously done some hard thinking. Phoebe and Richard would now be accepted as her parents. With Margaret on their side, they would hopefully have a much easier time with the other girls, too. After luncheon, Ned, Phoebe, and Sadie presented Essie with her gifts. A small Bible and teddy bear from Ned, a white leather prayer book from Phoebe, and a gold necklace with a beautiful cross on it from Sadie.

Essie said thanks for each gift and hugged the giver. When she got to Ned, she wrapped her arms around his neck. "Uncle Neddie, thank you for my 'Neddie Bear'; I shall keep him forever." She gave him a big kiss. He tousled her hair and then said farewell to her. Reluctantly, Ned took his leave. He had to return on the four o'clock ferry and still had to visit Eddie and Tim. He wished to spend a bit of time with them and see how Caroline Evans was coping as her husband was away at the moment. He often did a few small jobs for her if they were needed, but no one but the two of them knew how much he'd assisted her financially. Her brother, Thomas Tindale, came in weekly when Captain Douglas was off sailing, but sometimes, some little job just needed immediate repair. On each visit, Ned made sure she had enough money for the two extra boys to keep and often left a few pounds for extras for them all. Their parents did not know that he was doing this, although he promised the Evans family that when they were older, he'd tell them.

Eddie was now twelve and Tim ten. Tim had shot up and was slightly taller than Ed, but Eddie still had more bulk. Both boys were pulling their weight, and Ned had made arrangements with Major Downs at Hyde Park Barracks that the two boys were trusted and could be used for running errands. They made some pocket money by doing these jobs; however, they only kept enough for their ferry trip home. The rest they handed to Caroline Evans to assist with their keep. Caroline did not wish to take it, so she put the money aside to go towards replacing shoes and clothing. Her brother and his wife also supplied funds for the two boys. Thomas and Margaret had no children themselves, and they knew that these two young lads would have a chance in life if they only had an education. Thomas and Ned had nutted out their secret plan some years before. Tim had topped his class most years he'd been at school. Eddie was also doing well, not failing a single test or exam, but he was no scholar. He only desired to be back at the forge, blacksmithing with Thomas. Still, Eddie had to stay at school. His brother Charlie was currently working with Thomas.

While doing their charity work in the fabric storeroom, the women from the Benevolent Society sat around speaking of their children. Amelia stayed silent. More shiploads of Irish women had arrived, hundreds at a time. The Female Factory was well over capacity, and the situation was dire. Initially built for about one hundred and fifty women, it often had over six hundred. Many were expecting babies, and they had many a discussion of how to cope with the influx.

Amelia suggested that with some special counselling to both parties, marriages be considered. She trusted most of the women in the group, and they had all discovered that she was serving time. There had been no hiding her status when she said one day that her time was nearly up. She then explained her situation. Some were horrified, but most were highly supportive. Phoebe spoke up for her. "I have known about her since before I met her. I will continue to call her a friend. Remember, there but for the Grace of God…" She met the eyes of some of those willing to turn their backs on Amelia.

"Are you prepared to throw a stone? Are we all not sinners and have to stand before God in judgment? I know I will have to. I would like you to know I would stand shoulder to shoulder with someone like Amelia. I also know the charge against her is a trumped-up one. As a personal friend to both Governor's wives, do you think she would have been if they knew her to be guilty? Courts often get things wrong. Would our work have been effective without her input? No! Suffice to say, a certain duke, who shall remain nameless, pressed the charge, and I do not trust him. I do trust Amelia." After that, there was no more ostracising. This same duke had obviously been the centre of attention at some earlier conversation.

Amelia continued, "What I would like to see changed is the way marriages are arranged. I had no say at all in mine. If both parties are interviewed by, say, a group of independent women and then have the chance to meet the men in a less formal but supervised way, I think you will find many more women will agree to marry. Especially the Irish girls, even the expectant ones. If there were situations where prospective couples could meet and talk, fully supervised, then I think you would find it hard keeping enough in the Factory to work the looms. When I was married, the men walked past us and chose who they wished. We were not even introduced to them. Banns were read; we were not even informed about that, and they came back to collect us. It was all duly registered, and documents were signed by Reverend Marsden and by us. And for me, then the abuse started." She still teared up when she thought back to that horrific time. She brushed away an errant tear and continued. "It was such a traumatic experience that I certainly did not realise that I was actually even being married. My husband never even told me. I only found out after he died that we were legally married." Her voice broke, and she had to blow her nose.

No one interrupted her story, so she continued again. She saw a few wipe away tears.

"Truly, I had absolutely no choice of who my husband was to be. This must stop. The men also must be vetted, as I know from personal experience that not all are worthy. My husband was killed by his horse only three months after our marriage. If he had not died, I probably would have been the victim, like his previous wife." She heard the gasps of some of the ladies. Amelia finally lifted her head and looked around her. "My real married name is Black, but I will not use it as it is abhorrent to me. Hence, I am known here as Mrs West."

Phoebe, Sadie, and Caroline were by her side and supporting her while she told the group her story.

With the telling, the ladies listening were amazed at how she coped with the stresses of what she had lived through. A few began to ask gentle questions. Amelia shook her head at the questions; they could follow later. Now Amelia knew they were aware of her background, she continued. "We must get the men to listen to us. Governor Bourke is certainly in favour of the changes. Eight weeks after I left, there was a mass escape. The situation was so bad in there that they needed to get out to survive. Food was porridge or gruel if we were lucky; bread was only the leftovers from town the day before, and there was never enough. We had little water to drink and none to wash in, one bucket for every thirty women, supplied once a day. Blankets were so thin with many holes that they were almost useless. We'd actually relish being assigned two to a bunk as that way we could keep warm."

"Oh, Amelia!" Caroline exclaimed.

Amelia almost whispered her reply. "It's why I've been so passionate about aiding them. There are many like me, people of class who have been caught up by deeds, not their own making. I was, and am innocent. I promise you all." She finally met their eyes. "We need to do what we can to assist this reform."

By now, quite a few of the group were quietly weeping. Some had been forced into marriages by unscrupulous parents. But to not even know who they were to marry or even be informed that they were married, they were horrified. Some of the husbands of these women were the ones standing against Governor Bourke's proposed changes. Up until today, their wives had often supported those decisions. This would now change.

~

Things did indeed begin to change. Subtle suggestions by the wives started to change the attitudes of the men. Some months later, Amelia's suggestions about the 'marriage' market came into effect. Many of the girls in the Factory were willingly married, and numbers dropped to a more manageable number. Men interested in marrying were, after being vetted, allowed to meet women interested in the same. The couple were allowed to sit and talk, getting to know one another. Then, after a few meetings, they would only then agree to a union and the Banns be posted. The women were married to a man of their choice and released into their care. Even expectant women were allowed to participate. They trialled it for three months, and it worked so well that Governor Bourke gave permission for the program to continue. The number of women entering the Factory still outnumbered those leaving, and soon it was overcrowded again. As fast as they could be placed, more replaced them, something needed to be done and done quickly.

In October 1833, Amelia had finally gone on an inspection. Matron Findlay was still there, but Ned and the Governor and his daughter Mrs Anne Deas Thomson, who had very ably stepped into her mother's role as Vice-Regal First Lady, was with Amelia every moment. Amelia clung to Ned's arm. She had a nightmare the night before the visit, dreaming of all sorts of horrific scenarios that could occur. Sadie noted her pallor and stayed near her.

The memories flooded back to Amelia. Ned felt her flinch with various sounds they heard. Gates, clanging, bells, and slamming doors. The eerie sounds of the screaming women from third class and the swoosh of the looms being worked. He covered her hand with his and squeezed her fingers. Amelia had at one time drawn aside and cried in Ned's arms. "I can't do this, Ned; I have to get out of here."

Anne came to her and slid her arm around her shoulders. "Amelia, we're changing things for these women. Please do it for them. Now show me the women's washroom. I need to see how we can make things better." She turned to Ned. "Major, stay here with Papa while we inspect them. But please don't go far away."

Ned nodded. "We'll wait out here within earshot."

Amelia met her concerned eyes and drew away from Ned. "Okay, let's get this over with. The more I show you, the quicker I'll be out of here." She led them into the ladies' washroom. It was stark and dimly lit. Even in

October, it was cold in there.

"Is there any heating here at all?" Anne shivered. "It's so cold in here."

"No heating, no fires are allowed; it was considered too dangerous," Amelia said simply.

"How do you get warm?" Anne asked, puzzled.

"Haha, warm, are you joking? We froze, and they laughed. In winter, I had to break the ice from the water bucket inside. We had one blanket each, and if you had a friend, sometimes we'd slip into each other's pallet to double our warmth; even so, we'd get into trouble because we were not in our own beds." Amelia kept on with the description of the facilities, now answering their questions. "There was a brazier in the quadrangle, but in winter, it was worse out there than here. At least we had to sort and card the fleeces, which meant a layer of wool on our laps. I imagine that in the summertime, the lanolin in the wool would get so hot it would stick to the hands. The looms are upstairs, and that is always hot, summer or winter. But at least we were moving." As Amelia spoke, she did not realise that Matron had entered behind her. She stood listening and was not happy with what she heard. This woman was dangerous; Amelia realised she would have to watch her step. Amelia and Anne were pleased to leave and head home.

Chapter 10   The Final Year

$\mathcal{A}$melia reluctantly agreed to a visit to the Female Factory again. It was March, just two weeks before Easter and four months since the last visit. It was now only seven months before her time was up. Ned had promised to accompany her again to the Factory with the Governor, and he promised he'd stay with her. Essie was to stay with Sadie, and Amelia was to accompany the Governor and his daughter Anne to the Factory to check on the changes ordered. Anne was two years younger than Amelia, and they had become friends. She had married only the year before. There was now a tall wall around the Female Factory to stop breakouts. Another mass breakout occurred some eighteen months earlier, with over two hundred women escaping. They complained that there was no food and little water. Ned had checked with Charles and knew the food was being sent up. Many prisoners were rounded up, but some one hundred remained at large. The place was still overcrowded, and the noise was still oppressive. Ned took Amelia's arm as they entered Matron's office. The Matron rudely said, "Not a good day for a visit, Gov," She didn't like these snap inspections. "Ain't good for morale. Them women's don't like it and don't like strange men coming to gander at 'em."

Amelia clung to Ned even tighter. He could tell she was afraid. He shouldn't have made her come. The Governor was somewhat apprehensive as to his visit this day. Things didn't seem as cheerful as before. There had always been jeers, but this time, the atmosphere was different, silent and brooding. "Neddie, I want to leave. I can't go. Don't make me go in," Amelia said just before they entered.

"Milla, I'll be with you. It will be no different from before," he entwined his fingers with hers as they were sitting on his arm. "We'll all look after you."

"Something is wrong. I can feel it. It sounds, well, it's just different." She tried desperately to explain. "My heart is pounding, and I want to leave." Finally, Ned had promised that he'd take her out if anything occurred. Only with that assurance did she agree to accompany them. Many of Amelia's improvements had been completed, and she was pleased to see that each floor now had cooking facilities and washing facilities. There was a brazier to warm the rooms and a huge pile of folded blankets should the inmates wish to use them. She stood still, clinging to Ned's arm. He felt her fingers tighten on his arm when one girl walked up to her. Amelia checked with some of the girls she saw that they could actually use the blankets and other items.

"Yeah, we cud do with more tucker and mayhap, 'n' some new staff, but 'tis better than the ship out or them hulks," the unkempt woman said.

"It is that. They were horrible, weren't they?" Amelia agreed.

"You was in there too? You wus one o' us? A convict?" the woman said, stunned.

"Yes, I still am, but my time is up soon. I'm here with these people to see how we can better your conditions," Amelia explained gently. She saw the look on the girl's face.

"Yor really one o' us?" she asked, amazed. "Youse a convict?"

"Yes, I am, but you, too, need to be treated in such a way that you have dignity. Please trust us; help us, help you," Amelia pleaded.

The girl stood looking at Amelia. "Yus, I do, but how does youse think youse can help us?"

"Well, you now have a water pump and a brazier on each floor as well as washrooms. That was from our last visit. What else do you need?" Amelia asked.

"You did that?" the girl said in awe. Amelia nodded. The girl looked hard at her and then walked off. Amelia's hand relaxed.

Ned patted it and congratulated her. "You've done well, Milla," he whispered. The inspection continued. When they arrived at the ablutions area, Ned knew he could not accompany her into the women's washrooms. She looked fearful, but she went with Anne into the washroom. Two ladies were washing near the new brazier. As they entered, others followed them into the room. One was the girl Amelia had recently been talking to.

"I'm sorry, missus, but we comes to take you wiv us." She said apologetically to Amelia.

Anne was being held and a hand over her mouth, fear etched on her face. Amelia was escorted out the other door of the room and taken out of sight. She glanced back to Anne as she left. Anne saw the fear and panic in her eyes. Once out of sight, Anne was released and was pushed back out to her father and Ned. "They took her. They have taken her hostage," she said as she was taken into her father's arms.

"What do you mean 'they took her?' Who?" Ned asked. "Where's Milla?"

"The convict woman said that she would be able to understand that they needed help and that only she would know. Oh, major, I'm so sorry. I should not have forced her to come," Anne said.

"She didn't want to; even when we arrived, she said something didn't sound right. I made her come inside," he'd blanched. "Oh, Milla," he said softly to no one in particular while staring at the door she'd gone through.

At that moment, the Matron appeared. "They've taken Mrs West. They said they are holding her as a bargaining tool." She smirked.

"Well, if they harm a hair on her head, they will have me and the entire 48th Battalion to deal with." Ned glared at the rude woman in front of him. He'd had run-ins with her husband when he enlisted under his command. "Governor, Mrs Deas Thomson, please follow me." Ned turned and walked them back to the entrance. "Please wait for us at the Rear Admiral Duncan Inn. Tell Charles Lockley from the Jolly Sailor Inn to bring his wife and get Molly Miller to take the children." He saw them into the coach with an escort of four armed soldiers and then returned with six more into the Factory. He waited impatiently with them in the quadrangle, and soon enough, the sound of many booted footsteps was heard hurrying closer. Forty soldiers marched in to join them. Ned had them spread out in pairs with instructions: "Men, you are to pacify, not abuse. No women are to be hurt, and Mrs West must be rescued totally unharmed." Ned waited for Sal's arrival. He knew that she, too, had spent time in this place and knew where Amelia would be held.

Their arrival heralded the arrival of Molly Miller, too, "Where's Amelia? What have they done to my girl?" she bellowed. She and Sal stood arm in arm. "Don't you look like that, Major Grace; Amelia is my special girl. Mrs Anne is looking after all the children."

Ned welcomed the three newcomers. "The women have taken Amelia hostage, as for some reason, they think she will assist them. Ladies, I'm sorry, but I know this place is abhorrent to you as it is to her, but something more is going on here, and she's the lynchpin to understanding what it is. Charles, I'm sorry to involve you and Sal, but I know they trust you both. They have taken Amelia as a hostage, Charles; I have to do what they ask to get her released."

Charles nodded. "Major, we're here to be what assistance we can." He looked at his friend, seeing worry and stress etched onto his face and something he'd never seen there before… fear.

They were obviously being watched as two convict women approached him. "You boss here, mister?" they asked.

Ned nodded. "Yes!" Ned would not allow the Governor to be put in danger. "Where's Mrs West?"

"She's safe enough, Guv! She won't come to no harm, but we needed her, 'cause I seed her clinging to you, tight like, so I knowed you wants her back." The woman speaking had been the one who had entered with Amelia into the washrooms. "Will youse listen to our grievances? Honest like? She says you will and then do something about them."

"I'll listen, but if you hurt her, you will be sent to dig in the coal mines in Newcastle for the rest of your life. Do I make myself understood?

Your seven years will become life in chains, with no possibility of release." Ned was livid and scared for Amelia, such as he'd never been before.

Charles had never heard Ned so angry before. He shivered.

"Yes, I knowed; it's why we tooked her. You care for her." She stood her ground, hands now on her hips. "Now ya goin' ta listen or what?" She looked strange with a shawl over her head.

"Yes, tell me your grievances and your name," Ned said with such passive anger that Sal took a step towards Charles.

"No name, you'll find that out later. Well, first, that hussy has to go," pointing to Matron Findlay. "She's cut our meagre rations to half and pockets the rest, then she brings out the stash of fancy new blankets when youse come, then stores them away when you're gone. She's a big bit of no good," the woman said. "We get punished for our carnal exploits, but we're forced to it by the soldiers guarding us, not to mention her own Mr Robert's lusts. He be the worst of them all. Sneaking in while we're asleep and wiv a hand over our mouths, he bounces us gels. Them warders come and take their pleasure with who they want, and we gets no say in it. They gets us with child, and we is the ones wot get punished. Then they takes our kiddies away from us when they want. You want me ta keep going?" she asked.

"Yes, but first, Matron, please leave. I'll see you in the office. Rhys-Jones, go with her and guard her. She's not allowed to touch anything." Ned turned back to the angry woman. He waited until the Matron was now out of earshot. "Continue," Ned said.

"Fine. I will. Now, where was I? Oh yus, them pallets they has us sleeping on, they's ok wiv one but when two or three has to share, and we sometimes has a kiddy with uz, there ain't no room, even top to tail it's squashy." Sal knew about the hard, narrow pallets and knew what she meant. Far too many women had been housed in there when she had arrived in 1820. Now, even though the new Factory housed more, it was overcrowded, too. Thankfully, the major had claimed Sal as a servant himself. She had much to thank him for. He'd never laid a hand on her. Charles had asked him to rescue her, and Ned had. Charles married her soon afterwards.

"Thet Matron and her Mister, they ain't no good. Him 'specially, a nasty, lustful man he is. He be skimming from us and flogging the stuff for themselves. Most Irish gels here are political prisoners, here because of religion, not because of a crime. Then they gets *had-at* by the soldiers, and they get ruined. It's not fair. You've gotta stop that; we're not all fallen women. Most of us thieved to keep alive, not 'cause we're bad. We need food; thet's our biggest grievance, just some good, nourishing food. We're hungry. Real bad! We ain't had meat for a month. She flogged it all. We just need someone to listen to us." She wiped away angry tears. "Missus West said you'd listen to us. Will ya?" she pleaded. While she stood looking at Ned, she reached up and took off the shawl over her head. She'd been shaved. The four people watching her all gasped. "That woman put me on three weeks of bread and water for being raped by her man as if it was my fault. I was asleep when the creep came in an' jus' took me. I'd not been wiv a bloke before, and it hurt. Yet I'm the one wot's punished for reporting it. I was demoted from second-class to third-class prisoner and set to breaking rocks for a month. I 'spose I be thankful I wasn't knocked up. But if things don't change, I'll be dead soon. Ya gotta help us. Will ya?"

Sal stepped forward and hugged her. "Yes, dear, we will; we will make sure you are listened to, won't we, major." Sal turned to Ned.

"Absolutely! Amelia, um, Mrs West, told me of the conditions here; it's why we brought her. I shall see to some food immediately, but I need to know she's all right." Ned saw she was speaking the truth. Her emaciated condition was confirmation enough. Sal saw the concern in his eyes and watched him with amazement. She had no idea that he had a lady friend. Molly had hinted, but she now saw his concern himself. The angry woman motioned for one of the others accompanying her to bring Amelia out. They all stood waiting. Nothing would be done until Ned knew Amelia was safe. The five-minute wait was agonisingly long. Charles had never seen the major so agitated. The look of anxiety on his face spoke volumes. Ned saw his lifted eyebrow and said, "Charles, Sal, Amelia is my best friend's sister, no more, no less. I'm her daughter's godfather," Ned explained quietly. They heard, but did they believe?

Molly filled them in on some details. "'Tis true, Sal; I was there when he broke the news of her marriage to her. She didn't know she'd been married from this hell hole. Marsden did one of his batch marriages. Charles, Cyrus Black took her!" She heard Sal gasp. "The poor girls don't even get told what is happening." Molly looked at the angst on the major's face. "Major Grace, he's like a brother to her, that's all; a big loving big brother. They have met at our inn a few times. I have always been there. Nothing fishy and no hanky-panky. We trust the major, and I trust Amelia." With that, she nodded. "Yes, I trust them both."

Ned swung around when he heard the shuffling of feet. Amelia appeared between two other women. "Milla, are you harmed? Injured in any way?" He went to walk to her, but the others would not let him approach.

"No, Neddie, I'm fine. But..." she looked around her, "Where's Matron?"

"She's in her office," Ned replied, "under guard."

Amelia continued. "She's got to go, Ned, and him too. Neddie, Robert Findlay has been abusing the girls. It has become even worse than when I was here. She's allowing the soldiers free rein with the girls; the more innocent, the better, and then the girls get punished for being used. She's halved the already meagre rations, most are on bread and water at the moment, and they must be pocketing the balance of funds. Neddie, Ivy is speaking the truth. Please listen to her."

Charles saw a petite dark-haired woman with startling blue eyes and a gentle face. He watched Ned's face as it relaxed when he saw she was unharmed. Ned saw that Amelia was in complete control of herself. Her fears of the morning were well justified, though. "Milla, you're not being coerced into saying anything?"

"No, Neddie! It's all true. Ned, they say that Robert is in the 48th, too. Is he truly one of your men?" She was stunned when they revealed that to her.

"Sadly, yes, but I'll deal with him. He'll be immediately removed from this premises, and I shall arrange a trusted group to take over security." Ned was inwardly seething at the filthy man. He trusted Amelia and knew she was telling the truth. She had already told him much of her months there. "Thank you, Milla. I will get it sorted. Can you bear up for a little longer?" he asked, concerned.

"Yes, Neddie, but please be as quick as you can and replace them." Amelia met his eyes. "Ned, I told you things just weren't right. Matron has taken many of them off the looms and onto smashing rocks for mere spite. Even the first-class prisoners have been put on to carding the wool. Neddie, she's a nasty bit of goods."

Ivy went to her side. "You tells him, Missus. You're not being forced to say this. Them's yer own words. You tell 'em, I've bin telling the truth."

"Ivy, Major Grace believes me. I'd told him before today what it was like when I was here. As I'm sure has Missus Lockley and Missus Miller too. It's why I came, but you didn't need to kidnap me," Amelia said gently.

"We did, Missus, 'cause we've had promises before, and nuffin's bin done," Ivy said. "I don't wanna get raped again. I can't bear it, Missus." She started to weep.

Amelia hugged the girl beside her. "Ivy, I know exactly what you mean. I'll do everything I can to stop it."

"You too, Missus?" She asked softly.

"Yes, only it was by a man whom I didn't know was my husband, twice a day at least, for three months." Ivy's face softened. "Yes, I know. I will do what I can to assist you, but you have to let me go. I can't do it from in here," Amelia replied to the girl quietly. Ned heard and was horrified. From the corner of her eye, Amelia saw another lady appear. Amelia waved her over. "Neddie, this is the Factory midwife, Mrs Mary Ann Neale, ask her. She'll tell you what we say is true. Mary, tell the major, let him know what you told me."

Mary told him of the night visits by Robert Findlay and the other guards to the women's sleeping quarters. "Major, he takes his pleasure with them, even me too, in the dark, and they have no idea who it is. He's a bad man. He comes in and drops his trousers, then, with a hand over the mouth, does his stuff. No chance to scream until it's over. Then what does it matter? It's too late."

Charles gasped. Ned swung around and looked at Charles.

Amelia was momentarily puzzled until Charles said, "Major, he's my landlord. He owns the land of my inn," Charles felt ill. Thankfully, he'd never left Sal alone with him, and just as well.

The major nodded. "Leave it with me, Charles." He turned to the midwife. "Missus Neale, how many women are currently in here? What do you need most?"

"There are over six hundred in a place where three hundred is crowded. It's food, sir; we're desperate. We are all only on bread and water at the moment, and we had one die of starvation last week and three more the week before." Mary wondered if she'd get into trouble.

"Starvation? How? We send so much food here; what happens to it all? Charles, it does get sent, doesn't it?" Ned queried.

"Yes, absolutely, sir, I see to it myself. We send a wagon load daily, and when more prisoners arrive, we check numbers and supply per person. She's correct with the numbers, as I sent supplies for six hundred this week. I included six barrels of salt beef and pork. There should be ample."

"Meat! Ha, that's a joke! Well, sir, we ain't seen nuffin of that for weeks, if not months," Ivy said.

"She's right, sir; no meat has been on any menu for more than a month," Mrs Neale confirmed.

Ned's face grew red. "I'll get this sorted. Mrs Neale, please care for Mrs West. I'll return with food within the hour. Get the cooking fires ready and the women, too. Stop all work and prepare. Charles, ladies, we will go and raid the Government Store." He turned to Amelia. "I'll return soon, Milla. Will you be all right?"

She nodded. "Just hurry, Neddie."

"I will, with all possible haste," he nodded and turned to depart. Charles was surprised at her familiarity. He'd known the major for some thirteen years, and only in private did he dare call him Ned, let alone a pet name.

The town carriage had returned from dropping off the Governor and his daughter. It took them directly to the Rear Admiral Duncan Inn and dropped off Molly; Ned filled in the Governor and swapped a passenger, Molly, for the Governor. The four returned to the Jolly Sailor Inn, and Sal alighted. She'd get their thirteen-year-old son, Charlie, to harness up their horse and cart and meet them at the Government Stores. With the Governor and Ned giving directions, they soon had the wagon and the town carriage full to overflowing with supplies. So much so that the men had to travel up with the drivers; they stopped in at the bakery on the way and collected every cooked loaf they had. Within an hour, they were on their way back to the

Female Factory. Mrs Neale was waiting with Ivy and Amelia. They showed them in and then where to park and unload.

Ivy fell to her knees and wept. "I can't believe it, food, real food."

Amelia went to her and enfolded her in her forgiving arms. Ned walked up to them both. "Ned, we've been talking while we waited. There are some women here who have died giving birth because the doctor won't attend them. Others who have been ill are the same. The doctor won't come as they are not being paid," Amelia told him.

The Governor, too, had joined them and was listening. "But we pay him. I know because I see the bills from here. We pay Matron Findlay directly. You mean she's been making up his visits?" He directed the question to the midwife.

"Yes, sir," the midwife spoke up, "I've not seen him here for months. I've delivered twelve babies this last month and have not had his assistance. One lady died because the babe was stuck. It was born alive after the mother expired."

The Governor went red in the face with anger. "I can't believe it. She was recommended."

"Well, that may be so. However, I think Matron will need replacing. I think her husband should be banned from the premises forthwith." Charles said as he could no longer hold his wrath.

"He will be, and he arrested for embezzlement for a start. Major, deal with that, will you?" He fell silent, chewing his lips. "I want the books sent to the Board of Governors immediately, and Lockley, you send your records to them too, and let's see how much had been syphoned off. The books are to be audited." The poor man was livid. "Bread and water. How can anyone survive on that?"

"They can't," Ned muttered angrily. He arranged for the food to be distributed and more cooked for a sustaining meal for everyone.

"I feel a military presence should reign here until it's sorted. Major, you're needed in town, but I'll get Major Downs to send in a skeleton staff until we get this under control. Not the 48th; sorry, major, but we don't know who his friends are. Now, we should be returning. May I leave this in your capable hands?" The Governor was aware that the ferry needed to sail at full tide.

"Yes, sir, but I shall leave my two best sergeants in charge here," he called over Seargent's Brian and May and introduced them to the Governor. The Governor gave explicit instructions to the two men. Ned explained to them that he'd return after the Governor had departed on the ferry.

The soldiers were now overseeing the fair distribution of food for all. Peace had returned to the place. "Sir, we still have to see Matron Findlay. Can we spare a few minutes before we depart?" Ned asked.

"Yes, yes, of course, I forgot about her. Lead on." He followed Ned as they walked to the office.

The Governor gave her the benefit of the doubt but told her that her husband was no longer permitted to live on the premises nor visit it. He was permanently banned from the site. Neither were the guards who had previously been assigned to the watch duty. He asked for the books and walked out with them under his arm. "Major Grace, make sure these get to the Clerk of the Court. I believe he'll do a good job with the audit."

Ned knew Harry Moffatt and was happy that he'd been chosen. "Willingly, sir!"

On arrival back in the quadrangle, Amelia was released and went directly to Ned into his arms. "Get me out of here, Neddie."

Charles watched his friend embrace the petite, dark-haired lady. Totally enfolding her protectively in his arms, whispering comforting things to her. He kissed the top of her head and laid his cheek on her hair. He released her quickly, then took her hand and tucked it into his arm. "After you, sir," Ned said to the Governor.

"I'll stay for a bit if you wish, Major," Charles said.

"No, Charles, come with us, please. Things are under control here. I need to talk with you," Ned gave Charles a look that meant, "Come!"

"Yes, sir!" Charles said, following them out the main gates.

The coach stopped at the Rear Admiral Duncan Inn and collected Anne Deas Thomson, then continued on the way to the wharf. The Governor thanked the major for his protection and walked his daughter down to await the ferry's arrival. The three watched them leave.

"Charles, I wish to introduce you to Mrs Amelia West, well Black, actually. It's a long story, and I'll tell you later. She's my best friend Jimmy's sister, from home." Ned grinned at her in such a way that Charles gasped.

Ned then introduced Charles. "Milla, this is Charles Lockley. He and Jack Turner, Martha's husband, reported the attempted mutiny to me on the way out. Charles is my best friend, but we still have to keep it quiet for obvious reasons. You can call on either Sal or Charles should you need to. Now that they know of our friendship, they will do anything for you."

Amelia looked at the man in front of her and found it hard to stay silent. She was amazed at his looks. She smiled and said all the right things. She then said that she, too, had better join the Governor. They made their farewells to Charles and Sal and walked down to the ferry. Once out of earshot, Amelia asked, "Neddie, is he related? He's the image of David and Douglas. I found it hard to stay silent."

Ned had both a puzzled and concerned look on his face. "I don't know, Milla, and quite frankly, I'm scared to ask. Mind you, they do not know my real surname. I know of no other legitimate Lockleys, but as you say, we are too similar for there not to be a connection somewhere."

She saw the pain on his face. "Ned, you mean a by-blow? But of whom?" She felt terrible for asking.

Ned's eyebrows raised at her use of such a course term. "Milla, that's just what I'm scared to ask. He's the same age as Paul. I try not to think of it." Ned sounded sad. "He's my best friend, Milla. I'm not prepared to lose that to find out the truth."

Amelia gently squeezed his arm. "Oh, Neddie, I can see what you mean. I do hope there is an explanation. You can't exactly ask your parents, can you?" she said.

"Err, no, not the sort of thing to discuss. In the meantime, Charles will remain my best friend here. In a way, you could say I owe him my life. He gave me a reason to live. He and Sal pulled me out of my blue devils after Elouise Wickham dumped me. I presume you know about that?" He looked at her with an eyebrow raised.

"Yes, I had heard; I'm sorry. But Neddie, I'm also sorry for David; she has made his life hell. I've not seen her for some time. She had told Mother she was expecting and then was incredibly ill, but there was no child. Neddie, I've been praying that you will find happiness. I hope you can." Amelia gave his arm another squeeze. "I especially want to thank you for today. All I wanted to do was hide in your arms, then I realised that I had to stay strong, and I realised that I was about the only one they could trust enough to see things were sorted."

Ned was surprised at the emotions he'd felt. He looked down at this tiny woman on his arm. She meant the world to him. "Milla, I was ready to rip down every brick to get you back, but I, too, realised that when you were safe and standing strong, I knew I had to fix the problem to get you out. This is the fifth time they have rioted. Food seems to be a common thread. Not that they did any physical damage this time, but are you truly unharmed emotionally?" His concern for her welfare hit him hard. He was unfamiliar with the surge his heart gave when he'd seen her.

"I am fine, Neddie. I can't believe that I'm able to say that. But today, laid many ghosts. If I can cope with that, I can cope with going home again." She dropped her voice. "But, I'll miss you, Neddie, a lot!"

"As I will you, Milla, but you know I cannot offer you any sort of good life here. I will not do that. You deserve so much more." Ned had dropped his voice as they were getting closer to the wharf. "You need more than just a marriage of convenience. Maybe one day we will each find that special someone whom we will love as we desire."

"One day, Neddie!" she replied with a beaming smile.

"Milla, I will say that you have softened my heart, though. I didn't think it possible that I could care for anyone as I care for you, but not that way, and not after her. I think we both know that. You will always have a special place in my heart, Milla. You know that too, as well, Essie; I love her dearly. You are the sister I never had, but more than that, so much more. One

I will cherish until my dying day." He wrapped her hand in his. "I'll say my farewells for today now. I'll come and see you both next month as usual."

"Thank you, Neddie, my other brother." She gave him one of her sweetest smiles. "Never change, Neddie. You are all that is good and proper. You, too, are very special to me. Take care, my very dear friend."

"You too, Milla, you really have no idea what you have meant for me. You are someone who knows who I really am, and not only have you kept that quiet, but you treat me well, just as me, no kowtowing to a title. Here I'm not Lord Edward Lockley; I'm just me, Ned Grace at that, and not even Gracemere. That's to be David's name, not mine." Ned was still keeping his voice low. The ferry had not yet arrived, so they had a few minutes of private conversation.

"Why, Ned, why are you hiding? Is it because of David and Elouise? Does that still sting?" She looked at the hurt on his face and was somewhat unsure of what she should say. He remained silent, but he met her eyes apologetically. Taking a deep breath, she continued, "You are well out of that, you know? When I left, they had already been married for seven years. I think she lives in London now. She's a shrew and is hated by most who know her. Jimmy said David couldn't keep staff when she was there, and I think I was almost relieved when she left. I'm sorry if you still hold a flame for her, but you are well out of that relationship." As the ferry still had not arrived, they stood halfway down the hill to continue their private conversation.

"Yes, it was because of her initially. But, Milla, I saw her for what she was and was pleased she cried off. I might have run myself if she had not. I'm not brokenhearted over her loss but for the damage she did to David and my relationship with my family. He told me to leave, so I did. I came, for David's sake, Milla. Only Jimmy and the Duke of Malvern knew the name I enlisted under and that I was over here. I had to tell someone, and the duke overheard her crying-off. That in itself is a stupid term, as it was more of a gleeful cackle saying she had David in her pocket and wished to be a duchess. Duke James thought I was upset. I was, but only because she'd told me she wanted my older brother instead. When you are nineteen, one's heart is delicate at best. She's got her title. I hope it made her happy, but I'm sure she made David's life hell."

She so wished to give him a hug. "Ned, you need to move on. Let go of the hurt from both her and David. Find happiness."

"Milla, I might try. You being here has made me realise I am lonely, but I won't go home. At least not unless I have to, and you know what that would entail. When you leave, can you take word to Mother for me? Tell her I love her still and that I am well. Just let her know I care. Say hello to Father, too, but please don't let them know more than you have to. No details, Milla."

"I will, Neddie. I'll be praying for you, praying that you find your special someone."

"Thank you, Milla." He patted her hand and gave it a loving squeeze. They saw the ferry coming and slowly dawdled down to the others waiting. As they joined the others on the wharf, the ferry was tying up. Ned escorted the Governor on board with Anne, then returned to assist Amelia up the gangplank. "Take care, Milla, and give Essie my love. I am so glad you are safe. I'll not allow you back in there, ever. Just so you know," He bowed and kissed her hand, giving it a gentle squeeze again as he did so.

The gangplank was withdrawn, and Ned stood watching her face as they prepared to depart. She lifted her fingers subtly in a wave, and he saluted and then gave a small bow. He stood waiting until the ferry was out of sight, then returned to the inevitable twenty questions from Charles. Ned smiled as he walked up the hill; yes, he loved Amelia dearly, but not exactly as just a brother, but not enough to marry her. He also realised that should the horrible situation occur of him having to return and take David's place, a wife with a convict past would find life in England extremely difficult. He would not do that to her. He cared too much. She had, however, made him realise he was lonely and now open to the possibility of one day finding a wife, but it would not be Amelia. She was, as he told her, a best friend, no more, no less. He could not allow that to go any further. He had to guard his actions. He would miss her when she went very much. He gave a deep sigh, now to face Charles. He did so with a happy heart and a smile on his face. He had much explaining to do after the way he held her.

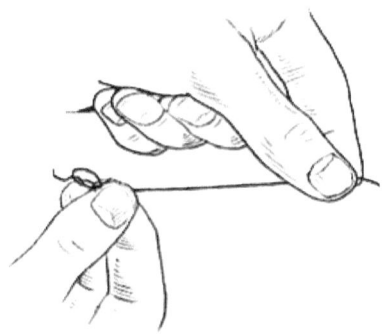

Chapter 11 Tying Up the Ends

*A*melia found that settling after the day in the Factory was not easy. She'd wake from nightmares and even woke Essie sometimes when she'd jump herself awake. She'd break out in a cold sweat and couldn't return to sleep. Many nights, she'd end up in the kitchen making herself a cup of tea, unable to sleep.

Mrs Endean knew, as although Amelia would wash the cup, she'd often leave it on the sink before returning to bed.

After over three weeks of this, Sadie took her aside. Mrs Endean had told her of her suspicions. The regular cups in the sink gave her away.

After breakfast one morning, Mrs Christopher took both girls from the room. "We need to talk, dear." Sadie saw the dark circles under her eyes. "You need to tell me what happened that day. You've stayed silent, and you need to release the emotions, dear."

Amelia was sitting with her head down. "I don't want to think of it, Sadie, but I can't stop. When I close my eyes, I can hear the doors slamming; I can hear the looms and the rocks being smashed. Oh, Sadie, it's come rolling back again. I can't believe that after all this time, I'm still haunted by it. When I sleep each night, it comes crashing back to me. They didn't hurt me, but I was so afraid that I'd be stuck in there again. Oh, Sadie, I was so desperate." She dug into her sleeve and took out an already damp handkerchief. "I've become a water fountain again. I can't believe it. I told Neddie I was fine, but I'm not; I'm far from it."

Sadie came and sat next to her and let her weep.

Amelia didn't hear the door open; she was too distraught. Phoebe entered and came directly to her. "I had a feeling you were putting on a brave face, Amelia. Richard has just been speaking to the Governor. You didn't tell us they actually kidnapped you." She saw the look of surprise on Sadie's face.

"They kidnapped you? Amelia, why didn't you say anything? No wonder you're not coping. Oh, my dear, dear girl. What a horrific experience," Sadie now understood her fears. Having seen that place once had given her bad dreams for a week. To have been locked up in there would be almost soul-destroying. She'd seen what Amelia was like the year before when she'd suggested that she visit with them. She'd practically had a panic attack that day. Finally, when she had gone to the Factory, she'd been kidnapped.

"Amelia, I know this sounds strange, but you need to talk it out. You need to voice everything. Tell us how you're feeling and why. If you can't get to that stage, at least outline what happened," Phoebe said softly. "Trust me, it will help."

Amelia nodded. "I know, but I haven't been ready to admit my fear until now." She proceeded to tell about that day and the trauma of first entering the gates. She spoke of her feeling that all was not well and then of the kidnapping. It was when she told of Ivy's rape that she finally broke. "Some men are beasts. They take, and they take, and they are not for the damage they cause. Poor Ivy had her head shaved because she was attacked. She'd been asleep, and Matron's husband forced himself on her. I wake, fighting off the blankets, thinking that it's Cyrus and that he's taking me again. How can I ever marry knowing what I've already gone through? I don't want Essie ever to know, but how can I hide it from her?" She shuddered.

"Has the Governor done anything about that man?" Sadie asked.

"He said he would, but honestly, I don't know," Amelia replied.

"Then let's find out if he has. Your major will know; how about we ask him for an update?" Phoebe added.

The door opened, and 'her major' was shown in.

He saw her in tears. "Milla, little one, what's wrong?" he asked even before he even greeted the other two ladies. His heart twisted.

"Nightmares, major; she's not been coping since the trip," Sadie said as she relinquished her seat to Ned.

Amelia turned to him, sobbing, adoring his endearment.

He drew her into his arms. He felt terrible as he'd made her go in on the trip. "Oh, Milla, why didn't you tell me?" He rubbed his hand over her back as she wept on his shoulder. "I knew I should not have forced you to come with us that day. You did not wish to go in; I should have listened. I'm so sorry." He laid his cheek on her hair as he'd done before.

"Neddie, I've had such nightmares of Cyrus again. And about Matron's comments from last time in the washroom. Then, the kidnapping and thinking I was to be hurt. Not that they hurt me, but it has just brought everything back. I've not had a full night's sleep since that night." Her hacking sobs started afresh. His arms were so comforting. She lay listening to his heart beating its tattoo.

He waited until she had wept for a while. He sat gently stroking her head.

The four sat silently, wondering what to say or do.

Ned continued while still holding her. "I've come to tell you what's happened, Milla. Can you bear it? I think it may help."

Not willing to move, she nodded. "I need to know."

"We've changed things already, and I've just given a report to the Governor. It's why I'm here. Robert Findlay has been removed from the premises and is no longer ever allowed there. Sadly, I can't charge him as he was not caught in the act, at least not for that. However, his removal from the premises was done that day. He was not even allowed back to collect his things. His wife, too, must now live off the site. Mrs Neale has taken over as on-duty Matron, but Mrs Findlay will remain as superintendent until the Governor can find a replacement. It could take some time, though. The books were audited, and their salary is to be adjusted until all is repaid. They won't have much to live on. I have also made sure he's forfeited his ownership of ill-gotten gains, and that includes ownership of a certain inn. It's been transferred to the licensee." He heard Amelia gasp slightly. "Much is missing. It does not tally with what Charles sent, and of the two, I know whom I trust. Over the past thirteen years, Charles has not been more than one penny out in his bookkeeping. He is now personally overseeing the distribution of food, and we have doubled the rations for every inmate. Milla, they are to get meat daily and even eggs and fresh vegetables and fruit. These are all the leftovers from the markets, boxes and boxes of fresh food. Previously, this was sent to the pigs at Rooty Hill. I think you may like this next thing. I have had Ivy promoted to Assistant Matron. She's thrilled."

Amelia finally sat up a little and gave a soggy giggle. "I bet she didn't expect that. What did she say?"

Ned released her but stayed close; he had an arm loosely along the back of her seat. "Milla, because of you, they will get some dignity, they will also be properly fed, and we are assigning many more of the girls as maids. There is a call out to any men who wish to marry to come and meet their prospective brides, but I have insisted on references for each prospective groom. Never will a man like Cyrus ever be allowed to be considered. Any suspicion at all will preclude them from being eligible. Again, thanks to you. Maids are being offered in pairs rather than alone. You again told me how afraid you were about going with a strange man alone. Amelia, it's because of what you went through that these women now have choices. Ivy sent a message, 'Tell that lady friend of yours that I send her a big clean hug.' It's just as well; it was a clean one. She smelled before."

He heard Amelia give another chuckle.

Ned continued, "They have heated bathwater available and can now wash their own clothes and cook their own food. We have an open-air undercover cooking area built for them. We are planning to enclose it, but it will do for the moment. Food is available as needed with the fully stocked storeroom accessible when required."

"Ivy, really? She'll keep things running in an orderly fashion. She'll also make sure no one will take more than their share." Amelia smothered a chuckle.

This time, Ned laughed with Amelia.

"Oh, Neddie, are they really safe now?" Her eyes sought his to read his expression

"Yes, Milla, they are, and what's more, I will make sure they stay that way." He was now relaxing on the settee. Amelia was sitting next to him but was now more relaxed, too.

"I think we all need some tea," Sadie said, raising her eyebrows enquiringly.

"Yes, please, Sadie," Amelia said.

Ned and Phoebe both gave a nod. Over tea, Ned filled them in on more of the changes made for the women.

"There is one more bit of information I've finally been given permission to tell you all. Anne and Edward Deas Thomson are moving permanently to Parramatta with the Governor. He wishes to be close to his wife's grave. He is not coping well, and Anne and Edward wish to be close to assist him as much as they can. So this, too, will mean he can keep his eye on what's going on there. In essence, he's stepping out of the social scene in Sydney. Anne and Edward will take over that. And that reminds me of my real purpose for my visit: a birthday ball is being planned for June. The Governor is planning to attend, but the Deas-Thomsons will be the official hosts for the evening. I have come to issue you all invitations." He let that sink in. He dug into his uniform coat and produced three handwritten invitations.

Handing Phoebe and Sadie theirs, he also had one for Caroline and Douglas Evans. He smiled at Amelia. "Yes, you too, Milla; I would be honoured if you would be my partner for the evening. Anne has specifically asked if I could bring you, but I would have asked you anyway."

"Really, Neddie? I'm still a convict." She was stunned.

"As you have an official invite from the First Lady, I dare not say no. I wondered if any of Mrs Darling's gowns were suitable for such a function by any chance. You mentioned that she had given you some when she left."

Amelia nodded.

Sadie caught her glance. "Amelia, you will finally get to wear that blue satin gown. It's exquisite. I'll answer that, major. Yes, she has a gown and a cape, too. I have some long gloves you may borrow, and that gown has matching slippers."

"Oh, may I? Thank you, Sadie. I have that and the green taffeta one, too, Phoebe. Do you have a gown? We're the same size, so I'm sure it will fit you. Would you wear that one? I'll never wear it, but it was far too beautiful to give away. Not very Christian of me, I know, but I just wanted something nice."

Phoebe was looking worried. "I don't have anything to wear, and with the girls, funds are now tight. Richard told me last night that when he did the books, the Benevolent Society is £150 lacking in funds. We've been called on so much with all the new convicts that we've overstretched the funds. So if I could borrow a gown, I'd be thrilled to come. Richard can wear his Clergy clothes. That excuses any formal attire. And thank you, major, for choosing us three of the new Irish girls. It made life so much easier since Margaret's behaviour had improved." Her smile made Amelia content.

Ned acknowledged her thanks. He stayed for a few more minutes before he made his excuse and left. He had yet to deliver the Evans's invitation and then return on the afternoon ferry. He gave Amelia a brotherly hug and then left.

There was a deafening silence for some minutes. "I should be so jealous, Amelia. Oh, to be held in arms like his. Just don't let John hear me," Sadie blushed. The three ladies laughed.

"I'll admit, it was nice, very nice." Amelia looked shy, then giggled. "Maybe I'll have nice dreams tonight."

Soon after he left, Phoebe brought up the lack of funds from the Benevolent Society again. "I think we should have a special collection in all the churches and see if we can attempt to cover funds by donations. I believe Archdeacon Broughton will be at St James this week. May I get John to speak to him?"

"I think we should also have some more working and sewing bees and build up some products for sale. John has just brought in some new fabrics. The bales were once more stored upside down, and the expensive fabrics were damaged. One is a light blue velvet." Sadie looked so sad. "Such a pretty colour too. It's so very sad."

"I'll get sewing, Sadie; fifty bags at £3 each is all we need. That bolt of blue velvet can be made into those. The dip-dyed ones sold well, too. I didn't even need much embroidery on those."

The three headed back to the workroom and started cutting up the blue velvet. They had sorted through the damaged sections of blue velvet cut into twenty proposed bags within an hour. This still left much of the fabric left over.

Amelia's eyes were still red and puffy from her emotional outburst on Ned's shoulder. However, she did feel much better. An idea struck her. "You know, the women at the Factory can sew. If I make one as a sample, they could make the bags; we can embroider them. Then they, too, are assisting their own help. Ned can sort the sewing bee ladies, and Ivy will work out who can do the work fastest. I wonder if we can get them to sew other things for sale."

They cut out various items: they had a sample made already, and they would send them to the Factory ladies to complete. There were other lovely fabrics, and Amelia suggested they include some yards of fabric for the women to experiment with. Also, some damaged straw bonnets were included and some trimmings. Amelia knew Ivy could read, as she'd told her when she was being held. So she asked for some paper and wrote a note to Ned, then another to Ivy with more detailed instructions. If this worked, it would benefit everyone. They packed a large crate of fabrics and cut-out items with samples, then pinned Ivy's note to the top.

Sadie called for some help to take the crate down to the afternoon ferry. It would probably be the one that the major caught, and he would take it up when he could. His letter sat on the top with his name in large writing. Captain Roberts would make sure it got to him.

~

A week later, Sadie was in the sitting room when there was a knock at the front door. Ned stood there with the large crate and a big smile. "Delivery boy!" he grinned.

"Come in, major, come in." Sadie welcomed him warmly. "Amelia is down at Phoebe's but is due back soon."

"That's all right, I can't stay, but this is a wonderful idea. Ivy was thrilled and asked if they could have more to do. It's treated as a reward. Now there are so many queueing up to do the 'special sewing' that the work was completed in three days." Ned smiled. "She wants more, much more. You'll find some amazing work here. The fabric lengths were devoured. Their creative juices were wetted, and they were eager to help. May I leave these with you, and I'll call back in about two hours from now? If not, you could send more by ferry."

"Oh, major, that is fabulous. And they have done them all? Truly?"

Sadie quickly looked through the top of the box. She gasped. "Not only did they make the bags, but they have embroidered them too. They will bring in a lot. Oh, and yes, I will get the next lot ready for your return." She was so excited. "Oh, Major, yes, yes, I will go directly. Is it possible for some of the ladies could come and see some of the fabrics for themselves? Could some be escorted in, and they could select some themselves? We have so much damaged fabric it's beginning to overwhelm me."

"I shall attend to it. I'll bring help this afternoon to carry things. Is any particular day more suitable?" Ned started moving to the door.

"Um, oh, I'm so excited. Today is Monday. Um, any day this week is suitable." She walked to the front door with Ned.

"I shall see you in a couple of hours." He turned to leave.

Amelia arrived as he reached the gate. "Hello, Ned. Are you leaving?"

"Yes and no; I'll return in two hours; I have a meeting at the Barracks. I'll bring some carriers with me. I have to take a small contingent back with me on the ferry; I may as well put them to good use. So you have a project for me to complete before my return. I must go, I'll be late as it is. See you in two hours." He gave her a slight bow.

"Okay, thanks, Ned." She waited until he'd gone, then turned and entered the sitting room to Sadie. "What's this all about?"

"Come inside and see what he's brought. It's truly amazing." Sadie led her to the crate. Sitting on the small table was the box Ned had placed there.

Amelia walked straight to it. "Oh, Sadie, this is astounding. What does he want us to do?"

"He wants more. He's returning in two hours." Sadie took another look at the finished goods. "We must hurry; this time, he just wants fabric, not cut items."

The two women went to the workroom and started sorting the bolts. The time passed too fast; they had chosen twelve bolts of suitable fabric. These would be sent uncut, and they hoped the women would make some useful things for sale. If what they had already sent was anything to go by, this would not be a problem.

They had chosen a gold shot satin, a brown velvet, two sprigged muslins, various taffetas and three embroidered damasks. They were tossing up if they should include the fine linen when Ned entered the room accompanied by four other soldiers.

When Ned saw the amount of fabric in the room, he suggested that while they had the manpower, they take more than just the twelve bolts. The women at the Factory could and would work miracles with some of these. The money for the items would soon fix the shortfall for the Society funds.

They quickly chose more bolts of fabric. One was a fine silk lining fabric and sewn into a calico cover to protect it. Sadly, it had been wet and was somewhat stained. Sadie was interested to see what the ladies would make from these. Sadie led out the laden soldiers while Amelia and Ned had a moment to say hello and goodbye. He was concerned that she may still be having nightmares.

"No, Ned, not since that day; I apparently needed a good cry. And it's such a nice shoulder to cry on." She chuckled.

"Anytime, Milla, I must go, though. I'll miss the ferry. See you on Friday, Milla." He gently stroked her cheek. "Release it to God." With that, he was gone.

Amelia stood in the middle of the slightly emptied workroom, thinking deeply about Ned's final comment. "Release it, too, God." It was one thing she had not done. She bowed her head as she stood in the now quiet room. She was still praying silently as Sadie re-entered.

Sadie stood waiting. Amelia felt rather than heard her. She opened her eyes to be met by Sadie's warm brown ones looking at her.

"Is all well, my dear?" Sadie asked.

"Yes, Sadie, Ned reminded me that I had not yet taken my problems to God. So I just did." Amelia gave her a beaming smile. "I told him that I enjoyed crying into his shoulder. Dare I say, he almost blushed." She gave a chuckle. "He's so easy to be with. He's kind, he's caring, and he's handsome, and he's cuddly; take it from me, I've benefitted from more than a few of those big warm hugs. Oh, Sadie, I do so hope he finds his true love. He so needs that special someone in his life." She smiled. "Don't look at me like that; it's not me. And, no, I'm not pining for him. I just wish for his happiness." Amelia was almost glowing with happiness.

"Are you sure, dear? You are always happier when he's either been or when he's around."

"Of course I am. Why would I not be? He's special to me, but as I said, not that way. Okay, more than a brother, but not as anything more than a best friend. I can be myself with him, as he can be the same with me."

"Amelia, you said that before. Is there more to both your stories from home?" Sadie said.

"We each have our own stories; we are only entitled to tell our own and no one else's. You say very little about your own." Amelia looked somewhat coy. "Nothing, actually!"

"Yes, Amelia, point taken. You are correct; it is none of my business. You are correct to keep his confidence." She took Amelia's hand. "It was wrong of me to ask."

"Sadie, many here are not who they seem to be; Sam Corbett, for example. Many are hiding behind masks; let me just say that he will reveal his if he wishes."

"Agreed, Amelia, I shall not ask again. Now, let us get on with our work." Sadie led her out of the workroom. "Let's unpack the crate and see what Ivy has sent us."

They spent the next hour unpacking and sorting the items and pricing them for sale. There were the twenty evening bags. They had varied the design from Amelia's, so each one looked different. There were also bookmarks, even spectacle bags. As they dug into the crate, deeper, more exotic items appeared. There were slippers, collars, sewn pictures and, of course, the reticules. At the very bottom of the crate was the most gorgeous patchwork blanket. As they pulled it out, a note fell from it. It was written in a simple script but written like a thumbnail had been dipped in tar.

Female Factory, Parramatta
June 1834

Dear Mrs West, Amelia,

Firstly I want to say sorry for that day. I will not say more except 'Thank you'. You did what youse said you would do; youse have not forgotten us. Your trust to do this sewing for you are amazing. Youse has given us hope and dignity, which is more than anyone has done for a long time. Give us a chance, and we shall not let you down. Many here sewed for a living. We are thrilled you wish us to help, and we shall do our best for you.

When your major delivered the crate and gave me your letter, I knew our lot here had changed. Things here are much better, and the food is now plentiful. Mary has said that no more babies have died either.

The Doctor even came and gave us all a complete medical check-up. He will now come each week and also will come when called for emergencies.

Thank you again.

Ivy Vine

(Don't laugh; my mother thought it funny.)

Friday came, and so did Ned. He was in his dress uniform with all his medals. He had arrived to escort Amelia to Government House for the June Ball. He waited in the foyer, turning at the sound of footsteps behind him. Amelia walked slowly towards him, down the staircase. He gasped.

Amelia had been primped, preened and dressed in the ballgown; beside her walked Essie. Amelia was always beautiful, but tonight she shone. He had caught his breath when he turned as he heard her coming down the stairs. She glowed with happiness.

John Landon had walked out of the sitting room and caught the look on his face when he saw her. A smile spread across both men's faces. John then lifted his eyes himself; he, too, gasped. She was a vision to behold. In Eliza's light blue ballgown, Amelia looked stunning. Neither John nor Ned even noticed that Sadie had appeared on the staircase above her. Ned found he had a lump in his throat. He finally found his voice as Essie took his hand.

"Uncle Neddie, are you okay?" she asked innocently.

He bent and lifted her up. "Yes, poppet, I'm just admiring your Mama. She's very beautiful, isn't she? Stunningly so!"

"Oh, I know Uncle Neddie; she's beautiful inside and outside, too," Essie said innocently, gazing at her beautiful mother from her new elevated position.

"She certainly is. Essie, may I have your permission to escort her to the ball?" Ned looked her in the eye.

"Oh, Uncle Neddie! How is she going to get there if you don't?" She then giggled and asked to be put down.

Ned covered the two steps to Amelia and greeted her. "You took my breath away, Milla. Tonight, you will be the belle of the ball. I'll be fighting off all the suitors tonight." He gave her one of his dazzling smiles.

"Hello, Neddie, so I'll do?" She gave him a smirk. "They have primped and preened me. It feels so strange dressed so, as last time was my come-out ball." That was the night she had seen the dark-haired young man who had dared ask her to dance; she had dreamed about him for so long. His face was now almost a faded memory, but he still had a place in her heart. He would always be her dream man. However, tonight was Ned's night.

Sadie made it to John's side without him even noticing. "What a couple," she said softly to her husband. "Pity they aren't actually one, though."

John bent and greeted her with a quick kiss. "You scrub up pretty well yourself, my love. I'll be very proud to have you on my arm tonight."

She chuckled.

Amabel was heard running down the stairs. "Mama, Papa, don't go without a kiss from me." She was in her father's arms as soon as she reached them. "Oh, don't you all look wonderful?"

The two little girls stood together and watched the four adults who were ready to leave.

Ned placed the dark blue velvet cloak around Amelia's shoulders, and John put a white fur cloak around Sadie's. They all turned and waved to the girls who sat on the bottom stairs, watching their own fairy princess mothers leave for a ball.

The ball was everything Amelia wanted it to be. She was welcomed by Anne and greeted, in front of everyone, with a kiss on the cheek.

Ned was, of course, the perfect escort. He danced only two dances with her and was the epitome of the perfect gentleman, as, of course, he was. Major Humphrey Downes and Major Tim Hinds each claimed two dances as Mr Landon. The evening ended at one in the morning.

John and Sadie allowed them to say farewell alone in the drawing room.

As the door closed behind Ned, Amelia turned, and Ned opened his arms to her.

She was in them in an instant and snuggled close. "Neddie, I had a wonderful night. How can I ever thank you?"

"You can thank me by always being happy, Milla; as Essie said earlier, 'you are beautiful inside and out'." He loved holding her, but she was so small that he always felt he'd hurt her if he held her hard. He kissed the top of her head. "I must go, Milla, but I just wished that this ball would be one for you to remember, too. I missed your come-out ball. The others never forgave me for missing that. Robbie met his mystery lady that night, you know?"

She let the comment slide. She vaguely remembered Robbie as a dark-haired boy with two big front teeth like a rabbit, but she'd not seen him since she was a child, but he'd always been kind to her.

"Thank you again, Neddie." She stepped back from his arms. "I had a wonderful time." Her face was serene and happy. She reached up and kissed his cheek. He left her soon afterwards and went to his friend Tom's spare room at Rock Cottage for the night.

~

The following week was busy with Amelia teaching both girls some of their letters. The girls both could now trace their names, and each could count to thirty. On Friday morning after the ball, they had just completed their morning lessons when Mrs Christopher came and said Amelia was needed in the sitting room.

Amelia left the two small girls with her, and they were taken to Amabel's Nanny, Miss Button. Amelia went into the sitting room, and Ned was there with Ivy and three other female prisoners. The soldiers had placed another huge wooden crate onto the floor. Ivy and Sadie were sorting through some of the items.

Ivy stood and greeted Amelia with a hug. "That's the big, clean hug I promised I'd give you. You haz no idea how wonderful it is to not only be clean but to be out and about. Sydney is such a different place to Lundun, isn't it? You can breathe. But oh, Mrs West, Amelia, to be doing some real work with some beautiful fabrics will be wonderful. It's been truly amazing, and then your major brings in them sixteen full bolts of fabric. Oh, Amelia, you haz no idea the joy that brought." She was almost bouncing with glee. She looked shyly at the major. "He's arranged for me to have a Ticket of Leave so I can come and go from the Factory. I still live in, but I'm one of the Assistant Matrons now. I'm even paid, Amelia. Oh, things are almost good there now."

Sadie called to her. "Amelia, have you any idea what they have made with what we sent them? Come and see." Sadie was still on her knees, unpacking the large crate.

Amelia joined her, and with Ivy and the others, they set to see what was included.

Ned and the accompanying soldiers stood watching the joy from the ladies. He had noted Amelia's acknowledgement of his presence. She'd given him a broad smile and a nod, but with so many present, more was not possible.

With the pile of items unpacked, Sadie turned to Amelia. "How about we show them what else there is? I think we can trust them, don't you?"

"You haven't opened the wrapped one yet," Ivy said.

"No, I thought I'd leave that until last. Amelia, will you do the honours?" Sadie said. "I figured it would be something special."

Amelia untied the string that held the parcel closed. Inside was the most exquisite gown, suitable for the most regal evening function. Even the soldiers gasped when they saw it.

"Oh, Ivy!" Sadie and Amelia gasped in unison.

"This should pay off the debt by itself. One like this, Madam

Genevieve, sold for over £200. She is the most amazing designer. She taught me dress design, and I have others there who can sew as well," Ivy explained. "We wanted to show you what we could do and so decided that the gold taffeta would be the best for that." She paused. "Do you like it?" She stood waiting for their reply.

Amelia turned and hugged her. "No, we love it."

"Is there any more we can have?" one of the other ladies finally asked. Most of them were silent, but they were all smiling.

"Yes, oh, could we. I was hoping you'd offer," Amelia replied. "You're happy to sew more?"

The four women nodded assent.

"Major, if you could accompany us, the rest of the soldiers can stay here as there won't be room for them all," Sadie asked. She hauled herself up gracefully and led them out of the room.

Ivy and the three other convict women followed her, and Ned and Amelia brought up the rear. She had little more time than to say, "Thank you for bringing them, Ned."

"These ones are the best sewers, according to Ivy. So I thought they'd know what's best to choose." Ned followed them into the workroom.

The four new ladies stood looking at the stock of fabrics. All had their mouths open, and Ivy could not resist fingering some of the shot silks. "Oh, ma'am, these are incredible. How many do you wish for us to use?" she asked Sadie.

"All of them, Ivy! These are the damaged bolts. My husband John is an importer, and these are the unsaleable items. We've been tearing some into the ten-yard lengths for the ladies at the Factory, but you can't exactly use silks, satins, and velvets while smashing rocks. So I've only been sending the drill, twill, and serge. If you can find better uses for the decorative fabrics, then the money we make from selling the items you make goes back into the Benevolent Society and gets used again. At the moment, we have a £150 shortfall, so before we, or you, do anything, we need to fix that. The gown you made from the good blue velvet will pay most of that in itself. I think it will sell for nearly £100, if not more. The gold taffeta one will bring in even more."

"Ma'am, we'll turn any of these into whatever you wish. All we need is some thread." Ivy turned to look at the other ladies and noticed the tears on their faces. She drew one to her and said, "We'll do magic things wiv these, won't we, Julia?"

The weeping lady nodded. "Oh, Miss Ivy, I've not seen such beautiful things for an age. I worked at Covent Gardens making costumes with Madam Genevieve, too, and she would also use damaged fabrics as the materials were cheaper. The damaged sections she'd hide so no one was the wiser. On stage, you could not tell." She sniffed. She walked to the huge stacks and fingered a blue moire taffeta. "This would make up into the most exquisite gown."

Ivy caught sight of a basket of laces, button shanks and other notions.

Sadie heard her gasp. "Lift it up," she said.

Ivy did; under it was sewing and embroidery threads and silks, pins, and needles.

"They are all heading out your way, too, dear. I presume you can use them?" Sadie smiled at the tears being shed.

"Julia, look!" Ivy handled the hanks of silks in many different shades and all the needles required for their use. "Oh, we shall enjoy working with these."

Sadie arranged for a cart to collect over twenty bolts of the very good fabrics, each still with damage. Also, a box of notions and threads and have them delivered to the Female Factory.

Within a week, the first of the items were returned, and each Thursday or Friday afternoon, the ferry brought more of the finished items. Sales of the exquisitely made gowns, bags and other things were selling faster than they could be supplied.

Phoebe, Sadie, Caroline, and Amelia did not let on who was making them; they just said, "Professional seamstresses, trained by a French Haute couturier," had been "employed" to do the work.

Once a week, Sadie and Amelia would send another cartload of fabric to the Factory.

Ivy sent a note back with a load of gowns from the damaged fabrics saying that they thought Mrs Landon should send in some of the better-undamaged fabrics, and they would make gowns for sale at Landon's store. They had heard of another ball to be held in October, and they asked permission to make some gowns for sale; John and Sadie thought this a good idea. Once the shortfall had been reversed and the stock in the charity store filled. John chose some perfect fabrics from the store and had them made up into off-the-rack gowns. All the dresses had seam allowances that meant they could be altered easily. With the Spring Ball coming up, a range of exquisite ball gowns were made and ready for sale, all of which sold. Ivy and some of the Factory ladies came for a special sale day, and as the seams were adjustable, did the alterations required before returning to the Factory.

The small shop for the Benevolent Society moved into a larger one. Word had spread about the quality of work now being sold from there. There was still some mystery about who the seamstresses were, but no one asked too many questions when they saw the gowns. The golden gown sold for £120 within a week of displaying it in the store. No one knew who had bought it, but the money was paid, and the dress was gone. So everyone was happy. The shortfall was repaired, and the balance was growing in the bank. With the women now sewing their own clothes from the bolts of work fabric, the workroom became a short-term storeroom. Phoebe had a basket at the back of the church for any donations of thread or notions that people had spare. Soon, this, too, was regularly needing to be emptied.

~

The weeks passed almost too fast for Amelia. Her life with Sadie and John Landon was drawing to a close. Her seven years were up. The Spring Ball came and went. Ivy had asked for Amelia's gown and said she'd refresh it for her for the ball. What arrived back was fit for a princess. Somehow, Ivy had found some blue georgette and made an overskirt scalloped and beaded. It shimmered as she walked. The tiny crystal beads alone would have taken hours to sew on. She wept when she pulled it from the box it arrived in. She and Sadie were alone. Ned had brought it and said he'd stay the weekend in town with Tom as he would collect her for the ball the next day. Ivy had made a matching sheer wrap for her from the georgette. She came down with this draped around her shoulders. Again, Ned caught his breath. She radiated happiness.

"Neddie, did you see what Ivy has done to my gown? It's glorious," she bubbled.

John's eyes were on Sadie. She was in the gold taffeta gown that he'd secretly bought her. He'd taken one of her other gowns and had Ivy and the girls adjust it for her. He had given it to her as a birthday gift the month before. He'd seen her admiring it as it hung in the workroom. She, too, was glowing. It made her fair hair look golden.

This Ball, too, was a spectacular event. Again, Ned danced only two dances with Amelia. She was unable to sit out any dances, though, as her dance card was filled quickly. Exhausted but totally happy, she whirled through the evening, knowing she'd get a hug from Ned on arrival home. She also knew that this would be the last time as her sentence was nearly over.

Ned once again was invited into the drawing room on arrival at the Landon's home. Sadie and John sat with them for a while, and then they excused themselves and said good night. It was nearly two in the morning when he went. They, too, had sat dissecting the evening but in a delightful way. Amelia stifled a yawn, and Ned knew that he must leave her. He'd well overstayed his time as it was. "I must go, Milla. May I just say how honoured I was to have you as my partner? You are truly beautiful; never forget that. Be the lovely person you always are. Never let anyone tell you otherwise." He stood and opened his arms to her. "Just a hug, Milla. No more, no less."

She went into his waiting arms willingly, "No more, no less, Neddie. Just to have you there is enough. One day, you will find her, though, one who will be more. I'll keep praying for you, be assured of that."

"As I will for you, Milla." He bent and cupped her face, brushing his fingers along her velvety cheek. He kissed her on her forehead. "I really must away."

They drew apart, and they walked to the foyer. He bowed a farewell without further conversation and then departed. Her heart was racing as she turned and made her way to her bedroom.

Two weeks later, towards the end of October, Ned arrived and waited for her in the sitting room. "It's over, Milla. You've done it. I've come to take you down and file the paperwork. Governor Bourke has made your release an Absolute Pardon, as promised. You only have to now get Major Downs to sign and file the final papers."

Amelia didn't know whether she should laugh or cry, so she did neither. She swallowed her tears.

Ned, however, held out his arms. "I feel this deserves a hug, don't you?" She went into his arms and leaned against his chest. She wrapped her arms around him. She barely came up to his shoulder. His thumb stroked the back of her neck.

"I'm scared, Neddie," she said after some time.

"I know, Milla, but you need to return, for Essie's sake. She would have no life here. I've made all the arrangements at home; Sam and Danny are expecting you. Jimmy and Dan will meet you in London, and you will return to Meldon Hall with them. The Darlings lived with them for nearly a year. It's the right thing to do, Milla. You need to go." He dropped his cheek to her hair. "I'll miss you; you know that. I don't get hugs like this from anyone else."

"Me too, Neddie! I haven't had a big hug since I was very little. We were not a touchy family." She was content in his arms for a while. Just relishing being cherished.

Ned spoke softly, "My last one was the night I was presented. Mother had me dressed in blue satin court attire. Jimmy was lucky he was allowed to wear black. Our other friends Gerry and Robbie were with us. They were in black, too. That was the week before Robbie saw his mystery woman that I told you about. I missed that ball as I was gone by then; I left the day after our Levee. However, we three teased him mercilessly for falling in love at first sight. He never found her, but back to that night. Oh, Milla, I felt terrible; the King had allowed our early presentation because I was a duke's son and Gerry, an Earl's son and Jimmy, a Viscount's son; also Robbie, well, everyone just loved him, so we dragged him along and finally your neighbour John Princhester. Mother dressed me like Gainsborough's painting. You'd think I was a little boy. Just before we left, she gave me a mother's bear hug. I left mere days later; you know Elouise and all that. Mother is all I really miss about home. If you get a chance, can you let her know I'm both well and happy? But don't let on too much more. She does not even know the name I'm under here. The Duke of Malvern will let me know if I'm needed. Jimmy also knows, and now you will know too."

She nodded against his chest. "I will, Neddie, I promise."

"As much as I'd like to stay like this all day, we'd better go," he said softly.

She drew away from him. "If we must! Thank you, Neddie." She took a deep breath, "Let's get this over with." She collected her bonnet and walked with him out the door. They walked down the road the few blocks to Hyde Park Barracks.

Major Downs greeted them and congratulated Amelia on what she'd achieved at the Factory. "The change in the women's behaviour there is astounding."

Amelia thanked him. "Matron and her husband still need replacing, and the numbers thinned out. They just wanted to be treated with dignity and have some respect. It's not too much to ask. I was in a position where I could do something to help them, so I did. I couldn't have done it without Major Grace, though." She signed the first document and dated it October 22, 1834; then, he handed her another. Then pointed to the ledger again, and she signed. Major Downs handed her one more that required three signatures. "This one is to say that you are known by other names. Please sign appropriately next to each name: Amelia Westaweller, West, and Black. This means that the paper trail will tally. You were arrested under Westaweller, shipped out under West and are leaving under Black. I also have a copy of your marriage certificate, your service paperwork and your release documents for you. Guard them well, as the Absolute Pardons are not common. Some would even kill for that scrap of paper." He countersigned the documents and filled in the ledger.

"Mrs Black, you are now a free woman, no, a free lady and may return home." He stood and congratulated her. "I believe the major is escorting you back to Mr Landon's? Are they happy for you to stay with them for a while?" he asked, concerned.

"Yes, I am still teaching their daughter and will do so until I leave. I'm not sure what arrangements Major Grace has made for me, as he's been in regular contact with my brother." She saw the look of surprise on his face.

"He told me of his friendship with your family. And that you know him well," he was obviously fishing for information.

"Yes, Major Downs, he is," she said, "And I do."

Major Downs raised an eyebrow and was about to enquire more.

Amelia forestalled him. "His story is not mine to tell. You know my name as you have my paperwork. He is a family friend, my brother's best friend, as it happens. He will tell you if he wishes you to know," Amelia said graciously. She was not aware that Ned, although out of sight, could hear her. He smiled, knowing that his secret was safe in her hands. If word spread that he had a title, his life in the colony would be made unbearable. She, too, was titled. He kept that under wraps for her.

Chapter 12 Heading Home

It had been nearly eight years since she was arrested, tried, then and transported. In November 1834, a month after her release, Major Ned Grace arranged passage with the £10 that Jimmy had given her. She had passed it over to him to purchase her ticket home.

Ned had even come to see her off, as had the Governor, accompanied by his family, Edward and Anne Deas Thomson. Sadie, John and Amabel Landon; Reverend Richard and Phoebe Hill, plus the five little girls, as well as many of the Benevolent Society ladies, lined the wharf. Amelia was going home, well, nearly home.

Sadie and Major Ned had assisted her on board and saw her adequately settled in her suite of cabins. When she saw the spacious rooms, she knew Ned had upgraded her ticket. Her £10 should have only provided a single room. Not the three she had been allocated.

Ned arrived and rearranged her luggage and the furniture for her so Essie was within earshot. He then introduced himself to the ship's doctor, also a military man, and asked that he take special care of them.

The Governor and Anne Deas Thomson then came on board, and Ned introduced them to both the Captain and the doctor. Then he presented Amelia as The Honourable Mrs Amelia Black.

Both raised their eyebrows when they saw Anne as the first lady, embracing and kissing Amelia. Their parting was sad.

Anne had been an excellent support to Amelia, and their friendship, although strange, as Governor's daughter and convict, was genuine.

From that first day, she was treated with the utmost respect by all on board. The fact that Ned introduced her by her title certainly didn't hurt. She'd not used it for nearly ten years. Even Sadie gasped quietly when she heard him introduce her to the doctor. He really should have just said Mrs Black, but she knew Ned was still paving her path back to respectability. After the Governor's entourage left, Sadie waited in the cabin as Ned said his farewells. She turned and exited to settle Essie in her room next door.

"Neddie, I will pray daily for your happiness as you've made my life so different from what it could have been. I have been praying that God will bring a special someone into your life. Someone whom you can cherish and bring joy into your future." She hugged him and gave him a kiss on his cheek. "However, from me, you're just like my brother." Her gentle laugh was tinged with regret.

He drew her tightly into his arms and kissed the top of her head, "Sort of like a sister, Milla," he said, then dropped his voice.

He had noticed Sadie had her back turned as she was still with Essie in the cabin next door. "However, I'm going to give you a quick, non-brotherly kiss." He stroked her cheek with his thumb in a very non-brotherly way, then drew her into his arms, and he gave her a very non-brotherly kiss on her lips. Not too short and not too long, but very loving.

"Shhh, don't tell!" His eyes were smiling. He placed his fingers on her lips and grinned. "I've wanted to do that for a while. Never undervalue yourself, Milla. Never! You are so very special." He released Amelia as he heard Essie returning.

Amelia turned her back and busied herself in the cabin; she wiped her eyes; her heart was somersaulting; Ned's care and compassion had once again been almost overwhelming. She felt cherished.

He turned to his goddaughter, who had just come back in with Sadie. He bowed and put out his hand to her. "Miss Esther, would you be willing to give your godfather a farewell hug and kiss?"

"I don't wanna say bye-bye to you, Uncle Neddie." She ran to him and threw her arms around his neck. "Will you comes and see us at our new home?" At nearly five, she was the image of her mother at the same age.

His heart skipped with joy with this captivating child. He truly loved her. "I'll make you a promise if I come back to England; I certainly will. But in the meantime, will you learn to write so you can send me letters?" Ned was looking the adorable child in the eye.

She didn't answer; she was pouting. "Well, will you write to me? Your Mama can help until you are better at it. But I expect at least two letters a year, preferably more."

"Oh, all right, Uncle Neddie." She gave a big sigh. "If I must!" Then she gave a giggle. "Of course, I'll write, Uncle Neddie, but I want to hear from you too. Okay? I've just put my Neddie Bear in my bed; Aunty Sadie helpeded me. Every time I hug him, I've really been hugging you."

"Okay, precious. Now give me a last hug as I have to leave for work." His eyes caught Amelia's and were met with a smile.

She hugged him tightly, giving a two-armed hug around his neck. He gently put her down. He leaned over to Amelia and said, "Here's a parcel for her bed for tonight and a book for you, too. Take care, Milla." He pulled a parcel from his coat. He bent and kissed her cheek again. "I'm proud of you. Remember that." He squeezed her hand and left.

Amelia suddenly felt very alone. Sadie waited until he left. "He's so special, isn't he? And so good-looking!" she commiserated lovingly.

Amelia found tears running down her cheeks with his departure. "Yes, he is all that. I do hope he finds happiness, though. I told him I was praying for someone for him. He's so alone here. He needs someone who will love him for just who he is." Amelia was watching Essie investigate their rooms. She opened all the doors and cupboards.

Sadie thought her comment was strangely worded but said nothing.

"My bed, Mama?" Essie asked

"Yes, poppet, but it is not time to sleep yet. We have to say bye-bye to everyone on the dock," Amelia explained.

"Okay, Mama, go now?" she asked.

"Yes, poppet, we're going now." She caught Sadie wiping away a tear.

"Oh, my dear Sadie. How can I thank you for everything? These last two years have been an absolute delight. Well, other than the riot and kidnapping, but besides that." Amelia gave Sadie a big smile.

"Is that all I get, Amelia? I want a hug, too. The handsome major got one from you both." She giggled delightfully.

"He did and a kiss, which surprised me. But I've known him for a long time. As to hugs, yes, of course." She went into her friend's arms.

Essie ran to them and said, "Me too, me too." They both bent and hugged her, too.

The three people headed out to wait for the ship to leave. Amelia carried Essie.

Sadie said her final goodbyes and was escorted down the steep gangplank by a sailor. She stood with her friends and the Governor's contingent.

Ned was standing behind them all. She could see his red coat as the ship slipped from the dock; he touched his fingers to his lips and blew her a kiss.

His action made her catch her breath. He was so crucial to the changes in her life, yet he had never overstepped the bounds of proprietary until today. Even when he hugged her, he made sure someone was in the room with them most of the time. She kissed her fingers and blew kisses to all her friends. Hopefully, Ned caught one. She smiled, remembering his kiss; she touched her lips.

He saw and did the same.

Essie was waving madly and also blowing kisses.

They stood watching until all were indistinguishable except Ned. She could still pick out his red coat. He had stayed until she was out of sight. Finally, the ship slipped around the point, and they were hidden from view. She wiped away an errant tear and then went down to her cabin to settle in. On the way, she met Hector and Fran Grey with their debonair fathers and four delightful children. They had taken six of the other cabins, and Amelia knew that as she would have five months on board with them, it was a good idea to meet them sooner rather than later.

It did not take long before the Grey family group absorbed Amelia and Essie. Essie was slightly younger than their youngest son, Alec. Their eldest daughter, Skye, was eleven and kept all the children entertained.

Amelia and Fran discovered they had much in common, and it didn't take long before revelations of their past drew the two together closely. With months ahead, the women drew close.

Amelia had experience in society, and Fran had none. So, lessons in how to curtsy and bow started, as well as the matter of dressing appropriately in all future situations.

London April 1835

The Grey family said their goodbyes in private just before Amelia and Essie disembarked in London. Mrs Amelia Black, a widow aged thirty-one, arrived at the end of spring after a five-month voyage on the *British Sovereign*. Captain Browne had cringed when he saw five children and their mother's board in Sydney. One small child and her mother were accompanied on board by a lady who settled her into her cabin. Then, a few minutes later, the Governor, his daughter and an accompanying soldier of some rank and standing boarded to bid her farewell.

Captain Brown realised she was no regular passenger. She certainly had not been. He remembered the evening he had shown her the magic lights in the sea foam, then the meteor shower that followed. She had joined her friend Mrs Grey and left him standing bereft and alone. She had certainly been special but not interested in him.

It had been a hot November day when they embarked from Sydney, and in all that time, he'd not heard Miss Essie misbehave once. The small, dark-haired girl had won his heart within the first few days. He had them dine at the Captain's table most nights, and she'd not once had a tantrum or misbehaved in any significant way. Her manners were impeccable, as were her mother's. As they alighted, he had the great pleasure of carrying her down the gangplank. He kissed the top of her hair and told her to continue being a good girl for her mother.

"Thank you, Captain Bwown; I will try to be good as gold." She gave him a beaming smile and a sloppy kiss on his be-whiskered cheek. "May I be put down now, prease?" she asked. Her slight lisp was even adorable.

"Of course, my dear." He placed her gently down on the dock. She stood still, holding her mother's hand. Her dark lashes and huge blue eyes were fixed on the face of her mother; her black curls were blowing slightly in the breeze. Amelia turned to thank the Captain for his care during the voyage. Standing watching the unfolding performance were two young gentlemen. One started walking quickly towards her. "Milla!"

"Jimmy," Amelia squealed in a very unladylike way. She wrapped one arm around her now skinny brother. He was even more handsome than she remembered. "Let me introduce your niece. Essie, this is Uncle Jimmy. Jimmy, this is Esther Martha Ruth West Black, known as Essie."

Essie curtsied perfectly. Jimmy looked at the adorable child and gave her a bow. "Pleased to meet you, Miss Essie. May Uncle Jimmy give you a welcome home kiss?"

"If you must, Uncle Jimney, but I'd raver a hug." She giggled. "Mama told me about you."

"A hug it is, then." He gave her a two-armed hug, and she settled into his arms as he lifted her above the crowds.

"Can I stay here? I can see everything from up here. You're nearly as tall as Uncle Neddie, but he's more cuddly," she asked innocently. "He's my Godfather, you know."

Jimmy looked at Amelia. "Oh, he's Uncle Neddie, eh?"

Amelia ignored his comment. "Poppet, you can stay up there if Uncle Jimmy is happy," Amelia replied. "Jimmy, I'd rather you carry her if that's all right. Then I know she's safe."

"Right, oh little sis," Jimmy introduced her to the friend who'd driven them to the dockland. He looked familiar, but she could not put a name to the face.

"Daniel, may I introduce you to my sister? Mrs Amelia Black, this is Danny …"

"Daniel Corbett, isn't it? You must be Sam's son. Um, Viscount Clarestow?" she finished.

"Err, yes. I am. Well, Garney actually now, but Corbett-Garney will do. I don't use the Clarestow. Do I know you? Have we met before?" He looked confused.

"No, but I met your father in Sydney, and I knew of him from home. And you really like him. Though, I had never met him before, of course." She turned to her brother. "Jimmy, Sam's brother Nigel was Papa's friend. Mrs Darling was on the same ship as them when leaving Sydney, and we met on board. Jimmy, do you remember Papa used to talk about being visited by Nigel and Sam Garney from school? Well, Sam is the Viscount's father." She smiled at the handsome, dark-haired man.

"Yes, I know that. I know them all, but well, this makes it easier. Milla, you're going to be staying with them. That's whom Ned has arranged for you to work for." Jimmy waited for her to question more.

"Thank you, yes, I know; Neddie told me, Jim." She gave them both a smile. "Oh, Ned's been so wonderful! I asked him to look us up if he comes back." Time enough later for her to tell Jimmy everything. "Are you coming too, Jim?"

"Not this time, Milla, but I'll stay later, probably with Robert, when I come for a visit. You'll be travelling back with Dan and Georgie, and I'll pop over when you're settled." Jim was waiting for her to ask about their parents. She had not, and he didn't want to hang around in case she enquired too much.

"Oh, thanks, Jimmy, and thank you too, My Lord," she said.

"Danny will do fine, ma'am," he said.

"Thank you, in which case I'm just Amelia." She met his eyes with honesty. The trip to their London home, Meldon House, was accomplished in less than twenty minutes. Jimmy stayed with the carriage and got the driver to drop him off at his destination. "I'll catch you later, sis. I'm so glad you're back and that things worked out how they have." He gave her cheek a quick kiss as she alighted, then climbed back in.

Essie broke the ice with her initial reaction to the enormous house. She walked in the front door and repeated something she'd obviously heard on deck: "Cor blimey." Her blue eyes could not take in the vastness of the room. The butler stood smirking at her comment, trying hard to control his laughter.

Danny's new wife, Georgie, greeted them in the foyer and asked if she could pick up the little girl to carry her upstairs.

"I thinks I'd like to walk if you please. I've been sittin' still for ever so long," Essie replied politely.

"Of course, my dear. How about I take your hand so we can see the toy room? And you can meet my baby son James and also Edmund, who's a year younger than you. You'll possibly want to stay there with the other children." Georgie led the way with Danny and Amelia hard on her heels.

Essie's eyes opened so wide when she heard about the toys. "You mean the toys get a room all to themselves? Does they come to life to play when the lamps go off?" Her innocent question made Georgie giggle.

"No, poppet, it's where they live so the children can find them." Amelia knew that Essie only had the four toys, and Ned had given her all of them. 'Miss Moppet' was the one Ned gave her when she was born, and 'Mrs Tuffett' came for a birthday, then the one he'd given her as they departed was a soldier. She also had 'Neddie Bear' from her Baptism, and he was carried everywhere while she was inside. Amelia had made a rule that the others were to stay 'on guard' in her room and couldn't be taken outside in case she lost them. They now sat in her carpetbag and were awaiting placement on her bed. His newest gift was a red-coated soldier doll she called 'Major'. He never left her bed. He was to guard her dreams.

Two days later, Danny, Georgia, and their five children, plus Amelia and Essie, travelled the forty-five miles to Meldon Hall. It was in Billingshurst, West Sussex, some four hours away. Ned had not been there, so she was totally unprepared for the magnificent edifice that she saw. It went on and on, reminding her of a visit to Stowe House when she was younger. "Ohh, Mr Daniel, it's incredible," Amelia gasped when it came fully into view.

Essie, too, watched the emerging house. Her eyes grew larger, and her mouth dropped open. "We's gonna live there? It's a fairy castle, Mama. Like one of Uncle Neddie's stories from his book."

Earl Sam and Countess Anne, Danny's parents, welcomed her warmly on their arrival. This was the arranged safe accommodation Ned had for her on return. Pittford Manor could have fitted ten times into the magnificent front edifice alone. And yet, she could see it went even further back than that. Danny made the introductions. Anne greeted her with a warm hug and kiss, ensuring her that she would be made welcome.

Sam greeted her warmly, saying, "You were so right, ma'am; we certainly learned to trust the Darlings. They ended up living with us for nearly a year; they have only recently left for their new house in Brighton. Hopefully, they will visit once they know you have arrived."

In the distance, Amelia heard a bell ring, followed by the running feet of many children. She looked puzzled. Anne stepped in and said, "It's the school, dear. Let's get you both settled, and then I'll tell you what we're doing here. Also, how you can assist if you're willing to."

"Neddie gave me a hint, but I'd love to know more." The Countess followed the housekeeper, whom she called Thea, up the stairs and into a lovely suite of rooms. "Oh, ma'am, I can't use these," Amelia said when she saw where she was placed. "They are... well, they are special or royal guest rooms," Amelia exclaimed at the overwhelming, exorbitantly spectacular suite she'd been put in.

"They are all like this. Well, many of them. It's not like the royalty is coming for a visit, is it?" She chuckled. "Thank you, Thea." She said to the housekeeper. "Now pop your bag down, and we'll sort Essie." She turned to the child. "Poppet, would you like to be next to Mama or in with the other children?"

"I finks with Mama prease," she said, "At least for a while."

Amelia then pulled the four toys out of her bag and set them on her bed. "They will wait for us here, poppet," Amelia said.

Essie watched her put her toys on the bed. "Fanks, mama, now can I meets the other girls?"

Anne smiled at the little girl, knowing she'd fit in well with Danny's children. "We have boys here too, sweetie," Anne said.

Essie's eyes opened wide. "Boys? Is they rough? I've never played with boys before, 'cept Mrs Fran's boys on the ship."

"No, they are not. Our two are both little. You've met James and Edmund already, but there are others. So you may have to help us look after them. But there are a few others who live here as well. They are our heart children."

Essie nodded. "I know what heart children are, too; Aunt Phoebe and Uncle Richard had five of them. Okay, I'se be a good helper."

"I'm sure you are," Anne said, a little surprised at the child's understanding.

Amelia's brother, Jimmy, was only sixty miles away and came for an overnight visit the week after her arrival. He stayed with his good friend Robert Styles. He lived in the next-door estate at Broome-Hall Manor with his father, Timothy, his mother, Sophie and his family. Amelia was astounded that Georgie was Robert's youngest sister. She and Dan had only married the year before. Georgie had been on her first outing since having their first child, James, known as Jamie. Amelia had been able to cuddle Jamie part of the way back from London. He was adorable.

Lady Anne explained that Danny's first wife, Vanessa, had died in childbirth, having Edmund in Sydney.

"Major Ned filled me in, Lady Anne. However, I didn't realise that Jimmy's friend Robert Styles was the brother of your daughter-in-law Georgie. Nor that he lived so close."

"Yes, he visits occasionally. I'd like to see more of him, but he's always busy doing something. Now, please call me Anne." The Countess was so friendly that Amelia relaxed.

"Thank you, um, Anne; I am Amelia, although I'm Milla to Jimmy, though." Just voicing her childhood name brought back many happy memories of her brother's friends visiting her home.

"Wonderful, well this is a rule in this house: if you're staying, we're all on first name terms, staff too. Hence, the butler is Victor; he's Thea's husband, by the way. Sam and I are Mrs Anne and Mr Sam, and our other guests are Lady Mari and Betsy. One other person who frequents the house is Lord James. You'll find out who he is soon enough." She waited for a reaction before adding, "Amelia, all but three of the staff are illegitimate children of peers. Thea and Victor's fathers were both Earl's." She saw a raised eyebrow but nothing more. "Are you still wanting to stay?"

A slow smile spread on Amelia's face. "Yes, please, sounds perfect."

Anne flopped herself onto the bed. "Are you sure? You'll be wiped from society."

Amelia threw her head back and laughed. "Lady Anne, sorry Anne, I've just finished seven years of servitude in the colony. Do you think I'll be accepted? Can you see me as a social butterfly in London?" she said with a twinkle in her eye. "Not even my parents will acknowledge me. No, I'll be perfectly content as long as I can have Essie here with me."

"Of course. I did my seven years myself, as did Sam. Danny was born free, as was his first wife. It will be wonderful to talk about things we know about Sydney and the like. I miss it, you know, the free life over there." She saw a flash of fear across Amelia's face. "Was your time bad?" Anne paused. "Amelia, don't answer unless you wish to."

Amelia nodded. "The beginning was bad, very bad, but I can't tell you now," nodding towards Essie. She was now at the age of repeating bits of conversation. "I'd like you to know. If you want me to stay, I want you to know it all."

"It took Sam and me over a year before we told each other our stories. Time enough for that later." Anne's smile warmed Amelia's heart.

When arrangements for her return had been mentioned initially, Amelia was very hesitant until the major had told her their story. Both had served time as convicts in Sydney and had reluctantly returned to take their place as Earl and Countess. They and their son now took in illegitimate children of peers and raised them as their own. They did not mix with London's Society, not because they were shunned, but because they shunned the shallowness of the immoral world in which they were expected to live, so society mattered not to them.

~

After three days, Robert came. He was everything Jimmy said: warm, caring and compassionate, and he looked more than familiar. Robert had delivered her note to Jimmy, saying she'd settled in well and would love to see him, and Jimmy had visited the week after she arrived. With everything they told each other, he still did not mention their parents. Conversations about home were quickly shut down by Jimmy. She did not press him. She'd taken the opportunity in the first days of her stay to give Anne a detailed version of her horrific experience. Little was left out, and still, she had been welcomed with open arms. Amelia had said that she refused to live under a lie and would prefer her to know everything. She also knew that Eliza would welcome her should this door close. To unburden to the older lady who had also been through such an experience, presumably not the abuse, but the gaol, hulks and conviction. Anne understood and had compassion for her. Amelia was still unsure of things and her acceptance; however, she realised she needed not to worry. The week she arrived, Lady Mari had admitted her own history to Amelia. She had an illegitimate daughter. Amelia was stunned but loved her all the more for her compassion and acceptance.

Georgie was everything adorable. Although her family lived nearby, Amelia had yet to meet all of them. Amelia had, of course, met Robert often. Georgie and Danny, having married only the year before and were like lovebirds, still sneaking away to be together whenever possible. The needs of five small children made those times valuable.

Amelia quickly made friends with Danny's three daughters. The three little girls loved being with Essie. They were one, three and five years older than her. There were fifteen other children at their school, and soon Amelia had settled into teaching regular lessons with the other ladies teaching their life skills.

Earl Sam and Countess Anne were everything that loving, godly parents should be. Anne's welcome of her with open arms was a reflection of how she treated everyone. Eliza Darling had mentioned Amelia to Anne the year before when they were living with them. She had come up in conversation on the voyage out, and Eliza spoke of her farewell.

When the major had written to his friend, the Duke of Malvern, the year before, the duke had suggested that she make her home at Meldon Hall as they needed teachers for "their little project". Ned only then realised the connections and wrote to Danny. At the time, he did not know Danny had married. Slowly, the pieces fitted together. The Duke of Malvern was the mysterious Lord James. She had yet to work out why he came regularly. Maybe it had something to do with Lady Mari; they certainly liked each other she'd even caught them hugging once. Neither was embarrassed when she'd walked in but offered no explanation.

Amelia was not expecting the fantastic welcome in class that she received. The children were so well-behaved and were all adorable. Here, she knew there would be no obnoxious parents making false accusations. She still needed to find out the reason for her own parent's abandonment of her. She'd not had the time nor the inclination to question Jimmy, but before she could move on with her life, she needed answers.

One of her first visits was to the church. She met Reverend Hugh Williams after church. He, too, welcomed her and said that he hoped she'd settled in well. She had; she was far more than just happy.

Robert Styles's visits became more regular, and after a month, he came almost daily. Ostensibly to visit his sister, yet, on his first visit, he had not been able to get Amelia alone fast enough to reveal his identity as the one and same Robert Styles to whom she'd been addressing Jimmy's letters. She had not realised the connection. He was the older brother of Georgina, now Viscountess Clarestow.

"You're that, Robert? Robert Styles? I had no idea. Why did it not gel? The Styles and Broome-Hall names, it just never occurred to me that you were the same person. I thought you must have lived there but not been one of the family. Thank you so much for being my liaison." She had caught her breath when first introduced. He epitomised every one of her daydreams of what a man should look like. He was tall, debonaire and very handsome. His manners were impeccable, and his gentle care for his family was adorable. His relationship with his step-nieces was charming.

What's more, Essie adored him too. "Robert, have I met you before somewhere? You look so familiar." His face was so familiar to her; she knew she'd met him before somewhere, sometime.

He gazed at her, obviously wishing to reply, but left her question unanswered. Amelia was unable to read his expression but saw a wave of joy pass across his face.

~

She saw him daily over the next few months. He still had not mentioned why he looked familiar, but now she knew she'd met him before; she just could not place where. She was also intrigued that Georgie had said that he usually only came about once a week at the most. Now, he'd arrive on some random pretext most days and end up always with some excuse to be alone with her. Carrying books, helping clean up after class, and walking with the children in the garden. He helped in every way possible, especially with reading classes. He'd take one or two of the boys, and they'd sit on the roof reading aloud.

As a widow, Amelia was given more freedom than had she been unmarried, so she did not need a chaperone. Each of his visits, her heart raced a little faster, yet, with each visit, he left having not touched upon the topic of recognition.

~

After some three months of his almost daily visits, as they were walking in the garden enjoying the sunshine, she said to him, "Robert, no Robbie, do you really wish to be seen with me?"

He gave a long sigh of contentment. He ushered her to a garden seat in a grove not far from the house.

The children were playing somewhere close, and they could hear their joyous squeals as they played.

He took her hand and sat holding it for a while before speaking. Theirs was a comfortable silence, though. "Why not? Amelia, nothing that happened to you is your fault." He gazed directly into her face. "I know all of what you've told Jimmy, so there's nothing that will surprise me in that. I hand-delivered each letter to Jimmy, and we met most of the time halfway, as I did not want them to fall into others' hands; I took them, and I read them after he did. I should apologise about that, but I won't." He grinned naughtily, his face lighting up with adoration as he spoke. "As I'm not really sorry, that would be a lie. I'll never lie to you, Amelia. I know about Essie and her full history. So yes, I know about you thinking her illegitimate, everything about her, Amelia. I know what Cyrus did to you, too. I also know I wished to have killed him myself." He caressed her hand. "Jimmy, let me read that first letter. Well, no, he didn't really; I snatched it from him and read it. His reaction told me the contents were not pleasant reading. I felt gutted. We sat outside in the sunshine on a day like this and grieved together. I saw the look of absolute horror on his face and the tears he shed while devouring the information you wrote. I, too, wept. Not with sorrow, although I felt that, it was with anger, but I was in awe of your strength and of your faith in such a dire time of adversity. I wept with anger for you, having been put through that in the first place. I wished to have been there and gathered you in my arms and made everything better for you, but that was not to be. After that first one, I could not read them fast enough," he admitted bashfully. "Amelia, I don't just wish to be seen with you; I want to get to know you much better, and I might add, with totally honourable intent. I'm just telling you so there is no confusion." Robbie looked at her adoringly.

"But Robbie, you'll be cut. Society will shun you. I may now be legally a widow, and yes, believe me, I was joyful when I found out about that. Even more so to find out *after* he'd died. But nothing will change me having been a convict, though," she said sorrowfully.

"You mean like Sam and Anne were? Nothing new about that! My dearest darling Amelia, when you hear what that same hypocritical Society is doing, those same people who will shun you and judge you, well, shall I put it this way, we have shunned Society. I presume you're not too interested in Society Balls and the like? I hate them. I never attended. I went for two seasons, then never had reason to return." Robbie waited for her to answer.

She shook her head. This man had come to mean so much to her, and he said he cherished being with her. If Ned's hugs were comforting, this man's mere touch could send her heart racing and make her breath stop, but she never dared dream he could ever feel the same for her. A mere accidental touch from him sent warmth shooting up her arm. His voice made her stop in her tracks, frozen with daydreams. His acceptance of her was loving, and she looked forward to his every arrival and was disappointed if he'd been held up or, for some reason, could not come. After Cyrus, she'd never expected to feel again, let alone to care. The mere touch of other men made her skin creep with fear. But with Robbie, she knew he would protect her no matter what happened.

"Amelia, I've not been to London for a season since my second one years ago. I went and fell in love with my dream girl the year earlier... and then she disappeared. That would have been when I was twenty-one; it was the year of your own presentation. I tried to dance with you, but your card was full."

She gasped. "That was you?"

He nodded; his smile lit her heart. He stroked her cheek so gently she hardly felt it. "I did go again next year, but you were nowhere to be seen." He paused, "That is where you may remember me from, although we'd met long before that. I watched you all that night and took a few chances to get close while your father wasn't looking. I hid behind plants and pillars just to be near you and whisper a few words of encouragement. I looked for you at other functions, but you never appeared. Even then, you stood out, as you were so different from the seething masses of shallow people. I saw you do what your father wished, and even though I asked you to forget another dance partner, you would not. During that season, many other 'Society Misses' would have just accepted the next man who offered, but not you. Amelia, I saw the shallowness of people in Society, and I want nothing to do with such hypocrites. All were so self-centred and none willing to step off their pedestals to help those less fortunate." He cupped her hand and now gently caressed it. "Amelia, then I saw you being swept onto the dance floor; fear was written all over your face. I was so absolutely jealous of that man, yet I knew I could not interrupt. I knew him to be a duke of unscrupulous reputation. I also knew he was hunting for another young wife. I knew Jimmy's sister was being presented, yet I never saw you two together, so I did not realise who you were until much later. I'd never met your father, and your mother was on the dance floor most of the evening. I did not see the adorable small child that you had been, so I did not recognise the stunning lady that she had become and so beautifully gowned at the ball. My darling love, I was smitten even then. I never realised that you were the adorable little sister of my own good friend Jimmy. I had been about ten when we last met; you only eight or younger."

She nodded, remembering Jim's friend Robbie so well. Even then, she adored him as he was never cruel to her.

Robbie kissed the tips of her fingers before continuing. "Jim, Gerry, and Ned teased me mercilessly about my mystery love. Some six years later, I eventually found out who you were, but you were gone. I saw a likeness of you in the Long Gallery at your house. Therefore, my dearest Amelia, I care not for their posturing. I do, however, care for you. That letter you sent to Jim telling him of Major Ned's discovery of the marriage is useful but makes no difference. I had made up my mind to woo you, court you, and marry you anyway. You are worthy in God's eyes and, therefore, mine too."

She caught her breath. She met his gaze as it fixed on her face.

As a tear slid down her cheek, he gently thumbed it away. Robbie then took both her hands and sat looking at her. "For a selection of a potential wife, I have been offered the crème of Society, the preened peers' spoilt brats, and the giggling Society misses. I have shunned them all. I rejected the selfish pea-gooses and the ladder crawlers loaded with cash that were thrust at me, for I had fallen in love with a girl who had a full dance card. A girl who had virtual rotten eggs thrown at her, thrown into a dung heap, and she survived; no, she thrived. One who stood brave against the world and still was proud; one who did not crumble at the first hurdle in her life but survived to jump many more. A girl who learned to cry and then dried her eyes and then got on with living. A girl who moved my heart in every word I read about her. One who turned her own adversity into aiding and assisting others who were in a similar situation to which you had found yourself. Oh, my dear, dear Amelia, when I read of your kidnap in that Female Factory, knowing how you didn't wish to enter in the first place." He heard her gasp.

"How do you know about that? I've never told anyone here." She gasped and looked at him, puzzled.

"Ahh, that was Ned; he wrote to Jimmy and filled him in on that day. I know about his secret too. Ned, Jim, and I were a terrible threesome when lads. Well, we were three of a foursome. Lord James told me Ned's pseudonym when he was not well. He knew we were best friends as lads. I was sworn to secrecy after I put one and one together. Jimmy was the link. Ned wrote and apologised to Jimmy for what he'd put you through."

Another tear rolled down Amelia's cheek. "That was not a good day," she said. "No, that was an understatement, Robbie. I was terrified. Yet they didn't hurt me. It was just being in there again and the clanging of the doors." She shivered.

He wiped that tear away, too, with a hooked finger. He gently caressed her cheek. "But back to those early days, when I read in your first letter what that pig, Cyrus, had done to you, I nearly jumped on a ship and came to your rescue then. Only I realised that he was dead by the time you penned it. Oh, Amelia, my dearest love, I so wished I'd been there to protect you from those hurts. I wished that I had the money back then to have been eligible enough for your father to have considered me a suitor, but I didn't. I cheered when I read about the demise of that brute in your first letter; I praised God hard for that. I have eagerly read of every twist and turn your life has taken since every hurdle you have jumped. I have envisioned Essie as my own daughter from before her birth and wish to make her so." He paused and raised her fingers to his lips. "Amelia, dearest Amelia, I wish to be far more than just a friend. I can't ask your father for your hand in marriage, but Jimmy has given his permission for me to pay my addresses to you." Robbie slipped off the seat and dropped to one knee. "My dearest Amelia, would you do me the greatest honour of becoming my wife?"

She sat holding his hands. "I want so much to say, *yes* Robbie, but …."

Her words made his heart sink; it nearly stopped. He thought she'd returned his feelings. Had he misread her kindness for compassion? Still on one knee, he listened as she continued.

"Truly, I do. You are everything I have ever dreamed about for a husband, but I can't just yet. I, too, remember you from that first and only ball I attended as a girl. Father would not let me dance with you. He wanted me to attract the duke, as you surmised. The duke was horrible; his hands seemed to make me feel dirty. When my father wasn't looking, he even touched me inappropriately. Father even allowed the duke to try to take me outside; I intentionally stood on my hem and fled into the retiring rooms. I refused his suit, and later, it was he who brought charges against me. I'm sure it was from malice. I feel he would have been no different to Cyrus." She'd never admitted her father's action before. "Robbie, my eyes followed you throughout the evening, too. I so wished to dance with you, but my parents had already arranged my dance card, and I did not dare break any of them. You did not know what my father was like; he drank a lot, and for one night, he was sober. I was so fearful something I did would set him off drinking." She could see she had broken his heart. "Robbie, I don't want you totally cast off from your family and friends. For you would be." Amelia met his saddened eyes with her tear-filled ones. "I also need answers from my parents. I have not braved them, and I have not even been brave enough to ask Jimmy. I need to know why; why they abandoned me. I'm not saying *no*; I'm asking for time. Time to get some answers," she finished with almost a plea.

Robbie held back a sigh. "Then don't reply yet, my dear. I will give you as much time as you wish. The question will remain, for I shall never withdraw it. I have waited so long for you. I will not give up now." He moved and sat beside her again, and as much as he wanted to take her in his arms to bring her comfort, he lifted her hand to his lips, then kissed each of her fingers, then turned it over and kissed her palm, then held it to his cheek. "I knew I had spoken too soon, but I wanted you to know I value you, I love you, and Amelia, I always have. I have loved you for a long time. Eleven years since I first saw you, I have never forgotten the smile you bestowed on me. I want you just as you are, and that means with Essie too." Robbie groaned as though in pain.

"Are you all right, Robbie?" she asked.

"Yes, give me a moment. I so desire to kiss you, but I will not. I have waited so long, and you have been used enough. I wish to bring you comfort, not more pain. If you knew how hard it was for me not to deck that twat of a peer who brought such allegations upon you…."

He saw Amelia flinch.

Robbie was not put off. "Yes, I know who it was, and no, I will not touch him, for I know he would call me out." He swallowed. "I'm not much good to you if I'm dead, am I? I'm not that good of a shot." He gave her a wry smile. He, too, wanted, no needed, to know why her parents had abandoned her. Something didn't make sense. He smiled at her bashfully. Jimmy never mentioned his family, and they never appeared when he visited, not that those had occurred recently. Their meetings for the past five years had occurred halfway between their houses.

She shook her head. "I think I'd like you to kiss me, Robbie, but not here and not now. Actually, I know I'd like you to kiss me, but it's too public. And no, that doesn't mean I wish to sneak away with you, but maybe soon. Robbie, I also need to tell you that I'm fearful of my responses. The only kisses I have received have been during abuse. I only say that because you read my letters. I know that deep down, that fear is still there, and I do not wish to hurt you either, and Robbie, I don't know how I will react to that side of things. Are you sure? After six years, I still wake and must throw off the blankets because they are suffocating me. He took evil delights in his versions of torture, and throwing my skirts over my head was one of them. Holding them so I couldn't breathe, and he enjoyed my panicking. Robbie, you will need to be really, really sure. I'm damaged goods."

She saw the compassion etched on his face. He said, "I am Amelia, my beloved. I know there are still wounds to heal. After what you went through, I expect no less. I would like to help if I can."

Another tear escaped. It ran down her cheek unheeded. She hesitantly asked, "So you'll wait? I need to know that you and your family will not be harmed by your association with me."

"I'll wait, my love. I'll wait forever if I know there's a chance."

"Oh, my dear Robbie, there's more than a chance." She looked lovingly at the wonderful man who sat next to her. "Can you give me a week or so? Or at least until I have seen my parents. I'll know by then, I'm sure."

Robbie released her hand and stood with his back to her, "Amelia, Jimmy has never said anything to me about the reason either; mayhap he does not know."

A small gasp of astonishment escaped Amelia.

Turning and looking down at her, he stroked her cheek. "Whatever happens, I'll not let you go alone. I shall come with you when you go. I'll wait in the carriage, but I'll be there for you. You know, Jimmy never actually even mentions your family at all. I've not been there for some years; he came halfway and collected the letters. I'm not sure why he even didn't get them sent directly to your home; mayhap it was an excuse to see me."

She held out her hand to him so they could walk back to the house. "Walk with me, Robbie. If I stay here, I shall sink into your arms as I wish to do. Just give me some time."

They continued their walk in the sunshine.

The smile he gave her warmed her to her core.

"Yes, Robbie, I am fearful of the meeting with my parents. I would love it if you could come and be near to comfort me, for I feel I shall need it." Her voice had a catch to it that nearly broke his heart.

"I shall be whatever you need, all the time you need. To know there is hope, that's all I ask. I wish to be your rock and support." He released a sigh of contentment. At least she had not rejected his offer. He tucked her hand in his arm, and he placed his other hand over hers. She walked as close as she could to him. "Amelia, it may be better to brave the lions in their den if we are engaged; think of that."

"Possibly, it's not my feelings I need to ascertain, Robbie, of those I am certain." She glanced at his face to gauge his reaction.

"You are?" he said, amazed. His gaze was one of delight.

"Yes, I am. I, too, fell in love on the night of my ball with a dark-haired man whose eyes followed me all night. I often dreamed of him. Robbie it was my one comfort in such a horrible period of my life. That someone may one day care as you had. I care so much for you that if I hurt you in any way, I could never forgive myself." She lovingly squeezed his hand. "Robbie, I do return your feelings. That is not in doubt; be assured of that. If things work out, then I would be honoured to reply *yes*, but I shall not give an answer until I am sure of your protection from a potential scandal. I have survived worse; you have not. Neither have your family. At least not the public scorn. There may be whispers about your great aunt, but that's all they are."

They meandered back towards the house, not hurrying. They were comfortable in the silence and their closeness.

Yes, she would be content to walk beside him for the rest of her life. She glanced up at his face. Yes, it was he whom she had seen at her ball all those years ago. She smiled at God's plan.

~

The next day, she was hoping Robbie would call, but he did not. She had been teaching in the morning, and he had not come. She was now having afternoon tea with the family. She sat looking at The Duke of Malvern and his son Nathan, then at Earl Sam. She said nothing but was stunned by the sudden revelation sweeping over her. Sam and Nathan could easily be brothers. Then she gasped; they were! That's where Lord James fitted in; he was Earl Sam's real father.

After the three men had left to discuss some improvements on the Estate, Countess Anne had asked her to accompany her for a walk around the garden. Danny and Georgie left the room together without even saying farewell. They just melted away.

Soon after, Amelia and Anne found themselves on the garden seat where she'd sat with Robbie only the day before.

Anne revealed the whole relationship between the duke and Sam as well as Lady Mari Broome-Hall and herself. "Amelia, the duke, is the natural father of Earl Sam, as you have guessed, and Lady Mari is my natural mother. What you may not realise is that they married soon after Danny married Georgie. That also meant that Lord James had a reason to stay here at the Hall. Recently, he's been back and forth to his house to finalise handing over the running of it to Nathan. Then he is moving in permanently."

Amelia sat stunned. "Lady Mari told me she had had a child, a girl; she did not mention that it was you."

"No, she wouldn't, as that was my story to tell. Robert knows, as do his parents, for Georgie was the one who guessed Sam's relationship to Lord James." Anne said bluntly, "Amelia, secrets such as ours are common in Society, hence our decision to host so many children at the Hall. I saw the wave of understanding pass over your face today, my dear. Here, we all have secrets. Sam and I were convicts, as you were. You started in a peer's family; Sam and I have ended up as peers. The previous Earl acknowledged Sam as his heir, knowing he was not his son, so even Sam cannot refute that. He tried; however, it turns out that the previous Earl was my own father. I don't even remember him, so in reality, Danny is in his right place."

Amelia again gulped.

Lady Anne continued. "We had not wished to return to England and no wish to take up lives here at all, but we had to. We were happy over in Sydney, for there we could breathe. But that's not what God called us to do. So here we are. Taking the illegitimate children of those same peers who shun us, we currently have ten, or it could be more, plus some belonging to the staff, and some of those too are illegitimate and some conceived by rape. Amelia, society is shallow. The men take their pleasures where they wish, regardless of the consequences. Do not live your life according to their rules. You and Essie are welcome to stay with us for as long as you wish; her legitimacy is neither here nor there with us. If you had not been married, you would still have been as welcomed, although it will be easier for her as she grows. Make your decisions for your own happiness, not theirs."

"Countess… Anne, it's Robbie. He proposed yesterday morning. I so wish to say yes, but I do not want to have Society shun them." Amelia was in awe of this amazing woman. She would not cry, even though her heart was hurting. She had no desire at all to reject Robbie's offer.

"Hmm, I guessed as much. I wasn't aware he had already proposed, but I knew his feelings. We all have known about his mystery love for a long time. He must have finally given her up. I gather he's revealed this to you?"

"He told you all?" Amelia looked stunned.

"No, we all guessed; no one knows who she was. Tim and Sophie will welcome you, though." Anne decided to tell her story with most of the details. "Amelia, what I'm going to tell you now is private, but I feel you need to know. It involves Sir Tim's uncle, who was Lady Mari's husband, Cecil. I shall only give you the bare facts, but Mari and Cecil had separated after their daughter was born. Betsy and I were sent to live with Sir Cecil in London and worded as maids; one thing led to another, and Ceccy and I became lovers. I was just seventeen, and he was forty-seven. Neither of us had any idea of my relationship with my mother. I was not related to him in any way. Now, add to the story of a violent and morally abusive grandfather. With one thing and another, I ended up being sent to Australia as a convict to protect me from being abused by my own grandfather, as both my mother and Betsy had been. Grandfather was, by the way, the Duke of Cheatham. He was part of the Hell-Fire club set; thankfully, they no longer exist, but some men still exhibit the same morals." Anne heard Amelia gasp but continued. "Mother knows what you've been through. She, too, had been violently abused the same way but at the hands of her own father. As had her friend Betsy, who is, by the way, Lady Mari's half-sister and, therefore, she is my aunt."

Tears dribbled slowly down both their cheeks. Anne still found her grandfather's perversion had to believe. Anne gave a small sob before she continued. "The day my grandfather died, my father, the Earl, filed my paperwork to rescind my conviction. Mother had already written a retraction just in case anything happened to her. Amelia, we each have sadness in our backgrounds. Sam, too, his time in the colony was worse than even yours. He had seven years of sheer hell. One day, he may tell you, but that's his story to tell, not mine. Then Danny lost his first wife, Vanessa, when Edmund was born. No one goes through life without these sorts of things happening. Some are really bad, some not. It's what you do with those pains that makes you who you are. You have two choices; you can turn these trials into one of two things: stumbling blocks that will hold you all your life or stepping stones that you walk on and grow strong from. Most of our staff have similar stories. Here, you will find acceptance and love. If Robbie wants you, then that's all that matters. He's had the pick of any of the belles and *incomparables* in London and rejected them all. If he's chosen you, then it's because he loves you. I do know he gave his heart many years ago but could never find her again. I do not know who she was."

Amelia gasped. She was weeping quietly as she spoke. "It was me, Anne! Robbie saw me at my come-out ball when I was nineteen. I had thought he looked familiar when we first met here. I didn't know where from. We were never introduced, so we never really talked, not officially. Anne, he knows all, for I told Jimmy my story years ago, and Robbie read each letter. I did not know. He also knows my accuser, but I have begged him not to do or say anything." She sniffed. "I love him, Anne, but I do not want him hurt. I love him so much it hurts." She clenched her hands to her chest.

Anne nodded, now fully understanding her fears. "Amelia talk to his father. I will join you if you wish, but Sir Tim will be able to assure you about your decision, either way and any effect on his family. He's due over tonight for dinner if you wish to see him."

"I cannot give Robbie an answer until I know. I cannot have them harmed by association with me or my family. Yes, I need to speak to Sir Timothy and Lady Sophie. As well as my parents, they need to tell me why they abandoned me." More tears dripped onto her gown. She let them flow unchecked.

"Personally, I wish to keep you, but this is the next best thing. Robbie is here almost daily now, anyway. I wonder why that could be?" Anne gave a chuckle. "For you to turn out to be his mystery love is absolutely wonderful. I wonder when he realised?" She chuckled again. "Hopefully, you will continue to come as often as you wish, should that be your decision. Be assured that you will always have a home here with us," Anne said.

"Thank you, I'm sure I will accept him, but it depends on… oh, I don't know. I do not wish to say *yes* and then find out something horrible from my parents." Amelia watched the wet patches spread on her gown. She had learned to cope with so much but was still fearful of that final revelation from her parents. Presuming they would actually talk to her, that is. Everything she imagined just didn't explain what they had done. Abandoned her.

Anne slipped an arm around her shoulders, drawing her into a motherly embrace. As they sat in the quietness of the garden, they heard a carriage arrive. "It sounds like we have visitors, my dear. It may be them. Let us return and see who's come calling." They walked inside arm in arm.

Robbie, Sir Timothy, and Lady Sophie had come early and were in the sitting room. As she entered the room, Robbie crossed the floor, took Amelia's hand and tucked it in his arm. He walked them to the side of the room near the windows, and he said, "I'm going to leave you with my parents. Ask them what you wish. The more I think about it, the more I think we should be engaged before facing your parents. It will give you some security and will give me some right to be there with you. However, be assured I shall not press you." He kissed her fingertips and then returned her to the others.

His mere touch was reassuring for Amelia.

He felt the squeeze of her fingers on his arm.

She wished to throw herself into his arms and stay there forever. However, she knew that this meeting was inevitable.

Robbie led her to a seat next to his mother and left the four of them to talk. He turned and smiled at Amelia from the doorway before he closed it behind him. "I won't go far. Call me if you need me."

Then he was gone.

Amelia's eyes stayed on the now-closed door. What does one say in a situation like this? She had met his parents before and knew them to be lovely and kind. Anne had already filled her in on Sir Timothy's importance in her own life. She sat nervously on the edge of the settee; she looked alternately into the three faces in the room with her. These two people could well be her parents-in-law in the future. She looked as nervous as she felt.

"We won't bite, dear," Sophie said.

Amelia gave her a wan smile but said nothing.

Sophie continued. "Robbie said he had asked you to marry him and that you were concerned with our reaction. Is this so?"

Amelia cleared her throat nervously. "Err, yes, ma'am," she finally managed to say. "I do not wish for any of you to be harmed by my association with you."

"Are you really thinking of us?" Sir Tim asked.

Surprised at his question, she turned to him. "Why yes, sir, why should I not? I have a great awareness of how even the association of friendship with me could harm you all irrevocably. I yet do not know the reason my own parents abandoned me. It must be dire, or they would not have done so. Until I do, I feel I shall not settle. If I accepted Robbie, it would be conditionally. I wish that to be understood. My feelings for him are not in doubt; be assured of that. I do know of my innocence about my conviction, but much still does not make sense to me about their actions or, should I say, their lack of actions. Being a parent myself, I would fight tooth and nail to protect Essie from anything." She dropped her eyes to her clenched hands sitting in her lap. They were twisting her handkerchief into a knot.

Sophie and Tim looked at each other, knowing that they, too, would fight for any of their six children. Finally, Lady Sophie said, "Amelia, we were wondering if the three of us could accompany you on your visit. Robert said he would go no matter what you say. He will not let you face them alone. If I came, that would lend countenance and also as a chaperone. Possibly not really required as you are a widow," Sophie said. "We will be there to support you, no matter what the outcome, do you understand? You are not alone in this."

"You would do that for me? I admit I am fearful of what their answers will be." She wiped away an errant tear, "Very fearful, ma'am." She met Sophie's concerned face with her own.

Anne said, "Tim will see fair play. No matter what your decision is about Robbie's offer. Amelia, no matter what the outcome of this meeting is with your folks, your place here is unchanged. You know our history, as do Tim and Sophie. It makes no difference to them either."

Unable to voice her appreciation, Amelia's eyes flicked from the speaker to the other two. Tim finally spoke, "Dear, you love the Lord, and as such, you are deemed worthy. Your worth, in our eyes, is therefore irrelevant. However, I will say this: I am astounded that with what you have been through, you have remained strong, both in your faith and in your steadfastness. You have not let the horrors that have befallen you bring you down; you have stood firm against the things thrown at you in your life, and please let me assure you that no matter what the outcome of the meeting with your own parents, we are happy to become your new parents. I know the colony and know how unjust it is."

He was only halfway through his words before Amelia released the pent-up emotions. She was shattered by a sob. In an instant, Anne was on her knees before her and enfolded her in her arms. Sophie had her arm around her. Both were bringing great comfort to her.

In choking sobs, Amelia said, "You would do that for me? You would stand by me without even knowing my full story?" she asked, amazed. "Without knowing why?"

Tim smiled reassuringly. "Yes, for we know enough to know that what you have said is true." Tim's gaze on her was sure and unwavering. "It may be not as bad as you fear, my dear, for just before that time, there was the great financial crash. It could well have been a financial issue and had nothing to do with you. Have you thought of that?"

Amelia's grief at all the things that could have occurred made answering hard. Every conceivable scenario had crossed her mind, but she had not known of this. Her face reflected amazement. "But they could have told me. Even Jimmy has said nothing."

"Mayhap, he does not know," Sophie said.

Amelia nodded. "That's what Robbie said. That is indeed possible; Father was a closed book." She paused, again looking at each in turn, "He lived in a different wing to Mama and us. And... he drank," she admitted softly with embarrassment.

"Many do, my dear. That, again, has nothing to do with you and our acceptance of you." Anne was still kneeling next to her, holding her hands. "The previous Earl and his wife before us lived apart. It is how the err situation that we are now in occurred."

Amelia's eyes were wide open. "You mean people do that? I wasn't the only one with an, um, unfortunate, um, marriage?" She said hesitantly.

Anne saw the sad look on her face, "Oh no, you, however, are in a way lucky, as he's dead and buried. You can now start afresh," Anne said. "Now, I must get up, for my knees won't take me kneeling for long," she explained with a smile.

Amelia assisted her.

While they were moving, Tim opened the door and beckoned Robbie in.

Robbie went directly to Amelia. She felt his hand on the small of her back. "Is all well, my dear?" he enquired with care, his soft, melodious voice reflecting his concern.

She turned to him and said, "Yes, Robbie, all is well. Just much to think about." He ushered her back to the settee and had now taken his mother's place beside her.

Neither had realised they were now alone in the room. The three older adults had left silently.

"May I... um, may I... darn it, Amelia, I wish to hold and kiss you, but I have no desire to force you to do something you have no wish to do." His loving look melted away the last of her hesitancy.

"I'd like that too, Robbie, very much," she whispered. "In fact, I wish it greatly." She flickered her eyes up to his. They were not showing coyness but desire. Her feelings for this man in front of her overwhelmed her. She wanted to be encased in his loving arms forever. She wanted to be caressed and loved in a way she had never been.

His heart skipped with joy. He had dreamed of this moment for years. He gently drew her to him with one arm wrapped lovingly along her shoulder. Then he stroked her cheek, brushing away the last of her tears in such a way that he showed his adoration of her. Then, slowly, so as not to rush her, he lowered his head and gently brushed her lips with his.

With her hand on his neck, she reached up and pulled him to her, deepening their embrace. Their need for each other soon had her sitting sideways on his lap, being hugged, cuddled, and kissed in such a way as she had never been before. In a way, she'd dreamed about it for years.

"Oh, my darling Amelia, this is not as it should be, for we are not yet engaged." He, however, kissed her deeply before she could say anything.

She drew back in his arms. "It is only for want of one word, Robbie, and that is a *yes*, my darling heart. That is if you still want me, or should I say us," she said as she snuggled onto his lap. "We're a package deal, as you know, two for the price of one," she smirked.

"Mmm, I do so like wrapped gifts." He kissed her again, "And your package, my dearest love, is a parcel I greatly desire to unwrap too, but not until we're married. My wonderful betrothed, my mystery love!" He proceeded to show her just how contented he was with her reply.

She had never known a loving touch like this before. Having never been kissed in such a way, she was thoroughly enjoying the effect on them both. After some time, she admitted to the not-quite-brotherly kiss of Ned on her departure. "Oh Robbie, I did not know... I did not realise the feeling that a loving kiss could have on one's insides. Very nice feelings, I might add. Ones I wish repeated." She then shyly added, "Often." Then she giggled.

He willingly obliged. Kissing her in such a way that he put to rest any lingering doubts about his feelings for her. She sat contentedly on his lap as they discussed many things. Her eyes were hooded with desire as he demonstrated his love for her.

They sat talking for some time; his eyes were often fixed on her lips, and he'd stop her mid-conversation, silencing her with a long and passionate caress. Their kisses were long, deep and profoundly satisfying.

She sighed contentedly. From this position, she fitted so neatly that their faces were on the same level. She relaxed against him, snuggling against his chest with her arms wrapped around him.

He was just content to keep her close. Neither had any idea how long they had been alone, and neither really cared.

They had been discussing Essie when they heard a knock. Amelia jumped up from his lap mid-sentence as the door slowly opened. He stood with his back to the entering person, attempting to master his own emotions. The physical effect of her closeness was obvious in his tight trousers. Her kisses were sweeter than he had even imagined, and after eleven years, he'd done a lot of imagining. She had never really been awakened, as he could tell by the innocence of her initial response. His mind and body were swirling with unfulfilled desires. He knew that the wait would be worthwhile; he just hoped that it would not be long in coming. He had not touched her otherwise; rubbing her back was enough to stir his raging feelings. More he dared not do as he knew he'd not be content to stop there; he also knew that his manhandling of her would be inappropriate. How he wished to touch her and awaken the loving physical side for her, but that would follow. However, when she willingly sat on his lap, he was almost overwhelmed with her closeness.

Anne entered slowly, giving the couple time to adjust themselves.

"Are any congratulations required?" Anne asked.

"Um, yes," Amelia blushed delightfully. "I'm glad it was you and not his parents." Amelia chuckled, embarrassed at being discovered in such a position and somewhat dishevelled.

Anne grinned with pleasure. "Amelia, they are waiting in the drawing room, along with most of the rest of the household. Congratulations to you both! She was worth the wait, wasn't she, Robert? She's a gem," Anne said while leaning forward to kiss Amelia on the forehead.

Robbie had walked up to Amelia and slid his arm lovingly around her waist, drawing her to him. "All that and more, Anne! If she didn't live here, I would not even be allowed to touch her. Let alone spend goodness knows how long we've been in here together. I could not even do that at home, I suppose." He bent and kissed the back of Amelia's neck.

Amelia leaned back against him. Safe and secure in his loving arms. She did not know contentment felt so good. She knew she had to do no explaining of her past either as he already knew everything, absolutely everything.

He bent and whispered so she alone could hear, "I love you. I will be here as your rock, but let's go and brave the masses."

She nodded, then, turning in his arms, she said, "There's one more small hurdle to cross, Robbie, but I think she will be a pushover, but dearest Rob, you'll have to ask her."

"I will, my beloved," he replied, his face showing his utter contentment. The stress lines were gone, as was the haunted look he had when they met earlier that year. "I can't believe I found you at long last." He dropped a quick kiss on her lips.

She moved again so his arm was around her shoulders. She was tucked close to his side with her arm around his waist. What an amazing household she lived in, to think that she could do this. That she could be with the man who had stolen her heart so completely.

As a girl, she had dreamed of his face gazing at her across the ballroom. She'd had no idea who he was. He had changed much from the very young boy she had known as a child. He literally had been the man of her dreams, too. Recently, she had fallen asleep at night dreaming of him, like a lifeline, and his care for her. He had come into her life early, as she had first met him when she was about six and then again so late. Yet, in reality, he had been caring for her from a distance and loving her always. He had been part of her life all those years, praying for her, and she'd never known. No wonder he had offered to be Jimmy's liaison; to have known who she was and not let on to anyone for years astounded her. She lifted her eyes for a sly glance and met his smile with her own.

~

The first pair of eyes set upon her was Essie's. She saw how they walked in, and she put her hands on her hips and had a frown on her brow. She said, "Why are you holding my Mama like that?" She paused, and then a revelation hit her. "Are we going to marry her?" she challenged Robbie.

Her comment caused everyone to fall silent. Her words were almost rude, but Essie was not the sort of child to normally speak to an adult like this. So there was absolute silence in the room around them, all waiting for the outcome of this crucial conversation.

Robbie knelt down to the little dark-headed cherub. "Well, Miss Esther, I really need to answer that with a question for you. Will you allow me to marry her and let me become your Papa? Because I'd love to have you both in my life." He was on one knee in front of her with Amelia's hand on his shoulder.

Essie frowned and looked from her mother's beaming face to Robbie's. Essie said, "You makes her happy, and you makes me happy too. And I've never had a Papa, and I fink you'd make a nice one. So yes, you can marry my Mama and me." She threw herself into his arms. "A papa, yes, I like that." She snuggled to his neck, "You smells nice too. Like warm hugs sort of nice."

With that, everyone laughed. Many had been holding their breath, awaiting the outcome.

He stood with her now cradled in his arms and reached again for Amelia. "Well, it's then official. We have permission from the second most important person; we are, therefore, officially betrothed." He bent and kissed Amelia in front of everyone.

Unbeknownst to either of them, Lord James and Lady Mari were sitting on the far side of the room. Lord James cleared his throat. "You may well be engaged, my dears, but some decorum is still required lad," the duke chuckled.

Robbie dropped his arm around Amelia, but he still held Essie, who had her arms around his neck.

Lord James bounced his walking cane between his legs as Amelia knew he did when happy. He continued. "We still are supposed to set a good example for others, as I'm sure my good wife will agree." He looked at Lady Mari and smiled lovingly.

Neither realised that he'd arrived back from his son's house nearly an hour earlier and had been awaiting the outcome of the afternoon's meeting.

Robbie and Amelia had been otherwise occupied and totally oblivious. In that time, word had spread throughout the household on the imminent engagement. The room was now filled with all the nineteen children, plus Essie and numerous adults. Danny and Georgie were sitting together with their baby James on Georgie's knee. Thea and Victor joined the happy throng when they delivered the afternoon tea, then stayed. The cook had rustled up a sumptuous feast, and even a cake had been made, and the cook, too, stayed.

A late arrival was Reverend Hugh, and he made his way to his own fiancé, Miriam Lock, who was one of the girls taken in to be trained. He would soon join the growing family of additions to Meldon Hall. Only Jimmy was missing. Amelia thought it strange that he'd not returned since his first visit. She realised she also wished to tell the Darlings. She looked forward to seeing them again, but that would have to wait until the visit to Pittford Manor was over.

Chapter 13 Revelations and Forgiveness

$\mathcal{T}$he day finally arrived for their departure to Pittford Manor at Aylesford.

It was only a week after their engagement. Before they departed, Robbie drew Amelia into the Blue Sitting Room. "My darling love, one is not officially betrothed without a ring." He handed her a small red velvet box. "Open it, my sweet."

She unlocked the hook catch and flicked open the lid. She gasped. A huge diamond ring sat glinting back at her, and it was not just any diamond. The central stone was at least two carats, and seven more diamonds circled it. It was set in gold.

Robbie lifted it from the box and took her left hand. "I do hope it fits." He slid it onto her finger. "Mine! Well, nearly so. We have yet to set a date. Hugh is reading the Banns for the first time this Sunday."

"I know. I still can't believe it," she said while fixing her gaze on his lips. "I still can't believe you want me, knowing everything about me that you do."

"Oh, my dear, believe it! I want all of you," he said, drawing her into his arms. "Every teeny weeny bit of you."

She reached up and wrapped her arms around his neck, drawing him to her. "Good!" She giggled just before she kissed him.

When he finally lifted his head, he said, "Oh, please say you won't make us wait too long?" He was kissing her neck, and she pressed her body close to him.

"No, as short a time as possible. I was thinking of the 22nd if possible," she said breathlessly.

"Hmm, 22nd of November, good, that's not too long," he said as he bent to kiss her again.

"No, not November, Robbie, but October. If Hugh's doing the Banns today for the first time and it's the 7th, then two more weeks means we can marry on Monday 22nd of October. Is that soon enough?" She smiled as he gasped.

"You mean it? Three weeks? Truly?" He was so excited that he swung her around. "Three weeks! Yes, I can work with that." With that, he bent and kissed her so passionately that she was weak with desire. When he eventually lifted his head, she nearly collapsed onto his chest. Her knees were wobbly. "Oh, Robbie, I didn't know love could feel just so darned good," she sighed dreamily.

"I can't wait to unwrap my present that you promised me. That is a mere taste of what is ahead for us." He kissed her again, then pushed her away from him. "If we stay here, well, let me say, you may need re-wrapping. We should depart."

Amelia didn't know what to say, so she chuckled. "Three weeks! We could always get a special licence. Do you know any Bishops?"

"Sadly, none nearby, but let's get today over with first. I might be able to pull a few strings on our return about the Special Licence." He bent and gave her another quick kiss. "Let's go before I forget I'm a gentleman."

She took a deep breath. "If we must," she said in such a way that he knew her very fearful of the outcome of the trip.

He led her into the main drawing room. Essie was waiting with Anne and his parents. Amelia had explained that she had to go away for a few days and that she was allowed to stay with Lady Anne and Lady Georgie and the children.

Essie looked at her mother. "Okay, Mama, you take care of her, Papa Rob." She had started calling him that from the day they became engaged. The day she had challenged Robert.

"I will try, poppet. May we have a hug before we leave?" She ran to him and kissed his cheek, then turned to her mother. "Come back soon, Mama." She gave her a kiss and returned to Anne's side.

"Take care, dear ones. We'll all be praying for you," Anne said. Sam lifted up Essie and walked with them to the waiting travelling carriage. Tim assisted Sophie in, and Robbie handed in Amelia. They waved as they moved off.

Robbie and Amelia sat with their backs to the road. For a while, they all chatted about the possible outcomes. None seemed plausible. Finally, Amelia fell silent. She knew it would take nearly six hours with horse changes to cover the fifty miles. Having not slept well the night before, Amelia was soon lulled to sleep and was resting against Robbie's shoulder. Robbie gazed at her lovingly. His face softened with his adoration of her.

Tim was watching his son's face. "It's her, isn't it? Your mystery lady?"

Robbie met his father's eyes across the carriage. He smiled and nodded. "I knew I wasn't imagining her. When I realised that she was Jimmy's sister and could do nothing to save her, Father, I was torn. I franked and then relayed their letters for all those years. Unable to tell Jimmy why I needed to be involved. My heart crushed more with every letter I read. If Ned could not arrange a full pardon for her, I would have moved to Australia. She has had my heart for that long. She said when she saw me that I looked familiar." He gently laid his cheek on her head. "I love her; I always have."

Timothy smiled at his son. Over the past eleven years, he'd seen his son pining over a mystery woman he had met just once in London. To have waited so long to find her, then having found out it was his best friend Jimmy's sister.

"You've known for that long? Seriously? Is that why you never went to London for another season?" Tim looked at him and smiled.

Robbie nodded. "I only found out soon after she was transported. I would do anything for her, Father. No matter what they have done, I'll be there for her." She murmured in her sleep. He lifted his arm, and she snuggled to his side. He drew her to him. His parents smiled as they watched the contentment on his face. Wrapped in his arms, she relaxed. Robbie put his head back on the headrest and napped.

In her sleep, she turned and wrapped her arms around his waist. She stayed like this for the next ten miles, stirring only when they stopped to change horses. "Oh, Robbie, I'm so sorry; I'm used to sleeping with Essie in my arms while we're travelling." She looked embarrassed.

"You might be sorry, my darling, but I'm not. I enjoyed the cuddle. I was wondering if you'd like to stretch your legs or refresh yourself. They will be a few minutes yet." His parents had already alighted and were walking inside. He bent and gave her a long lingering kiss. "Come, let us walk for a while."

She needed to use the facilities inside the inn, "I'd like to go inside and refresh myself if I may, Robbie; I shouldn't have drunk so much tea at the last stop." He handed her out of the carriage and followed her into the inn.

The coachman said, "Only five minutes, sir, or we'll not make the last stage before nightfall. There's no moon tonight." They headed inside, and Amelia headed to a private room to refresh. Sophie, too, had utilised the facilities, and once both refreshed, they headed back to the carriage. The final ten miles were accomplished, with everyone staying awake. Amelia was nervous, and Robbie could feel her anxiety in the tight grip of her hand on his.

They pulled into the yard of the old Chequers Inn in Aylesford just at dusk. They would have the entire day tomorrow to find Jimmy and hopefully get some answers. He'd gone to ground. Not answering notes or letters. Amelia was getting very concerned, Robbie realised, as she'd almost crushed his hand.

That night, she did not sleep well and woke early when the rooster crowed. She dressed and went to find some tea. She'd become spoiled at Meldon Hall, being brought a cup of tea every morning.

~

The kitchen staff were up and awake and were surprised when she came downstairs just after dawn. She was directed to the private parlour Tim had booked. As she entered, she was equally surprised to find her three travelling companions already downstairs. It seemed that all were somewhat anxious about the outcome of the day. She was met with three pairs of worried eyes.

"What's wrong? Robbie, what's happened? Is it Jimmy? Is he all right?" She turned to Tim. "Sir Tim, you've heard something; what is it?"

"It seems that our suppositions of the financial problems may well be the answer. I heard in the taproom last night that the prosperity of Pittford Manor is now as we all expected. Robbie, how long is it since you've been there?" Tim said carefully.

Robbie slid his arm around Amelia and drew her to him. "It's some six or seven years now, Father. It was when I received Amelia's first letter. Why?"

Tim nodded. "Did you see any staff of family other than Jimmy?"

"Um, no, actually, we sat in the garden and read her letter, then came down here to the inn." Robbie was stunned. "But why, Father? What did they tell you?"

Again, Tim nodded. He pursed his lips and then said, "I think Jimmy has been doing some false bravado. I gather he's not mentioned his problems to you?"

Amelia felt her legs weaken and sank onto the settee.

Robbie shook his head. "After that, we met halfway. We swapped letters at the *Kings Arms* in Westerham. He said it used to be on the far edge of their estate, but the land was sold. That much he told me."

"I think that when we go, we should take some supplies for him as, from what I've heard, I do not think there will be much in the house." Sir Tim paused, then said, "If the house remains at all."

Amelia gasped; she looked up at Tim from her seat. "But the school?"

"Closed years ago, just after you left, it seems," Tim said with compassion.

"Oh no! That was mother's life." Her head was spinning. Jimmy kept it from her. "Where are my parents?" She felt dizzy.

Sophie stepped up to her. "We don't know, love, but we'll find out." She knelt at Amelia's feet, "Dear, if money was the big problem, men have their pride and will not admit these things. As Jimmy has not told you anything, I'm guessing he protected you from some bad news. Did he never, in all those years, say anything?" Sir Tim and Sophie knew of rumours about Amelia's father, but they were just that, rumours.

Amelia shook her head; her eyes were swimming.

Robbie was comforting her as best he could. "Milla, sweeting, this would explain everything. We know the duke pressed charges against you, and the charge was theft. Suppose the item did indeed go missing… What was it, by the way?"

"I confiscated a solid gold bracelet that was obviously not hers. Obviously, it belonged to an older woman. No child would ever wear anything like that, and a book that also did not belong to the child. I could never find the bracelet, but the book was there. But why?" she asked him.

"Think, sweeting. Mayhap you didn't lose the bracelet; mayhap, it was stolen from you too and sold." He saw the frown on her face, and that was replaced by puzzlement.

"Oh! Robbie, do you think that's what happened? But where are my parents?"

The look of confusion on her face worried him. He wished he had answers. "Milla, darling, I think that further speculation is pointless. It's only upsetting us all; I suggest we eat, find supplies and be on our way. If things are as bad as I've heard, he will need all the assistance he can get."

"Oh no! But he sent me money." She felt giddy.

"Recently?" Robbie asked.

"Ned told me…" she stopped mid-sentence and looked at him, shocked. "Would Ned have paid for things for me? Robbie, would Neddie have done that?"

"Milla, Ned would not have let you suffer; he knew Jimmy would pay back any money he expended on you. I have no doubts at all that Jimmy did send money. But how much or how Ned spent it and what he bought is something only Ned would be able to tell you. Jim certainly had enough money to give you £10 in coin and then another £10 note. These questions will all be answered in time."

"But, Rob…" she protested.

"But, Rob… nothing, my love. If Ned did, then he shall have my eternal thanks. I shall repay him myself." He drew her into his arms and comforted her. Neither said anything, but both were full of questions.

She rested on his shoulder; she felt safe and protected, yet all sorts of things were flying around her head.

Two hours later, they had eaten breakfast and filled the coach with everything edible they could obtain in town, including two stone flagons of ginger beer and a case of wine. They had a vast picnic hamper, which contained an entire ham, loaves of bread, pickles, butter and everything the kitchen could spare.

The short trip to Pittford Manor was taken in virtual silence. Tim and Sophie had changed seats so Amelia could see forward. Her first glance at the ordinarily beautiful facade was one of horror. It showed on her face. Silent tears dribbled unchecked onto her gown. Robbie took her hand and covered it with his own.

One gate was half off at the entrance. The road, pot-holed and filled with weeds, and the formal gardens were left to run riot. At least the two-story house still stood. It had not burnt down. She started noticing some broken windows that had been boarded up and that the hedges, too, were overgrown along the front of the house. As they passed the fountain, they saw that it was green and still. The carriage pulled up at the front door; the knocker was wrapped. There was no sign of life. No one was around at all, and it looked like it had been abandoned for some time. Robbie assisted Amelia out of the carriage, and together they stood looking at the facade. He would not drop her hand. Eventually, they walked up to the front door.

She pushed and, of course, found it locked. "Come with me." She led Robbie around to the side of the house. "There's a secret door around here." Robbie knew of it, having used it once or twice himself.

They walked along the front of the house, and just around the corner, there was a strange aperture sticking out from the side like a buttress. Behind it was a very narrow door. Strangely, it was unlocked and well-oiled. She opened it, and Robbie insisted that he enter first. She followed him inside, then, realising no one was around, she led the way through a narrow hallway, then through the formal rooms. She could see signs of someone having been in there recently. They stood gazing around them in the main foyer. Many things had been covered with dust cloths, but even those had not been left untouched.

They were standing hand in hand in the foyer when they heard a voice at the top of the stairs above them. "Who's there?"

"Jimmy? Jimmy, is that you?" Ignoring Robbie, she ran to the staircase and, hitching her skirts, took them two at a time. She saw him sitting on the top step. Head in hands and looking bedraggled in filthy gardening clothes. "Jimmy, dearest, why didn't you tell me? Why hide it?"

"Why? Because you didn't need to know. You had been betrayed by our parents, and I was determined that you would be spared the humiliation of this...." He waved his hands around at the cobweb-draped chandelier.

A few moments later, Robbie joined them. He had unlocked the front door for his parents and then came upstairs. He sat on the other side of Jimmy.

Amelia met his eyes and mouthed, *thank you*. She was afraid to ask, but she had to know. "Where are Mother and Father?"

Jimmy looked at her with swimming eyes. He knew that now he would have to tell her all.

"On the day you were arrested on the duke's false word, Milla, Mother collapsed. Then, the day afterwards, the bailiffs came and arrested Father. He's in prison for embezzlement of Government Funds. Mother has been in Bedlam Hospital for eight years. I visited them when I could, but I can't afford the time away from here to go often. I need to milk the cow twice daily. If I don't, I don't eat at all. I can't afford any help, and it takes me all my time to scrub myself clean at the end of the day before I fall into bed exhausted. Mother just sits in a daze. She does respond, but it's an effort. It's as though she's half-asleep all the time. She's just not herself."

With those words, she drew him into her arms. "Oh, Jimmy! You should have told me when I returned. I could have helped."

"Jim, how long is it since you've eaten a decent meal? You're as skinny as hell and look much the same," Robbie asked his friend.

"Food! Ahh yes, well, that's not a commodity that there is much of anymore," Jimmy said.

"There is today. Come, we brought you a hamper. We shall have an early picnic. Mother is setting it up now." Robbie pulled his friend up from his position on the steps. He smelt the earthy pong on his friend. "Sweetheart, go ahead and let them know we'll be down in a few minutes. I'll get him cleaned up."

"Got no energy now, Rob." Jimmy looked at his friend with glassy eyes. He was exhausted. "She accepted you then?"

"Yes! Now, let's get you sorted out." Robbie took his friend and led him into his bedroom. Thirty minutes later, a scrubbed and neatly dressed Jimmy walked out with Robbie. "Father guessed it was the financial crash from a few years ago. This has been going on for too long for that."

Jimmy nodded. "I'll tell you all together. It's harrowing. Sorry, Rob, but I could not stomach the truth getting out." He was so weak that the effort to talk was almost too much.

Rob assisted him as they walked down the stairs sometime later. He didn't want him passing out on them. Jim saw the food laid out on the table, and again, tears welled in his eyes. "How did you know?" It took all his will not to race to the table and devour the delicacies set in front of him. Meat! He'd not eaten meat other than a rabbit for over two years.

Amelia took his hand. "Jim, I know it will be hard, but don't eat too much at once. Your stomach will not handle it. Trust me. I know. Just little bits, let it settle, then more."

He nodded.

"You had no food?" Robbie looked aghast.

"Not much in the Female Factory; I got that sorted before I left, though, and in my first three months with Cyrus, we ate a rough porridge of some sort, salt meat and beans. I brought up the first few meals there as I'd not even eaten that much in the Factory. It didn't settle too well on an empty stomach. We'd been on bread and water for three days. When I went to the Turners, Martha nurtured me. Mind you, I was with child, but that wasn't the problem. Just take it easy."

Tim and Sophie had welcomed him.

Tim said, "Jim, I do wish you had confided in us; we could have assisted."

"Pride, sir. You know it *goeth before the fall* and all that. Well, I can't fall much further. I'm rock bottom now." He gave Sir Tim a wry smile.

Sophie pushed him gently into a seat and handed him a plate with buttered bread and ham. "Just nibble it, Jim."

Jimmy nodded, taking a bite of the delicious food. "Mmmm, oh, nectar of the gods!"

Amelia moved and sat next to him. "Can you talk and eat? What happened to Father? It's no use hiding, so tell us all."

Jimmy nodded; he'd just taken another bite and then put the open sandwich down. His stomach was already rebelling. He took a deep breath. "Father gambled and speculated. That's how it started. It's also why Mother made him move into the other wing. She was disgusted at him for selling one of the big blocks at Westerham, but it was done, and they had no money to get it back. Father then started drinking. We kept that from you, too. We managed to get him sober for your ball, but even that didn't last. Anyway, he met with your accuser, the duke, at the ball; he even tried to marry you off to him in lieu of his debts. If you'd not trodden on your hem, he would have given permission for the duke to ask you for a third dance."

Both Amelia and Rob gasped. They realised that was as good as announcing an engagement.

Jim continued, "Both were gamblers, and Father gambled with him that night and lost heavily. I still can't bear to mention that man's name. Father couldn't pay a debt of honour to him, and then there was that damned gold bracelet." He groaned, blanched and said, "Excuse me." He ran from the room and out the front door.

"Oh dear, we have our hands full here, dear," Sophie said to Tim.

"I've been thinking about some of Sam's soldiers and their wives. We need more accommodation for up to a hundred, which could work out as a win for Jim. A bit like the Chelsea Hospital situation." Tim finished speaking as Jim came back in.

"I see what you mean, Milla." He took a mouthful of ginger beer and slowly swallowed. "Ham is a bit rich, I think." He slid off the ham and ate the rest of the bread. He bit into some cheese then and nibbled on an apple. He then continued his story. "Now, where was I? Oh, that bracelet! Father hocked it and let you take the fall for it. It's what sent Mother into her decline. You were her pride and joy, Milla, and he did that to you. When you were arrested, she collapsed. I tried to tell the constables, but there was only the duke's word against mine. The duke informed on Father, too and then had the audacity to foreclose on a debt of honour. I managed okay until the crash happened. The last of the money went overnight. Father had it tied up, so I couldn't move it. Being only the heir, I had no right to touch it, even though he was in gaol. The bankers, while sympathetic, were legally unable to do anything. Then they, too, went bankrupt. Everything is gone. Nothing left. Even your dowry is gone. I have a feeling Father used that too." He put his head on the table, exhausted. After a few minutes, he continued. "The solicitors sent along with a sheaf of paperwork, but I haven't gone through it extensively as they assured me there is no money in any of it. But I left the documents in the office."

Amelia laid her hand on his shoulder lovingly. "And through all this, you protected me? You never let on. Even Robbie didn't know, or Neddie."

He shook his head and mumbled, "Too much pride to ask for help. Now I can't go on. I'm done for Milla. I don't even have a farthing to my name, so I couldn't come to see you."

Amelia dug her hand in her reticule and gave him the sovereigns she had left from the money he had given her. She took his hand and placed the few coins in his callused palm.

Robbie felt as though he'd been kicked in his guts. "How could you not tell me? I would have helped. You know that? Even if you locked the place up and came to us, we would have welcomed you."

"Pride, Rob. My damned pride. Sorry, ladies!" He took a laboured breath. "Now I have no choice, you know. I'm done for. Too weak to work." Too weak to even cry, he thought.

Tim had sat listening with his arms folded. He had been deep in thought. "Lad, I'm saddened that it's come to this. I've been thinking while you have been speaking. Your mother started the school to help out with finances. So things were tight for some time?"

Jimmy nodded.

"How much land do you have on the estate?" Tim asked, knowing there should be much more arable land around a house of this size.

"One thousand acres is all that is left; it was entailed, so he couldn't touch that. The rest was freehold, and Father squandered it. Over fifteen thousand acres gone! Many, if not all, of the cottages are either empty or in such bad repair that they soon will be. I can't afford labour even though we have trees and all the materials needed to fix them up." Jim turned and stared out the dirty French doors. "I've managed to keep the glass unbroken in most of the main rooms. But a storm came through and smashed a few last months. I have boarded them up."

"Jim, will you sit and listen to an idea that's been going around my brain?" Tim said.

Jim nodded. "I have nothing left to lose. Now Milla knows I have no point in hiding anything."

"Do you know what Sam Corbett Garney is doing?" Tim asked.

"I've heard whispers about illegitimate peers brats." He replied softly, looking at Amelia. "You said something, Milla, when I came that first week."

"Well, yes, but I certainly didn't put it like that," she said moodily.

"No, sorry!" Jim had the courtesy of looking embarrassed.

"Yes, but that's just one thing they are doing. After the various wars, many of the soldiers returned injured, burnt, and disabled. They can't all get into Chelsea Hospital. A philanthropy group in London started this after the Napoleonic wars. Some have families, many don't. They can't get work or even find places to live. Do you see where I'm going with this?"

Jim shook his head, his brain not capable of grasping where he was leading.

"Jim, the house is in reasonable repair. There are beds and rooms galore, and I presume bedding for each one, from when the school was here, but no money to pay anyone. What you need is a stack of "freeloaders". People who will work for their keep and a dry, warm roof over their heads."

For the first time, Jim was beginning to understand. "There are people who will work for no pay?"

Tim, Sophie, and Rob all nodded.

Tim continued. "Sam has been training them and then placing them, but he needs somewhere for them to, shall I say, practice and heal. Perry and Katy White started this. Perry is Sam's friend. Sam focuses on their abilities, not their disability. He teaches things like gardening and repairs; he can't take in more who really need help until this lot is gone. This is where you come in. You could be the next stage. The London Domestic Bureau had discovered that his clientele never caused any trouble to their employers, and they are in much demand. Sam would supply transport and the people, and I will throw in food for six months for you all. Jim, first get the kitchen gardens sorted so you can all eat. Then, buy some livestock. If you have excess funds from the produce, plough it back into food production first, then the profit side later. You have the work sheds and all the tools, I presume?"

Jim nodded, absolutely stunned. "Yes, I just locked them up. I didn't go into debt, so nothing is owed. Just no money to pay for anything."

Robbie looked at his friend. "Jim, would you object if Amelia and I moved in here with you, Essie too, of course, and helped with the… well, if we just helped? We were talking this morning about a Special Licence. Father, do you think Uncle William Howley could arrange one? I know Hugh has started with Banns, but it would be better if…" Jim interrupted Robbie.

"No, Rob, no Special Licences, not even from your uncle, the Archbishop. If your Reverend Hugh has started with Banns already, then it's only a few weeks." Jim turned to Tim. "I was wondering if I could come and stay with you and get my strength back?" He waited for some sort of reply but again flicked his eyes to Rob. "After you are married, then we can all return with the first lot of men. I could do with the break, the food and yes, the help." He raised his eyes to the four, and they rested finally on his sister. Meeting her loving smile, he returned it.

"We're hoping to be married on the 22nd, Jim. Now you can give me away." She came and knelt before him. "How can I ever thank you, Jimmy? If I had known about all this, I think it would have been the final straw for me. As it was, you kept my hopes up. But to bottle it up all these years? Oh, Jimmy, we'd love to help. Won't we, Robbie?" She turned and met his smiling face.

"Too right we'll come, but it won't be much of a honeymoon, love." Rob grinned and raised his eyebrows.

"Hmm, okay," she chuckled. "Well, we might leave it until mid-November. Give us a week together first. But then we'll all come and get cracking on things. You're not alone anymore, Jim."

He bent and leaned his head on her soft, clean hair. "I'm so sorry, Milla, so very sorry. I could not bear to tell you." Tears dropped onto her lap. His tears were her undoing.

She wrapped her arms around him. "I love you, Jimmy. Even more for protecting me, just as a big brother should." She cried onto his shoulder as they embraced each other.

He relished her care and compassion. She felt the wetness of his tears on her neck. "I love you so much, little sis. I just wish I could have done more," he whispered while still wrapped in her arms. Later, he sat nibbling more food, letting it digest. He started feeling a bit better. A honey sandwich helped, too.

~

Two hours after their arrival, Jim took them all on a slow walk around the outside of the house. Then, after some more sustenance, on an inside tour. The condition of things was reasonably good.

"Jim, you've done an excellent job battling on alone," Tim said as they walked around. "Can you show us the staff quarters? I need to assess how many we can send." Tim asked; he was quite impressed with what Jim had managed to keep going. A house like this would typically have had at least forty outdoor staff and more indoors. Jim was totally alone.

They had walked to the back of the house and out to the north wing. "These are not exactly staff quarters, but they will work well. They won't need much work either." He opened the connecting door to the wing, and mustiness met their noses. "Just needs an air, so I'll leave this door open." They walked through the connecting door, then room after room, throwing the doors open of some fifty rooms. Each bed had a pile of folded blankets and linen on the bed. All was ready for immediate occupation.

"I'm surprised that these bedrooms are on the ground floor, Jimmy,"

Rob said.

"These were where the children stayed. But they will do fine for the staff, especially if they are disabled. There are many more rooms up in the attics, but I've not been up there for ages. There may be leaks." Jim led Tim and Sophie through more of the rooms.

Amelia took Robbie's hand and kept him from following them. "Robbie, are you sure you don't mind helping Jimmy here? Living here until he's back on his feet?" she asked as he pulled her gently into his arms. "It could be a few years, Rob."

"Why would I mind, love?" He bent and kissed her, taking the welcome opportunity of being alone. "As long as I can be with you, I don't care where I am. Let's call it an unusually long honeymoon." He silenced her with a long and passionate kiss. Eventually, he said, "My darling, Father has everything under control at home. He knows that I'll come if needed." They didn't hear the returning footsteps and eventually looked up to find three pairs of smiling eyes watching their passionate embrace. Somewhat embarrassed, Amelia hid her head against Robbie's chest.

"Mayhap a Special Licence would not be so bad for you two after all," Jimmy said, grinning at his best friend and sister. "I just can't fathom that I never realised who your mystery woman was all those years ago. I knew you met her at Milla's ball, as I saw you talking. I dare say I had my mind on other things. Sorry for the teasing, Rob!" Jimmy looked from one to the other. "That day you came for my birthday with another hamper and then fled, that's when you found out, wasn't it? You saw the painting and then left."

"Yes, I went to see Katy and poured out my heart." Chuckling, Robbie slid his arm along her shoulder, and they continued their tour. He dropped another kiss on her lips as they turned to walk off. They found themselves walking back through the Long Gallery. Robbie stopped at the foot of a portrait. "This is what I saw and when I realised who you were. My dream mystery girl. It was just after your transportation. I stood staring at it, and my heart pounded. I had found you. Jimmy came in and told me it was of you and painted the year before. And yet, even then, I didn't tell him that you were my mystery woman. I let them tease me. At least Gerry and Jim did; Ned was gone by then, but he was still in London for a while, so he did his teasing by letter." Rob chuckled. "I get the last laugh, though, as I have found you."

She nodded and smiled. She remembered the artist who'd made her sit for hours. His lecherous gaze was as though he was undressing her with his eyes. Thankfully, her mother had never left them alone. She shuddered as she stood gazing at her own younger reflection.

"Bad memories?" Robbie asked.

"Yes, but he never touched me. He wanted to, though. I think Mother realised, as she never left us alone. Not even for a moment, Rob." She turned and walked along the corridor further. She stopped in front of a portrait of her mother. "Robbie, do you think we can visit her? If she knows I'm alive and well and back again…" She couldn't finish. She turned to Robbie and wept again. The overwhelming rawness of the emotions ate at her. All these years, she thought she'd been abandoned. When all this time, her mother had been ill and in hospital. After some moments, she lifted her face to his. "More tears, Robbie. I am not usually so, um, liquid." She gave a soggy laugh.

"Any excuse to hold you is a good one." He was about to drop a kiss on her lips when he realised they were again being observed. He didn't release her and proceeded to give her a quick kiss. "Well, she's kissable." Not embarrassed at all. "And what's more, I've waited long enough for her." She smiled, and they followed them all out of the room.

Robbie helped Jimmy pack for a month-long stay at Broome-Hall Manor. The house would be locked up, and they would all return to Billingshurst together. Jim had one last job to do, and that was to call by one of the cottages on the estate. The old butler, Vincent Eggleton, and his wife, Mildred, who had been the housekeeper for the Manor, now lived in the near-derelict cottage.

"I'm leaving for about a month, Vince. Amelia is getting married, and I'm to give her away. Do you remember my friend Robert Styles?" Jimmy said to the old retainer.

"I do that, Mister Jimmy. Congratulations to Mister Robert and Miss Amelia, too," Vince said. He smiled as his wife joined him.

She smiled a greeting to Jimmy as Vince said, "Mister Jimmy, I was wondering if you'd like us to move back to the big house while you're gone? There be rains expected, and the thatch over our bed is leaking. I've not told you about it as you've had enough worries, but we'd be happier if we can move back."

"You'd do that, Vince? I was going to suggest you bring the livestock down here, but that would be even better." He dug into his pocket and pulled out the six-inch-long front door key. "I'll hand this back into your safe hands then, Vince. Move back permanently, but do you mind if you take over the Crimson Suite upstairs? That will give you three rooms and a washroom for yourselves. You'll find out why when we return. We three are coming back with a hoard of disabled staff, and they will need all the ground floor rooms."

"Oh, Mister Jimmy, really? You're going to reopen the house?" Mildred said. "That be the Royal Suite, Mister Jimmy."

"Yes, it is. And it's because you stuck with me all these years. My way of saying thanks. It will be yours as long as you want it. It's not like royalty will come for a visit, will they?" He chuckled. "Help yourself to whatever you need re provisions. Rob's parents brought some things, and you can use all of them too. We left them in the larder. You know what's there even better than I do." Jimmy put out his hand to shake the butler's hand. "Vince, you made me keep my sanity. You helped with Father when we knew how difficult he was.

Mildred, you, too, made me keep heart when everything had fallen around my feet. I do not know what I would have done without either of you. I'll send a cart from the inn in two hours. Pack and take what you can for tonight, and then it will return tomorrow for the rest of what you wish to keep."

Just before he left, Jimmy handed a coin to Vincent. "This will cover it and keep the change. I owe you way more than this. Vince, do with the house what you like. I'll see you in November."

Vince and Mildred stood arm in arm, watching the carriage depart. Vince looked down at the wonderful woman under his arm. "Are you thinking what I'm thinking, love? He did say do with it what we liked, didn't he? Feel like a working bee?"

She looked up to her beloved husband of thirty years. "Yes," she giggled, "it seems we are thinking along the same lines. The rains are due tonight. Can we move the mattress off the bed and go up tonight?"

"Like minds, love. Crimson Suite, eh? A bit different to here?" They turned to head back inside. Both stood and looked at the sunlight streaming through the thatch in the roof above them.

Mildred stood and clapped her hands gleefully. "We're going home, love. Vince, can we tell some of the others? Their cottages are worse than ours."

The mischievous smile he gave his wife was all the answer she needed.

"Yes," she gave a little dance of happiness. "You go and tell them while I throw some things in a bag. It will take an hour or so for the cart to arrive. Be as quick as you can, though, love."

He set off for one of their close neighbours, all of whom had worked at the big house over the years. Now, they were all on the Parish for living expenses. Some of the cottages were so bad that the occupants slept, ate and lived in one room. They all knew Jim had no money for repairs. Some had no fireplaces, and one was barely habitable. Vince only went to the first cottage and told them to pass the word around. Come when they could. They were only to come if they were prepared to help get things in order.

An hour later, a cart arrived at Vince and Mildred's house. Driving it was their son, Joe, and he quickly assisted in loading up everything he could. He also lifted their horsehair mattress off their bed in case it could be used later. He turned and looked back into the nearly empty cottage and then shut the door. He hopped up with his parents and headed off up the bumpy driveway. "Things could turn around; at least you'll be warm and dry up there, Ma. I'll come back and bring up the rest tomorrow. What about the stock?"

"Bring them up too. Lord Jim has kept the hen coops in order so they can go straight in there. Daisy can join Bessy in the dairy yard. Actually, I'll tie her to the back. By the sound of it, we'll need what food we can get. So empty the larder and bring everything, especially all the preserves. Oh, and the big milk tin, too."

As Vince turned the huge key in the front door of the Manor house, another cart was arriving. The three stood looking at the magnificent foyer. "We're home, love."

Soon, some twenty people had chosen rooms on the top floor or gone back to their old rooms. It was all hands on deck in the kitchen as they unloaded what food they each had brought. With the daylight closing in, the kitchen had once again become a hub of both warmth and friendship. Over the next week, more of the old staff came, and each brought supplies and their stock. They pooled their resources and then got to work. The front gate was the first thing repaired. It was oiled, and the driveway was weeded. The place needed to look different when they came back.

~

Tim insisted Jim eat a small plain meal and only an apple for dessert. After his last trip outside to bring up what small amount of luncheon he'd eaten, Jim saw the wisdom of what Tim said. The meal served him was smaller than what a child would eat. Even then, they made Jim eat slowly. He managed to keep it down. For the first time in years, Jimmy fell into a dreamless sleep and woke refreshed at dawn when the rooster decided his room's window sill made an excellent dawn perch. He awoke smiling. He lay in bed for some time before rising. There was a gentle knock on his door, and a maid brought in some hot chocolate and toast.

"Morning, sir. Drink it while it's hot, sir," she said before immediately departing.

It was just what he needed. He slowly downed the delicious beverage and hot buttered toast. Then dressed, re-packed and headed downstairs.

"Sleep well, Jim?" Robbie asked when he entered the parlour.

"Hmm, yes, delicious dreamless peace," He grinned, "And with a full tummy. Sorry, Rob, I know I should have said something. I tried a few times but just couldn't spit it out. Father in gaol and Mother in Bedlam is not something you can just say, is it? Not to mention my sister as a convict. Add bankruptcy, and well, the facade just had to be kept up as long as possible. I managed until the crash. Father even speculated with shares. I found he'd purchased some £5,000 of shares in an oil venture in Burkesville, Kentucky. A total waste of money. I found the certificates in his desk. There were other things, too; I can't remember offhand what they were. I just shuffled through them and couldn't believe how he wasted the funds. Fry's bank actually was his broker, so when it went under, we lost the lot. At least they sent him the certificates for what they purchased for him." He wiped his hand over his face. "Rob, I just felt ill. Really, really ill."

Robbie put his hand on his friend's shoulder. "We're here for you. You'll be helping Sam and Danny, too and doing them a favour."

The five departed from the inn soon after dawn. The trip back to

Billingshurst was far more relaxed. Jimmy had managed to nibble most of the afternoon and was feeling much better by nightfall. The trip was uneventful. Jimmy filled them in about how he survived for two years, trying to maintain the entire Manor himself. Vincent and Mildred had stayed until there was no longer food for three. By leaving and living in a cottage, they had gone to the Parish for support. Jim just hid, not even collecting mail. He subsisted on what he could find. The only time he had left had been the two visits to Amelia, one in London and one to Billingshurst; each had been for just the one night while Vince milked the cow.

Chapter 14 A New Beginning

*A*melia was in expectation of visitors who'd announced they were coming for the wedding. Eliza had heard about her engagement from Anne Garney the week before. She sent a message that all of them, including her mother, were coming to the wedding uninvited. When they arrived, Amelia fell into her arms.

"Oh, dearest Eliza, thank you so much for coming. I was so looking forward to seeing you all again. I'm so keen to meet your littlest one. Charlotte, wasn't it? Did she come?"

"Yes, dearest, she is now four, and Cornelia has her in the playroom. I can't believe Essie is six." Eliza stood holding Amelia's hands. "Oh, my dear, it's so good to see you again. I knew the Lord would have someone special for you. Well, someone else special. Have you heard from the major?" Eliza asked softly. She wasn't sure this family knew about Ned Grace.

"He wrote to Jimmy. I have written to him to let him know. Robbie was the third friend of their group of four. Later, there was another boy, Gerry, but I have no idea where he is now. Eliza, Ned was never 'my' anything, you know that. We were just there for each other, and he was a good friend. He still is and always will be."

"Well, you can't say we weren't all just a tiny bit jealous of the attention he paid you." Eliza chuckled.

"Caroline, Sadie, and Phoebe said the same. I'm still praying he'll also find the love of his life." She gave a deep sigh.

Amelia led Eliza to a settee at the far end of the room. They sat comfortably as Amelia filled Eliza in on how the work at the Female Factory was continuing. After checking to see if the rest of the family was still at the other end of the room, Amelia told Eliza of the day at the Factory when she'd been kidnapped. Only Jimmy and Rob knew about it, as she'd never mentioned what had happened. Ned had told Jimmy, and he'd let on to Robbie. With her back to the room, she unfolded the entire story to Eliza. Even Anne didn't know what had happened that day. As the story unfolded, Amelia realised that the retelling of a year ago was much easier than she had imagined. She did tear up once. But it was with compassion for the girls still there. When she told Eliza of Ivy Vine and the amazing sewing circle, sewing the damaged fabrics that Sadie and John Landon donated, Eliza clasped her hands together with joy.

"Oh, dearest Amelia, that is wonderful, just what we were trying to do. And the horrible matron, is she still there?" Eliza saw a strange look flick across her face.

"No, sadly, she's still there. In a way, it wasn't her fault. She thought that supplies had been cut, but in reality, her husband was skimming the profits and then, as a bonus, would be helping himself to the women in the Factory. Many of the illegitimate children are reported to be his, but there is no proof. He denies most of it, of course." Amelia paused, thinking. "So she's still in charge, but he's never allowed on site again. Since he's gone, no women have fallen with child."

"Oh, Ralph will not be pleased to hear that. She came with recommendations."

Amelia shrugged, daring not to say more than needed. "He was in the 48th under Ned."

Their talk turned to the wedding. Amelia asked if Eliza would mind if she wore the ball gown she'd given her in Sydney. "It's the blue one, Eliza; I left most of the other things with Phoebe as she had none. I knew you wouldn't mind. Ivy 'make it over' for a ball just before I left, and Sadie gave me a long length of lace, and I plan to wear it as a long veil. It's sort of involving you both."

"I'd be delighted, my dear. You know that they say blue for true love. May it be so."

So Amelia wore the pale blue gown that Eliza Darling had given her in Sydney and the beaded georgette overskirt Ivy had made for her. She had not been able to bear to leave it behind. A much healthier-looking Jimmy assisted her into the Earl's town carriage. Two loads of the family had already been taken down to the church. The carriage had returned for the flower girl, the bride and her brother.

One thing that astounded everyone was that Amelia wore a veil. A short length covered her face, and the lace extended as a long lace train past the end of her gown. A garland of ivy leaves and rosebuds held on it.

Jimmy escorted her to the church entrance.

She stood with the sunshine on her. Her gown reflected light into the church. The crystal beads on the gown made rainbows all over the ceiling of the building.

Reverend Hugh Williams' mouth dropped open at the amazing sight. She almost glowed. The lace veil gave her a floating, practically angelic aura. Those watching him turned, and they, too, were in awe at the shimmering sight they beheld.

Danny nudged Robbie. "Cor, Robbie; look."

Rob was so nervous that he'd kept his eyes off everyone. When Danny told him to look, he did. He first saw Essie walking down the aisle, carefully scattering rose petals from her basket. Then he lifted his eyes to Amelia, and he caught his breath. Her face was hardly visible at all. She was totally shrouded in the veil. He could see a graceful bouquet of carnations and roses. All pure white, but in the middle of the bouquet were two pink roses. They stood out and were a pure symbol of love to all watching. Essie carried something else in her petal basket. A third pink rose.

Straightening Amelia's veil as she stood at the door was Robbie's second younger sister, Alexandra. Georgie had suggested that she take the opportunity to be a bridesmaid, as she'd never been one. Georgie had baby James in her arms, and Sophia Jane, Robbie's oldest sister, was heavy with child, sitting next to his brother Tim and his wife, Mia, and their brood. She was Perry and Katy's daughter.

Robbie didn't even notice his middle sister Alexe. His eyes never left Amelia's veiled face. His radiated joy.

As she arrived beside him, Amelia leaned over and whispered, "A parcel for you to unwrap later as promised."

He couldn't help himself; he chortled softly. He took her hand and interlocked his fingers with hers. "I can't wait," he whispered.

It was her turn to giggle.

Hugh gave them both a dirty look as he heard both comments; however, he tried not to smile.

Robbie murmured, "Jealous?"

This time, Hugh stifled a smirk, knowing that it was a month until he and Miriam married. "Yes, shhh!"

In his most resonant voice, Hugh read from the Prayer Book. "Dearly beloved, we are gathered together here in the sight of God, and in the face of this congregation, to join together this man and this woman in Holy Matrimony, which is an honourable estate, instituted of God in the time of man's innocency, signifying unto us the mystical union that is betwixt Christ and his Church: which Holy estate Christ adorned and beautified with his presence, and first miracle that he wrought, in Cana of Galilee; and is commended of Saint Paul to be honourable among all men: and therefore is not by any to be enterprised, nor taken in hand, unadvisedly, lightly, or wantonly, to satisfy men's carnal lusts and appetites, like brute beasts that have no understanding; but reverently, discreetly, advisedly, soberly, and in the fear of God; duly considering the causes for which matrimony was ordained."

Hugh caught Robbie's grinning countenance. Hugh smiled and tried not to laugh. Someone needed to update these words, he thought.

The service continued. Hugh then asked, "Who giveth this woman to be married to this man?"

Jimmy stepped forward and said, "I do and about time. He's waited long enough." It was his turn to chuckle when he met the eyes of his soon-to-be brother-in-law and long-time best friend.

Hugh smirked again. He continued. Rob handed him the ring for Amelia, and Hugh had blessed it. Eventually, he reached the part Robbie had waited so long for. "Forasmuch as Robert and Amelia have consented together in Holy wedlock, and have witnessed the same before God and this company, and thereto have given and pledged their troth either to other, and have declared the same, by giving and receiving of a ring, and by joining of hands; I pronounce that they be man and wife together, in the name of the Father, and of the Son, and of the Holy Ghost. Amen."

Everyone else said, "Amen."

Hugh gave a slight discernible nod. The congregation erupted in applause. "I suppose you can kiss your wife, Robbie."

"Really?" Delighted, he turned to Amelia, lifted the short section of lace, and folded it back over her head. The smile she gave him nearly melted his heart. He slid his hand along her jaw and cupped her cheek lovingly with one hand while the other slid around her back. He gently brushed his lips across hers. He groaned and drew her entirely into his arms. "Oh, Milla," he uttered, then he passionately kissed her in a way such as he had done in the sitting room on the day they became engaged. Weak at the knees, she leaned into him, returning kiss for kiss, her arms sliding around his neck.

Finally, Hugh's clearing of his throat broke through into their consciousness. "Robbie, enough," Hugh whispered but was smiling.

Amelia had the courtesy to blush. She had just been kissed passionately in front of nearly everyone she knew. She clung to her new husband's hand. Every word she said she had meant wholeheartedly this man she could and would honour and willingly obey. This man would love and cherish her until they were parted by death. This one she adored.

"Sorry," Robbie said, grinning from ear to ear, then clearing his throat, not that he was. He had enjoyed every moment of it, as did she.

Amelia gave his hand a quick squeeze.

Hugh finished the service quickly; then, after they had signed the register, he led them forward and introduced "The Honourable Robert and The Honourable Lady Amelia Styles." The church congregation erupted in applause again.

Jimmy had wanted to be the first to congratulate Amelia, but someone else had beaten him to them.

Tugging at Robbie's jacket tails, Essie stood looking adoringly up at him. "As my new Papa, now can I hug you?"

"Yes, poppet," Robbie bent down and picked her up, walking back down the aisle with her in one arm and holding Amelia's hand in the other.

"Do you like kissing Mama?" Essie asked in quite a loud voice as they passed the Darlings. She stroked his cheek.

"Yes, poppet, I do. One day, you will find your own Prince Charming and want to kiss him, too. I waited a long time to marry your Mama; I hope you will find your special man when you grow up." With that, Robbie bent and gave Amelia another quick kiss.

Outside in the autumn sunshine, Robbie gently placed Essie down. "Poppet, I'm going to kiss Mama again. Is that all right?"

"Oh yes, 'cause it makes her so happy." She stood watching them.

"This is going to take some getting used to, the being watched, I mean. The rest is going to be easy to accept," he whispered to Amelia. "As will the unwrapping. I'm very much looking forward to that." He'd just released her when they were swamped with rose petals by most of the guests.

Amongst much joy, laughter and jocularity, Essie was bouncing from foot to foot as, for the very first time in her life, she had a father, and he loved her. Everyone Essie spoke to, she said, "I have a Papa, and we are a family."

Danny's three girls eventually persuaded her to join them for some games while the adults stood around talking and kissing each other.

Danny's oldest child, Jo-Anne, called Jo-Jo, astounded her as she told Essie, "Ess, you don't only gain a Papa, but you get us too, as we're now your cousins as our step-Mama, and Papa are your aunt and uncle. You also get grandparents."

"You mean I get to keep you all forever?" Essie looked astounded. "And Uncle Jimmy, too?"

Jo-Jo nodded.

"Do I have to give any away?" Essie's wide open in the excitement of the discovery.

Jo-Jo shook her head. "No, you can keep us all. Forever."

Essie hugged her, and then, as it sank in, she ran off and soon played with her new family.

Finally, Robbie assisted Amelia into Sir Timothy's travelling landau. He and Dan had arrived in it with the hood up. Now, the hood was folded back, and they headed back to Meldon Hall for the wedding banquet to be held in the Great North wing. As they drove past all the villagers and staff, the open carriage slowly filled with thrown flowers. Robbie and Amelia, in turn, threw out handfuls of small coins. There was, of course, a mad scramble for all of these.

Miriam and a couple of the other girls from the Hall stayed back and assisted Hugh in cleaning up the church. They, too, would then head up to the Hall for the party in his four-seated buggy. Robbie's words during the service had hit home. He was so looking forward to next month as Miriam turned eighteen, they could finally marry. He had the Rectory whitewashed inside and out, and although she was never allowed there alone, she and the family had rearranged the furniture how she wanted it. Much of the previous tenant's furniture Hugh had left was stored in an unused room. Other rooms sat empty after the repaint. He let her set up the place as she wished. He'd only arrived with a case of clothing and had more pressing things to attend to over the past twenty months or so since his arrival. The Rectory sat virtually untouched as Hugh mostly ate at the Hall. It was only a few minutes away, and he would take any excuse to be there. Hugh knew there was always a place at their table for him, and he didn't have a cook. He had no idea if that would continue, but as long as he was with her, he really didn't care.

After the church was clean and tidy, he assisted Miriam up next to him in the driver's seat. The mere touch of her hand upon his stirred his passions. Whoever the others were, they never complained; he had not even noticed them. One day, he would be able to kiss Miriam as Robbie had just done with Amelia. He had once before, on the day he proposed, in front of the entire family. His new family had adopted him, too.

On arrival at the Hall earlier in the week, Earl Sam had taken Robbie aside. "Have you planned where you are going to spend your week-long honeymoon? As I was wondering if you'd like a suite in the south wing. Food will be delivered with the pull of the bell cord." Sam gave him a knowing look. "I can guarantee you won't be sightseeing, so no use paying to go anywhere."

Robbie smiled. "No, true, sounds like heaven. I'll run it by Milla if that's okay."

Sam saw them with heads together and her look of astonishment, then a nod and another. Robbie caught his eye and gave Sam a big smiling nod, then a wink. He had been planning on something similar at home, but this was far more comfortable.

So now, after the ceremony, they only needed to walk down the corridor to their room. Neither had seen the room in which they were to stay. Amelia's clothes were already there, and the rest were packed for the next trip. Robbie had also brought his luggage, and one case was unpacked, and the rest was awaiting removal to Jimmy's place.

Amelia needed to remove her veil, and Robbie offered to escort her, so, "So you don't get lost, love." He smiled lovingly at her. "In reality, I wish to see where they have put us, but I'm going to wait until we don't have to reappear before I unwrap the rest of my gift," he whispered as he walked in behind Thea.

Amelia blushed. She was still slightly fearful of the physical side of marriage. Having been forcibly used and physically hurt, she'd never enjoyed the conjugal act. She had, of course, never even known she was married at the time she was so abused. Sometimes, she still woke throwing off the blankets, thinking she was being forced again. She had confided this to Robbie, and he knew that as much as he wanted and needed her, he needed to be gentle and compassionate. Their first time together would not be a quick tumble.

Having shown them their suite, Robbie asked Thea to stay. He then quickly brushed his lips over Amelia's forehead. Her look of disappointment nearly broke his heart. "We have the rest of our lives, sweetheart. Tonight, after we are alone, your wrapping will be thoroughly admired, trust me." Another quick kiss, and he was gone. "… And then disposed of." He whispered.

Thea removed her beautiful veil and pinned the train of her gown up so she could dance. "He's a good man, Mrs Amelia. One of God's true gentlemen. There's not many like him."

"I know, Thea. I only really know of two others; one is my brother Jimmy, and the other is their friend Neddie. I'm praying Ned will find his soul mate, as will Jimmy. However, Jim needs to get the Manor in order first and make it pay."

Thea said she'd pray for him.

Amelia returned to her new husband and the extended family after freshening herself and manoeuvring her ball gown-cum-wedding dress over the chamber pot.

Essie greeted her entrance joyfully. "Mama, have I really got a Papa now, really truly for keeps and forever?" The six-year-old was so bubbly and joyful that Amelia still found it hard to believe such an adorable child came from such a hideous person. Hopefully, Robbie would be the only father she ever wanted. Hopefully, she'd never need to know the truth of her birth.

"Yes, my poppet, he's ours to keep forever. And the only one you will ever need. And talking of him, look who's behind you." Amelia's face was showing such extreme happiness that Robbie thought she'd burst.

Essie wasn't far behind. "I love you, my new Papa." She put her arms up for him to pick her up.

"I love you too, poppet, but tonight is Mama's special night, and I have to look after her. She and I will have a little holiday together; then, we can be a family forever. Would you like that?" he asked while down on one knee.

"How long will you be away?" she asked, concerned, with her hands on her hips.

"We'll be back before church next week. Can you spare her that long?"

Amelia was standing behind her daughter, chuckling. This child certainly had an attitude.

"Hmm, yes, okay," Essie said, "And then you'll stay?"

"Yes and no! Yes, we shall be together. We're all moving in with Uncle Jimmy for a while until his house gets fixed. It will be dusty and dirty, and great fun making it nice again. It takes a whole day in the carriage to get there. But we'll be together for always," Robbie assured her. "You will have to help them get organised and even help pack your own things while we're away."

"Okay, are there other children there?" Amelia knew that her questions would go on forever, so she broke in. She motioned for Rob to put her down.

"Poppet, Uncle Sam and Uncle Danny are arranging who's coming with us, so some of the children from here may also come. You'll have to go and ask them." She pushed her towards Danny.

Robbie laughed. "I forgot how many questions small children ask. Alexe and Georgie were both like that."

Amelia said, "You should have heard her when she was two. I'd get ones like Why is the sky blue? Who makes the grass green? She certainly kept me on my toes."

The party went on all afternoon. Finally, half an hour before dusk, it broke up. Rather than everyone leaving the tidying up to the staff, as the staff had been most of the people attending, the clean up was nearly all hands on deck. Amelia did notice that Alexe was often found either watching for or working with Jim. She smiled and pointed it out to Robbie. He nodded, watching his sister.

Only the bride and groom escaped the cleanup.

Lord James was left holding his sleeping namesake, his great-grandson that he would never be able to acknowledge outside these walls, and Lady Mari had a sleeping Essie on her lap. She and Lady Mari's great-granddaughters, Mary-Anne, along with her older sisters Jo-Anne and Lucy-Anne, Essie's new cousins, had danced and danced that they were all now asleep. At six, seven, nine and eleven, they were all exhausted.

All the rest of the family had gathered in the foyer as Robbie escorted Amelia up the curving staircase. He knew where they were going, and as they drew closer, he swept her up in his arms and carried her along the final corridor. "Now, my darling wife, I believe you promised at the altar that I have a parcel to unwrap?"

She nodded. "Yes," she blushed adorably. "Robbie, I'm still nervous. I've never experienced this side of a marriage lovingly. It's silly, but I'm scared stiff." She blushed. "But I do want you."

He had gently placed her down after he carried her into their room. "Well, before we do anything, we're going to pray because this marriage is a God-centred one. Built on trust, not lust. If that side of things is not to your happiness, then we'll sort that out later. But for tonight, we'll take things easy, and I'll be led by you. Just be honest with me, Milla. If you're scared, talk to me. We can work through all of this."

She nodded, tearing up from happiness.

They stood together for some time and dedicated their new marriage to God. Together, they finished with *Amen*. They were both hesitant about what to do next, so Amelia sat on the bed and slipped off her shoes, as did he. She then stood and willingly walked into his arms. His kisses occupied her while she was busy unbuttoning his shirt. Soon, the trail of clothing was spread across the room. Her gown swished off into a silken heap, and it was followed by petticoats, stays, and drawers until she stood in her 'altogether'. She, too, had fully divested him of his wedding finery. They stood enfolded in each other's arms, naked as the days they were born. Amelia had never been fully undressed with a man who loved her, unfurling unfamiliar emotions in her.

He asked, "Are you sure you're ready?"

She nodded. "Yes, I want you."

He gently lifted her onto the bed, and he proceeded to ease her fears with his kind and loving caresses. This would be no repeat of her abuse. His gentle touch was so different from her earlier horrors. Their union was beyond her wildest imaginings; he waited and held back until an explosion of fireworks shot through her body.

"Oh, Robbie, what just happened?" She was still gasping in the rapture of her discovery. He then released, and together they enjoyed their initial joining.

"That, my dearest darling, is true loving. Call it 'the joys of marriage,' my sweet. It is how God made marriage to be. Giving, not taking, makes the union enjoyable for both. Was it?" he asked, concerned.

"Oh, yes," she was lying contentedly in his arms, one of hers wrapped around his torso. "Way beyond my wildest dreams, Robbie,"

She lay wrapped in his loving arms; he gently caressed her soft, downy cheek. She was so contented and relaxed that she had no desire to move. They both dozed.

She woke when he brushed a lock of her hair from her face.

"You were not frightened? Did I hurt you?" He looked at her sleepy eyes. "Was it bearable, my darling one?"

"Oh yes, So much so…" she reached over and kissed him, "…that I'm here when you wish to, well you know… If this is what real marriage is like, then I'm content to make a glutton of ourselves for the rest of the week, if not our lives."

"Oh, my dearest love, are you sure?" His relief was overwhelming; he burrowed his head into her neck. "Good," he chuckled, "because I've waited years for you, and well, I've some catching up to do." As he spoke, he finally did something he'd been wanting to do for a long time. He brushed his hand over her stomach and then her breast. He noted her response was not with abhorrence, but she responded with her own sensual desire. Now he asked her if he may not only look but touch.

She knew now that touch by a loved one was a very different experience from how Cyrus had gawked, mauled and manhandled her. So again, she said, "Yes, for there never will ever be a comparison between you and him. You are as the sun and the moon; he was the dark stormy nights."

He gently pushed back the sheet a little and gazed at her superb body. His loving caress evoked a groan of desire from her. "Oh, sweetheart, you are just perfect. I've dreamed of you like this. Of letting me see what's under those amazing gowns you wear. I never realised, I never imagined how absolutely exquisite you are."

His hand shook with both desire and awe as he gently caressed her glowing skin. This time, she reached for him. All barriers were now gone; her only tears were of happiness.

Chapter 15 Swept Clean

*A*melia and Robbie emerged from their room after two days. Food trays had been brought and removed, as had tea trays. Both of them now needed to stretch their legs. Thea showed them a way out to a back garden that was rarely used. Thea was delighted to hear giggling coming from their room. They relished the newly discovered intimacy that their marriage brought to them. Amelia found a new and more caring side to Robbie, one only she would ever really see or understand. She also was far more relaxed as she now knew there was nothing to fear in marriage; her haunted look was now completely gone. He also made their lovemaking fun. His compassion for what she had been through and his knowledge of her abuse they discussed so that he'd be aware of things not to do to rekindle those memories. This had been brought about once by her instant reaction to him calling her "wifey".

He did this only once, and she froze. "Oh, my sweet, I'm so sorry, I had no idea. That will never reappear in my vocabulary." He cradled her in his arms, and she relaxed again. He learnt there were some other words not to say and names not to call her.

She realised that if she did not tell him, he would not know.

On Sunday morning, six days after they married, they emerged from their honeymoon suite and joined the family for church.

Essie greeted them joyously. "Did you enjoy your holiday, Mama?"

Amelia snuck a quick look at Robbie. "It was wonderful, poppet. Did you work out which of your friends were coming with us to Uncle Jimmy's?"

She certainly had and joyously filled Amelia in on the week's happenings nonstop until they reached the church gates.

Hugh welcomed them and asked, "Get your present?" He asked

naughtily.

Rob had confided in Hugh. He had anxieties about the treatment that Amelia had suffered at the hands of her previous husband. Hugh felt quite useless in discussing this side of marriage, not having experienced it himself. Like Rob, he, too, had kept himself until the sanctity of marriage. Hugh's only recourse was to refer to and focus on his words in the Bible. "Focus on 1 Corinthians 13, Rob. God gave us that chapter for a reason. Just be as kind and gentle as you can be. Love her and, above all, cherish her. It's what she's missed, Rob. Cherishing is a wonderful word. If more did it, we'd have a lot fewer problems, especially in marriage."

Rob knew Hugh was anxious for his own marriage. Miriam, too, had a rough upbringing, having been orphaned as an older child. She'd been taken in by a family friend. Sadly, that lady had died after Miriam had been with her for little more than a year. Sam and Anne opened their doors to her, and as she had some education, she assisted in the classroom, teaching the children. Thankfully, she'd not been forced onto the streets. She'd been rescued before that had happened. Hugh had fallen in love with her when she was sixteen. He'd patiently waited for her to be old enough to marry for over a year. He had proposed one luncheon in front of the entire family. Now, in two weeks, they, too, would finally marry. His uncle, Reverend Hector James, was coming across from Maidstone to perform the ceremony.

Robbie whispered something as he passed. "Yes, and well worth waiting for, too."

"Two weeks and counting, Rob," Hugh laughed, and then Rob led the way into the family seats.

Jimmy had saved a seat next to him on the pew, and they joined him. Amelia noticed that his eyes were smiling and his face fully relaxed. "We've been busy while you've, err, 'been absent'. Sam and Danny have arranged a full team. A food wagon is loaded, and they leave tomorrow at dawn from here with three other wagons of the first people from Sam's place. We four will go in the carriage on Tuesday."

She smiled and sat holding Jim's hand. The Jimmy of old was back, her beloved, caring brother.

On completion of the service, the extended family stood outside catching up on the week's happenings.

Sam had already sent to London to his friend Perry White for some new, needy ex-soldiers. They were to arrive from London on Monday, soon after the forty had departed for Pittford Manor. They arrived late in the afternoon on Monday and had a day to settle in; then, their first-day orientation was set for Wednesday. More were due once the next departing group vacated the rooms. The forty had departed at first light on Monday, with forty more leaving on Friday. The first group would prepare rooms for the next lot. The disabled ones were to have the ground floor and the rest of the old upstairs staff quarters if they were habitable.

Amelia saw Jimmy's eyes light up, then fade. She knew that he wanted to accept the assistance he so desperately needed but wouldn't.

Sam had come over to see them off. He offered to go with them, but Jim politely declined, saying that he already felt indebted to him. Sam tried to explain that it was the other way around. Taking on these people allowed Sam to rescue more from the streets and their desperate poverty. Some of them ended up in the various gaols, and then eventually the hulks and transported to Australia.

Jim was only assisting in their training, Sam financed the entire project, and Tim was supplying food; Jim felt humbled. He rejected the offer of equipment, as he knew they had much in store. However, he promised he'd let Sam know if they needed anything.

"Sam, hold that thought," Amelia said. She took Jim aside and admonished him. "James Westaweller, this is a way you can get back on your feet with no cost to you. Accept what the good Lord has provided and be thankful."

Jim looked at her somewhat chastised and apologised to Sam as soon as he saw him again with Tim. He explained the situation. "Sam, Sir Timothy, I have all the tools and equipment, and most of the equipment and raw materials are already on-site, but I require workers. And especially a thatcher if you have one. The cottage roofs need urgent work."

Sam gently spoke to him. "Jim, we are all here to assist in whatever way you need. I am following my friend Perry's example. I had the Darlings help me and then Tim, too. I'm not offended, but you need to realise that if you leave yourself without assistance, you are hindering their rehabilitation."

Jimmy nodded. "I'm sorry, sir, my pride still sticks in my throat." He looked as guilty as he felt. "Send what you think we need, sir."

"Thank you, Jim. I will." Sam put a caring hand on his shoulder. "Jim, you are giving far more than you are taking. Do you understand how important you are to what we're doing here?"

Jim's look was one of puzzlement. He then shook his head.

"You think I'm just doing this to assist you? Seriously, that's what you think, isn't it?" Sam asked.

Jim nodded, "Yes, sir."

"Oh, James! Dare I say, 'silly boy.' Jim, I need you. Well, I really need your house, actually and your rooms and your willingness to take on these needy men. Yes, I started doing this because I wished to rub the Earldom in the faces of the peers who willingly begat children, then ignored them. I wish to train them and place them in the gentry's houses to haunt them. Then I realised that God put me in my position to assist them. We are all pawns on God's chessboard. We, however, have free will to move how we wish. Personally, I'd rather be moved by the Maker's hand than be taken off the playing board. Am I getting my point across?"

"I think so, sir. So you didn't plan this?" Jim asked

"Oh, heck no!" Sam walked to the window. "God made it happen, and now, with your assistance, I can make this work grow and assist many, many more. Are you willing to work a full partnership with Tim and me? I need to know now, Jim." Sam turned and stared at the young man in front of him. "Well?"

"So this isn't charity?" Jim asked.

"Of course, it is charity, Jim; only we are the ones giving to them. Get off your hobby horse and swallow that pride; remember, *'Pride goeth before destruction, and a haughty spirit before a fall';* it's from Proverbs 16:18. James, if you don't accept assistance, there are forty families I will have to turn away. Think hard before you reply, as I won't ask again."

The shocked look on Jim's face spoke volumes. "You really need my house? If so, then I'm in; I need them too." He blanched and then looked Sam in the eye. "I'm sorry, sir, my pride is now swallowed." He managed a smile.

Sam grabbed his hand. "Deal done, then."

The next day, they spent packing. With Jimmy accepting Sam's assistance, another wagon was loaded and sent off mid-afternoon. The following week would be exciting.

Essie and one of her special friends, Danny's youngest daughter, Mary-Anne, were tearfully saying their goodbyes. She had packed her special toys, all given to her by her Uncle Neddie. And along with her special blanket, then informed her mother that she had packed all her own things. The contents of her bag included her two rag dolls, Neddie Bear, her blanket and Major. She made sure that his head poked from the top of her bag so he'd be able to still be on guard duty. Amelia packed all the rest of her things as she'd not included any of her clothing whatsoever. Amelia chuckled as she told Rob.

With only the three adults and a child, the trip was accomplished with more comfort. For three of the five stages, Essie slept on the rear-facing seat while Amelia leaned against Robbie and dosed.

Jim and Robbie sat whispering as the girls dozed.

"You should have hinted, Jim. You covered it too well. I had no inkling at all." Robbie looked at his friend mournfully.

"That's what I intended, Rob. I tried hard to keep it all from Milla. Imagine if she'd known? I don't know what she thought had happened, but surely, to have a mother in St Mary's Bethlehem lunatic hospital and a father in Fleet Street Gaol would be about the worst I could think of. Rob, I know why they call that place 'Bedlam'. Oh, it's awful."

"She wants to go, you know. She wishes to see her mother," Rob said quietly, not wishing her to hear.

Jim's eyes turned to his, flabbergasted. "No! You can't let her. Don't take her, Robbie. It's a horrific place. I'm still haunted by the screams. I'm pleased that Mother is out of it most of the time; she's unaware of what's happening around her. She's just groggy."

"I thought I'd put it off for a while, but she needs to see her. I will not let her see your father, though." Rob said, "I gather they were not close?"

"No, he dropped out of our lives before we were fully grown. Alcohol! I'd still go down to his rooms and see him, but I kept Milla away. He'd often be so drunk in a pool of vomit that it would take Vincent and me hours to clean him up. His valet quit, and Vince and I took over his care. On the few times he was sober, he'd go to London and gamble. It was, in a way, how he fell in with the duke. His daughter had already been asked to leave from three other schools, and the duke sowed the seed of starting a school at the Manor. Mother knew the funds were low as she'd taken over the finances when she moved Father out. She didn't realise that his gambling IOUs were eating away at the non-entailed land that was the money-producing fertile farms. One by one, the parcels of arable land went. I'm only left with grazing land now."

"Jimmy, is she beyond care at home? Could we bring her back and have some of the new ladies and Milla look after her at home?" Rob looked at the astonishment on Jim's face.

"Yes, Rob, that could work. She just sits in her room all day. She eats, sleeps and walks, but it's as though her mind is vacant. She'd be no trouble, but I just didn't have the means to support her. No staff, no food and well, just nothing."

"I think if we prepare her rooms first, then we can get her home as soon as possible." Rob smiled at the joy on Jimmy's face.

They sat silently for a while.

"Don't say anything to Milla. Mother's condition may have changed." Jim noticed Amelia stirring.

They were due to pull in for the last change of horses. It was mid-afternoon, and they still had ten miles to go.

"Good afternoon, sleepyhead," Rob teased her as she opened her eyes. He kissed her lovingly as she fully woke.

"What a nice way to wake." Returning his kiss. "Where are we? Did I sleep long?"

"Yes, it was, in answer to your first statement. An hour away in answer to your second, and we still have one stage to go, so ten miles and a bit over an hour." He stretched his arm. He would never admit it was stiff, but holding her close was a delight. He could never get close enough to her. To marry his best friend's sister was ideal. To be in the position to assist them was even better as it would draw them closer. In all things, he knew he had to protect Amelia. She was still so fragile and vulnerable. She would flinch if a tone of voice were angry or hurtful, walking away rather than admitting her hurt. Even knowing her history, it was so hard not to occasionally cause her unintentional pain.

Twice at night, she'd woken with nightmares. He'd learned that holding her was not the way to soothe her. When he'd tried that, she'd struggled more. Gently stroking her cheek was a way to wake her, and then once awake, he could then bring her comfort. Her sobs would nearly break his heart, but together, they would work through her pain. She would cling to him and weep.

Essie was woken at the last staging post and taken for a privy break. Danny had sent word through yesterday for the inn to prepare a large hamper for them to take, and it included a cold roasted haunch of venison, beef, hogget, six cooked chickens and many other prepared dishes. The inn had also included some forty large pork pies. The quantity of food would be enough to feed the new staff until the kitchens were put back in order. The larder was virtually empty, and this was used to restock the perishable foodstuffs. They had been sent with enough fresh food for a few days. Nothing would be able to be prepared there until the kitchens were again serviceable, and that included cleaning the chimneys.

Also included was a smaller hamper of ready-to-eat foods and selections of small buttered bread rolls and a loaf of whole-grain locally made bread—a small container of relish. At the bottom of this was a level of freshly picked apples and a bottle of cider.

They nibbled on the delicious ham picnic as they watched the miles pass. Essie, now wide awake, was getting bored, and so Jim played a game of eye-spy. She had not played this before, so they had the joy of teaching her the game. Grasping the idea quickly, she soon had them stumped when she chose 'dust'. She could see it and smell it, but as she was sitting facing backwards and they weren't, it was not visible to them, so she won the game. Her childish laughter and joy made the time pass quickly. Soon, they were drawing into the road towards the Manor house.

"Rob, look." Jim was amazed that already the front gate had been repaired and tree branches on the driveway removed. He knew the gate was just a matter of lifting it back onto the swivel points, but he'd been unable to do this alone. Astonished at the change in the house, he looked at Rob, puzzled. "Did you send someone earlier?"

"No, I thought you must have arranged something with Vince. Then who?"

"No!" They gazed at the gardens that were already being trimmed, and other signs of repairs were visible. The changes in the month were astounding. Neither had a clue until the carriage pulled up at the front door under the covered portico. Vincent and Mildred were there with quite a few of the old familiar staff faces.

"Welcome home, Mister Jimmy. We hope you didn't mind, but some of the cottages are so bad that they'd rather live here with no pay than suffer through wet nights. So to earn their keep, I set them to work." The old retainer grinned. "Do you mind, sir?"

"No, you did the right thing, Vince. Absolutely the right thing, thank you. Do you mean some of them want to come back? Did you explain that there are no funds to pay them still? Did the others arrive yet? Have they settled in well?"

"Yes, yes and yes, sir! All according to your instructions or lack of them. I do hope things turn themselves around, sir." Vince welcomed Amelia. "Miss Amelia, or should I say, Lady Amelia, congratulations, and Mister Styles."

Robbie greeted the old butler. "Evening Eggleton, Mrs Eggleton; you've done wonders already."

Mildred dropped a curtsy to them all and added, "Thank-ee sirs, ma'am. I had them prepare your old rooms if you don't mind. They were the easiest to clean. We can move to anywhere you wish later."

"That's fine, thanks, as long as the bed is dry and the sheets are clean," Jimmy said. "Vince, the carriage is stuffed full of fresh foods. We will eat like kings for a while, and then we're on rations. Can you deal with them, or do you need assistance?"

Mildred then clasped eyes on Essie. "Oh miss, I mean, M'Lady, I didn't know you had a child. She's the image of you at that age, ma'am."

Essie, who had been eyeing off the older lady, had finally emerged from behind Amelia's skirts. Her enormous blue eyes took in the new people in front of her and saw she was the centre of attention. Robbie felt her tug on his jacket. "Papa? Up, please." Her beseeching gaze was his undoing. He bent and lifted her. Once in his arms, she hid her face in his neck. He wrapped a loving arm around her, bringing her the security she craved. He understood that new things and places were always scary to children.

Amelia led the way inside and up the staircase to her old room.

Robbie placed Essie on the ground, and she walked with them to the room.

Jimmy had taken Vincent into the study and, got a run-down on what had been done and given group assembly instructions for later that afternoon. Then, he inquired how the new folk had settled. Once briefed, he returned to find his sister.

~

Two hours later, all gathered in the large drawing room. Jim knew that all the furniture from this room had been moved, and it was currently empty; hence, he'd chosen it. The eggshell blue and white walls with gold trim were as beautiful as ever. All but the old retainers knew what the plan was, but he wanted everyone to meet to hear directly from him what the strategy would be.

With Jimmy now in charge, they set the women to assist the old retainers in scrubbing the food preparation areas. The men showed them the storerooms, stables, gardening sheds and tool rooms. Each had training from Sam, and their skills were chosen for specific talents. Jimmy set only six to work on the front driveway and entry gardens, and the rest were sent into the kitchen garden; this was vital to feed the many mouths that now required food. They had brought enough food with them for a month, but fresh produce was still needed. Each of the old staff had brought with them what livestock they had at their cottages. They had combined them with Jimmy's cow, his ducks, and chickens. Some even had pigs.

The men doing the kitchen gardens realised that the hen house needed extension and repair. They were able to straighten the posts and fox-proof the coop. Hopefully, no more would be lost to the wily predators.

Over dinner of the cold roast chicken brought from the inn and some of the remaining picnic packed for them, they discussed the things that needed to be done. Mildred and Amelia had walked throughout the Manor house and listed these things. Robbie and Jim had also decided to itemise the necessary repairs. After dinner, the three prioritised them. Two of the expectant wives were in charge of the children, and Essie was content to stay with them.

Amelia remembered a large chalkboard that used to be in the nursery, and Jim took Rob up to retrieve it. They also found a tin of coloured chalks. Jim found an easel, and they carried this and set it up in the foyer; they carried the board into the dining room and sat it on two chairs. With a line drawn down the middle of the board, they started listing jobs in order of priority. The two columns were Inside and Outside jobs. Amelia wrote as the men dictated. Once completed, Jimmy took the board out to the foyer and set it up on the easel.

Essie was by this time in bed, asleep in the room next door to Amelia and Robbie. Mildred had quickly arranged for a bed to be set up in there for her. The next morning, with Mildred's assistance, she'd found her way down to her friends staying in the lower rooms of the north wing. Essie had spent the remainder of the day in the care of one of the mothers. After playing outside all day, she was exhausted. She had discovered a love for the chickens.

After a month, the jobs on the board had been replaced numerous times. The kitchen garden had been dug over, and the untended vegetables were now thriving. Two of the amputee soldiers had been given the job of tending this, and both were skilled gardeners. Neither could climb ladders to do hedging or tree lopping, but knowing that they would now be in charge of the supply of fruit and vegetables for the household delighted them. Both already knew how to prune the unproductive and dead branches off the neglected kitchen trees, and soon, with the advent of the cold weather, they put the trees to sleep for winter and set to prepare the garden for spring bloom.

Amelia and Essie took the opportunity to visit Ned's mother to fulfil the promise she'd made to him when she left. On arrival at the Gracemere Castle, she was welcomed with love. Duchess Susanna couldn't sit her down fast enough. Essie was hugged and then sat next to the older lady. The duchess's maid brought in a small bowl of freshly picked warm glasshouse strawberries and handed them to Essie. She'd only ever eaten one before and loved it. To have an entire plateful herself was a treat. Amelia would have loved to have met the duke. However, the duchess explained that he wasn't well. She saw a painting at the top of the stairwell when she entered and gasped. It could well have been Charles Lockley. He looked much like this when she had met him. No wonder Ned had questions that he needed answers to.

Without saying much about where Ned was, Amelia told her about his life in the colony. Including that Ned was Essie's godfather. Amelia explained that she saw him mainly in Sydney when he came in for meetings, so she gave nothing away about either his name or his location. Her Grace already knew he was in New South Wales, but that was all. Amelia then gave her the short note Ned had given her for his mother, telling of his love for her, but no more hints. Amelia then took her leave after the prescribed fifteen minutes. Essie had eaten all the strawberries. They returned to the Manor house. Sadly, a week later, they heard that the old duke had died. Amelia grieved for the lovely lady and for Ned. The new duke would be David, Ned's older brother; Elouise would finally be the duchess.

~

One of the wounded men was poking around an overgrown lump of vegetation he'd come across in the yard. He found it hard to tear away the vines as he had a hand missing, but he persevered. What he found was the remains of what had once been a dovecote. Many wild birds still use it. Squab pie was something many still enjoyed, so he reported his find to Jim, who had totally forgotten about it. One group got to work repairing it. Another group knew how to lay down live fencing hedges, and others still, how to coppice the woods. All the soldiers and sailors used their latent skills from their youth on their various farms. Jimmy and Rob were astounded at the collective group knowledge. The only trouble was making the two groups sometimes work together. Jimmy eventually found that letting them sort out who was doing which jobs and leaving the work team arrangements worked much better. They each knew their own skill sets and were prepared to pass jobs on to others. Specific jobs needed more able-bodied men or different skills. The most needed men were the ones who could climb ladders, and this included thatchers. The majority were either limping or amputees; the scarred and burnt ones ended up trimming trees and hedges and even learning how to re-glaze some of the few windows that had broken in the storm. Only one man in the group had the required thatching skills, and he was set to work on the cottage roofs with others as ground crew to pass things up to him. The job was daunting as there was so much to do. There was lots of wheat straw as the crop had been left in the field, and the birds ate the grain as no one was there to harvest it. They scythed the straw and used it for the thatch or gave it to the women to make bee skep hives. If they could make their own honey, that would help. As straw was free, so were the hives.

Seven weeks after their arrival, they celebrated the first Christmas that the house had seen for many years. Jimmy was beginning to see the light at the end of the tunnel. Jobs that he'd been unable to do for years were now completed. Everyone had gone out to collect the Yule log. On the way, Essie asked what it was all for, "This seems to be a lot of fuss, Mama, for a log of wood for the fire," she said to Amelia.

When each tried to explain that this was an English tradition and that it was to be placed under the bed and then burnt on the twelfth night after Christmas, they realised how silly the custom was. Even more so when they realised it had nothing to do with Christianity. So rather than gather a Yule log, they loaded up a wagon with firewood from various fallen trees and decided to deliver it to a needy family or two. Vince had told him of some in the area who could do with some assistance. Jim had never been able to do much before other than give them access to trapping and hunting in the woodland. As thanks, he occasionally used to find a dead rabbit on his kitchen doorstep. It had been his only source of meat. There was a long way to go, but if these people were prepared to assist, he'd take all the help he could get. In the process, they were gaining experience and training.

When New Year came, so did some visitors. A fancy travelling carriage arrived, and the passengers were greeted with much joy and celebration. Sam had decided to accompany the second wave of staff. This meant Anne wanted to come too. Tim and Sophie wanted to see what was happening, so they, too, decided that the time was ripe for visiting.

Some of the more experienced trainees had been asked to head off to paid jobs on other estates. Sam had taken on more of the recently wounded soldiers, this time from the Royal Marines from the Ashanti wars. He was now bringing the ones who'd come from London when Jimmy had departed some three months ago.

Sam was now able to take on forty new men at a time. Each visit to London revealed more and more who needed assistance. He always chose the most injured, the most unemployable and the ones who needed the most care and the most dejected. Nursing them back to health was also something that the rescued street women did. Many of those had fallen on hard times when their men had been either killed or injured. A group in London assisted such girls and women and tried to farm them out to places like Meldon Hall. Sadly, there was so little being done for them that the problem was almost overwhelming. Sam would only take the ones prepared to follow the house rules and participate in the church activities and Bible study groups. Each was offered the opportunity to learn to read and write. Most relished the door opened to them. Many of these women had illegitimate children through no fault of their own. These were often hard to place unless they married. So, although no immoral fraternisation was allowed, relationships and marriage with the soldiers and sailors were encouraged. It settled the men and gave the women the chance of a promising future.

The arrival of Tim and Sophie, in particular, was a boost to morale. Sam and Anne had not seen the state of disrepair, but having had Tim describe what it had looked like, they were all astounded that the place, although in its winter sleep, looked beautiful. The trees had now all shed their leaves, and the buds were visible on the branches. Soon, all would spring back into life.

Their arrival coincided with Amelia becoming ill. For the past three mornings, she had cast up her accounts after breakfast. So far, Amelia had hidden her condition from Robbie, but now she knew it was time he was told he was to become a father. She knew from what she went through with Essie what to expect. Martha Turner had taught her well.

The morning after the unexpected visitors arrived, Amelia lay in bed and stroked his stomach. She had woken with such lustful desire for him that he'd woken to her hand creeping down his stomach, then lower and lower. This had not been the first time she'd instigated things recently, and it was becoming a regular morning occurrence. He willingly obliged her desires, and they lay entwined in the afterglow.

She was twisting his chest hairs around her fingers. "Robbie, you know how much you love Essie and that she's not yours?'

"Hmm," he said in a very distracting way. He was thoroughly enjoying the effect she was having on him. "Why, love?"

"Well, I wondered how diverted you'd be with one of your own?" She looked at him shyly.

"Oh, I suppose quite…." He stopped. "You mean you're expecting? Are you kidding?" He sat up, stark naked, and spun to face her. "We're going to be parents? I'm going to be a father?" He was on his knees before her and searching her face for an answer.

"Yes," she smiled meekly.

"But we just did… I mean, can we still do…? You know what we just did?" He had no knowledge if marital relations could still continue if she was expecting.

"Yes, we can, but it apparently becomes more difficult as my size increases. I never had to worry about that before. Cyrus died when I was but three months gone with child. As I'm still ill, I must only be about two months along. We did enjoy ourselves somewhat after we married. I was surprised when I got my menses two weeks after our marriage. But that would make me about nine weeks along."

Robbie was lost for words. He'd not even been sure that marital relations would continue after their first joining. That, however, had not been the case, far from it. And now, her desire for him was even more than on their all-too-short honeymoon.

He finally lay back down beside her and adoringly drew her to him. "We're to be parents. I know I should not be surprised, but I am. I'm astounded."

She giggled when she said, "Robbie if you don't want them to guess, wipe that ridiculously wonderful grin from your face."

He laughed heartily. "Of course, I want them to know. I want to shout it from the rooftops."

They emerged from their room much later than usual.

Before the rest of the family was told, Essie first needed to know. She had got into the habit of dressing herself and beetling down to her friends and often helping out with the hens. She loved them. So to the farm kitchen, they went. Sure enough, she was sitting in the hen house with a chicken in her lap. It was eating grain from her hand, and she was patting it.

"Essie darling, do you think it could eat on its own for a while?" Amelia said.

"Yes, Mama." She gently eased it off her lap and shook off her skirts, then joined them on a garden seat.

"Morning, possum, you were up and out early this morning," Robbie said.

"Yes, Papa, the chickens were hungry. Do you mind?" she asked with her huge blue eyes, seeking approval from him.

"No, of course not. We just needed to have a little chat before we go into breakfast," he said. He loved her so very much.

"Oh, yes, Papa?" She sat between them.

"Essie, you love having friends, don't you?" Amelia started.

Essie nodded.

"How would you like ones that never went away? Ones you could keep for all your life?" Robbie smiled at Amelia as he spoke.

"What? You mean like a brother or a sister?" she asked.

"I told you she was quick. Yes, darling, just like that," her mother answered.

"I'd like that. But how?" She looked from one to the other. Suddenly, her eyes opened even wider. "Mama, are you going to get me one I can keep?"

Amelia nodded. "We can all keep it. It should be here mid-next year. It's got some growing to do yet, but it's coming." She sat with her hand on her stomach.

"So, will you get fat like Frances's mama? Is it growing in your tummy, too? Or is it a heart baby like at Uncle Sam and Aunty Anne's place?"

"This one is a tummy baby, darling. And there might even be more later. We'll see what God sends us," Amelia explained.

Essie reached out and took her parents' hands. "As long as we can always be together, we can fit lots more into our hearts. Aunty Anne told me that. She said that every time she thought her heart was full, God brought another child into their lives who needed love. Each time, room was made. When you were away on your holiday, I knew I'd like to keep some, but the heart babies belonged to the others. If God has sent us a tummy baby, they can't take it from us, can they?"

"No, poppet," Robbie said, astounded at the little girl's wisdom. But this child had experienced much hurt and heartache, such as none he knew had seen. "God has chosen us to be this baby's family, and we'll need your help. It will cry a lot for a few months, but it will grow into a wonderful friend for you."

"Is it a brother or a sister? I don't really care too much, but I'd like a little brother." Her big blue eyes searched her parent's faces.

"Ahh yes, well, you don't really get a choice with a tummy, baby; you get what God sends us," Amelia explained.

"Oh, that's all right, as God never gets things wrong, as I do." The adorable dark-headed cherub looked from one parent to the other. "Is it just one? Can we have more than one?"

"How about we start with this one and see what God sends us later? But we'd like more." Amelia sought her husband's eyes. "Many more, poppet," she responded when she saw the look on his face. "Sweetie, we're going to tell everyone later at breakfast, and we wanted you to know first."

"Okay, Mama. I'll go and wash up." She hopped off the seat and went to the chook's water to wash her hands.

"No, no, poppet, not in there! We'll use soap in the kitchen, with clean water," Robbie said.

Once she was cleaned up, they joined the rest of the family, now assembled in the dining room. Mildred and Vince had even polished what remained of the silverware. Vince had unearthed that from some hidden repository.

"Sorry, sir, but I hid this from your father," he grinned at Jim. He had candles under the warming tureens, keeping the food hot. One of the soldier's wives, Bertha Fernwood, had turned out to be an excellent cook. She'd been an assistant cook at a castle before she married. Deferring to her vast knowledge, she had unanimously been voted in as chief cook. She was thrilled. Thinking she'd never be allowed to work again because of her married status. Everyone was fed with a minimum of fuss. Her husband

Edgar was one of the two disabled soldiers who now worked in the kitchen garden; they had four children already and another on the way.

Bertha had a warming dish full of soft eggs cooked just how Robbie loved them, just about set, so he helped himself to two and some toast and bacon.

Amelia only had some buttered toast and some plain porridge.

She was sitting next to Robbie, and when he dug his fork into the gooey eggs, it had Amelia fleeing from the room. Robbie kept on eating and said nothing. She had warned him of this happening.

One look from Sophie and the smile Anne gave her made them both wonder if they had a secret. The realisation hit both ladies at once.

Robbie met his mother's eye. "Rob, is there something you need to tell us?"

"No, dear Mother, why would you think that? Nothing I 'need' to tell you at all." He kept eating, ignoring their speculation by talking about inane topics.

Finally, Amelia returned; Robbie met her loving look and lifted one of his eyebrows as almost a question.

She nodded.

Robbie cleared his throat, "Dear all, there is nothing we need to tell you; however, there is something we 'want' to tell you all. We three are to be four in about August. So everyone is to make sure she is not to do any heavy lifting."

"I am getting a brother or sister. Ain't that grand?" Essie said, grinning.

Everyone started talking at once and offering their congratulations. As Robbie had spoken, he'd gone to stand behind her. He absentmindedly caressed her neck. He was still in some shock. They were having a baby. The absolute joy on his face was visible for all to see. At thirty-one and thirty-five, he did not expect that such a blessing would occur so quickly. He bent to Amelia and whispered, "Are we really having a baby, my love? I'm... well, I'm delighted. So excited and absolutely overwhelmed."

She smiled adoringly at him, and Amelia leaned her head back against him, thinking of the different reaction from her first confinement. Robbie's response was of care and consideration. The thought brought her up short; she must absolutely stop comparing them. There was no future in that. There was in Robbie; he was her future. One thing that concerned her was what she was going to do with herself if she were not allowed to continue cleaning and assisting in the refreshment of the house. Essie's innocent comment had shed light on where her talents could be used. She'd let the teaching of her own child lapse. She'd teach again. Essie's education had been sadly lacking during her courtship, and now there were other children on the estate often. They were underfoot. They already had a classroom set up, and she'd taught in it before. It would just be a situation of getting it cleaned and dusted. She'd talk to Robbie and Jimmy about it after breakfast.

The repair activities for the day were somewhat delayed as they sat around discussing the forthcoming baby. Finally, when they all rose from the table, Amelia had stopped Robbie from leaving and called Jimmy over to discuss her idea about re-opening the school and the possibility of her teaching the resident children. She had not asked Robbie first, but if it meant that she would not be doing any lifting or scrubbing as she had been, she was sure he wouldn't worry.

"I've had an idea, and Jimmy, I've not even run this by Robbie yet as it only struck me while we were eating, so I want you to discuss it before you make a decision. Rob will have the final say." She saw a puzzled took wash over Robbie's face. "There are so many children; they are beginning to run riot and get underfoot." She saw both men nod, but neither spoke.

Both knew she would have a good point to her reasoning. They waited.

"Well, as you both know, I was teaching here and also in Australia, and as I'm no longer allowed to lift or scrub, why don't I re-open the classroom and teach the children, thus solving both problems. Everything we need is already here. I happened to be in the room last week and saw all it needed was a good cleaning. It was exactly as I left it, only dusty. If that were done today, I could start tomorrow." She turned to her husband, "Don't just say no, Robbie; please talk to Jimmy about it. It's not like these children are the 'Peer's brats', as Jimmy crudely called them. These ones wish to learn, and it will mean I can continue Essie's education, too."

Robbie opened his mouth to say something, but Amelia gently put her hands on his lips.

"Darling, please don't just say no without making some effort to see how it's really needed," she pleaded with him, beseechingly looking at him.

Robbie caught her hand and lovingly kissed her fingers. "Actually, my love, we had been discussing how the children were quite annoying. Some are pestering the workmen, and many are unaware of dangerous situations. If you could remove them and teach them, we would be most appreciative." He'd not released her hand, and he kissed her palm again. "And it would also mean that you are lifting nothing more than chalk."

"You mean I can do it? Oh truly? You don't mind?" She walked into his arms.

"I mind. Of course, I do, but I know that this is something you love. It's not like it's work. I will say, though, it's only temporary. We will try to find some more people who can assist you and eventually take over. I want to return home before the baby is born. Sorry, love, but at home, there are good doctors and far more help than here. We'll stay here only until June, Jimmy. I won't allow her to travel after that."

Jim nodded and agreed wholeheartedly.

Amelia was a little sad but knew the wisdom in his words. She was Robbie's wife, and it had never been their intention to live at Pittford Manor permanently; it had only ever been short-term. However, they knew they would always be welcome. They may even come back for a while.

"That's fine, Rob. I might come for an extended visit if things here are working as they should." Jimmy looked at his brother-in-law and sister, grinning widely. "I'll arrange a team to set to work there now. It should be ready after luncheon today. For some reason, I thought if I could get the school back up and going, it could be the means to an end—a way to make some money for the estate. Robbie, with your permission, 'Pittford Manor Children's Academy' will re-open today. I'll set Amelia's classroom to be done first and Mother's tomorrow."

"I'll get things started. This will give me about four months." Amelia was so excited.

"Yes, love, you can start. From little things, big things grow. This could well be the means to put the estate back on its feet, Jim. Once we have the estate cleaned up, Jimmy, I think that you can expand the classrooms to local children, no boarding, just day students. What do you think? Can you handle them, sweetie?" Robbie had again put his arm around Amelia's shoulders and drew her to him.

She lifted her face to him for a kiss. "Thank you, my dearest love. I was wondering what I was going to do."

He willingly obliged her unvoiced request for a kiss. Oblivious to all watching, he drew her into his arms. "Just don't overtax yourself, sweetheart. When you feel tired, dismiss class and rest. Send Essie to me whenever you want me."

Amelia nodded. "I will, Robbie, I promise; I'll not jeopardise this child for anything."

His parents, plus Sam and Anne, all watched their intimate moment.

Essie walked to Sophie. "Grandma Sophie, Papa makes Mama so happy. She used to cry a lot, but now she laughs and smiles all the time. I like her like this."

Sophie bent and picked up her adorable step-grandchild. "Darling, that's what being in love is like."

Essie wrapped her tiny arms around her neck. "I smile too 'cause I now got grandparents like other children." She laid her head on Sophie's neck. "And I love you muchly, Grandma Sophie."

"As I do with you, my poppet," she said while hugging her back.

Within an hour, a working team had been sent to spring clean the schoolroom. When word spread of the possibility of the children being educated for free, all the parents were keen. When the children found that Lady Amelia was the teacher, all the children pitched in and assisted in the cleanup. Both rooms were utterly spring-cleaned and scrubbed by lunchtime.

By midday, the classroom floor was nearly dry after being mopped. The blackboard had even been washed, dried and re-chalked. Amelia loved the priming or seasoning of the board; She'd always make it fun. The big blackboard was ready for use. All the slates had been washed, and Amelia's first lesson was to teach the children about chalking their boards. All of her teaching manuals were still in the room, sitting where she had left them when she had been arrested. When she entered, it was as though she'd left the day before, not many years ago. Even the school bell sat on the desk.

The room held forty school desks. The school was only for the younger girls in days gone by, so ink wells were not used. Slates were all that they had required. Amelia knew that one day she'd love them to learn to use graphite pencils, but that day was far off. This school would be basic. These children were from a cross-section of backgrounds. A few had an elementary education, but most had none. This time, she would have both boys and girls of various ages. She sat in the room thinking about how she'd sort the children. She worked out to sort them by age. The youngest children would be at the front and the older ones towards the back.

Both Sam and Tim had assisted in various plans, including cleaning the library. This had not been on the to-do list as sitting reading had not been a required activity until the school opened.

Amelia started coughing when she went in to retrieve a book. Rob and Sophie heard her.

When Sophie had heard her, she mustered some help and set about cleaning the room from head to foot. It was so dusty that they had to all cover their mouths and noses. They threw open the windows and let in the late cold winter air, but it certainly helped.

Within a month, the school had fifty children regularly coming. With only forty desks, the ten youngest were taken into the next-door room and taught some basics, like how to hold the chalk. One of the younger women had basic writing skills and at least knew her alphabet. Sophie and Anne oversaw her lessons and said she was doing a good job and knowing that Amelia relaxed.

A month later, Amelia was well over her morning sickness. Robbie insisted that she have a comfortable armchair installed, and twice a day, she had story time, where all the children from both classes would come and sit around the chair while she told a story.

Tim had sent away for any children's stories he could find, and one that was included was a new book by the author Hans Christen Anderson. Unfortunately, it was in Danish, but the bookstore had included a handwritten translation of four stories. The book was a fairy storybook for children. The first time Amelia read *The Tinder Box*, the children sat spellbound. They kept asking for it until she read a second one from his book later that week, "The

Princess and the Pea", which became an equal favourite.

Just before Tim and Sophie departed, the second book of the series arrived. Again, the bookseller had included a handwritten transcription of this and their favourite from this was once called "Thumbelina".

Sophie and Anne each sat and took a copy of the stories to take home with them. They, too, enjoyed the delightfully entertaining stories. They knew, too, that their grandchildren would adore them.

Chapter 16 Blue Skies Ahead

*S*am and his coach load departed after a glorious three weeks of vigorous cleaning activity. Sam made arrangements for the next group of workers to arrive after Easter. He told Jim he'd see if he could find any women who could teach. Jimmy was now back to his usual exuberant self and handling the management of the growing household well. Vince was a treasure as he knew the way things should be done. Jim referred to him for many things.

Jim, Sam, Robbie, and Tim had sequestered themselves in the study for some time and worked out how the training regime would work. It had to take a more formalised approach now as more households were involved. Perry and Katy White dropped in from their hideaway farm, Blackberry Cottage, next door. Perry's father, Duke of Cheatham, had died. For their year of mourning, they escaped from their Ducal duties in Warwickshire for a few months to Jimmy. His mother and son had things well in hand at home.

Sam would take over the financing of the food, and Jimmy would continue the training. The accommodation was not a problem, and as long as they had food, they could take many more of the walking wounded. Within four months of making the bee skeps, they had their first honey harvest. More were nearly ready for that, and that would bring in some money.

Each man and his wife, if he had one, were sent with a written list of skills and areas in which they needed more supervision. Tim's role was now to find positions for the fully trained people. He had a team to assist him in London; the Darling's friends were assisting with this, and many new jobs were found for their new charges.

Jimmy explained bashfully that he'd beaten his ego down with a stick and would now take all the assistance he could get.

As both Sam and Tim had now seen the estate for themselves, they knew who would be best suited to send. After perusing the cottages, Sam could well understand Jimmy's need for a thatcher. As there was an experienced one in Billingshurst who was currently not working, he thought that he'd send him and his family along for a busman's holiday. The family of seven would arrive next week, and Sam had asked Jimmy to prepare a royal suite for them; when he explained why, Jim willingly did just that. Angus Hebblewhite and his wife and family had never had a holiday, and Sam knew the man would be well paid on his return home; just in case Jimmy questioned him whilst there, he was to say that he was doing the work in lieu of a holiday. The job would be done, and the cottages once more become habitable. As he re-thatched, others in the team did other repairs. He taught others while he worked on big jobs. Soon, windows with broken glass were replaced. The chimney that had fallen was replaced, and the cottages were almost rebuilt. One by one, the remaining four tenant farmers had their complaints attended to.

At the end of that month, those four farmers came and paid Jimmy some rent. Each was so appreciative of the work done that they had given him some back rent, too. He stood with £4 in his hand; each had paid a quarter year in total. This was his money. Not subsidised by Sam, but his own money. His fingers clenched around the precious coins. He walked into the office and recorded the payments in the rent book that he'd found in the bottom drawer of the desk. The coins he slipped into the cash box, wondering as he did so how long it had been since it had held any money at all. He owed so much in back wages that they were unlikely ever to have enough funds to pay those. This would go towards some fresh food for everyone.

One of the men had been a cavalryman in years gone by. He loved to work with horses but, as yet, was not quite well enough to do so. He may never be, but he knew the work well. The tack room had not been touched at all, as there were no resident horses. Albert Winterbottom could sort and repair the tack until that time came. The man was a skilled leatherworker. He soon had the tack room in complete repair. The smell of Neatsfoot Oil became a familiar smell as Albert worked all the leather. Every bit of neglected leather was polished with his sheepskin squares that were soaked in the Neatsfoot Oil. He reworked and replaced all the broken sections. The tack was soon as good as new.

While there, Sam suggested that they send a team for a complete, stable clean-up. Some six stalls had been cleaned for visitors' nags and carriage horses, but the rest remained in a state of neglect. He had an idea about getting some horses, too. Even visitors' horses needed a clean stable, so it was added to the to-do list. Many horses, post-was, were sold at a ridiculously low price as they, too, were battle-weary or had ugly sabre injuries. He wasn't sure if the Ashanti wars involved horses, but he'd find out. Tim and Sam suggested that they head to stock sales and see what was on offer.

If available, these beasts needed a quiet place, and this area was perfect for them. Often, these were tough beasts and had years of work in them. They just needed the love and quiet that Pittford Manor could supply. Sam and Tim had discussed getting Jim some other stock, too. But that would be a surprise. Sam had men already working on the fencing and hedges. If Jimmy complained, Sam had already worked out what he'd tell him. The soldiers needed experience in how to work with animals, so they required animals to work on. Jimmy could keep any born on the property. Sam intended to buy all expectant beasts and a calm bull. They also needed a small dairy herd, as two dairy cows were not enough for the household. Tim, Sam, and Anthony Jenkins, Sam's head coachman, would head to the Smithfield markets and select an appropriately mixed herd for Jimmy.

Anthony had risen from the muck-out boy as a lad of six to, at nearly seventy, he was the go-to man if you needed to know anything about any stock or knowledge of how Sam's estate was run. He was some sixteen years older than Sam and the only person at home who'd befriended him as a boy. Anthony was the only staff member Sam had kept on when he inherited the title. He was far more than just staff; he was a friend of both Sam and his father, Lord James.

The three men headed to London three weeks after their arrival home from Pittford Manor. As they departed, another wagon followed them out the gates. Sam's next set of workers headed to Jimmy's house contained a thatcher and his family. With most of the thatching now complete by Angus Hebblewhite, the new man's job was to keep the buildings in good repair. They were a small but select group of workers. The three wives on the other two wagons were all literate and would eventually take over Amelia's teaching. Their three husbands were all victims of the same fire and were severely burned. All were friends, and Sam knew that they would work well together. They were chosen people who were all stock lovers. A fire had been in a hay barn where they were all working. The fire had taken hold, and rather than let the stud horses die, these men risked their lives to save them. All were so severely burned that all shunned them but each other and their wives. Sam took on the entire group, presuming that they would be with him forever. Now, he'd found them the perfect home. Here, they would all have a home forever. Their faces were so severely burned that when in public, they each wore full-face covers. Sam was not sure how they even lived. Their faces had just melted, much like Perry's, and in the same way. He, too, had been caught in a fire.

With staff now awaiting animals to work on, Sam set forth to supply such beasts. Instead of going to Tattersalls for the horses, all the livestock were purchased at Smithfield markets. They also visited the knackery; they were given some scrawny beasts from there. Anthony and Tim led Sam through the markets. They had intentionally chosen the worst animals and ones that no one else wanted, commonly known as Welsh runts. All were bought for only shillings each, some even less. The mixed herd of cattle, horses, sheep, and some goats was more significant than they intended. All bought for less than £50. Included in this were over a dozen horses of various breeds: one plough horse, a riding nag, and others for multiple uses.

The group of Welsh drovers, who'd initially herded some stock from Wales, were employed to drove the stock to Jimmy's place in Kent, some thirty-eight miles from London.

Sam had also purchased a large wagon with a bench seat and a pair of sturdy, healthy horses to pull it. Sam would own this vehicle if Jim complained, but he intended that it remain at the Manor for use there. On this sat assorted cane cages of poultry and two large cages with two nanny goats; both were expectant and docile enough to milk, and they were loaded on the back.

Anne and Sophie knew that the men planned to accompany the stock to Jimmy's and would be gone for over a week. In the end, it took ten days to buy and drove all the stock to Pittford Manor, settle them in and then return home after a few days' rest. The herd of cattle arrived first with the Welsh drovers. A hired cart was bringing up the rear of that as it carried the fodder drums for the stables. Some were full, and four were now empty, having been used on the trip. The stock would now have to survive on the field grasses until the hayloft was restocked next season.

Sam drove directly to the stables and handed the vehicle over to Albert. They prepared him for what was following. The look of excitement on his face was a delight. From tonight, the stables would be used again. The three stable hands were delighted and readied themselves for the new livestock.

The work done in the month that Sam and Tim had been away was astounding. Hopefully, Sam's instructions would have been thoroughly carried out and that the fencing was at least stock-proof.

Jimmy heard the carriage; however, when he looked out the front windows, nothing was there. He called out to Vince, "Did I just hear a carriage, Vince?"

"Yes, sir, the Earl. Sir Timothy and Anthony drove in. They went directly to the stables." Vince had been warned by Tim what was coming. He'd been making sure that jobs not on the chalkboard were completed in time.

Amelia, too, had heard the vehicle. Knowing what was to arrive, Robbie came and told her to dismiss the class and follow him. She was followed by all the children. A month ago, they would have run riot, but they walked in an orderly double line and followed her as she walked on Robbie's arm.

As they walked the long distance to the main entrance, Robbie explained, "I must warn you that you may have some talking to do to Jimmy." Rob knew that Jim may not like his father's plan, but it was a way of restocking with virtually no outlay. "Father and Sam have, if their plan has been followed, brought a herd of bedraggled animals to nurse back to good health, fatten and breed. These are often Welsh animals that they can't sell, brought over by drovers and sold cheaply. These could be horses, cattle, sheep and even occasionally goats. I'm itching to see what they could get. Father said the deal is to fatten and heal them, and Jimmy can keep the babies. Now, this is a dual purpose as the new men have to learn to tend stock. If they only have healthy animals, they will learn little."

"Oh, Robbie, do you think he'll accept them?" She was concerned knowing of the conversation she'd recently had with him about accepting charity.

"That's where we come in. Father is not giving these to him, not unless he's been given them himself. Sometimes, old horses are given away, especially by the knackery. But many still have a year or two in them."

By the time they made it to the front doors, the cattle were arriving. Perry had heard of their imminent arrival and ridden over to take a look. Anthony took his steed. Perry was just walking up the steps. Sam, Tim, and Jimmy stood watching the stock and the Welsh drovers. Robbie greeted his father, Perry and Sam. They stood watching the bedraggled mob as they trundled along the gravel driveway.

Jimmy stood chuckling. "I was going to complain, Sir Tim, until I saw what a dishevelled mob they are. Where did you get them?" Jimmy could not believe what he saw.

"Well, no one else wanted these. There are sheep and also what's on the second wagon. It's for here, too, as you'll need to get around. The second wagon and horses are a sort of gift, as are the poultry and goats. The rest of the stock is training material and part of the rehabilitation programme, although you can keep any of the progeny born," Sam said. "I was going to buy a bull until I realised you are not going to need a stud bull. Keep one of the male calves and use him as a breeder. Sell the mother, though. Some of the cows are a South Devon cross; their male calves should be docile. You can also milk the cows."

"But sir, I can't accept that; it must have cost you thousands of pounds. I know a horse alone costs about £50, and how many did you say there are?" Jimmy felt ill. If his pride was wounded before, it was now stomped on thoroughly.

"I told you, they are not yours, Jim. Well, that's not quite right. The draught horse stallion has string-halt, and the riding nag was free from the knackery, so you can have them. The string-halt is mild, and with proper feed, like lots of yeast, the horse may be able to recover and then breed him. That leaves twelve others; the wagon horses were £12 for the pair, and I needed some good ones. There were ten that were skin and bones; The knackery rejected them. They'll need nursing back to health. The rest of the herd, cattle, horses, the sheep that are coming, oh, they will need shearing soon, so that's something else you can get the men to learn, and the poultry and two goats all cost less than £20 together. They almost paid me to take them off their hands. Many of the sheep were so thin, they did actually did a 'buy one, get one free', so half of the flock are yours already," Sam said. He was standing with his arms folded, watching the entry of the sick-looking beasts. Sam chuckled to Tim. "I've personally never been much an animal person, but even I can tell that this mob was a sorry bunch of air suckers such as I've not seen since West's farm during the drought in New South Wales, where I served my seven years." Sam then said to Jim, "You'll have your hands full keeping them alive. It's taken us four days to get them thirty-eight miles from London. We lost one on the way; it dropped dead overnight. I hope the rest pull through. Some are even due to drop their offspring; I've no idea how far along, but they will test the metal of the trainees. If they can heal this mob, they'll be earning their keep." Sam took a glance at Jimmy. He saw the confusion on his face. "Jim, this is part of the men's training. They need to learn how to handle sick animals. You had none at all. If this works and we sell at a good price, then we've made our money back. If not, well, they will have learnt a lot. If it does work and you can get some young from it, then build up your own herd and start making some money. There are a few odd dairy cows among them; they'll need bringing into the kitchen yard for milking. One of the girls, Maywyn, I think her name is, used to be a dairymaid, so she knows her way around a dairy. Start making some of your own cheeses, butter and things like that."

"How can I ever thank you, sir? You've done so much more than put me on my feet." Jimmy was getting a tad upset.

"Jim, spit that pride out, will you." Sam said, "These are a cheap means to an end. You're repaying by working and supplying a roof over their heads. You are the missing link in our programme. A way we can help many, many more neglected men. Thankfully, we've had few conflicts of late, but more will come, and more wounded will need long-term rehabilitation. Jim, this way, they can all heal together."

Jimmy couldn't answer. He followed the men down to meet the Welsh drovers, Dylan, Rhys, Alwyn, Glynn, and Huw. All were bright, cheery men and anxious to return home. They were stunned that this group of peers living in such a beautiful stately house would be interested in this woe-begotten lot of animals. Then, the burnt stable hands came out to thank Sam. The Welshmen's chins dropped. They had heard about the injured workmen; now they saw it was true.

Sam gave the Welshmen directions to bring the next bedraggled herd directly here. Jim saw Sam hand them the £15 for these animals. As they had a herd of thirty more cows that were too ill to bring, they rubbed their hands with glee. Once the flock of sheep arrived, they would all leave together, returning soon with what stock survived the trip.

As they walked down the front driveway, the wagon slowly trundled in. Another Welshman named Edwin sat on the driver's seat. He greeted Tim and asked where he was to take the wagon. Tim turned and looked at Jimmy enquiringly.

"Oh, the kitchen garden, I suppose. Hang on, and I'll come with you." He hopped up beside the Welshman and directed him around to the back of the building. As he drove, he turned to see what was in the back.

Edwin said, "Sorry I was a bit late, sir. One of the goats dropped her bundle, as you can see, or should I say, bundles. Giving birth to twins in a cage can't be too easy, but they is big cages, and she seems no worse for wear. Got yer money's worth with that one. Three for one," he chortled. "I think the t'other one's not far behind her. And she was the bigger of the two. She might even drop triplets; who knows? As some dairy cows is coming, you may need to feed one kid by hand if she drops triplets. Goats only has two 'what's it's' you know, sir. They can feed three, but one has to wait, and they doesn't always do too good."

Jimmy learned more about goats in that five-minute ride than he'd ever known in his life. He hopped off the wagons and instructed some of the men nearby to unload the crates and deal with them as they saw fit. "Just make sure the goats can't get into the kitchen gardens." He knew they ate everything.

Edwin suggested that if there was a place that needed weeding with walls, that would be the best for the goats. "Them is escape artists, sir; them beasties can find their way out of a locked box."

"I'll fix 'em, sir," one of the men named Jonas said. "I knows goaties and will deal with 'em." Thus sorted, Jimmy left them all to it and took a shortcut through the house to meet up with Perry, Sam, and Tim again.

"I've just realised the fences were never on the list. They are not…" Jimmy saw their smiling faces. "Don't tell me; you told the men anyway, didn't you?"

The older gentleman nodded. Sam said, "I told you we sent the necessary men. Tim told me the state of the fences when he first came. They started on them before you arrived. I had actually sent along with a crew of three as soon as you came that first time. They stayed at the inn in town, so Vince didn't even know about them. They just got on with the job and then returned. They fixed the perimeter ones, and the rest of the men who came down later did the internal ones." Sam grinned, pleased that his plan had worked. "Leave off, Jim. Can't have my plan work if I can't restrain my own stock."

Jim had nothing to say, but he gave Sam a huge grin. The stock was sorted into dairy and meat, and the ones who needed more care than the others were kept closer. Jimmy saw that they were in good hands with their new carers and left Thomas to get on with their work. Perry couldn't stay, so said his farewells.

Sam and Tim waited until the flock of sheep arrived. They took two more days. Some had dropped lambs on the walk, and some had even had twins. Many were in poor condition. As well as being expectant, their walk had, by necessity, had been slow. The flock had increased by ten en route. Two sets of twins and six singles, more were to come.

The two drovers accompanying them with their working sheepdogs greeted them smilingly. "Sorry, sir, lost one en route but arrived with ten new ones, so in all, not a bad walk."

Sam paid them their dues, thanked them profusely and pointed them to their friends. They were offered beds in the loft if they wished. They were used to sleeping rough and said their thanks and, without further ado, departed. Jimmy insisted that they at least have some provision for their journey. This they accepted, and all went via the kitchen to see what the cook could spare.

Sam and Tim said they would stay a night or two to help settle in the stock; then they, too, had responsibilities at home.

All the while, Amelia and Robbie had stayed back. Neither had a chance to talk to Jimmy since the first of the stock arrived. Amelia saw the office door closed one morning and gently knocked.

"It's open," came the reply, so she entered.

"Jim? It's only me," Amelia said as she entered.

"Oh, Milla, there is nothing 'only' about you. You are so very special." He held his arms out to her. She walked into them.

"Jimmy, how are you coping? I'm serious. To have all this thrown on you, I know it must be galling," she said, quite concerned for him.

"It was, but Milla, as I said before, I was so down because of my pride that I'd forgotten to trust God. Both Sam and Tim said I don't own the majority of the herd, only the babies born here or on the way here. They didn't have to pay for them, so they are the beginning of my own herd. I shall swap or breed from them and build up from scratch." The sound of his voice was no longer the melancholy one where he had no hope. She could hear a spark come back.

"Jim, if we now have a dairy herd, Maywyn can make cheeses, and we can bring the dairy back to life, too." She pulled back in her brother's arms. "What do you think?"

"I think we're too slow. She's already doing it." He bent and kissed her on her forehand. "Milla, I'm not a good farmer; I need someone who knows what they are doing. Father never taught me anything. He was always too drunk. I'll pay for one when we get some money to employ a real steward for the estate, someone who actually knows how to run things. I have no idea how to find one, though. Tim or Sam, again, I suppose." She was still standing in her brother's arms when another knock came.

Robbie came in without waiting. "Hello, you two. I hoped I'd find you together. Just as well, he's your brother and my bestie. Or I might get jealous," he smiled, not at all jealous. "I've just been talking with one of the burned lads, the newest lot that Sam sent up. His papa has been laid off from the farm he's been on for twenty years; he was wondering if you could use him here. He could pull his weight; he might even be able to assist, as he was the estate manager for the Marquis he was working for." He noticed the strange look the siblings gave each other.

"Well, Jim, God can work quickly; how's that for speed?" Amelia said, grinning at her husband as he walked to her and bent to kiss her.

"It could have been marginally quicker; I mean, he could have walked in while I was actually speaking," Jim smirked.

"What are you two talking about?" Robbie asked, confused.

"I have just finished swallowing the very last of my pride and saying I will have to employ an estate steward. I have no idea how to run a farm, Rob. Papa was so drunk that he never taught me. Not that I ever had any access to money, but if I'd had some knowledge, it might not have got this bad."

"It seems God does indeed know what we need before we even ask Him." He saw the peaceful smile settle on Jim's face. "As you'll be offering him free accommodation, you realise you won't even have to pay him for a while. If he stays on when you're sorted, then yes."

Amelia giggled. "God has that covered too, Jim."

"Oh, all right, that is this fellow's name? He can come; I have no problems with that, but don't say anything to him about the job until I enquire into his background. And Robbie, I want you with me for that."

"Fair enough, but don't laugh when you hear the poor chap's name; it's Cuthbert Mainwaring. He'll fit right in, as he's also somewhat disabled now. It was why he was laid off. His son said something about a broken leg that didn't heal properly. He now has a major limp."

"Good, so he'll fit in well with this motley crew." Jimmy was chuckling. "I'm beginning to enjoy this, Milla. I feel like I'm fleece throwing like Gideon in the Bible, though."

"No, you're not, Jim. Gideon tested God; you are trusting God. He's just better at knowing what you need than you are yourself."

The next three months flew past too soon. At six months with child, Amelia said her farewells to Jimmy. He promised he'd come to visit soon. Cuthbert had proven a treasure and worked with Jimmy sorting the estate out. His son Albert was offered the job as assistant estate manager but refused, staying with his horses instead. He did, however, say that he'd always been able to be his father's legs when required. Jimmy worked out why the poor man had been sacked; he could hardly walk. His son was so severely maimed with facial burns that Jim knew he'd never leave, so together, they made one brilliant estate manager. Cuthbert also decided to train Albert to take over the running of the entire estate.

A month after Robbie, Amelia, and Essie left for Broome Hall Manor for the birth, Jimmy followed. However, it was not specifically to see Milla. His goal was much more tantalising. Robbie's younger sister, Alexe, had caught his eye at their wedding. He'd known her for many years, but being aware of his situation at home, he had gazed in adoration from afar. At Robbie and Amelia's wedding, he'd seen her watching him. As this time he'd be staying with Robbie, he would try to find out if she was taken. Financially, he was still in a very delicate situation; he had £4 to his name. He thought that he'd have a chat with Robbie before he said anything. He decided that he'd stay at least until the child was born and then maybe a week or two later. He'd not make any rash decisions. He still had no income, but there was still that light at the end of the tunnel. Only this time, it wasn't a steam locomotive.

Robbie and Jim also had the plan to bring Mother home. They had delayed, as they thought it better to have everything back to normal before she arrived. Jim felt that they were nearly at this stage.

Chapter 17˙ New Life

Once ensconced at Broome-Hall Manor, Jimmy said he had some visits to make while in the area. One was to his mother. Tim offered Robbie a gig and a lovely high-stepping roan mare. He took it more as a treat to himself than a need. His arrival at Bedlam Hospital caused no little fuss. It seemed that Lady Caroline Pittford no longer wished to be in residence. He could hear her voice as he walked along the corridor to her room. It was certainly not the sleepy voice he'd heard the last few visits to her.

Caroline said loudly, "I need to get out; she needs me; where's Jimmy? Where's Horace? No, on second thoughts, I don't want Horace. Contact Jimmy for me."

Jimmy had not heard more than a few words from her in nearly ten years. To hear her thus was a good sign.

His arrival at her door took in a scene of utter chaos. Her possessions were strewn around the room as if she were packing. A large carpet bag lay on her bed, and as she stuffed things in, a maid pulled them out again. Lady Caroline's eyes lifted, and she saw her son standing in the doorway.

"Jimmy-lad, good boy, these silly people won't let me get to Milla. She needs me, and I want to see her." She grabbed him just below the shoulders and was staring into his face. "She's back, isn't she?"

Jimmy nodded. "Yes, Mother, she is, but how did you know? She's well and happy, and yes, she needs you. Are you up to leaving then?" he asked as he smiled at her. This was his mother, whom he knew when he was a child. Thoroughly determined.

His mother hugged him, "Yes, oh yes, Jimmy boy. I've been praying for you both all this time. My mind is still somewhat fuzzy, but I've not been drinking that vile potion they've been feeding me most days; I wait until they are gone and pour it out. Since then, I've been much clearer. Jimmy, take me home."

Jimmy dismissed the maid and told her to bring a case for Her Ladyship's clothing and to get Matron as he was taking his mother home. "Her Ladyship will be checking out. Permanently!" He turned to his mother. "I'll take you out, but not to home, but not directly; we'll see Milla first. How do you feel about being a grandmother? She has one already and is due to have another."

The delighted smile that spread across his mother's face soothed him greatly. No, this was not some fleeting clarity; she was healed.

"She's married?" his mother gasped.

"Yes, for the second time. But don't ask about Milla's first marriage yet. I'll tell you everything on the way, but accept that she is well and happy. She has married Robbie."

"What? Your friend Robbie? Robbie Styles? How? She's in… where is she? The last time I saw her, she was being arrested." She was full of questions.

"Mother, wait until we're underway, and I'll tell you all. There are too many ears here," Jimmy said.

Caroline assisted with the packing, and soon, they were on the way. Thankfully, it was a beautiful August day, as travelling forty miles in a gig was not normal.

Jimmy got the giggles when, outside of London, his mother told him, "Spring 'em, lad."

If he'd been in a phaeton, it would have made more sense. However, he flicked the reins, and the mare quickened her pace. He turned and checked her trunk and bag were firmly attached and kept the mare at a trot for as long as he could.

Lady Caroline relished the speed. She had not really been outside for more than a gentle walk for nearly ten years. She flung her arms above her head and, laughing, shouted, "Weeeeeeee," as they trotted along. Jimmy chuckled. He remembered her doing this when he was a child. She loved the speed and, in a very un-ladylike manner, then threw her head back and gave a heart-warming belly laugh.

After some miles, she said, "I'm free. Jimmy, and I'm me again. I woke two weeks ago, and I felt that I was not to drink the warm milk they brought me each morning. It tasted disgusting anyway, like smelly shoes. But they would stand there until I drank it. I would start feeling fuzzy, and then all I'd want to do is sleep. I couldn't focus, and I'd have a headache. So, I stopped drinking it. For the first time in a long time, I could remember things. So I started praying again; the last two weeks, I've been so clear. I even remember the day they took her. How long ago was it, pet?" She looked at the flash of angst on his face. "Tell me, Jim. I need to know before I see her."

Jim did, spending the next three hours filling her in about the past ten years. His mother wept bitter tears of regret, sorrow, and remorse about what Amelia had to cope with and then about Robbie. "I always loved that lad. I loved it when the four of you were home at once. I also loved Neddie. What happened to him?"

"He enlisted and moved to Australia; he's been watching over Amelia for us. He's the one who sent her home." He turned to look at his mother's face.

"And Gerry? What happened to him?" she asked.

"I heard he married Emily someone; she died in childbirth, and then I lost contact with him. Have not heard for over a decade." Jim felt guilty he'd not followed up with his friend.

"So Neddie sent her home, eh? Trust him. I'm surprised he didn't marry her himself. Another lovely lad, that one! Not so keen on his eldest brother. Daniel? No, David! A bit toffy-nosed that one. Too full of his own importance."

Jim smiled, agreeing, but remained silent. If Amelia wished to go into more detail, she could. It was enough that her mother was being returned to her in full sane mind. It had never occurred to Jimmy she was being drugged. "I bet it was Valerian," he thought to himself.

The remainder of the trip to Broome-Hall Manor was accomplished with much laughter. Jimmy told her about the restoration of Pittford Manor and that it was now officially a halfway house, training disabled people for useful work.

Lady Caroline smiled and nodded. "Jim, that's even a better use than a school."

"Oh, that's still going too. Milla started teaching when she fell with child; Robbie would not let her do any cleaning, so she took control of the children. It made the work proceed much quicker, too. Robbie brought her home six weeks ago, and she's due to deliver your second grandchild in a couple of weeks."

"I can't wait to see it all, son. Did you notice I've not asked about your father? I'm just not interested," she said. "He had his chance, and I hope they keep him locked up for a long time. I won't talk about him any more, son. Except to ask if he's still alive?"

"Yes, he was last time I heard. And still locked up."

Lady Caroline nodded, content. Then she sat back and enjoyed the passing scenery.

Jimmy turned the gig in through the large iron gates and past the stone gatehouses, over the bridge and down the sweeping driveway to Broome-Hall Manor.

"Oh, Jimmy, this is nice. This is Robbie's home? He was such a nice boy; is he still so? Is he good enough for our Milla?"

"Yes, Mama, he's all that and more," Jim said simply. They were drawing up to the front door. A groom took the reins.

Lady Caroline was assisted down from the gig by Jimmy. "Oh, Mama, you have lost so much weight; you're as light as a feather."

"Nothing time won't fix, son." She took his arm and walked inside with him.

Jim was wondering where exactly to take her when Sophie and Robbie came from different rooms. With a minimum of fuss, Jim explained the situation. Sophie greeted her warmly and told her she was welcome.

Robbie welcomed her and ushered her into the drawing room. He'd just taken Amelia in there as it was lovely and sunny. He motioned for Jimmy to follow him. He opened the door, and Amelia turned when she saw who stood there. It was as if she'd turned to stone. "Mother? Mama, is that really you?" Amelia moved as fast as she could and soon was embracing her mother. It was many years since her arrest. So much had changed; none of it mattered; they were together again.

Robbie was just about to leave them alone when Amelia called to him. "Robbie, please stay; you are now part of us. We are all family."

He came to her side and walked her to the settee. Jim took his mother's arm and sat her beside Amelia.

Over the next hour, much that had confused everyone was made clear. With the drugs out of Lady Caroline's system, she remembered the incidents of that day with great clarity. It was her last clear day. She confirmed that her husband had indeed stolen the gold bracelet and pawned it. They had had a blazing row, and before she knew it, the constabulary had arrived. The bracelet had brought a mere fraction of the amount he needed to pay off the latest gambling debt. Everything else not entailed had already gone. At her instruction, Vince had hidden the remaining silverware and refused to tell his lordship. Then, before Lady Caroline knew what was happening, Amelia had been arrested. She had collapsed, and poor Jimmy had been left alone in the house with a drunken father. Jim admitted that he tried to set the record straight for Amelia, but it was the duke's word against hers. Jim told her that more constables came the next day and arrested Horace for embezzlement of the Parliamentary Funds that he'd been supposed to be banking. Then, the duke foreclosed on the gambling debt to make sure he was locked up. Amelia had been almost overlooked by all but Jimmy, and he had no idea of what had happened. Now, it was all too late. The duke had recently died, Lord Horace Pittford was locked up, and Amelia now returned from the colony a free woman.

While Lady Caroline was talking to Robbie, Amelia asked Jimmy how much he'd told her.

"The bare minimum, none of the bad stuff. I didn't think she needed to know that just now. Time for that later," he said softly.

Amelia nodded in agreement.

Alexe, Sophie, and Tim came and told Lady Caroline that a room had been readied for her for as long as she needed it.

Jim introduced them all.

Alexe blushed each time Jim caught her eye.

He'd not said anything to either her or her parents; Jim knew that soon he'd have to talk to Sir Timothy. He so wished to court her, but his suit was not that promising, with lack of prospects and no funds. He knew that to have any chance, he had to prove himself worthy. He'd not done that yet. Alexe was his ideal woman; she was everything he admired. At twenty-four, she was also considered on the shelf. This gave him hope that there was a slight possibility to consider his circumstances. Now, however, was not the time to ask. He'd just arrived unannounced with his uninvited mother directly from a lunatic hospital. No, now was not the time to ask.

The seven sat around the drawing room chatting about the weather and other topics, avoiding the one they all wished to ask.

After the tea tray was brought in, Jimmy broached the subject bluntly. "They drugged her, you know. The stupid people at the hospital have had Mother on a twice-daily dose of strong Valerian or something similar. No wonder she was in a mind-numbing stupor. Once she stopped taking it a few weeks ago, her mind cleared." He got up and was pacing the room. "Why didn't I not check earlier? Why didn't I do anything before?"

"Jim, come and sit. Beating yourself up is not going to help anyone. Your house was in no fit state anyway, so move on." Tim was just as blunt. "You can't change the past; we can all change the future. Jim, quite honestly, you could not have looked after her. You could not have cared for any more than you did. So now we move on, all together, do you understand?"

Jim ignored him, trying hard not to hear.

Tim said again, "Jim, I said, do you understand?"

Jim nodded reluctantly.

"The past is just that: gone. Now, we work to change the end. Your mother can stay here for a while until she, too, is back on her feet. If she were to go home now, well, she'd want to be doing things there. Let her heal. I'm sorry, Lady Caroline, but things at your home are still in some need. We'll tell you all about it later, but you will be here with Amelia and Robbie in the meantime. I have a feeling they will wish to return when the baby is born, though. Even Alexe has said she wanted to assist, but that is down the track."

With Tim's last comment, Jimmy's eyes flew to Alexe's, "You wish to come and help?"

She blushed and nodded. "At least there I can be useful. Here I sit and twiddle my fingers, embroidering, and I'm totally useless. If the new staff can learn things, so can I."

"Sir?" Jim left the unvoiced question with just that one word.

"If she wishes to return with you all, then that is her prerogative. Your mother and sister will be ample chaperones." Tim grinned and lay back in his chair. He'd watched the two eyeing each other off for some weeks, and if that were the way the wind blew, he'd welcome Jimmy as a son-in-law. Broke though he may be, he was a hard worker. What was more important, his faith was growing again. Alexe had never given her heart before. Her interest in the work being done had always assisted where she could. It usually involved helping out with the children.

Jimmy's face said all that was required at the moment. He couldn't wipe the smile from his mouth. His heart was racing, too. Now, he'd have to speak to Sir Timothy. He could not live in his home with her unless he had some sort of understanding.

Lady Caroline was shown to her room. She was left to settle in, and a maid was allocated to assist her.

Amelia asked Robbie to escort her to their room. Emotionally exhausted, she wished to rest.

Robbie would not even leave her alone to rest. He removed his coat and shoes and lay down next to her. She snuggled into him, and they chatted for a while until her deep, rhythmic breathing told him she was asleep. He lay with her in his arms. A year ago, he could not imagine she'd be here with him like this. All his wildest dreams had come true. Now, her mother was well and in sound mind. Robbie lay with his sleeping wife cradled to his chest. His mind thinking over the past ten months since his marriage. The only thing now was to persuade Jimmy that Alexe loved him just as he was. He'd seen the joy on Jimmy's face when he heard she was coming with them.

~

Surprisingly, Amelia breezed through the confinement. Towards the beginning of August, she was very sick of being large. She waddled as she walked, and her backache was constant. She could no longer stand up without assistance. Robbie was like her shadow; he was with her constantly and mothering her.

Her mother had been with them for six days when Robbie noticed that Amelia was holding her back as she walked. Robbie lay in bed watching her walk around the room. "What's wrong, love? Did you hurt your back?"

"Oh, I'm so glad you're awake because I think it's time." Her back pain was getting worse. She remembered Martha just before she went into labour saying, that Jack had to get Maureen as she was having back pains. With Essie, she did the same, and then when the pains really started, she knew about it.

He stretched. "Time for what, love?"

Amelia smiled, "Time that you became a father, in reality, love. It's time that this child is born." As she said the final words, the first of the severe contractions hit. She groaned in pain. Martha had taught her to breathe through them and lean on something. "Robbie, you'd better get dressed before you leave the room. You're still naked. Please don't shock Mother any more than she has been."

"Cripes!" He had jumped out of bed and come to her aide when she'd groaned with pain. "I'll go... um, where do I go? Milla, what do I need to do?" The panic on his face was almost laughable.

The contraction was passing. "Darling, this is going to take hours. Please come here." He walked to her, all his glorious body showing through the open dressing gown he had tugged on. She gently took his face in her hands. "Robbie, sweetheart, first you need to dress. As I said, this will take hours. As I asked you before, I want you with me. I don't care what they say; you got me into this; we'll see it through together."

He nodded. "Um, yes, okay. If you insist." Sweat beaded on his forehead in fear.

"I do. Now dress in comfortable clothing and loose-fitting trousers. You'll find out why after about six hours... and no shoes." She knew her waters had not yet broken; when they did, she also knew things would speed up.

There was a knock at the door; Robbie closed his dressing gown. The maid, Netta, was bringing her morning chocolate.

"Netta, could you please ask Lady Sophie to come when she can please?" Amelia asked.

Netta had just closed the door when another contraction hit.

Robbie heard her groaning and returned to her, hopping with one sock on. "Love, what can I do?"

"Rob, I need to be able to lean on you later. Then you will be sitting on that chair, and I will be squatting for the birth with you holding me up; I'll be leaning on your knees. Just trust me; it's far easier this way. Essie would not budge. I'd been in labour with her for hours, and finally, Maureen and Martha had Jack hold me. Don't worry, love, I was fully covered. Only the ladies saw anything. Jack had his eyes closed anyway, or else he'd get sick. He'd held Martha this way for each of her six births. They were old hands at it; it's the way the local aboriginal women birth, squatting. It's far easier for everyone but the midwife."

Sophie arrived within minutes. "I didn't think you were far off delivering. I noticed the babe had dropped."

Sophie went to send Robbie out when Amelia put her foot down. "He's staying. I'm going to need him."

Sophie tried to argue.

"He stays, or I go outside to deliver." Amelia was adamant.

Robbie and Amelia had already discussed this, and she was worried he'd renege at the last hurdle. "Rob, I need you." She knew that she did, and this would cast the die in their favour.

"Mother, if she wants me here, nothing will move me. We've discussed this. I'm staying, scared stiff, but staying." He was sheet white.

"Rob, I'm the one with the pain. You just have to hold me. From where you'll be sitting, you will not really see anything. However, you will appreciate what we go through." She chuckled.

Sophie departed the get the doctor, midwife, and other required persons to assist. Amelia was leaning on Robbie through the contractions, which were now only fifteen minutes apart. They were slowly getting stronger. She'd shown him how to rub her lower back as Maureen had done. It eased the pain incredibly. Hot towels were also placed on her back and stomach at various times.

Sophie, having had six children herself, knew that the delivery would probably take hours. However, she still dressed quickly and sent word for the doctor and midwife to arrive as soon as possible. Lady Caroline was also informed. She, too, had dressed and gone to help if she could.

Five hours after the start of her labour, Amelia was being held up by Robbie. He was sitting in a leather chair with his arms wrapped around her. She was being supported by him yet could both brace against him and lean on his legs. Timothy Robert James Styles was born at 2:02 p.m. on 11th August. Robbie had a son and heir to the Barony. Sir Timothy was over the moon that he had a grandson and heir as well as one named after him. Her mother had stayed with her, as had Sophie. They had been amazed at how easy and quick the delivery was. However, the midwife and doctor were not impressed. Both had to sit on the floor to catch the child. Both did acknowledge that it did seem quicker and easier on the mother.

Amelia bounced back from Timo's birth quickly. At thirty-two, she should be feeling weak and wan, but she wasn't. She was up and down stairs three days later, horrifying everyone but Robbie.

He knew her strength, and although in awe at what he'd experienced, he knew she would have said if she wasn't up to it. "She's a big girl. If she's feeling fine, then why should she be confined to her room?"

Timo was a wonderful baby. He slept through from the end of the first week until he was four months old and started teething. When that started, Amelia gave him the toast crusts to chew on. That, too, horrified Robbie's parents. She would leave them until they were hard and stale, and he'd happily gnaw on them until his mouth was covered in ooze. His first two teeth caused some pain for her as he kept biting her. The finger taps on his cheek, and he'd grin and try it again. It took nearly a week before he stopped biting. And only because she wouldn't put him back on the breast after he drew blood. Finally, he got the idea and stopped biting her.

~

Jimmy returned home after a month. Ostensibly to prepare for his mother's return, but also for the visitors. Amelia insisted that she was well enough to travel and refused the retinue of staff to assist her with one small baby. Essie was a tremendous help. She loved her little brother and cooed over him constantly; Timo was her baby.

Lady Caroline was determined to go home. Six weeks after Timo's birth and two weeks after Jimmy had left, two travelling carriages departed for Aylesford: Lady Caroline, Essie, Robbie, Amelia, and the baby in the first carriage, and Tim, Sophie, and Alexe in the second one.

Sir Tim had finally spoken to Jimmy about Alexe. He'd given his permission for Jimmy to court her if he wished. Alexe apparently had refused every other man who'd looked at her. Tim already loved Jimmy as a son and knew that he would make a wonderful husband for her. Yet Jim had departed without speaking to Alexe.

On arrival, Jimmy welcomed them all. However, it was Alexe's arm he drew through his as they entered the refurbished foyer. The entire house had been spring-cleaned in his absence, and all the rooms were once again readied for visitors.

Lady Caroline's suite was also repainted, and one of the new ladies had painted peony roses on the soft green walls of her room. The effect was a delight to her. Her old life had been completely washed away.

Tim said he could only stay a week; however, they finally departed two weeks later. Alexe had begged him to have a quiet word to Jim. Tim gave Jim a verbal nudge, and Jimmy had finally declared himself to Alexe, and they were officially courting.

Lady Caroline said she'd watch them like a hawk, and she did. Alexe was never allowed to be alone with Jimmy. He never overstepped his self-made boundary of honouring his beloved. He felt she was far above him in every way but title. But you can't eat a title.

Jim and Sir Tim had discussed an engagement, but Jimmy wanted to have some form of income coming in before he even considered it. If Alexe would wait, he wished to have things more settled. Tim wondered if they should mention the £ 3,000 dowry that Alexe would bring to the relationship but knew that wouldn't change things. He wouldn't touch her money.

Sir Tim decided to let Jimmy have his own way. He wasn't ready; no use forcing his hand.

~

It took until just before Timo's first birthday for Jimmy to feel things were settled enough for him to have a wife. He took Alexe for a walk in the evening gloaming and asked the long-awaited question.

Lady Caroline had told him to stay within sight all the time. He had. She saw him drop to one knee in the rose arbour, and moments later, Alexe was in his arms. "So, I'd say that's a *yes*," she said almost to herself.

"What is, Mama?" Amelia asked.

Lady Caroline beckoned her over. "That is, look." She pointed to Alexe being thoroughly kissed by her brother.

"Ohh! Well, that's about time. It must have been because she said she would leave to go home next week. Stirred him along a little. I wonder if she'll still leave?" Amelia chuckled. "Sir Tim and Sophie are coming for baby Timo's birthday on Wednesday. She was going home with them."

Alexe stayed for two more months, only leaving because the wedding needed to be planned. She wanted no fuss, just family. Even that meant that all of Meldon Hall, Lord James' Ducal abode of Malvern Hall, Broome-Hall Manor, Sam's cousin Charles Garney's household from Oakwood Park and, of course, anyone from Pittford Manor who wished to make the trip. She refused to have a sit-down banquet. Instead, she wanted to join the staff at the party in the barn. She said the money could be put to much better use. Her father agreed, so a staff barn dance was arranged, and as the evening was perfect, much of it overflowed to outside.

~

One year, then two passed.

Finally, Jimmy's stock was breeding, and he had enough to sell. The goats had bred to such an extent that they went first. They had, however, cleared the grazing lands of the weeds, so they had served their purpose, and they could already buy more. The stock on the farm at Pittford Manor steadily increased. His bull was now a wonderful sire, and Jimmy's first sale had been the new bull's mother.

The school was now open for paying attendees. All the staff and their children were guaranteed an education while in residence. The possibility of a free education overtook the desire to earn a wage. Here, the adults would not be ridiculed due to looks or disabilities. Even though all could do brilliant work, the looks they received made them feel repugnant to others. If their children could work in a paid job later, it would bring in much more income for their families.

Sam still insisted that if they could work and were offered a position, they must take them. If that position didn't work out, they could come back to either property, but after being fooled by one man, they decided they could not go back into the same work they had previously trained in. They would have to start from scratch, and in a new field and not one they chose. This ensured that not only did they try hard in their new positions but that the desire to return had to be genuine.

Jimmy and Alexe welcomed Robert James Westaweller into the world on their first wedding anniversary.

A week later, news arrived that Viscount Horace Pittford had died in hospital three weeks before his proposed release date. Sad as it was, he was not much mourned. His death meant that Jimmy now had the right to use the farm legally as he wished. A sheaf of paperwork was ready for collection from his solicitors, and with the birth of his son, Jim put off going to London straight away. Prior to this, the bankers had refused every petition to them.

Jimmy and Alexe had the house running like clockwork. He would not go into debt, *per se*, but asked for an advance, which was immediately granted. He required £100, and from that, he knew that by buying more of the ill Welsh stock, he could fatten and re-sell them for massive profit. The goats had done their work but had caused more trouble than they were worth.

Others in the area had heard he had goats and gave him more. Soon, a herd of some thirty and their young were devouring the estate's precious fodder. They had to go. They were now a fine herd, and again, many were expecting. The billy goat was one of the most cantankerous animals he'd ever worked with. The kids are not much better.

In the end, Jim returned the money to the bank as the Welsh farmers had brought one hundred thin and bedraggled beasts with them, and they swapped these cows for the goats as a clean swap. Jimmy was pleased to see the back of the goat herd and welcomed the new skinny beasts. There were probably better ways to do business, but one healthy cow sold in this situation would produce a good income.

~

Alexe delivered their second child, Alexandra Amelia, on 9th July 1840. She would be known as Lexi.

The farm was now almost self-sufficient. They swapped grains and fodder for produce with Sam's farm. It was not yet fully paying, but it was well on the way to doing so. Their honey and cheeses were becoming much sought-after commodities. They had gone into production with a range of them. Cuthbert, the Estate Manager, encouraged Jim to put a field under crop to try it out. He was stunned when the yield of this field was double what it should have been. The field now produced much of the fodder for the animals. Part of it was now also under grain crops. This, too, was producing well.

~

With Amelia's third child's coming and Robbie's second, Robbie finally said that Jimmy was now able to handle everything alone. He was moving his family home permanently, but they would still come for visits. Lady Caroline came with them. It was time for Alexe and Jimmy to forge their path alone. The parting was somewhat sad; however, they knew that the two pairs of siblings would always remain close. Lady Caroline asked if she could accompany them for the birth and spend a few months at each house, keeping in contact with both families.

Eliza Anne Caroline Styles was born at Broome-Hall Manor. Another dark-haired, blue-eyed baby. Essie, at nine and a half, claimed her the moment she saw her. "This one is all mine, Mama. My own sister. Oh, Mama, she's so beautiful." Eliza clung to Essie's finger. She was such a placid babe, rarely crying but rarely having the chance to, as there was always someone near her. Her older brother Timo was "free and a bit," as he told everyone. He was the apple of his father's eye. Rob still adored the company of his adopted daughter, too; their bond remained as strong as ever. Amelia insisted on continuing Essie's education herself. Her time hung heavily on her hands; teaching Essie filled much of this. Timo, too, was learning his letters, and soon, others in the household asked if their children could possibly join in.

Sir Timothy sat down with Amelia and asked if she was happy to take on some of the staff children along with their own. He'd already spoken to Robbie, and they had decided that it was a simple way of slowly changing their own estate for the better. Many of the old retainers had been with the house when he inherited it from his Uncle. Some had recently retired, and some still stayed. The new ones were bringing in families. Many were from Sam's pet project and had previously been soldiers, sailors, or rescues from hospitals. Some of Tim's existing staff had found working with the new ones awkward.

Amelia sorted this quite quickly one day when she announced that she'd teach the new children to read and write, as they had little chance of ever looking for work elsewhere. The other children had not made them welcome. She had seen so much hurt and pain in her short life that her compassion was stirred to assist where she could. When the existing staff thought that they would have their children excluded from learning, their attitude changed discernibly. Peace reigned again. Life settled, and the family grew. By 1842, Amelia had just realised she was expecting their third child in October; she had yet to tell Robbie. At thirty-eight, she was surprised she'd fallen with her fourth child.

In April, Amelia was teaching a class at Broome-Hall. Robbie interrupted one morning and waved the letter he brought with him. She set the children's writing and followed him outside.

"Robbie, what is it? Who's it from? You look so excited that you're ready to burst." She'd not seen that look since the birth of their son. Robbie had cut the cord that day and then been first to cuddle the newborn babe that he'd helped to deliver. He'd wiped an emotional tear from his eye, and Amelia smiled at the smile on his face. Today, his face showed his absolute happiness.

"You have to read this for yourself, Milla. Your prayers have been answered, but in far more ways than even you expected."

She took the letter and recognised the handwriting on the front. "Neddie, is it from him?"

Robbie nodded. "But wait until you read it." He stood and walked a few feet away, letting her read the screed in peace.

Since finding out what Ned had done for her, Robbie had been in regular contact with his childhood friend, who was still in Sydney. Initially, as a thank you, but he'd been delighted to reconnect with Ned. Jimmy, too, had written and kept him abreast with the "old news" from home. By the time it arrived there, it was already nearly six months out of date. "Robbie, he's the duke now. I did not hear that David had died. Did you know?"

"No, love, but keep reading." Robbie smiled.

Phillip Street,
Parramatta
19th December 1841

Robert and Amelia Styles
Broome-Hall Manor
Billingshurst England
Dearest Robbie and Amelia,

Thank you for your amusing letters. I always enjoy reading your 'old news.' I can't believe that you now have two children (Not including Essie, of course. – Uncle kisses to my poppet; I can't believe she's eleven). Milla, I send my brotherly love to you, too, no Rob, don't be jealous. Tell Essie that Uncle Neddie is coming home and that I promise to visit her (yes, and you all, too) as soon as I can. Also, thank her for her regular letters to me. I love the drawings she always does for me. However, I will not be coming alone. I am to be married next week on Christmas Day, just a mere six days away. To say I am excited is a vast understatement. Milla, thank you for all those beautiful prayers of yours. They worked.

I know you have been praying for a bride for me for many years. You told me so twice, at least, but back then, I wasn't sure this would ever happen. God actually sent her two years ago. She was also the reason I retired early – to be near her and surreptitiously care for her. However, I thought I would not be able to offer her anything and did not intend even to ask to walk out with her. Rob, our friend Gerry Winslow-Smythe's news that I'm now the Duke of Gracemere changed all this. David is dead and has no children. Father died five years ago, as you know, so now I'm the duke. The only reason that I'm happy about this is it allows me to marry my beloved. She is a queen amongst women.

Robbie, do you remember our various country jaunts? Gerry, Jim, you and I went on one to Tunbridge Wells? Do you remember our run-in with the Earl of Riverdale? Christina Meadows is his daughter. I could wax lyrical about her; suffice to say, I adore her. She's one of the most beautiful women God ever made, but you would expect me to say that, wouldn't you? Milla's prayers are indeed answered.

Christina, too, was a widow and found herself in dire financial circumstances. She had no children, but if she had, that would not have stopped me. We will not book our passage until we are married, as we're keeping our new identities under wraps for as long as possible. (She had not admitted to anyone she was an Earl's daughter. She's just been here under the name of Mrs Meadows.) Milla will understand what it would be like here; if they found out either of us had a title, life here would be unbearable. Charles and Sal were the only ones who knew, although we have had to let the Minister and his wife know. Harry Moffatt is here too, of course, and has known since he arrived, but I swore him to secrecy. I've not yet told him I'm the duke. I dare say I will have to before I leave. Poor Sam Corbett Garney had a terrible time when news about him being an Earl leaked out. The Governor, George Gipps, has sadly already been informed about me. I dare say I will have to front up there and pay my dues as I should. Oh, how I hate that side of society. Why can't they just leave us alone? I'm the same person. Sometimes I wish to be that carefree child again, Robbie. I relished those carefree days at your place, Milla. We could be children and have no responsibilities. Sadly, my older brother often took that too far. I'm sad he had such an unfortunate marriage.

Milla, I wish to tell you that Jenna Turner married Eddie Lockley two weeks ago. So God has drawn another pair of threads together. Rob, it was Jenna's parents who rescued Amelia on that life-changing day. It was the beginning of your new life, Milla. I knew you were in very safe hands with them. Rob, she knows both families. Liza, Eddie's oldest sister, married Tim Miller last month so that family is another family now brought together by marriage. Milla, Molly and Bill send their regards and hugs, too. The community here is so tiny that many know each other well. It will be so exciting to see where this town heads. I shall certainly keep in contact with Charles Lockley after my return home. Milla, I shall also look into finding some answers about him too.

I shall send word when we're due to arrive. Rob, please give my goddaughter, Essie, a big hug from me and one for Milla too. To say I'm excited *is an understatement to see how she's grown.*

I am looking forward to seeing you all later this year. I'm sure you will adore my Christina as much as I do . . . and Milla - thank you!

God Bless

Ned, Gracemere

"Oh Robbie, Neddie is coming home, love, and he's getting married. Oh, Robbie, he'll be on his way by now. That was four months ago. Did you know the Earl of Riverdale? And is this Gerry, your friend, you know, the fourth of your group? Oh, I have so many questions, and I can't ask any of them now." She giggled excitedly. "I have to go back to class. Prepare yourself for an inquisition afterwards, sweetie."

As Robbie was as excited as she was, he looked forward to the discussion. He bent and gave her a long, deep kiss before she left him.

Amelia dismissed the class early as she had not been able to concentrate all afternoon. She was lightheaded with excitement. When she released the class, she kept Essie back. "Poppet, do you remember Uncle Neddie?"

"Yes, Mama, I do. I still write to him, but his face is fuzzy now. I remember he gave me my toys. Major still sits on my bed and guards my dreams. I remember his uniform and his light hair like sunshine, and I remember I loved him. Why Mama?" At eleven, she was heading to be a beautiful young lady. Her big blue eyes fringed with long dark lashes were still the most startling feature of her heart-shaped face. Her dark hair was in long natural ringlets and was tied up from the sides of her head to a graceful arrangement at the back and tied with an oversized blue bow.

"He's coming home, poppet, and what more, he's married, and also he's not just a major anymore, he's…" she paused and smiled to herself. "He's the Duke of Gracemere."

Amelia still found this hard to believe. She remembered David coming with Neddie. She didn't really like him all that much. Although only a year or so older than Ned, he seemed to like bossing people. Ned was always kind and gentle. David was authoritative and autocratic. When David once said something hurtful to a maid, Ned apologised on his behalf. The difference between them was vast.

Her eyes grew as big as saucers. "Uncle Neddie is a duke? Didn't he know before?"

"No poppet, as he had an older brother who has recently died. He had no idea. Do you remember visiting his Mama when we arrived back? It was when we first went to live with Uncle Jimmy. We saw the lovely lady who fed you strawberries. That was Uncle Neddie's Mama."

"Yes, I remember her, Mama. She was so sad that you wouldn't tell her more about him. I remember I gave her the big hug that Uncle Neddie told me to give her. She sat and cuddled me. I remember that. She was nice. She told me to call her Aunty Suze."

"Yes, she is lovely. Now that Uncle Ned is coming back, we might all go and revisit them. Papa would love to catch up. Anyway, I must go, poppet. Papa and I have to sort a few things out. Can you take Eliza to the nursery with the other children? Timo is with the boys in the chicken yard, so he should be fine."

"Sure, Mama, I'll watch them both." She gave her mother a kiss. "I love you, Mama. I just want you to know that." She threw both arms around her mother's neck and gave her a hug.

Amelia stood and watched her leave with little Eliza. She was about the same age Essie was when they lived in Sydney. So much had changed. As the door shut behind them, she turned to clean up the room. As she did so, the room started spinning. She grasped her stomach and collapsed. She hit her head on the table leg as she fell and blacked out.

~

Robbie knew that the children had been released, but Amelia did not appear. Knowing how keen she was to talk about the letter, he went in search of her. He bumped into Essie and Eliza, who told him that she'd left her in the classroom.

Robbie went straight there and was horrified to find Amelia on the floor, unresponsive and in a growing pool of blood. He went directly to the bell pull and rang it three times quickly, then returned to her side. "Milla, my darling Milla! Talk to me." He gently eased her into his lap and checked to see she was breathing. She was, thankfully. All he could do was wait. He did not want to just lift her too much in case she had hurt her neck. He held his clean handkerchief on her head wound to stop the bleeding.

The urgent three-pull summons had been heard, and moments later, feet came running from various directions. Sir Tim listened to the ruckus and running staff and followed. Finding his son sitting cradling Amelia, he arranged for a narrow door to be removed, and she was gently carried to their room. Robbie was holding her head still. "Father, she fell and hit her head. That's where all the blood is coming from. She hasn't moved, but she's breathing evenly."

Tim had everything organised in a matter of moments; someone had been despatched for the doctor, and four able-bodied men lifted the door. Robbie held her head still as they moved through the house. Tim opened the various doors until the convoy reached their room. Taking great care not to move her much, they eased her off the door and laid her on the bed. Robbie covered her with a quilt and sat beside her until the doctor came.

She didn't move or murmur. She was white as a sheet and still immobile. The oozing blood was dried in some patches. How long had she laid there? Minutes? By the time the doctor arrived, Robbie was reclining beside her. He'd not moved her but lay with his arm carefully caressing her cheek. "Milla darling, wake up; we need you, my darling love."

Sophie came and asked him to leave while the doctor saw her.

Robbie refused. "No, I will not leave her. I went through everything with her; I'll go through this too." He assisted in disrobing her by cutting off her clothing himself and carefully putting on her nightgown. The doctor was of little assistance. There was nothing he could do except bleed her. Robbie refused that, too, as she'd lost enough blood. Robbie ended up sending him out. All that afternoon and all the next day, Robbie kept his vigil. He sat beside her and had been reading. He read her favourite Psalms and was currently reading her the book of Luke; she could quote entire passages of that book. Her favourite verse was from Philippians 4:13 *I can do all things through Christ who strengthens me.*

It was a strange verse to be her favourite, but she claimed it as her own. She felt it was what God had called her to do. She relied on God for everything she told Robbie often that God was a brilliant crutch and He'd never let her down. Robbie now prayed that, once again, Jesus would not let them down.

Come night time, she finally gave a single whimper.

Robbie was instantly attentive. "Milla, darling one, open your eyes, love, don't leave me like this, sweetheart."

Her eyes were firmly shut, but he felt a flutter of pressure from her fingers. "Darling one, did you squeeze my fingers? Do it again." He felt the momentary pressure, then nothing. "Don't rush it, sweetheart. I need you to sleep, all right? Just sleep and heal." Again, the slight pressure, then her breathing eased into a deep rhythmic pace. Her head was cradled in a feather pillow as he still needed to stop her moving, just in case something had happened to her neck. He'd seen it before, and the person had not been able to move again. So he insisted that she be kept as rigid as possible. Her body was jammed into the bed with pillows, and he was on the other side of her. He'd dozed the night before, and he knew he needed to sleep now. At least she was able to respond.

Lady Caroline came and sat in their room for a while, never taking her eyes from her immobile daughter.

Rob didn't even know she had come in. He, too, slept a sleep of relief. He had changed his clothing but slept with his dressing gown on.

Sophie relieved Lady Caroline after a few hours, and then Sir Timothy, too, sat on guard should he be needed.

When morning came, Robbie awoke to Amelia's eyes open. "Robbie, thirsty!"

Robbie was instantly awake. "Don't move, love, don't even turn your head."

Sir Timothy left to find Sophie and Lady Caroline. They both bustled in moments later, both still in dressing gowns.

"Okay, why?" she asked weakly.

Caroline was by her side, too. "You had a fall and hit your head. You've been unresponsive for nearly two days," her mother said. "Robbie has not left your side for a moment, love."

"I heard him. He spoke to me, telling me to squeeze his hand." She did just that now. "Mother, it was like I was in a tunnel. Robbie was at one end calling me." She spoke in a dry, soft voice. "I need a drink."

"I'm coming, love; just trying to work out how you can drink lying down. You are not to try to move. Do you understand?"

"Yes, Rob, can you scratch my foot? It's itchy."

He scrambled out of bed and gently untucked the sheets so he could gently scratch her foot. "You can feel that?"

"Yes, it tickles." She smiled. "Rubber tube, some in the classroom. Why can't I move? What's wrong?"

Robbie felt like he'd been kicked in the guts; she couldn't move. "The doctor wants to make sure you have not hurt your neck. He'll be here soon, so you have to lie still until he comes, and I'll get someone to get the tube."

With his mother and mother-in-law staying with her, he ducked into their dressing room and quickly changed, used the privy and returned.

"Robbie, I think it was the baby. I fainted, that's all," she said to him so only he could hear.

"You're expecting? Oh, Milla, how far along?" The look of concern on his face just doubled.

"Only a little bit, love. Can I be that? Not really, I suppose; I'm either expecting or not, aren't I? Oh well, about eight weeks, I think, if that." She lifted her hand to her nose and scratched it.

"You can move your arms," he said, startled. "I thought you said you can't move?"

"No, Rob, I asked why can't I move? You told me to lie still. Is scratching not allowed either?" A tear rolled down her cheek.

"Oh no, love, it's wonderful. Absolutely blooming-well wonderful. I thought you meant you couldn't move." He buried his head in her neck and wept with relief.

She lifted her other hand and caressed his prickly cheek. "Silly, wonderful man, you told me not to move."

The doctor walked in to find them like this.

"She can move, doctor. Both hands and her foot are itchy." Robbie bent and kissed her.

"Then she's fortunate, lad." The doctor bustled around her, feeling her pulse in both arms, checking her eyes and listening to her heart.

Robbie explained their earlier communication breakdown and gave a mild chortle. "Doctor, she's also with child, about eight weeks along. She hadn't told me."

"Ahh, that explains the faint then. That's good! Now let me check her neck." The doctor gave her a thorough check-up all over. He tested her reflexes and also looked at the wound on her head.

"Ma'am, you are to stay in bed, if possible, for at least a week, if not longer. Any pain, and I mean any, pain at all, and you must call me. I don't mean where you hit your head; that should heal just fine. It quite honestly is the least of your worries. But if your neck hurts or your feet or hands tingle, you must let me know. If that occurs, you get back to bed and stay still. Do you understand?" He very gently checked the movement of her neck. He had his eyes closed and was concentrating as he ever so gently touched and pressed her neck. "You are a fortunate lady, if I may say so. Everything seems to work normally, but we won't really know until the swelling fully goes down. I'll check again tomorrow to make sure, bed rest for the week, though. Support your head at all times, even by wrapping a towel around it if you sit up or use a commode, do you understand?"

She was about to nod but remembered his instructions; she softly said, "Yes," instead.

When the doctor left, she waited for the door to close behind him. Sophie and Caroline left them alone for a while. The urgency of her situation had passed, so they went to get changed.

Robbie said he would stay with her for a while.

Amelia met Robbie's eyes; the look of love in them made her catch her breath. "Rob, I need to tell you something."

He came, and she motioned for him to lie down with her again. "Robbie, you called to me and told me to squeeze your hand, didn't you?"

"Yes, sweeting, why?" His head was on his hand as he rested on his elbow, gazing adoringly at her.

Tears were cascading down her cheeks. "I didn't want to come, Rob; I wanted to go to the white light. It was pure and Holy, Robbie, and was drawing me so close. I just wanted to be wrapped in that warmth. I was nearly there when I heard you calling me, telling me you needed me. I knew I would be safe with you, too, but it was so hard to make that decision. I couldn't hear exactly what you were saying, but I remember hearing the word 'squeeze', so I did it as hard as I could. Darling, the next bit is going to sound crazy."

"Go on, tell me." Rob's emotions crashed; he realised how close she had been to death.

"Jesus came and stood beside me. He told me it wasn't my time. I had to go back." A sob escaped her, and tears oozed down her pale cheeks. "Wasn't I good enough? Rob, that light was God's light. It was so inviting and not at all scary. I think I nearly died, Rob. I can't work out what else just happened." Another tear escaped. "Hold me, Robbie, I just need to be held."

Rob lay holding her. If he'd felt gutted before, it was nothing to how he felt now. He realised just how close he'd come to losing her. They quietly talked about her experience. Rob realised how sick she was and was aghast at her reluctance to return. Only her love for him had made that decision. He knew it had been touch and go, but not that it was that close. He felt ill, totally shattered. He gently gathered her in his arms, and together, they became lost in their own thoughts. Finally, they both dozed. She stayed in bed for two weeks. They worked out a way to wrap her neck so she could use a commode. He would not let her turn her head at all. He had even held her neck as she used the chamber pot. She cried each time with the indignity of it.

He chuckled. "It's no worse than you giving birth, love. Much less mess, actually, and no yelling."

Chapter 18 Starting Over

$\mathcal{A}$melia's recovery took time. She had continual headaches for some
weeks, but as her condition progressed, they became less frequent. Ned's
letter had been forgotten until another one arrived. The information was they
were leaving on the *Sarah Botsford* in early March and had them counting on
their fingers. They were due in June or July sometime. It was already late May.
The long-delayed conversation finally took place. Amelia had mentioned
Ned's assistance, but she finally filled Rob in on everything, including that
very final farewell kiss. It certainly was not brotherly, yet it was not lover-like.
It did, however, give her hope that she could respond without abhorrence to a
man's touch. It was the real beginning of her healing. Over the next few
months, as they'd lie in bed at night, they would talk about her time in
Australia. All the good things that had happened to her, working with two
Governors assisting at the Female Factory. Of her being in such a unique
position that they would listen to her. Then the day of her kidnap, looking
back, she really could not call it that, but yet it was. She'd been taken against
her will and held to ransom. She then thought of being assigned to the
Landons and finding all the fabric they donated to whoever needed it. Then,
of use it to make money for the Factory and to pay off the debt for the
Benevolent Society by getting the women themselves to sew and use many of
the exquisite bolts of fabric. The sale of one gown in particular nearly paid
off half the debt. This then gave the women the dignity to have their abilities
recognised.

"Rob, I can see God's hand in my involvement over there." She was
snuggled against Robbie as she spoke. "We now have three children; with this
one on the way, how can I help out any more?"

"I have no idea, love, but we'll watch for the opportunities God sends us. There will be doors for us that He's preparing." He did not want her worried, so he silenced her with a long and loving kiss.

The more she told him, the more she realised how vastly different her life could have turned out. "Rob, there are things I will not tell you at night. I don't want it playing on your mind as you go to sleep. But I will never intentionally keep things from you; sometimes, it just takes some time to get my head around things. Never be afraid to ask me, though. I want you to have no unanswered questions." She had never spoken in detail about those first horrific three months of her placement. He only knew what she'd written in that first letter. So, one afternoon rest time, she poured it all out. She told him everything. Had it really been such a short time? It had felt like an aeon whilst she lived through it. Then came Cyrus's death and Essie's life. She started to live again. She told Robbie of Martha, Jack, and the children. Of Maureen and Finn Murphy, who were happy living in a dirt hovel.

They, too, slept on a straw-filled sheet of canvas, but they were so lovely. The lack of money reflected little of a person's worth. Amelia had long since realised that poverty was not related to money but to attitude. She said, "Rob, you can have no possessions at all and still be rich." She knew as it had once been her own situation. She owned the dress she wore and her bible. It still sat on her bedside table, and it was used daily. She loved Maureen's simple faith. "God says, that's it, I believe it." It had kick-started her faith again. She'd become so busy with life. She knew she had to reply to Martha's letter. It said that Maureen and Finn now had nine children, and she was expecting another.

Each of Amelia's revelations made Robbie more and more protective of her. Her healing occurred as she released her story; it was liberating. Sharing it with him and holding nothing back brought them closer together. Robbie listened while holding her close and comforted her as she related the past. Together, they prayed and released the pain to God. Amelia finally found peace.

Eight weeks passed, and word finally came that Ned and Christina were home.

Gracemere Castle,
Maidstone England
18th July 1842

Mr and Mrs R J Styles
Broome-Hall Manor
Billingshurst England

Dearest Robbie and Amelia,

We're home. What a wonderful welcome we received. Thank you, dearest Amelia, for letting Mother know I was well. It was such a relief for her to find I was settled and happy. It was from your information that Gerry eventually set out to find me. All he knew was what you'd told Mother and that I was not using my real name, but I was still known as Ned. That much Gerry had ascertained before his departure. Why did he not ask you for more information? I have no idea. Especially after David died. Mother knew that you knew where I was.

As I mentioned in my last long letter, I am now married. That was in itself enough of a surprise for me; however, we believe we're having twins. Honeymoon babies. They are due about the end of September, but if it is actually twins, they usually come earlier, so sadly, we will not be visiting for a while. My poor darling is somewhat immobilised. I find I am still dazed that I am married, let alone that I shall be a father at forty-three. By the time we made it here, she had found the ship's cabins very cramped due to her growing size. For such a petite lady, she can sit a teacup on her stomach and walk around. I should not say that, but I know you both so well you will laugh at the image this creates. I do so look forward to catching up with you all. Danny also has asked us for a visit, so once the birth has occurred, we shall attempt to come before the winter months.

Gerry, too, found a wife on the voyage home. He is married to Annabella Derbyshire, Viscount Ellison's daughter. Her first husband died from a snake bite. Anyway, she is from Ashford. Do you remember the cantankerous Viscount Matthias Ellison, Robbie? There is a younger brother, Matthew; I do not remember either much, just the father, a somewhat ferocious gentleman. Anyway, Gerry and Annabella, too, are now expecting, some two months behind us. As Gerry is an Obstetrics Doctor, he's staying close until both ladies have delivered. They are, therefore, living here with us. Hopefully, I can get him to make his home here forever.

Amelia, do you remember my conversation with you about Charles? I have done the digging I said I would and have found him to be a legitimate third cousin. My relief was intense; however, my guilt was now immense that I had done little to assist him for over a quarter of a century. His mother and sister (incidentally, both named Elizabeth, although they are known as Elle & Lilabet) were almost starving. I could have assisted them if I had swallowed my pride. Milla, I'm telling you, as you know, my reasons why I did not follow through. To know they were unfounded was a great relief. But to have made them suffer, to salve my pride and ego is not a cost I wished to shoulder, but I must so do. I am at fault. Please explain to Robbie as I will not put this on paper. I will do everything in my power to now ease their burdens. There is far more to his story, as Charles is, in reality, an Earl. His grandfather was bestowed the title for his work in the Carnatic Wars (I had not even heard of such a war!) for the British East India Company, but he never used it. So Charles has been an Earl longer than I, a Duke. Christina's brother, Matthew, seems to be showing some interest in Charles' sister, so this will be interesting to see where it pans out. He visits regularly, but little of his time is spent with his sister. Lilabet is here to assist my Christina as they have become firm friends; she is forever within her company.

Milla, I thank you for your prayers and for confiding in me about them. To know someone is praying for your happiness is happiness in itself. It did change my own attitude so that when Christina came to my notice, I was open to my new feelings.

When I met Christina in church one Sunday, I was smitten in an instant. She was in such a pitiful state of hunger that she nearly fainted from lack of nourishing food. She found mysterious parcels of nourishing food that appeared regularly on her doorstep. (I imagine you smile, Milla) I walked her home that first Sunday and realised her malnourished state. Her skin was tight, and her bones protruded from her cheeks, and her hands were skin on bone.

I still thought her beautiful. That week, I purchased the cottage two doors down from her, in Phillip Street and resigned my commission just to be near at hand for her. I knew I had met the woman you prayed for. We drew close, and as she ate the food I had left secretly at her door (she took it because she did not know who sent it), she regained strength. Does this sound familiar? Finally, I hired a maid for her so we could be seen together. I was then able to invite her over for meals or, better still, arrive with a surfeit of food that I could leave for her. I similarly assisted you; only you had food; you needed moral support. I had that in droves. Anyway, Christina finally started feeling and looking even better. Her beauty is... Well, you will understand when you meet her. We officially could only see each other publicly on Sunday mornings when I could walk her both up and back to church on my arm. Suffice to say, we dawdled both directions. It wasn't far, as you know, but I could hold and touch her and talk to her.

I had little loose money; most of what I'd earned I gave to Charles' family as their needs were greater than mine, and I ate with them often. They had even less than I. Is it not amazing how little we actually need to survive? We gather the worldly trappings through life and discover how unnecessary they are to our existence. My darling Christina, however, had none at all. I had some money in the bank and eked it out as needed. I had so much at home and in comparison to them all, and I knew if things got bad, I could write to either Mother, Father or David and go on the family pension. I never needed to. Poor Christina could not even do that as she had no money even for the post. I did not know how lacking she was in that regard! She eventually took in sewing and taught piano at two of the better homes in town. I, too, assisted in sending work her way.

When Gerry told me I was the duke, I proposed to her that night. The next day, she tells me in front of Gerry, Charles, Sal, and Eddie who she was. I nearly fell off my seat.

Dear friends, there's lots more to that story, but I'll tell you of that when I see you all. My dear Amelia, if you think I was protective of you and Essie, then you will understand my gut-wrenching concern to find the one that God had sent me was so malnourished and that she is now carrying my twins. Although her health has much improved, we are taking no chances. She and Annabella are walking daily with Gerry and me. He is overseeing their every move, well, almost.

In the meantime, we are now at the Castle awaiting the birth of the babes. I shall endeavour to come when we can.

Yours in His ever-loving service.

Pray for us, please.

Neddie

Amelia finished reading the letter. She was leaning against Robbie on their bed and rubbing her growing tummy. "If I was not also expecting, I'd be tempted to make the trip. Can we send a reply, though? Love? I'm so pleased he's no longer alone. I could see the unacknowledged need in him. He felt so lonely but was a continual source of comfort for everyone else. He just gave, and gave, and gave."

"He was like that as a lad, too, Milla. Did I ever tell you how we met? Jim and I were a couple of years younger than him. His youngest brother, Dougie, was in our class at Christ's Hospital, and Jim's invitation to visit was issued to Doug. The four boys came: David, Ned, Paul, and Doug. David was a prig, and I never really liked him; he was some four years older than us. Paul and Doug were nice but were content with each other's company. Ned stood out even then, and he was only ten. Jim and I were about two years younger. We three became friends. I don't even remember the others coming back, but Neddie came often. He'd arrive in the Castle coach and stay for up to a week. I think… no, actually, I have no idea why he came, but he did. And I loved it. Father let me come to stay with Jimmy as he had business in the area, and I'd be allowed to stay with your family while he went off to do what he had to. It was always school holidays, and it was great fun. I also remember Gerry coming with him; he was Ned's special friend. As we grew older, the four of us would head off on some cross-country drinking jaunt. We were loud but not really doing harm to anything. That's when we had a run-in with the Earl; Jimmy and I were eighteen; Ned and Gerry would have been about nineteen or twenty. The Earl threatened us, and if we ever trespassed on his land again, he'd call the constables. Last I saw, Ned was at a Hunt Ball at the Earl's place, so we had actually gone back. Just to prove to him we could behave. We were very well-behaved. I remember Gerry was taken with the painting of the most beautiful child. Fair-haired and blue eyes to melt the heart. Funny how that memory stuck with me. The two older boys just stood staring at it for ages.

Personally, a dark-haired child had already stolen my heart. Even then, I loved you. You were about fifteen and still really a little girl. Your mother kept you well away from us all by then. It just never occurred to me that my own mystery girl was the same adorable child I already loved." They lay entwined discussing what happened at a Hunt Ball. "Cripes, love, I know who she is. Christina must be the child in the painting of the angelic-looking child, much like Essie's, only fair-haired. They called her 'Tiny Tina', but that would be Christina. I bet it's her. I think the child in the painting would have been about eight or nine. I didn't really take much notice of it, so the memory is admittedly somewhat hazy, but it's who Essie reminds me of when I saw her, only a dark version."

"Rob, he really does sound smitten. I do hope she is as nice as she is, apparently beautiful. Sometimes they aren't." She snuggled into his shoulder. "I hope she's as besotted as I am with you, my beloved." She lifted her lips to his. He responded to her unvoiced request.

Eventually, he asked, "Milla, did Ned say anything about why he went?" Robbie was wondering how much she knew.

"If you mean about Elouise, then yes, we spoke about it at length, and also David, he left before their wedding, though. It's why he enlisted as quickly as he did. Lord James knew; I wonder why he said nothing. Mayhap, he had not heard that David had died either. I certainly didn't know; surely Neddie's mother knew I would have told her his direction in such a case."

Rob heaved a sigh of relief. "Good, I'm glad he told you."

"Robbie, he didn't go because of her; he was relieved to get out of the engagement. Darling, Ned went because David asked him to go. So he did." She said, "I can't work out why Lord James didn't say anything, though?"

"Neither did I; David's death surely must have been in the papers. I'll ask Father; he might be able to shed some light."

"When did David die?" she asked quietly.

"Um, I think it was about the time Eliza was born because I remember thinking one life snuffed out as another started. So that would be about November '39." Robbie lay looking at the roof, thinking.

"Rob, that's when Lord James took Lady Mari to Scotland. I remember as they missed Eliza's birth. Her daughter and I share a name, Amelia, and her middle name is Elizabeth, only up there, she's known as Elspeth." Amelia leaned over and lovingly occupied her husband for some time.

He could tell she was still thinking of Ned. "Tell me the rest, love."

She nodded against his chest. "Robbie, Ned was so hurt. Elouise only became engaged to him for his title. Being only nineteen, he would have been so vulnerable. Then, to be dumped for your older brother. How cruel is that? No wonder he was bitter. No wonder he stayed single for so long."

Rob gasped; he had not realised the reason for the breakup, only that

Elouise had married David on what she'd called the rebound. That one word had put the fault with Ned. "Being titled is not always beneficial; you know that to be true." He trusted Ned over Elouise any day.

Later, they sat together and composed a letter back to Ned. They let him know that Amelia was also with-child and unable to travel. They also wrote about her accident. They promised that they, too, would catch up when they could.

~

The last months of Amelia's confinement passed without incident. Her knock on her head caused no further trouble. Ned wrote again in September saying that his twins had been safely delivered, Charles Edward John, called Chip, and their daughter was Sarah Christina. Christina, too, was well and suffered no complications. They arrived on Sept 1st. Amelia was due six weeks later. So, she didn't expect to see them until about November at the earliest.

Letters were sent backwards and forward between the three houses. Jimmy and Alexe were also expecting their third child. Their oldest child, Robert, called Bobbie, was now four, their daughter, Lexi, was two, and the third was also due in November. Ned had been over to visit him and had been astounded with what Jim was doing. When he heard it was Sam and Danny's project, he chuckled. The wounded soldiers in rehabilitation sparked his interest, though. On the way home from Jimmy's, he'd come across one such man, his old friend, Reg Hawkins. Ned hired him on the spot, took Reg up in his carriage, collected his things from his rented room, and took him to the Castle. Reg had been in his old 48th Battalion before the injury, where he lost his leg. He knew so much about organising an estate; Ned knew nothing. Due to Reg's leg being amputated at the knee, he never thought he'd work again. Ned couldn't write to Robbie fast enough. When Ned found out the full extent of what Sam and Danny had achieved and that it had now spread to Jimmy's estate and even put it back onto its feet. Ned said he wanted more information as it's what he was thinking of doing, too. Jimmy said Robbie had worked with him for over two years, so Robbie, too, knew the project.

Amelia woke with back pain soon before dawn. She quietly drew on her nightgown and brocade dressing gown. After three births, she knew what was to come. Robbie would need his sleep. She would, too, but knew that would not happen today. She breathed through the first contractions, but after two hours, the pain made her groan.

It was loud enough to have Robbie out of bed and at her side. "How close, Milla?"

She answered breathlessly, "Been going for a few hours, love. They are about twenty minutes apart now."

"Okay, sweeting, I'll get things organised." He was nowhere near as panicked as he was with Timo's birth. "Yes, and I'll dress first." He saw her notice his state of undress and gave a wicked grin.

"I wouldn't want our mothers shocked, sweetheart." She chuckled. Their time together last night had been everything-loving. His gentleness with her still made tears spring to her eyes. She thanked God for him daily.

Once dressed in what he termed his birthing clothes, he pulled the bell pull three times and waited. This was the sign for assistance to come quickly. He knew that she would need him again. She wished to walk around the room, so he walked with her through the dressing room and back again. By the time they made it back to the bedroom, Sophie and Lady Caroline had both arrived, as had the maids with some hot water. Robbie had learned that soaking a towel in hot water, wringing it and holding it onto her lower back was terrific relief. There was little more they could do. Sophie had called the doctor but was not too worried if he would arrive or not. They had become used to assisting with her births. Amelia had taken at most six hours for either of the other two deliveries.

The midwife usually had arrived after an hour or so, yet she still had not come. Amelia was normally down to fifteen-minute contractions by this stage, but this time had stalled. By mid-morning, Amelia was already so tired that she leaned heavily on Robbie as she stood and breathed through each contraction. Still, neither the doctor nor the midwife had appeared. For two hours, the contractions stayed constant at fifteen minutes apart; then, they stopped completely. An hour passed, and Amelia took the opportunity to sleep. Robbie lay with her, leaving her only for a few minutes at a time. He insisted that she have some tea and keep up her fluids. "So tired, Rob; it's not happening fast enough." She lay in his arms as another one hit. Groaning into his shoulder, she wept. "The last births were so much easier; I'm getting too old for this, Rob. My waters have not even broken," she whispered.

Robbie felt so bad. There was nothing he could do but hold her.

Sophie and Caroline bustled in and out; both were somewhat worried that neither of the medical personnel had arrived. Another contraction finally hit. She again managed to sleep between contractions for about fifteen minutes. It gave her the energy to walk more. Robbie had her up off the bed again; he was about to stand her up when a maid appeared at the door.

"Ma'am, His Grace the Duke of Gracemere and Her Grace have just arrived." She bobbed a curtsy and disappeared.

Sophie apologised and left the bedroom. Minutes later, she arrived back with both Ned and Christina in tow.

Ned stuck his head in the door. "We're not coming in, but I personally wanted to tell you we will be downstairs praying for you all. Milla, stay strong and trust God like you always have," he said.

"Thanks, Neddie, I will; I mean, I do," she managed to say before another contraction hit.

Christina could not stand back and do nothing. She had just been through it herself twice in one day. She entered and walked to Amelia as the contraction pain was easing. She leaned in close and asked softly, "Have the waters broken yet?"

Amelia shook her head.

"Thought so!" Christina spoke to Robbie, "Get them to prepare a bath, quite hot, and get her in it. It will relax her, and hopefully, it will speed things up. She looks exhausted already; I found them wonderful. We'll be downstairs praying. We're not leaving until this baby is here." She squeezed her hand, turned back to Ned with a smile, and waved him away.

She stopped and spoke to Sophie, "Do you have a large bath she can get into? Also, the waters haven't broken yet. I think that's why it's slowed down. I've just had twins and have delivered my share in Australia. I found it always relaxed the mums and hastened things along."

"You've delivered babies, Your Grace?" Sophie asked, astounded.

"Oh, fluff, I'm just Christina. Yes, I have, and when you have no choice but to help or let the baby die, you do what you need to." Christina saw that no one was there to help Amelia other than Robbie. "Can you arrange a bath for her?"

Sophie nodded and sent the maid standing behind them for lots of hot water for a deep bath.

Amelia turned to Robbie and whispered something; he nodded in reply.

"Your Grace, um, Christina, will you stay? Neither the midwife nor the doctor has arrived," Amelia asked. "This one is just not moving along. I'm getting too old for this; I have no energy left." A tear of exhaustion escaped. "I'm just so tired."

"Yes, I will. Tired you may well be, my dear, but we need to get this baby born. So it's bath time. Robbie, you may stay; she'll need you. Lady Caroline, as her mother, she may wish you near, too. But even if she has contractions in the bath, she won't deliver there. She needs to relax, and the hot water should work."

"But your Grace, your gown, it will get dirty," Sophie said with a fluster.

"Then bring me a large apron, please. I'm Christina, and I'm staying." Christina would now not take *no* for an answer. Considering Christina came for a visit, she was now about to assist with a birth. Thankfully, she had just fed her twins, so she had three hours before they needed her again.

"Edward, if you can watch Chip and Sarah while you pray, I'll see if I can hasten this one along." Christina saw the look of anxiety cross his face. Then he relaxed.

"Anything you say, my dear. Milla, she knows what she's doing, so trust her," he said with affection.

"I do already, Neddie. You chose her, so that's enough for me. Pray it comes quickly, please." She moaned as another contraction hit.

Christina stood behind her and massaged her lower back.

"Oh, that's wonderful! Martha did that, and it felt so good." She could feel herself relax. The bath came and was filled to the right level. Robbie assisted her into the warm water, and the tub was covered with a towel, so she had some privacy. "Oh, Christina, this is so good. It's easing all the pains." She lay back and relaxed. Even a contraction in the bath was not as painful.

Sophie, Christina, and Lady Caroline stayed in the next room while Amelia stayed in the hot bath. The three heard the groans as the contractions hit.

Amelia stayed in the hot bath while she had two more contractions, only ten minutes apart; the water had been topped up twice and was again getting cold by the time she needed to get out.

Christina waited in the next room; she called, "I give you a warning; once you step out of the tub, if your waters have not broken before, they will probably do so then. The pains will come quick and fast." Christina said, "Don't forget to breathe through it, dear. Deep breath in, release, again, release. Did Martha teach you the importance of deep breathing? I'm sure Maureen would have known."

Amelia nodded. "I forgot." After that one passed, she asked Robbie to lift her. "I need to get out, Rob."

Robbie stood her up. As she stepped out of the bath, she knew that, finally, her waters had broken. He wrapped her in an oversized towel and dried her off. She lifted her arms, and he slipped on her nightgown again. "Can you walk, Milla?"

"Yes, Robbie, things should be quicker now. The bath has refreshed and relaxed me." She had just finished speaking when another contraction hit. The violence of this one took her by surprise. "Oh," she groaned as she leaned onto Robbie.

Christina heard, and she came in. "Waters break?"

"Yes, that one was bad," Amelia said.

"Good, it means that it has speeded things along. They should get quicker now. Remember to breathe through them; mouth open wide to get the air in."

Amelia nodded; she started to draw in deep breaths.

"Another already?" Robbie asked. "That was less than five minutes."

Christina smiled. "I said it helps. Are you thirsty? Lots of little sips; drink a little, often." She handed Amelia some sweet barley water that had been brought up on a tray. Robbie was also brought some food. He grabbed some toast and marmalade.

"I could drink a tank dry, Christina," Amelia admitted. She'd barely finished her drink before she was groaning in pain again.

"Three minutes apart; walk around the room for a bit while we get things ready." Sophie and Lady Caroline were hovering in the room but not doing much.

"What's your preference, lying or squatting?" Christina asked.

"Oh, squatting; Robbie knows how to assist." Amelia chuckled. "He got me into this; he can see it through again."

Robbie gave her a smile like a guilty five-year-old. "Love, you really shouldn't say things like that, let alone to a duchess." Robbie was so embarrassed.

"Oh, phish, Robert! Amelia and I have many things in common; time in the colony is one. The edges get a little rubbed off there, don't they, dear? We did things slightly differently in Australia, didn't we, dear?" She smirked, knowing exactly how different. "Good on you for insisting that Robbie stay, though. Poor Gerry would have died if I had wanted Edward with me. Plus, with twins, it does complicate things." Christina turned to the others, "Lady Caroline, if you could lay two towels on the floor there, and you and Sophie find scissors and some thread or cord, please."

Caroline placed the towels and then stood near Amelia with a basin. After a few more contractions that were now down to less than a minute apart, Amelia grabbed the bowl, retching violently, then grinned, knowing delivery was imminent.

Robbie turned away, unable to watch. The miracle of birth certainly dumfounded him, but the actual process turned his stomach. How she wished to do this so often astounded him. He'd seen her throw up each time, and it never became any easier.

"Okay, places everyone," Christina said after Caroline had cleaned Amelia up.

Robbie sat in the chair, and Amelia stood between his legs. "I need to push Christina."

Robbie eased her back to a squatting position and hoisted up her nightgown, with his arms now wrapped around her as he had done before. She crouched with her arms on his legs, supported by Robbie's arms. He was praying and whispering loving words to her. The head had just presented when the midwife and doctor finally arrived together.

"Who are you? And what do you think you are doing?" the doctor asked Christina brusquely.

Caroline was like a defensive mother cat. "That, sir, is Her Grace, the Duchess of Gracemere, and you'll mind your manners, please. She knows what she's doing," Caroline said in awe of the beautiful woman in the process of delivering her grandchild.

"It's a boy!" Christina announced to them both. She caught Amelia's smile as she held the child.

The doctor harrumphed. He stood watching as she delivered the healthy baby boy. "Humph, anyone would think you've done that before."

"I have, six times, and I've just had twins myself, so, sir, please assist or move aside. The cord is now empty, and I need to cut and tie it." The doctor was about to tie the cord in the middle when she said, "Seriously, you're going to tie it there?"

"Why not? It will fall off in a week anyway." The old doctor muttered, "I always tie it long."

"Well, I don't. Amelia, what do you prefer? It's your baby." Christina asked the new mother.

"The others were all about two inches, Christina. That worked fine. I cleaned them with strong alcohol," Amelia said. She was watching the tussle between the duchess and the doctor.

The midwife stood silently apart, taking neither side. The cord was tied twice, about two inches from the baby, and once secured, the baby was wrapped and handed to his parents.

Robbie leaned down and whispered something to Amelia.

"Are you sure, love?" Amelia asked with such a look of happiness that she almost glowed.

"Yes, absolutely, my choice, as it's a boy." He sat with Amelia, still half squatting between his legs, as she had yet to deliver the afterbirth. Rob had dropped the front of her nightgown to cover her somewhat.

Lady Caroline was hovering, ready to take the baby when the final contractions hit.

There were always the worst as the pains were far more intense. Robbie felt her flinch and throw back her head. He motioned for Caroline to remove the baby, then braced himself. These he absolutely hated. The agony she went through tore through him. He wasn't wrong. She emitted a scream; her fingernails bit into his legs through his trousers. He then felt her relax against him. He was so pleased he couldn't see entirely what was happening. It was gory enough as it was.

Christina looked up. "All done, Amelia, Robbie, get her to bed."

Sophie had the bed turned down, and Robbie stood her up and carried her to their bed. He laid her on the rubber sheet and towel placed there for her and settled her on the pillows. "Christina, can you call in Neddie after you've washed up? I hope you'll stay for a few days. Today has been a somewhat unusual welcome." Rob gave her rueful a grin.

"I had hoped you'd invite us to stay. Danny has too, but I'd love to stay for a few days," Christina said.

Ned walked in a few minutes later with their twins in his arms. "So we're staying, love?"

Christina nodded. "Yes, sorry, Edward, but wild horses won't tear me away from this little lad for a few days."

Amelia finally had a chance to look at the stunningly gorgeous lady who had married Ned. She was everything he said and more.

Tim had followed Ned into the room.

"I thought you'd like to meet another namesake, or almost. Everyone, please meet Edward Ralph Daniel Styles." Robbie grinned at his long-lost friend. At forty, he's not expected to become a father again when Eliza had been born. Now, to have a second son, he was in seventh heaven.

"You're calling him Edward? After me?" Ned asked in awe.

"Why not Neddie? You're godfather to Essie, so why not to another child named after you? You are Eddie's Godfather, too, aren't you?" Robbie asked, knowing the answer already. Amelia knew that to be true.

"Um, yes, I am, to all four of Charles' sons, but not the girls. Fancy you remember that, Milla?" Ned grinned like a cat that got the cream. It suddenly occurred to him. "I haven't officially introduced you to my wife yet." He did so.

Tim, Sophie, and Caroline all cooed appropriately over the tiny infant, and then Christina shooed everyone but Robbie away. "He needs to be fed, Amelia. See how he goes, then let the children in."

Amelia put out her hand. "We may not have met, but I feel I know you so well already. Neddie has told us so much about you. But to me, you are an answer to prayer." She saw a look of concern across Christina's face. "No, not for today; for that, I will be forever grateful too, but for loving Neddie. He was so alone out there. He cared for Essie and me and did so much for us after Cyrus was killed. I hope he told you everything?" Amelia saw a glance of understanding between her and Ned.

Christina nodded. "He told me enough to know he's like another brother and that you love each other as such." Christina bent and kissed her cheek. "Enough talking for now; the babe is hungry. I'll tell your mother to give you some time together before the children come. She's gone to get them."

Rob met her concerned look with a big grin. "Ned would have me to deal with, ma'am, if he felt more than brotherly love for my girl. I, too, can't thank you enough, both of you, for what you have done for us both." Robbie looked admiringly at the graceful lady standing in his bedroom.

"Oh, pfaff, Robbie, and enough with the ma'am or m'lady stuff. I feel I know you both well enough to be on first-name terms. Now I'm going." She said, "Do what you do so well, my dear." She took off the large apron, revealing her stunning sprigged muslin gown. She rolled the bloodied garment into a ball and left it with the dirtied linens, and with that, she was gone.

"Neddie wasn't wrong. She is the most beautiful woman I've ever seen, and so nice and kind. I love her already." Amelia turned her attention to the baby in Robbie's arms. He was trying to nuzzle Robbie.

Robbie smiled. "No, my sweet, only the most beautiful blonde woman," he bent and kissed her forehead.

She unbuttoned her nightgown and took the babe from him. Robbie was watching the procedure in awe. "Love, I was thinking. This may well be our last; why do we not add another name to his, Edward Christian Ralph Daniel? What do you think? Edward means 'protector', so adding Christian next to it, you could say it means 'protector of the faith'."

She grinned at Robbie. "That's beautiful, Rob, I love it." Amelia put her newborn son to her breast. "I'd really love that, sweetheart, and how about asking her to be his godmother, too? Your brothers TC and Simeon are godfathers for Timo with Georgie, and your sisters, Alexe and Rosie are godmothers for Eliza with Jimmy."

Little Edward knew exactly what to do and was soon quenching his thirst. His dark hair was nearly dry. He had both hands grasping her breast. She chuckled. "He's clinging on like a teddy bear. I think that's what we should call him, Teddy, at least while he's young. We still need another godfather for him. What about your other friend, Gerry Winslow-Smyth? He can be one by proxy; Jimmy can say the promises for him."

Rob agreed willingly; the four childhood friends would keep in contact with each other from now on.

After little Teddy finished his first meal, Amelia prepared herself for the onslaught of their three other children. Sure enough, the door burst open, and Timo followed by Eliza and then, more sedately, Essie came in.

"Sorry, Mama, but he was too quick for me. Is it true you have had the baby?" Essie asked.

"It's all right, poppet. Yes, he's arrived. All of you, up on the bed and come and meet Teddy." Essie lifted Eliza up; Timo needed no assistance as he'd launched himself into his father's arms.

"Careful, little ones, you must be gentle with him. Even more so than with the chickens."

"He's so little. When can he come and play? Is it really true I've got a brovver?" Timo was so excited his questions were tripping over each other.

Eliza just sat looking at the dark-haired baby with a frown on her brow. She had not seen a tiny baby before. "He's too little. He's not cooked enough to play wiv us."

"Actually, darling, he's 'cooked' just right. This is how babies start. Ask Essie; you were both this little when you were born," Amelia replied, smiling.

Eliza adored Essie. She looked at her big sister standing beside the baby, her eyes enormous as Essie answered her mother.

Essie nodded. "Yes, you were both this little, and I loved you even then."

Robbie sat looking at the faces of his own three children. Each perfect and small version of their dark-headed parents. Then his eyes fell on his stepdaughter. He could not love her more if she were his own. He'd known *of* her all her life, although he had not met her until she was nearly five. He was the only father she had ever known.

"Papa? Is everything all right?" Essie asked. She had seen what she thought was sadness on his face.

"Yes, poppet, everything is fine. I was just thinking how much I love all four of you, so very much. God has truly blessed us with a clutch of the most adorable offspring." He met Essie's eyes across the bed.

"That's all right, Papa. I was wondering if we should give God thanks for Teddy's arrival?" she asked.

"I was thinking the same thing, poppet." While the little children sat on the bed, Robbie bowed his head and gave thanks for Teddy's safe delivery and Amelia's safety.

All said, "Amen" at the end. Teddy had fallen asleep, and Timo and Eliza had lost interest in the sleeping baby.

Amelia was exhausted and finding it hard to keep her eyes open. Robbie took the sleeping child from his mother's arms and laid him in the crib near their bed. He had been surprised when Timo was born that Amelia insisted on mothering the child herself. She refused a wet nurse and a nanny but was content to allow the staff to assist her with everything else. The children were only moved to the nursery when weaned. By then, they were sleeping in the dressing room. In a house as large as Broome-Hall Manor, there were always other children to play with.

As at Jimmy's house, both little ones loved the chickens and were often found in the hen house or near the feathered animals. The maid assigned to keep her eye on them was eighteen, and they adored her. However, she was amazed that these children were allowed to get as dirty as the staff's children. They were even encouraged to play with them and help with the morning chores.

Robbie kissed Amelia and suggested she rest. He then ushered all the children outside and left Amelia to sleep. Lady Caroline came in and said she would stay with her. She had her knitting with her. She sat, and the clicking of the needles was heard. He bent and kissed her cheek. "Thank you, Mama Caro," he said and walked down to find Ned and Christina.

Essie was waiting for him outside the room. She walked with him, holding his hand. "Papa, is Uncle Neddie really here? What if I don't remember him?" she asked anxiously. She'd not seen him while he waited for Teddy's birth.

"Then stay near me, poppet. He's as lovely now as he was then. He's your godfather. So just treat him like Uncle Jimmy," Robbie said.

"But he's a duke now. Should I bow?" she asked.

"I think he would rather have a hug from you, poppet. You're special to him. He's been keeping you safe from before you were born. He loves you, darling, and so will Aunt Christina." Rob gave her hand a gentle squeeze. "Do what you feel is right, poppet. Hug him if you wish, or stay close to me."

She nodded and clung tighter.

The door to the drawing room opened, and Essie saw the fair-haired man at the end of the room. Suddenly, all the memories of his loving hugs came flooding back to her. She ran across the room and into his waiting arms. No words were necessary. He was down on one knee and holding her lovingly. "I was wondering if you would remember me?" he said softly.

"I did too; I was saying to Papa, what if I didn't, but I do. I remember always feeling safe with you, of being loved and knowing everything would be all right, and I remember being so sad when I had to say goodbye. My major doll still sleeps on my bed and guards me every night." She rubbed her hand on his cheek as she used to do as a small child. "Yes, I remember." She snuggled to his neck. "I remember best your big hugs and how you smell nice."

He chuckled. "Well, you've grown somewhat in the past six years."

"I would hope so," she giggled. "Children, do you know."

She heard a soft giggle behind her. She turned to find a beautiful lady sitting with two tiny babies in her arms. "Hello, miss; I gather you know my husband quite well. I'm not used to young ladies throwing themselves into his arms, but I'll make an exception for you." She smiled, so her entire face glowed. "If he's Uncle Neddie, then I'm Aunt Christina. Would that be all right?"

Essie nodded. "I'd love that." Then, she hardly believed what she saw. "You've got two?" Her eyes grew as she took in the fair-haired babies. "Twins. I've never seen twins before."

"Yes, twins. That one's Chip, Charles really, but we call him Chip, and this one is Sarah. She's about twenty minutes younger."

"Oh, they are so different to mother's babies. We're all dark, but so is Papa. I never met my own Papa, so I don't know about him."

"He was dark too, poppet; I knew him in Sydney. You have his eyes." More than that, Ned would not say. He certainly would not mention that he'd met him while being arrested for being drunk in Parramatta just before he'd chosen his newest wife, her mother. Nor would he say what a brute Cyrus Black was. He had told Christina about the evil man, but it was for Essie's mother to tell her everything. Milla was a sister to him, like the one he never had. His sister, Sarah, had died at birth.

"Thank you, Uncle Ned. Mama doesn't talk about him much. I see her face when someone says his name; it makes her look sad, so I don't ask," Essie said in a very matter-of-fact tone.

"Poppet, one day Mama will talk to you about him, though not until you're grown up, but now is the time for happy things," Robbie said, trying to divert the topic.

Ned now sat with Essie on the settee next to Christina, and she was allowed to hold baby Sarah while Ned cuddled tiny Chip.

Robbie sat watching Essie's face. At eleven, she was extremely bright. Amelia, Ned, and Rob had almost obliterated her bad start in life. A child whose conception was so horrific, she had been loved from the moment she was born. It was that love she remembered. Ned would always be special to her, as she obviously was to him.

Christina asked Essie if she could take her up to her mama as it was time to feed the twins. Ned assisted her to stand and helped place a baby over each shoulder; she and Essie left the men alone.

Essie assisted Christina by lifting her skirt as she walked up the stairs.

~

Ned and Robbie sat looking at each other for a while. "Perfect timing, Ned. Your wife is perfect, too. You're right, though; she's stunning and a perfect foil for Amelia's dark colouring. Who would have thought that we'd each marry two of the most beautiful women and have children so close in age?"

Ned gave Robbie one of his big grins. "I think it's funny that after all these years, you finally married your mystery woman and that she was no mystery at all. How did you never meet her as a child?"

"Oh, I did; I just never put one and one together. She looked so very different when made up for her debut. Nothing like the scruffy child who had shadowed us when we were children. Maybe that's when I fell for her. Who knows? I certainly adored her as a tiny child, but Ned, she's always been the only one for me." He offered Ned a drink from the grog tray. Ned shook his head but accepted some lemonade from the large jug on the tray. Rob poured two. "Oh Ned, when you arrived today, I was beside myself with worry. The baby wasn't coming, the birth had stalled, and no one knew where the doctor was. If something had happened to her, I have no idea what I'd do. When Christina came in and suggested a hot bath, things just kick-started." Robbie broke out in a cold sweat again, just thinking of the agony Amelia had been in. "She was exhausted; the bath not only relaxed but revived her."

"It's horrible, isn't it? You're lucky you could be with her. Because it was twins and also Gerry would have had a fit, I was not allowed in with her. The poor love was surrounded by many strangers. Having said that, I don't know if I'd cope." Ned commiserated with his friend. "What a strange welcome, though, 'Hello? Nice to see you after twenty-two years, here; help me deliver a baby'." Ned chuckled.

It broke the ice for Robbie. "Ned, it's as though I saw you yesterday. We've both aged, but otherwise, you've not changed much. I think you're more at peace now than you were. I lost track of Gerry decades ago. I gather you haven't?"

"No, well, I had, but I'll tell you about him later. He's living with us now."

Rob continued. "Poor Jimmy has been through hell and back with his family problems. He's on his feet again now, thanks to Sam and Annie Garney."

Ned looked puzzled. "He told Milla he broke his leg. I gather that wasn't so?"

"No, broken pride, maybe, but no physical injury other than hunger. More likely no money for mail." Rob paused, thinking of his friend. He still felt guilty he'd not visited him. "The land is paying again, and he's rehabilitating and training disabled people to work. Re-training them, I should say. Father and Sam are doing the same. Perry White started it with Elizabeth Fry, and Sam joined in, more as a poke in the eye to the previous Earl, however, it's working out brilliantly. Then Sir Ralph and Eliza Darling have come on board with her mama, Ann Dumaresq and the group she works with in London. All are well vetted before they are sent to whichever place they are best suited to. Sam gets the majority of them, though. They are such a sorry sight when they arrive, sick and emaciated. They are now sourced from the streets and docks around the country. Jimmy initially needed the most abled-bodied ones, and his staff are certainly not the most beautiful, but they are sure the most appreciative. They have burns, scars, and horrific injuries; they suffer and are shunned by others because of it. Oh, Ned, I shake just thinking of what life would be like if I had suffered such wounds." He did then actually shiver. "Sam focuses on their abilities rather than their disability. He quizzes each one and finds out what they can already do or what their interests are. There are jobs for all. Most are working for bed and board, especially at Jimmy's place, but they love it compared to life on the streets. Even his estate manager is a rescue. Considered too old to do his work, and he's disabled too. He's fitted in beautifully."

"I love it, Rob. I think I'll join the circle too. I've been thinking of something like this. I have to re-staff the entire estate as most left when David was in charge. I gather he was mostly an absentee landlord, and the younger staff ran riot. Mother sacked most of them, keeping a few old retainers. Many of the others left when Elouise returned for her year of mourning. She ended up with a skeleton staff. The butler stayed on, although he too went to work for Mother and a few outdoors staff. Elouise brought her personal staff from London, and they all left with her when she went home. When my letter arrived to say I was bringing my wife, she scarpered. I have a feeling she thought she would have another chance with me. Anyway, when we arrived, there were very few left, but it means we can start from scratch." He fell silent, thinking of what was ahead of him. "I have, in a way, started already. Reg Hawkins was in my Battalion in Sydney. He had to have his leg amputated and was shipped home. He was in desperate shape when I met him on the road back from Jimmy's, but I employed him on the spot as I know his organisation skills. Reg is my estate manager now. He has some of his friends from the hospital that he wants to employ." Ned fell silent again.

Rob asked, "Ned, did you notice that some of the maids here are, well, um, not exactly as you'd find in a big house?"

"Sorry, Rob, I haven't noticed. Should I?" Ned looked puzzled.

Rob looked around to make sure the doors and windows weren't open. "Ned, some were streetwalkers. They had fallen on hard times. Eliza Darling's mother, Ann Dumaresq, and her cronies have been 'rescuing' some of them. Oh, Ned, it's been eyeopening, to say the least." Robbie was finding it hard not to laugh. "Some of the things they do are absolutely hilarious. We've managed to stop them from taking food from the table. Assuring them there is plenty more. They are so appreciative. Their language is, well, blue, to say the least. Others are orphaned children of soldiers, rescued before they had to turn to the streets. One such is our minister's wife, Miriam. She was rescued before harm befell her. And then there are the illegitimate peers' offspring. Sam, Anne, and Danny started focusing on that, and it's grown out of all proportion. Not only the minister but his butler, housekeeper, and probably ninety per cent of his staff have that background. So, thank you for sending Amelia to work there when she returned.

At last count, Sam's estate had some twelve children with similar pedigrees. Sam and Anne train them and place them in good positions."

Ned smiled; he knew what they planned to do but had not realised how much it had grown. "Trust Sam. Being a peer did not sit well with him. He and Danny had a rough time in Sydney when the word got out."

"Ned, have you heard from him recently, or Danny?" Robbie didn't know how much they had been told about his situation.

"Dan said a bit. Apparently, Sam is the Duke of Malvern's son, and Anne is the Earl's daughter. Also, Danny is married to your youngest sister, Georgie, and Jimmy to another." Ned had a twinkle in his eye.

"Phew! I was wondering how to ease into that tidbit of juicy gossip." Robbie relaxed back into his chair. "Perry and Katy too, of course, their daughter, Mia, married my brother Tim, or TC as we call him."

Ned chuckled, "So, all one big family now, as Paul married Louisa, Mia's sister."

Robbie smiled, "Sam and Anne's paternity is not exactly a topic of discussion in front of the ladies, is it? Okay, well, in front of most ladies, our two would be the exception, don't you think?"

Robbie nodded in agreement. "Milla astounds me. How she copes with what she has been through and has come out stronger."

"Christina, too. Who would have even thought an English duchess knew how to deliver a babe?" Ned chuckled. "I don't imagine many could."

"Ned, I want to thank you for everything you did for Milla. I realise now that Jimmy could not have sent you money, for he had none. I owe you so much for what you did."

"Rob, he did send money. He sent £15, and I stretched it and added a bit. Over there, things are much cheaper if they are locally made. Yes, I added a bit, but as Essie was my goddaughter, I had the right to assist them. I refuse to be called to account for my expenditure, but I will take your thanks. I just wish that I'd been around when she arrived. Jimmy knew where I was and what I was doing; I wish he'd let me know she was there. I'd seen her name on the list of assignees, but as she was under West and not Westaweller, I didn't realise it was her. Oh, Rob, I would have had her assigned to myself." Ned fell silent for a while. "Rob, it was just as well that stinker was dead when I found out; I'm sure I would have done something back to him, even just arrested him." Thinking back to those days when his heart was frozen solid when Amelia needed him, he released a long sigh. "Rob, she restored my faith in women, and without her, I would not have my Christina." Ned sat thinking of the change Amelia had made to him and his life. "No, Rob, I have her to thank, truly. So let it be."

Rob had seen the flashes of emotion cross his friend's face. "I thank you from the bottom of my heart, Ned." Rob smiled at his friend. He knew he had no need for the few pounds, so he accepted gracefully.

Ned met his eye with a twinkle. "Robbie, Jim tried to pay too, you know. He felt it was his responsibility, I refused him too. It really was my pleasure. She paid it back in a way, as I insisted that she partner me for a few balls. She'd only ever been to one, and that was her come-out ball, which I'd missed. So we went to a couple of the Governor's Balls together. She wore the most astounding blue gown."

"I know it well, Ned, for she wore it for our wedding. She positively glowed." Robbie smiled at the memory.

Both men were thinking deeply about the lovely lady asleep upstairs.

Chapter 19 The Ship Comes In

*N*ed and Robbie had been talking for about an hour when they heard approaching voices. The door flew open; the butler stood holding it open. Robbie heard his mother's voice echoing to them. "But, Amelia, you should be in bed. You've just had a baby," Sophie said.

Lady Caroline followed. "Amelia Mary Styles, it's just not done."

Robbie heard Amelia's joyous laugh. Then her reply was, "Rubbish."

"See, they certainly toughen them up over there," Robbie said to Ned before the newcomers entered.

Ned nodded in reply, still secretly in awe that Christina had delivered his good friend's child. They stood and waited for the group of ladies to join them.

Amelia continued talking as she entered. "Yes, I've just had a baby. And then a really good sleep. After I had Essie, I had to help babysit five other children, then I milked a cow and churned butter. I feel fine, truly. I had a baby, not lost a leg." She arrived with baby Teddy in her arms. She'd just fed him for the second time.

Sophie bustled in after her with Christina and Lady Caroline in their wake, each carrying a twin.

Robbie greeted her with a kiss on the lips. "Hello, love. Feeling better?"

"Yes, thank you, sweetheart," she replied.

His mother was horrified. "Robert, that is not appropriate," she said, aghast.

"Mother, this is Neddie. If I cannot kiss my wife in front of one of my best friends..." He chortled.

"Well, it's just... he's a duke," Sophie said quietly.

Ned was nearly in stitches. "Ma'am, I may well be a duke, but it's not by choice. I'm also best friends to Milla and Robbie; I shall excuse them both as I'm sure my own dear wife will." Ned bent and proceeded to give Christina a peck on the lips in front of both embarrassed ladies. "May I remind you that my duchess just delivered your grandson," he chuckled, "We are not a normal Ducal couple; we are just friends."

Sophie shrugged, then blushed. "Are you sure?"

"I am," Ned said.

"As am I," Christina added. They sat discussing the recent birth and some of the others Christina had delivered. "Bush-babies, I called them."

Sophie and Caroline were speechless.

Amelia, Ned, and Christina were at one end of the room discussing life in Sydney and how things were changing.

Rob sat listening, enthralled.

Sophie rang for tea, and as they waited, a carriage pulled up at some speed. Wondering who it could be, they were all astounded when Jimmy and a very heavily expectant Alexe and their children walked in.

"Hello, everyone." Jimmy was almost hopping with happiness. "Hey, Neddie, you here too? Oh, this is just perfect. I can tell you all at once." He froze when he saw three tiny babies. "Milla, you had three?" He stood looking at the little bundles.

"Firstly, hello Jimmy and Alexe. Secondly, no, just one, this one, his name is Teddy, and he was born this morning. These two are Neddie's and Christina's twins," Amelia said, laughing. "What's brought you both in hot-footed? Alexe, should you be travelling in your condition? You must be nearly due. Jimmy, you pulled up like the house was on fire." She answered his questions one by one, and then Amelia asked, "What's happened?"

After he'd acknowledged everyone, he said, "I've just had a letter. Well, Milla, we have, actually. You and Mother get a share, too."

As he spoke, the afternoon tea tray arrived. He fell silent. Alexe had moved to sit next to her mother, smiling broadly but staying silent. Her lips were obviously being bitten with excitement. She was eight months gone, but still relatively compact and fighting fit.

Amelia watched her face, almost exploding with excitement.

"Two more cups, please, and can you take the children to the others?" Sophie said. Jimmy and Alexe's older children, Bobbie and Lexi, followed the butler out.

Once the door closed, Ned introduced Christina to both Jim and Alexe. Rob officially did the same for his mother and mother-in-law, although they had already met in Amelia's room.

Caroline had been astounded that the duchess, too, refused to employ a wet nurse.

The butler returned with three extra cups and another tea tray, duplicating the contents.

As the door shut behind him, Jimmy, who'd been pacing the room like an expectant father, turned around to the group and focused on Amelia's face. "Mama, Milla, Father's ship actually came in." He grinned as though he'd explained everything.

"Jimmy, I have absolutely no idea what you mean. What ship?" Amelia looked as puzzled as did the rest.

The door opened again. Sir Timothy, returned from his trip to wherever he'd been, entered the room as Jimmy was speaking. He nodded, acknowledging his new guests. Recognising Ned, Tim smiled a warm welcome. However, he helped himself to some tea, then sat in silence and let Jim continue.

Jim waited until his father-in-law settled, then continued, "Robbie, do you remember I told you Father was speculating and bought some strange things? I found those documents in his desk. One of which was some shares in a company in Kentucky?"

Robbie nodded but said nothing.

Jimmy continued, "It was supposed to be for a saltwater well. But the company had just notified me that the capital used to sink the well is now producing oil. Another one Father invested in was the company behind the Drake Oil Well in Titusville, Pennsylvania. For years, they found nothing, but seven years ago, in 1836, they dug a nearly seventy-foot deep well, again for saltwater production, but they have struck oil too. Father was apparently one of the major investors." Jimmy's face was so animated that Amelia was giggling. He continued. "Milla, in the past six years, it's grown more and more productive; they expect it to become huge. They asked if they could buy out our shares for over £1,000,000. I said, *no* to an absolute buy out but that I would be prepared to sell them ten per cent of my holding. That will bring us in £100,000 in cash. Another one of Father's speculations was to give a man named John Rathbone some £2000. After correlating the dates, that was from the sale of the land on the boundary at Westerham. He's just written to me to say that he too had previously purchased one hundred acres in America, with Papa's money, and he's dug a small well on this land which is already beginning to produce more oil than saltwater. He wants to sink more wells on his land and wanted permission to use Father's investment. Of course, I have said yes. I explained that Father was now dead. They expect this to be even bigger than the other Drake Well field."

Alexe was by now giggling along with Amelia. Sophie and Caroline sat in a very unladylike pose with their mouths dropped open.

"How much did you say, Jimmy, £10,000?" his Mother asked.

"No, Mother, one million pounds value, he said, spelling it out and increasing daily. I will liquidate only ten per cent so we have working cash and leave the rest for income. Amelia, that £5000 was the money from your dowry and some of the arable land he sold. So we share fifty, fifty in that. Mother, don't worry, you won't miss out either. There's more than enough. You put up with so little for so long, you are now going to reap the reward." Jimmy punched the air with joy. "Can you believe it? Sir Timothy, Rob, Ned, I brought the huge bundle of that paperwork with me. Can you help me go through it? I am now in well over my head." He caught the look on his mother's face.

She was sitting weeping with her head in her hands. He flung the sheaf of papers onto the seat and was on his knees in front of his mother. He gently drew her into his arms and comforted her. She sobbed into her son's shoulder. All her worries of how to support her children had come to naught. "Horace had always said one of his grand schemes would come good. Now his ship has come in." Jimmy would be safe, as would Amelia. She cupped her son's face in her hands. "Son, you have protected us all for so long. I'm glad some benefit can finally come from his schemes."

Amelia already married to Robbie; would be safe anyway.

Caroline's tearful outburst had not lasted long. Her wet eyes were quickly dried, and she gave an almost hysterical giggle. "Jimmy, you're rich, as rich as Midas himself. Wouldn't your father be both delighted and also livid that he now can't touch a penny of it?" Again, she gave a wet gurgle of laughter. "He'll never ever get to touch a damned penny of it." Lady Caroline threw her head back and laughed joyously. She, too, punched the air gleefully.

Ned and Christina had sat listening. Slowly, a smile spread over his face. "I'd be delighted, Jim, but I feel Sir Timothy may be in a better situation to assist than I. I suggest that we retire to the office and discuss the bounteous blessing. Mayhap your mother may wish to join us?"

"No, no, our Grace, my children are well and happy; that is all I ever wanted," Lady Caroline said.

"Ma'am, I was 'Neddie' to you as a child; may I continue to be as familiar? I would be far more comfortable as such," Ned asked.

"Are you sure? Then I'd be delighted. But I shall still leave the finances to you men, if I may." She gave Ned an affectionate smile. "Thank you, Neddie," she said as she clasped his hand as he passed to attend to the paperwork.

As tea had been poured and drunk during this discourse, the four men excused themselves and departed. Robbie had caught Amelia's eyes, and with a raised eyebrow and a nod of his head, he briefly questioned her about if she wished to retire. She shook her head and waved him to follow the men. She watched him lovingly as he left her with the others. Her adoration of her husband was clearly visible for all to read. Her heart was still pounding from the news just revealed.

Christina moved and sat next to her. They finally had a chance to discuss much of their pasts.

Amelia told Christina of Ned's assistance in the Colony and of her first memories of him as a child.

Christina admitted to a tiny bit of jealousy. "Amelia, when I first heard about you, I do admit I could not believe your relationship with Edward was as innocent as you both insist. Now I see you together; he really does mother you, doesn't he?"

"Yes, Christina, you have no worries there. Neddie is like another brother. I love him dearly, but only as that. There was only one time he kissed me, and it was on the day I left. It was not quite brotherly but nowhere near a lover-like one either, somewhere in between. Our relationship was exactly as he said, platonic. I was for him, someone who knew his background, and he did not have to put on a front for me. I was Jimmy's little sister, no more, no less, but Christina, we were vital to each other's sanity over there. We could knock down the barriers with each other. Otherwise, every word we uttered with everyone else had to be vetted and guarded."

Relief flooded Christina, but she only said, "Oh, Amelia, I do know what you mean; I, too, had to do that. I was Lady Christina, daughter of an Earl when I first married over here. I left here as 'The Honourable, Lady Christina Meadows', then over there, I became just Mrs Meadows. Can you imagine what my life over there would have been like if word of my title had spread?" She relaxed, knowing that not only did their stories correlate but that she could see the adoration of Amelia and Robbie for each other. "I didn't even tell Edward until we were already engaged."

She heard Amelia gasp. "But why? He wouldn't have cared."

Christina laughed. "It was not really like that; we had been secretly seeing each other for nearly two years then, and he surprised me and proposed late at night. We, um, were occupied in a more pleasant distraction for some time before he reluctantly returned to Gerry. I told him in front of Gerry, Charles, Sal, and Eddie when he revealed his new status the next morning. Eddie was recovering from a highwayman attack, and we arrived to see them, and I revealed who I was." She heard Amelia gasp again.

"Eddie got injured? Is he all right? What happened? I've known of him since he was a child. Caroline Evans was a good friend in Sydney. I got to meet the five boys often." The look of concern on her face spoke volumes.

"It was more of a rotten character trying to get his horse back after he'd abandoned him. I don't suppose you ever met 'James', the black stallion?"

"No, I didn't get to know the Lockleys all that well. I spent the few times I made it to Parramatta with Bill and Molly Miller. I met Eddie regularly in Sydney with Caroline Evans, but he was only a boy then."

Christina smiled and filled her in on his story. "An untrained black stallion had been left at the smithy in lieu of payment. Thomas Tindale, Caroline Evans' brother, gave it to Eddie, who then trained it. They are an absolute sight to behold and are jokingly called Ebony and Ivory. The previous owner, one Erastus Black…" She heard Amelia gasp but continued her story, "...attacked Eddie to try to get the horse back. Gerry was coming from visiting his sister at Orchard Hills and came across Eddie, wounded and bleeding quite badly. When he brought him home, Edward was there, and Gerry told him he was the duke. That night, Edward proposed."

"So Eddie is all right?" Amelia asked in a sort of strangled, scratchy tone.

"Yes, he was well enough to get married that next weekend. It was only days before his wedding to Jenna. Amelia, I saw the panic cross your face when I mentioned the highwayman's name. Do you know him?" Christina looked puzzled.

Amelia's eyes were glassy, "Before I answer that, did Ned tell you of my assignment and my first husband?" Amelia looked at Christina anxiously.

"Yes, do you mind?" Christina looked embarrassed.

"Oh no, not at all; it just makes it easier to tell." Amelia took a deep breath. "Christina, his name was Cyrus Black. His only living relative was a brother, Erastus, and they'd not seen each other for years. I never met him. There can't be too many with that name. What happened to him?" Amelia asked in a slightly panicked voice.

Christina reached out and covered her hand with her own. "Amelia, he was sent to Hobart for life. He'll never be released. I'd be surprised if he lives out the first year from what I've heard of the place. He was a bad man. You should have heard the list of crimes he was eventually convicted for." Christina shuddered.

Amelia released a held breath and relaxed. "Oh, thank goodness."

"Was Cyrus that bad?" she asked in a lowered voice.

"That and much more, Christina; I'll tell you the full story later, but please continue," Amelia said, almost relieved to hear he was locked up for life.

They continued their discussion for some time, and soon, the men returned. Sir Tim came in and closed the door.

Jimmy was almost sheet white and shaking but was grinning, too.

"Jimmy, what's happened?" Amelia saw the stunned look on Robbie's face and wondered if it was bad news.

Ned spoke as he stood next to Jim. "It seems God is in his firmament, and all is well with the world. We sorted through the paperwork. Lots of documents still have to be investigated, but we did find one more interesting document. I don't suppose the name of Matthias Barringer means anything to you, Lady Caroline?" Ned waited, wondering if she'd met him.

"Yes, he was another of Horace's so-called 'fair-weather' friends. He's one that I'd remember in particular as Horace sold him one of the best fields and gave the man money. It was the final straw. I refused to allow him near us after that. Then Horace started drinking heavily as the man cleared out with the money." She had gone somewhat red in anger just thinking of that situation.

Sir Tim looked at Ned then continued the saga. "Ahh, well, the documentation from Barringer seems in order, and it also seems that Barringer actually came good on his word. There was a letter with the documentation. He found gold and lots of it in Montgomery County, North Carolina. Horace apparently was the major investor in that, too but didn't know it. I remember hearing recently that the mine is now a going concern. They are mining by tunnelling, and it's reaping a great reward," Sir Tim said. "We'll have to take it to London and verify the claim for Jimmy, but from what I remember hearing, Jimmy will be part owner of a very successful gold mine, a very, very successful one. I only knew about 'some English Lord' who had invested heavily and could not be traced. By the paperwork that we have here, Horace invested heavily in the exploration and set up of the company."

Jimmy felt dizzy; it still had not sunk in.

Rob led him to a chair and sat him down, pushing his head between his knees.

After a few moments, he sat up, grinning. "Cor blimey, from pauper to a virtual prince in the space of a day," Jim said; he felt ill.

"Oh, 'Cor blimey' are the words that Essie uttered when she saw the house in London. I believe they are quite apt today," Amelia said with a laugh as she met her mother's smiling face.

~

Alexe stayed with her mother while Sir Timothy and Jimmy made a trip to London. Ned and Christina stayed until the men's return a week later.

Amelia and Christina had become firm friends during this time, and while feeding their babies, Amelia had poured out her entire story to Christina. Amelia told her everything, far more than any of the others knew, for only then could Christina understand the need she had for Neddie's friendship and healing presence. Things that only a woman who'd lived in that sort of situation could understand. She also told Christina of the day at the gaol where she'd been kidnapped. How Ned had consoled her afterwards, yet never had been alone with her. "Yes, Christina, I adore him, I even love him, I always will. But, I was never 'in love' with him, nor he with me." Amelia also revealed that she was Robbie's mystery woman. "Robbie had fallen in love with me when a young man at a ball in London. He had discovered my identity soon after my transportation. He never even told Jimmy, but they all knew he'd met someone and then lost her. I, too, remembered him. We were never introduced, so I never knew his name, but he was the man who held my heart through all those sad years." Amelia then told her of another friend, Fran Grey, who had returned on the same ship with her family.

Christina also opened up to her about her physically abusive first husband and living with a drunken husband. She told Amelia of her life and how she coped. Together, they shared the painful emotional wounds that each had carried unwittingly into their new marriages. Each knew they now had an understanding friend to confide in fully. That their husbands were already best friends certainly helped.

Sophie had allocated a smaller sitting room for the two nursing mothers to use when required. It was set up as a mini nursery and had a changing table and a large pile of napkins. The three tiny babies needed copious quantities of these, but the Manor was well stocked from the numerous children born there over the decades. It gave the two mothers much time to converse. Their differences, as well as the similarities, gave them a strong bond.

The ladies' time with the children also gave Ned and Robbie time to reconnect. Rob again thanked Ned for his care of Milla, and then Ned apologised for his teasing Rob about his mystery woman. "What an astounding coincidence," Ned had said.

"No, Ned, not that," Rob met Ned's piercing, vivid blue eyes with his laughing, light blue ones. "It was a 'God-incidence.' I know that through all this, God has been leading us. When we wander from His path, sometimes it brings more good for others than it does for us. I withdrew from society and entrenched myself here assisting my father and then later Perry, Sam and Danny; I love their work. I knew God needed me to be here for Amelia on her return, although I was itching to go to her out there. God can use our errors to strengthen our lives. I never looked at any other woman, but Milla, and trust me, enough threw themselves at me. I just knew when we met at that ball that she was the one for me. Then I lost her." Rob sat looking deeply into his quickly cooling cup of tea. "Ned, I still can't believe that I did not recognise her from when she was little. My only excuse is that with her hair up and 'grown-up', she looked vastly different, yet subconsciously, she is what I was looking for."

"True, I could easily have married Milla, but I knew she was not for me. I had no idea about you then either; well, what I mean is your feelings for her. Oh, I did know about your mystery woman, but not that it was Milla. I love her dearly, but was never 'in love' with her. Gee, cripes, Rob, you know what I mean." Ned looked flustered. "But when I met Christina, I too just knew. She completed and complemented me. My other half, as some say, but it's true."

"Oh, I know Ned; trust me, I know! Jimmy and Alexe were just the same. I had no idea she had a tenderness for him. She turned down enough offers to make Almacks unnecessary. She only wanted Jimmy right from the start. She'd fallen in love with him when he came here once. She was only about sixteen. None of us ever knew they'd even met."

~

Sir Timothy and Jimmy's return caused a stir. Following Sir Timothy's travelling carriage was a brand new coach with four magnificent matched dappled grey horses pulling it. On the coach were three men in livery. Amelia and Caroline gasped as they recognised their family uniform. However, the outfits were brand new. It brought admiring gasps of astonishment from the family. As the entourage arrived back, the family group happened to be ambling through the front gardens.

Jim grinned as he introduced the three new men to his mother and the rest of the family. They were three more ex-soldiers, brothers who, due to injury, had fallen on hard times. Grayson, Wesley, and Maxwell Remington would join the growing clan at Pittford Manor. Jim left the carriage in their care and directed them around the back to the stables.

Ned and Robbie were escorting the wandering group and welcomed home the two men. "I gather the search went well?" Ned asked.

"Oh, rather, Ned," Jimmy greeted his friend with a big grin. "Along with what we already know, Father also invested in the Reed Gold Mines. And that was before they had even turned a sod. Apparently, he had a mutual friend to one Conrad Reed, the fellow who found the first gold in North Carolina. So I suppose Father invested with some knowledge. They, too, are a gold-making concern, a huge one. Apparently, Father had set up a new bank account at Schroder's Bank and then forgotten about it. He probably had done it while half-drunk or, more likely, half-sober. Anyway, all of the dividends and share payments have been building in that account for over forty years. There was money there all the time. He was loaded and didn't even know it. There's some £80,000 in there already. And it is just as well, as he would have spent the lot on hair-brained schemes and more gambling." He turned to Alexe. "As I intend for us to visit often now, I bought us the best travelling coach that money can buy. The children have their own seat. It even has a fold-up footrest facility that you can lie down and stretch out. The coachman and grooms are undercover, too, with a foldable hood, and can get out of the weather. I have bought more horses too. There is now a team of horses at each of the staging posts between us and there. I like greys, so they are all grey teams. I also ordered some new livery. Like it, Mother?"

Without waiting for a reply, Jimmy turned and took Alexe's hands. "My darling, we have everything we need already; that is just each other and our children, but, my darling heart, now we really can assist Sam in his project. I'll try to buy back some of the lands Father sold and really throw ourselves into this in a huge way." He saw Robbie's face, and smiling, he said, "No, Perry can keep Blackberry Farm. It was never that productive, and I like him close. We have been entrusted with an astounding fortune, my beloved. God has let us become keepers of his money so we can use His wealth to help so many more."

While still standing on the lawn, Alexe wrapped her arms around his neck in front of everyone. "As long as I have you, Jimmy, that's all I wish for." She proceeded to ignore her Mother's protests and kiss her husband. She drew back and said, "I married you when you were poor because I don't care about money. I care about you. I always have."

"Alexandra, some decorum, please," cried her mother, "James, please, not in front of everyone." Sophie huffed, obviously upset that no one listened to her. "Caroline, these young people have no respect for what's acceptable."

Caroline herself was trying hard not to laugh. Tim caught her eye, and she saw a twinkle of humour he was not able to completely hide.

Robbie then decided that it was some time since Amelia had been kissed, and he proceeded to rectify this situation. If it was good enough for a Viscount, then a Baron's heir could kiss his wife, too.

Ned looked at Christina. "If they can, why not us too?"

Christina giggled as she walked into his waiting arms. Ned silenced her chuckle with a passionate kiss, too. Christina wrapped her arms around Ned's neck and drew as close as she could.

"Oh, dear! Oh, dear, really, all of you?" Sophie gasped at the duke kissing the duchess on her front lawn. "This really won't do."

Tim caught Caroline's smiling face again, but he felt for his wife's embarrassment. "Oh enough, all of you! You three boys should know better. If Gerry were here, he'd sort you out," he said laughingly to the trio of forty-plus-year-old men, each still embracing their wives.

Ned finally came up for air. "Actually, Sir Timothy, if Gerry were here, he'd do the same to Annabella. He's even more smitten than us. We are always catching them." Ned chuckled when he finally released Christina from his embrace. He still kept her tucked under his arm.

Tim sounded angry but was secretly trying to stop chuckling, He harrumphed! "And Gerry seemed to have more sense than that the rest of you. Anyone would think you are all seventeen again and not peers of the realm and in your forties. Come along inside, and we'll tell you the rest," Tim said with a big grin on his face. He really wanted to clasp Sophie and do the same to her.

"There's more?" Amelia asked as she finally pulled herself reluctantly from her husband's arms.

"A bit more, but wait until we get inside for that," Tim said.

The three romantic couples ambled inside behind the three older people. Sir Tim had an older lady on each arm; they led the way into the drawing room and rang for tea.

The tea tray arrived shortly afterwards. The nine were talking about their children until the staff departed. As the door closed behind the butler, Tim explained the last discovery. "This is about Horace's conviction for 'Embezzlement of Government Funds'. Apparently, Horace must have had a whisper that the crash of 1825 was likely to occur. So, the year before, he moved a single Government account from the Bank of England to Schroder's Bank in London. This bank had only started twenty years before, and it was considered a non-trustworthy company. He transferred the funds he had access to into a new account under the Government's name, not his own, and added a few of the other dignitaries as people who could access monies. They were the same names as on the original Bank of London one, so in reality, he didn't actually do much wrong, except he did do it without permission and forgot to tell the other signatories. The money was not lost in the crash the next year when the Bank of London found itself short of money, and his actions eventually gave the Government the funds it needed to see it through. In essence, you can say he actually saved the Government. Again, his drinking problem got in the way. It must have addled his memory. He forgot the name of the bank. Many banks failed, and others started. Over six hundred companies shut their doors in a short space of time. Horace must have forgotten which one he'd invested in. When I read the court papers, he kept saying it was Fry's Bank, but it was Schroder's Bank. There were so many banks before the crash that it's really quite excusable. What with all the names like Fry's, Thorntons, Everett and Co, Rochester, and Baldock, it's no wonder he became confused. Even I get confused with the Bank of London or the Bank of England. In a way, I feel a bit sorry for him. The Government had enough funds for some years, but it was after he'd been in prison for some three years, and therefore now sober, that he remembered it was Schroder's Bank. He directed them where to find the funds. Lady Caroline, I have made sure his name has posthumously been cleared of embezzlement."

"Thank you, Sir Timothy, for the children's sake and, therefore, yours too, as they are both your in-laws. I'm glad. But he was still a drunkard. Jimmy and our butler Vince will vouch for the state he would get himself into." She turned to Amelia. "Sorry, love, but he was. I wouldn't say that out of this room, but you all know everything else," Caroline said without grief or anger.

"Mother, I saw what the rum did to Cyrus and also what he was like when he could get any. It wasn't pleasant. You will get no condemnation from me, Mother," Amelia said.

Christina met Ned's eyes, but they stayed silent. She had finally confided in him about the abuse she, too, had suffered at the hands of an alcoholic husband.

Small cries of the three hungry babies disturbed the afternoon's peace. Amelia and Christina made their apologies and left the others together.

The maids had changed them and brought them to their mothers for their feed.

The two women sat chatting while they fed the babies in the privacy of the special room. Little Teddy was fast catching up to the twins in size. There was only a bit over six weeks between them.

Christina said that they had the whole story and that Jimmy was now able to move forward finally. She was thrilled that all had turned out so well. She knew that they would have to head over and visit Danny and Sam. She had yet to meet them and was somewhat anxious.

Amelia assured her that she had no need to be. "They, too, love the Lord, and they are wonderful Christina, absolutely wonderful. It was like meeting family. I loved living with them so much. You know Danny is married to Robbie's sister? So, in reality, they are now my family too."

Amelia was still in awe that Christina could feed the two babies at once.

"It took some getting used to, but it's easy now. The two pillows help greatly."

After half an hour, the maids returned and removed the three sleeping children again. The ladies adjusted themselves and then returned to their families.

Christina walked to Ned as she entered and spoke privately to him. He nodded, then turned to the group and broke the news. "Dear friends, our visit has been one of the most interesting and exciting I could ever imagine. Fortunately, I can guarantee any visit to the Castle will not be anywhere as gripping. No emergency births or discoveries of lost fortunes. However, you are all invited whenever you wish. Robbie, Milla, as you are virtually free agents at the moment, come in the New Year for an extended stay." Ned gave one of his devastating heart-melting smiles. "Do you mind, Sir Tim?"

Tim laughed. "As if it would matter. They'll go anyway. I'm surprised they came home from Jimmy's at all. They seemed to be having too much fun there." It was said with good humour and a laugh in his voice. "Who knew that dusting and scrubbing could be so much fun?"

Ned turned to Robbie. "We'll be at Dan's, Rob. No, sorry, I should say, Sam's place at Meldon Hall for a couple of weeks, so if the Baptism of our godchild is on during that time, we'll still be here."

"We'll sort it for then, Ned," Robbie said.

"Thank you, that would be wonderful. Now, I also have a gift for my only goddaughter. Amelia, I have missed many of her birthdays, and as she's now too old for dolls, I had something made for her in Sydney. I'd like to give it to her tonight at dinner before we leave." Ned pulled a blue velvet bag from his pocket and passed it to Amelia.

She opened it and tipped the contents into her hand. A gold chain and a heart-shaped pendant sat in Amelia's hand. The blue of the topaz stone was precisely the shade of Essie's eyes, and it had a small diamond sitting on top. "Oh, Neddie, it's beautiful. She'll love it." She held it up for all to see, then carefully slid it back into the bag and handed it back to Ned.

~

Dinner that evening was a joyful event. After dessert was cleared and the meal completed, Ned stood and made an announcement. The children turned to look at the fair-haired giant they had all come to love.

"Miss Esther, over the past years, I have missed your birthday at least six times and so wish to make up for it. I could have posted this in one of our many letters, but I wished to give you this personally. I brought you something made in Australia, just as you were. Something for you to wear and remember you are loved. Even though I now have my own little girl, you will always be special to me, to all of us, actually. This is just to remind you of that." He walked to her chair and handed her the gift.

Amelia had dressed Essie in a gown of exactly the same shade as the stone in the necklace Ned was going to give her, knowing what was to come. Essie took the bag and untied the ribbons. She upended it and tipped it out the same way as her mother had earlier that day.

"Oh, Uncle Neddie, it's perfect," Essie gasped. She held it to her lips and kissed it. "I'll remember Uncle Ned; I'll remember forever."

Ned took it from her hands and clasped it around her neck. He then kissed the top of her head and went to sit back down. "You can hug me later, poppet."

"No! Now, Uncle Neddie!" Essie was up and in his arms in a moment. On the way back to her chair, Essie met her mother's eyes with her own. Both were filled with tears. Happy tears fell with joy.

Robbie slid his arm around Amelia's shoulder. "What's wrong, love? Are you not happy?"

Amelia turned to Robbie and cupped his face with her hands. "Oh my darling Robbie, I'm so very happy; these are happy tears, my darling Rob. I have absolutely everything I want. God heard my prayers and answered every one of them, especially about you." She leaned over and kissed him. "You, my darling husband, are quite literally the man of my dreams."

Robbie, regardless of who was watching, gathered his beloved into his arms and, drew her to his heart and kissed away Amelia's tears.

A Lady in Irons is the next book in this trilogy
Find out more about what Robbie and Amelia do
and who else comes to join their work.

ISBN: 9780645110784   eISBN:9780645441505
https://amazon.com/dp/0645110787   https://amazon.com/dp/B0BCWSXB9Z

Author's note:-

This story was inspired by a mix of my two great-great grandmothers, Sara Ellison née Watkins.

and Amelia Harlow's convict stories. But there, the similarity ends.

I do, however, know that Sara ended up with a child from either her first placement or a sailor on board the convict ship. John Ellison married her after their third child, John <u>Thomas</u>, was born. John snr brought up her first child, William, as his own. Amelia Harlow married Joseph Huff (they inspired Bill and Molly Miller), and both men were publicans in Parramatta. Later, their children married <u>Thomas</u> Ellison and Elizabeth (Betsy) Huff.

Thomas was a blacksmith in Parramatta, and he was the only one of the Ellison children to receive any official education, the others being educated at Miss Marsden's charity school. Thomas was sent to Cape's Academy in Sydney with two other boys, George Thornton and James Martin. Thomas and Betsy started the Arms of Australia Inn in Emu Plains, and it is in this inn that I have placed the Turners, Martha and Jack. This inn was the Cobb and Co coach stop on the Parramatta run; prior to that, Thomas and Betsy had one at Linden named Ellison's Pinch Toll Bar. It was reclaimed for the railway.

Arms Of Australia Inn, Emu Plains 2009

For more of Hetty Walker and Martha Turner's stories,
watch for 'The Vine Weaver'
(Martha Turner spent six months there recuperating)

Characters

Viscount **Horace** Pittford d Aug 38 of Pittford Manor Aylesford
m **Lady Caroline**
    #1**Jimmy** Westaweller b 1800 m 7 November 1837 Alexandra Styles (Alexe)
        #1 Robert (**Bobbie**)James Westaweller b 7 Aug 38 -on 1st wedding anniversary
        #2 Alexandra (**Lexie**) Amelia b 9 July 1840
        #3 James John (**JJ**) Timothy 9 November 1842 (b after story finished)
    #2**Amelia Mary West** b 1804 Aylesford Kent.
        m1 1829 owner/husband – Cyrus Black – brother Erastus
Convicted 1827 – aged 23 – Shipped on "Morley" 1828
        Dept Nov 1834 Arrived back in Easter /March 1835
        #1 Esther (**Essie**) Martha Ruth West Black b 9 May 1830
m2 22 Oct 1835 **Robert Styles,**
        #1 Timothy(**Timo**) Robert James Styles b 11 August 1836
        #2 **Eliza** Anne Caroline b 6 Nov 1839
        #3 Edward (**Teddy**) Christian Ralph Daniel b 14/10/1842 bp 6/11/42

Mary Adams, the other convict lady, owner/ husband, James McTavish at Castlereagh
Dr **Reid**, Dr on the 'Morley – convict ship

John (Jack) **Turner** b 1800 Transported 1820
Martha Turner b 1800 (Pa and Maa) -Arms Of Australia, Emu Plains,
  #1 Marcus (called **Marc**), b 1820
  #2 Alexander (**Alex**) b 1821
  #3 Jennifer Martha (**Jenna**), b 1823 m **Eddie** Lockley Dec 1841
  #4 Victoria (**Vicky**) b 7/1825
  #5 Catherine (**Cathy**), b June 24 1827
  #6 Nicholas (**Nicky**) b 26 Apr 1830
  #7 Malcolm (**Calum**) b 1832

Finn and **Maureen Murphy** family – Emu Plains
Eion b 23; Colleen b 25; Deidre b 26; Connor b 28; Brodie b 30

Major Edward (**Ned**) Grace aka Edward Lockley aka Duke of Gracemere, from Kent UK b 16/10/1799
m Dec 1841 **Christina** Meadows b 1808
  #1 Charles (**Chip**) 1/9/1842 twin
  #2 **Sarah** 1/9/1842 twin

Bill (Bill) Miller and
Molly Miller (Par and Ma) "Rear Admiral Duncan Inn"
Timmy   b 1822
Gracie   b 1824
Samuel   b 1828
Ellen   b 1830

<u>Charles</u> **John Lockley** b March 1800 and d 27April, Easter 1870 *Dad John Lockley m Mum Elle Staverly d 2/9/1855 m2 1846 Richard Childs d 1855*
m Feb 1820 <u>**Sally**</u> (Sarah Shannon) **McCarthy** (45) (Dar and Mama) '<u>Jolly Sailor</u>' Sally's mother:- Shannon McCarthy *parents Eamon (Edward) and Nioiclín(Nicola) O'Shane. Ireland*

Charlie John **b Nov 1820** m Nov 1841 **Gracie Miller** b 1823
Eddie (Edward John) b 16/10.1821
m Dec 4 1841 **Jenna** (8)- Jennifer Martha Turner
#1 Edward (**Neddie**) Charles Gerald and b 15 Aug 1842
#2 Christina (**Tina**) Sarah Martha b 15 Aug 1842 m Mar 1859 **Chip** Gracemere
#3 (**Liza**) Elizabeth Shannon **b 1823** m Nov 1841 **Bertie** Ellis
#4 (**Anna**) Susanna Grace b **1824** m Nov 1842 **Tim** Miller.
#5 (**Wills**) William Lockley b 20/4 /**1826** (Wills) m 14/2/1845 **Cathy Turner**
#6 **Luke** John b March **1828** m 2/8/1856 **Ellen** Miller, b 4/10/1830;

Thomas Tindale - m Margaret - blacksmith in Parramatta with Eddie
Mrs Caroline (**Caro**) **Evans,** Mr Tindale's sister (Eddie's & Tim's foster parents)
m Captain **Douglas** Evans – supply ship captain Pitt Street
Phillip b 1819 Phil
Stephen b 1821 Stevie
John b 1822

Reverend **Richard** and **Phoebe** Hill – St James Sydney (real people)
Five fostered children **Margaret**, Julia, Charity, Frederica, Mary Blenheim (fictitious)

Governor **Ralph** and **Eliza** Darling to Oct 1831 (real people)
Mother – **Ann** Dumaresq in Cheltenham, UK (real person)

John and Sadie Landon – from Sheila Hunter's book Ricky.
Amabel Landon b 1830
Sir **Timothy** Broome-Hall m to **Sophie** Broome-Hall Manor Billingshurst. West Sussex
 #1 **Robert (Robbie) Styles b 1801** m 22/10/1835 **Amelia** Black nee Westaweller
 #2 Timothy Charles (**TC**) b 1804
 #3 **Rosemarie(Rosie)** b 1807 married and pregnant
 #4 **Simeon (Sim)** b 1809
 #5 Alexandra (**Alexe**) b 1811 **m** Viscount **Jimmy Westaweller**
 #6 **Georgina (Georgie)**b 1814 (m 1833 **Danny** Garney)
              #1 **James** and +5 more. 6 children, 2 boys 4 girls
Reverend **Hugh** Williams m Nov 1835 **Miriam** Lock – eng Easter 1834
Samuel James Corbett Garney (Lord Garney/Viscount Clarestow then 6th Earl Meldon)
Meldon Hall-mother Anne Corbett – served time West's farm arr Royal Admiral 1792
#1 **Daniel** James Corbett Garney b 1803 Sydney
m1 1824 **Vanessa** Comfrey
              #1 **Jo**-Anne b 1824
              #2 **Lucy**-Anne – b 1826
              #3 **Mary-Anne –** b 1828
              #4 **Edmund** Daniel James b 29/5/1831 (m 1852 **Essie** Black b 9/5/1830)
m2 2 July 1833 **Georgina** Styles – 6 more children 2 boys 4 girls
              #1 **James** Samuel Daniel Garney b March 1834 West Sussex
                   +5 more. 6 children, 2 boys 4 girls
Staff at Pittford Manor
Edgar & Bertha Fernwood, - Gardener soldier and cook
Vincent and Mildred Eggleton; Butler and Housekeeper at Pittford Manor
Albert Winterbottom - Tack room and stable hand.
Cuthbert Mainwaring - new estate manager - at Pittford Manor (son Albert, badly burned-
Taught Jack O'Neill the job)
Maywyn- dairymaid
Grayson, Wesley and Maxwell Remington. Brothers, carriage drivers/footmen

NOTES:-
The Convict ship, *Morley*, actually went to Tasmania on that trip.

Real People

Reverend **Richard** and **Phoebe** Hill – St James Sydney (real people)
NB Richard died of a heart attack on May 30th 1836
The children are fictitious
Governor Bourke
And Deas-Thompson (Gov Bourke's daughter
Governor **Ralph** and **Eliza** Darling to Oct 1831 (real people)
Mother – **Ann Dumaresq** in Cheltenham, UK (real person)
Elizabeth Fry and Philanthropy group of trilogy (up to 20,000 volunteers at its height)

And others…

i loved you at your darkest

- *Romans 5:8*

Bibliography

Philanthropy
https://dictionaryofsydney.org/entry/charity_and_philanthropy

Eliza Darling
https://en.wikipedia.org/wiki/Eliza,_Lady_Darling

Betsy Bourke
https://stjohnsonline.org/bio/elizabeth-bourke/
died in May 1832 after only six months in the colony. She was never well enough to make any visits, and her daughter Anne stepped in as first lady.

Female Factory Parramatta
1 http://www.parragirls.org.au/female-factory.php
2 https://historyandheritage.cityofparramatta.nsw.gov.au/blog/2015/07/28/the-second-parramatta-female-factory-1818-1848
3 http://www.parragirls.org.au/female-factory.php
4 http://www.parramattafemalefactoryfriends.com.au/wp-content/uploads/2014/04/PARRAMATTA_FEMALE_FACTORY_HISTORY_FAST_FACTS.pdf
5 https://www.records.nsw.gov.au/archives/collections-and-research/guides-and-indexes/female-factory-parramatta

Matron Gordon
1 https://historyandheritage.cityofparramatta.nsw.gov.au/research-topics/female-factory/matron-ann-gordon
2 https://adb.anu.edu.au/biography/gordon-ann-12943

Transport of innocent girls
https://trove.nla.gov.au/newspaper/article/2216828?searchTerm=benevolent%20society

Grantley Hall, Ripon, North Yorkshire (used for Pittford Manor description)
https://www.grantleyhall.co.uk/?utm_source=mybusiness&utm_medium=organic

Hans Christian Andersen
https://en.wikipedia.org/wiki/Fairy_Tales_Told_for_Children._First_Collection.

USA Oil History
https://en.wikipedia.org/wiki/History_of_the_petroleum_industry_in_the_United_States#Appalachian_Basin

Gold in USA
https://en.wikipedia.org/wiki/Carolina_Gold_Rush
https://en.wikipedia.org/wiki/Reed_Gold_Mine

Schroders Bank started 1804 London
https://en.wikipedia.org/wiki/List_of_oldest_banks_in_continuous_operation
(story of government funds is made up)

A First Fleet Convict Story 1788

A First Fleet story with the descriptions taken directly from the Journal of Doctor Author Bowes Smith who was the doctor on board the Lady Penrhyn.

Gentle Annie Soames

Her dreams lead to unexpected outcomes. An Australian First Fleet story.

Annie Soames is a girl beloved by the community but not afraid to voice her desires. That leads to trouble, illicit love, and a world turned upside down.

Oliver Quilpie, the recently married Marquess, discovers his arranged union is not to his taste; he is drawn to his wife's companion. Unfortunately, he is unable to keep his hands off her. For revenge, Annie mimics his every move while riding but is dressed as a highwayman. However, she had now fallen in love with him. This action finally leads to her arrest and transportation to a faraway land.

After some years, Oliver's wife dies, and his thoughts turn to Annie. He seeks to find her, but she has vanished. He is horrified to discover she was transported to New South Wales as a convict on the *Lady Penrhyn*. He follows with a shipload of supplies on the *Kitty*. Will Annie want to see him?

ISBN 9780645441574   ISBN ebook 9781923097063
July 2024

The Hunter to Macquarie Collection 1795-1822

When Upon Life's Billows

Sydney 1795-1821 - Governor John Hunter

Captain John Hunter was born to a life at sea. The wind blows where no man knows, and John is caught up in the tempest. Although wrecking his ship, the *HMS Sirius*, in 1790, he became the second Governor of the rough and filthy penal settlement of New South Wales. He always seems to be in the wrong place at the wrong time, trusting the wrong people.

Helena Rosedale is not a typical female convict. She fights tooth and nail to stop the men from abusing her. She gains the name of Helena the Hellcat.

Crispin Milroy is alone in the world and one of the new Governor's security detail. Can he win the fair lady's heart? Life in 1795 in Sydney Cove is raw at best. Food is scarce, and disease often ravages the settlement. Life throws everything except death at these three, yet somehow, they survive. Why does John trust this young couple when others betray him?

What trials must Helena and Crispin endure to make their new lives in this raw town bearable? How can John ease their path?

ISBN: 9780645783339   ebook ISBN: 9780645783346
Coming 2025

Saddler's Song

London 1790s to Parramatta 1840s

George Ellis is a tanner's son living on the outskirts of London. When disease takes his family. Alone and hurting, he seeks to find a new life for himself. Hearing from a friend about the possibility of setting up a business in New South Wales, he sells up and leaves all he knows. His beloved violin is his most valuable item, and his talent for making beautiful music is hidden from all but a few.

Ben Parker is a saddler, like George; he is also alone in the world. Ben also sells up to move to the new colony. The two young men meet and combine their skills to start afresh in a new world. During the journey out, George's skill as a violinist is revealed. On arrival, they find accommodation with a family with many lovely daughters. Two of these girls steal their hearts, but how will the business survive in an animal-starved land where access to leather is limited? What is the saddler's song?

ISBN : 9780645783353   eISBN: 9780645783360
Coming 2025

Tuppence to Pass

London 1800s to Parramatta 1820s - Governor Lachlan Macquarie

Josh Callan is a London lad who makes the best of the life that has been dealt to him. Stealing from the man who killed his father gives the family a change of direction. Josh is arrested, but the judge belittles him, saying he's not worth tuppence. He is transported to the penal colony of Sydney as a convict just as **Governor Macquarie's** term starts. He proves his worth and falls on his feet, becoming the Governor's groom and confidante.

Life in the Colonial town opens opportunities they could never have dreamed about in England, but can Josh find his niche?

Where will this strange friendship take Josh and his family?

ISBN : 9781923097070   eISBN: 9781923097087
Coming 2025

His Majesty's Pageboy
London to Emu Plains, Australia, in the 1800s

Jack Turner was born into a life of pomp and privilege that was not rightfully his. He was brought to the royal court for his own protection. By the age of ten, he was King George the Third's pageboy and known as Lord John. For years, Jack roils against the immorality of society and the shallowness of people; then, he meets an unspoiled young girl amongst the mire of humanity whose purity stands out. He is unable to pursue her before his life hits a wall.

Martha Alexander is the daughter of a wealthy shipping merchant. She has been presented to London's second tier of society, where she meets the young man of her dreams. She is expected to marry well, and Lord John sets her heart fluttering. However, her father's drinking shatters her future. He was made to sign all his possessions away while drunk, unknowingly including his daughter. Refusing a forced marriage changes her life. How do these two end up as convicts in Australia?

Paperback ISBN 9781923097308   eISBN 978192309792
Coming 2026

Far From the Whispering Sheoaks
Set in Australia in the 1820s

Fanny Little was in the wrong place doing something she thought was legal. Her actions see her arrested, tried and banished. She is assigned from the female prison to ex-soldier Gordon McKenzie and soon finds herself in a despicable and humiliating situation of being sold in the public marketplace.

Phil Bentley is a man running from his jealous uncle, and he finds solace in a secluded farm half a world away. With the community on their side, can Phil save Fanny from Gordon's vile abuse? Why is their relationship destined to court controversy? And who is Jas? Why does Gordon wish to harm the child? Will they ever escape the shadows that are chasing them?

Paperback ISBN 9781923097315   eISBN9781923097322
Coming 2026

Bound Down in Iron Chains
Set in Australia in the 1820s

Howard Marlow was a studious and honest London bookkeeper. He is asked to help a friend's brother, and he finds himself arrested, convicted and transported. Who are the men involved in the Cato Conspiracy? How does he become involved with some of the worst criminals in the penal colony of New South Wales?

Naomi Buckingham is a convict maid assigned to a man who has no respect for women. Rather than used as a cleaner as she expects, her duties include warming his bed. She wants to escape his oppressive household but has no one to turn to but his new accountant. Can she trust him? Howard is assigned to a retired soldier and gets tricked into using his skills to keep a double set of books and therefore, avoid paying the extra taxes on his boss's illicit rum profits. Being new to the colony, he doesn't know who he can trust.

Naomi turns to him after she overhears a violent altercation between them. Can he use his brains to save them both?

Coming 2026

Unlikely Convict Ladies Trilogy 1792-1840s
Dancing to her Own Tune
Co-authored by Sheila Hunter and Sara Powter
Sydney 1790s to England 1830s

Annie White is released after serving seven years as a convict in Sydney. She gets a visitor who, with his help, she can start a baking business. She is then asked to assist another sick man, **Sam** Corbett. Annie nurses him back to health, and a relationship develops. They settle into a life together, barely making ends meet; she realises she's expecting a child. Sam has his past laid bare and must adjust to the revelations. They both must face their accusers and find that the answers to their questions are not what they thought. Their life experiences seem to cling to them, and unable to shake them off, they end up back in England. They must face their ghosts and discover they are not who they think they are. How can they turn their anger and spite into love and forgiveness? The Dance of Life goes on.

ISBN 9780645110715   ISBN9780645110722

Long-listed in the Historical Fiction Company Competition 2022

Amelia's Tears
Parramatta 1828 – England 1840s

Amelia Westaweller awaits her assignment in the Parramatta Female Prison. Forced to leave the relative safety of gaol, she is assigned and now faces her worst nightmare. A foul man claims her and makes her life a living hell. Then, her world goes black. A glimmer of hope arises when she hears from her brother, Jim, who has enlisted a friend to help her. She writes to Jim, pouring out her heart and telling him of the horrors of her new life. He encourages her to stay firm in her faith. All she can do is pray. When Major **Ned** Grace, her brother's friend, enters her life in Parramatta, he starts to ease her path. Things have changed, as now she has a child in tow. How can Amelia forge a new life for herself? What man could want her with her background and a child at her side? Who is the gentleman who turns her tears of sadness into tears of great joy?

ISBN: 9780645110739   eISBN: 978-0-6451107-4-6 Hard Cover ISBN 979-842061-7953
https://amazon.com/dp/0645110736   https://amazon.com/dp/B09SS855BR

A Lady in Irons
England 1800s – Parramatta 1808+

Katy Harrington is mourning the death of her husband after he died in a shooting accident. Barely coping, she awaits the birth of their child. If it's a girl, she must hand the family home to her husband's brother. The day after giving birth to a daughter, she and her daughter are left on the side of a road. She collapses and is found by someone she thought had died in a fire ten years before. **Perry White**, badly scarred himself, nurses her back to health. They marry and move in with her widowed friend, Mary.

After some years, she discovers her husband and friend in each other's arms. Now living in a love triangle, she flees. Grasping the only straw available, she intentionally gets arrested and is sent to a colony far away. By doing this, her marriage can be annulled.

What happens in the Colony is different from what she expects. Governor Macquarie comes to her rescue, but what of Perry and her children?

ISBN: 9780645110784   eISBN:9780645441505
https://amazon.com/dp/0645110787   https://amazon.com/dp/B0BCWSXB9Z

The Convict Birthstain Collection 1830-1840s
NO MORE, MY *Love*
Hunter Valley, NSW 1820s

Jess Elkin is distraught when tragedy ravages her family. She becomes the victim of a carriage accident and is nursed back to health by the driver, **Marcus Ryan**. Marcus was not expecting to fall in love. Yet, when Jess's fortunes suddenly turn for the worse, Marcus must decide how far he will go to pursue her. As time passes in Newcastle, Australia, Marcus must take a business trip and is taken by pirates. Jess is left wondering if her will keep his promise to return to her… Will she ever see him alive again?

ISBN: 9780645441536   eISBN 9780645441581
Long-listed in the Historical Fiction Company Competition 2023
https://amazon.com/dp/0645441538   https://amazon.com/dp/B0BSBH143Q

The Vine Weaver
Hawkesbury River area 1820s+
New Beginnings and Old Threats

In the 1820s, Australia, **Joel and Hetty Walker** live on a secluded farm on the Hawkesbury River, which becomes a healing haven for the protection of young convict women. A series of events brings **Fran Rea** to Hetty's attention, and she is taken to the farm. Fran and Hetty develop a cottage industry under the compassionate eye of farmhand **Hector Macdougal;** Hector's loving words change lives. It is to him that Fran turns when threatened.

The vines now must draw them close to survive the future revelations, and of those, there are many.

ISBN: 9780645441512   eISBN: 9780645441529
Long-listed in the Historical Fiction Company Competition 2023
https://amazon.com/dp/0645441511   https://amazon.com/dp/B0C6Z552Y2
The story continues in Scotch at The Rocks…

Scotch at The Rocks

Glasgow, Scotland, early 1800s to The Rocks, Sydney 1830s

Orphaned children Brodie Stewart and Heather Anderson live on Glasgow's streets. Although hungry, somehow they survive and keep out of trouble. Heather finds a job and looks to be settled; things go pear-shaped for them both. Eventually, they marry by declaration, yet even that gets messed up, and they are both arrested soon after they make their vow. In 1838, they were transported to Sydney as convicts. Heather arrives within weeks of Brodie, and they are assigned close to each other. They are now living on the docklands in Sydney, called The Rocks. They now have to forge a new life halfway across the world from their homeland.

Adventures abound, and Brodie gets press-ganged. While he's away, Heather's life changes and soon, she's officially selling Scotch Whisky at a shop in The Rocks.

You can take a Scot out of Scotland, but where did the Scotch come from?

ISBN 9780645441550 ebook 9781923097001 Large Print 9781923097254

Waiting at the Sliprails

The Bathurst Road 1830s

A Convict's Tale

Bea Dawes's term of conviction nears an end, and she has few options other than marriage to a stranger or going on the street.

Jack Barnes, the hired drover, wants a wife. Bea accepts his offer; then, she discovers that he could be gone for months, leaving her alone with **Billy and Netty**, part of the tribe of an Aboriginal tribe who live on his secluded farm. Bea learns to love her husband and also this wonderful aboriginal couple.

Drought ravages the farm, and Jack must hit the long paddock with the flock. In his absence, a visitor arrives, threatening to destroy everything she has worked so hard for. Can Bea touch her heart? Can she cope? Will the drought ever end? And when will Jack return?

ISBN: 9780645441543   eISBN: 9781923097032

August 2023

Convict Shadows of the Past

Two Jennifers, two hundred years apart

Eight year old, **Jenny** Kellow learns of her convict family history and discovers that she was named after a convict from nearly two hundred years ago. Her grandfather's stories inspire her to dig deeper into her ancestors' convict past. From her grandfather, she hears stories of bushrangers, convicts, and life in the infant colony of Parramatta. She sets about retracing the footsteps of her convict great-great-great-grandmother to honour her. Jenny's search starts with microfiche back in the 60s, and she learns about the small tin mining town in Cornwall and the production of a cheese that sets London afire. She discovers her ancestor, **Jennifer Kellow,** has brought these cheese-making skills to Parramatta, where she taught others her craft. Echoes of the past can still be heard if you know where to listen.

Who was the first Jennifer, and what does she have to do with cheese? Why is she so elusive? Did Jenny's ancestor, Jennifer, ever see those two small crosses carved into the bricks of the Female Factory? Would Jenny ever find out her ancestor's story?

ISBN: 9780645783315   ISBN ebook 9780645783322

A NaNoWriMo 2022 book winner

January 2024

In Defence of Her Honour

London 1800s to Parramatta 1819

Bill Miller had been raised and educated with the sons of the family. The youngest, Bert, had been his best friend. However, jealousy intervenes when Bill's excellent schoolwork curtails their friendship. He wins a scholarship and enters Oxford University. When Bill's father, the old butler, dies unexpectedly, Bert insists that Bill take over the position, but it's more to oppress him. Bert's jealousy grows and festers. Now looking for a way to rid themselves of their new butler, a ruckus ensues, and Bill is arrested for assaulting Bert. The housekeeper and her daughter, **Molly Ross**, vouch for him, but it's too late; Bill has been arrested and sentenced to be transported. With Bill gone, Molly now needs to defend herself from Bert. After hitting him with a pan, she is arrested and sent to Sydney. Bill and Molly arrive with letters of introduction and compensation from Bert's father. Soon, they will be running the best inn in Parramatta with an endorsement from the governor.

ISBN 9780645441567   ISBN ebook 9781923097049

April 2024

I can't stop Tomorrow
Irish Famine 1840s to Avoca Beach, Australia

Escaping bigotry and prejudice in Ireland, the **O'Shane** family lives on a secluded farm on the west coast of Ireland. The potato blight soon decimates their farm. It's always darkest before dawn, and the two remaining girls cling to the hope of a new life. With the kindness of strangers, the eldest girls, **Clare** and **Kerry O'Shane**, head to their cousin, Sal Lockley, in Parramatta, Australia. A new, wonderful life awaits them both. **Shéamus Connor** is the annoying teenage boy who reluctantly draws Clare's affection. However, living in a convict town means ruffians abound.

John Moore is an angry and troubled Irishman, content to live alone on another secluded farm until he discovers Clare and two other lads need rescuing.

Can John protect her from the pain inflicted by an evil world?

Can Shéamus find his lost love who had fled?

ISBN: 9780645441598   ISBN ebook 9781923097056

October 2024

Madeline's Boy
England 1830s to New South Wales 1840

All is not straightforward when money and a title are involved.

Madeline Brougham is asked to care for her best friend's orphaned son when his life is in danger. **Christopher Downes** is the pawn between a greedy, unscrupulous uncle and his inheritance. Maddie must do everything she can to keep him safe, including moving halfway around the globe to take Chip to his guardian, Major Humphrey Downes, in the Australian Corps in Sydney. Humphrey's best friend, another soldier, **Major Tim Hinds**, meets Maddie, and with the support of these two men, a chase around the colony ensues. Will Maddie and Tim be able to find happiness together?

Can the three adults keep Chip safe until he's old enough to claim his inheritance?

ISBN: 9780645783308   ISBN ebook 9781923097094

Dec 2024

Jam or Marmalade for Tea
England 1820s to New South Wales 1825 (Governor Brisbane Era)

Martha Hamilton is the eldest of four orphans struggling to survive on their own. Caught stealing, she is tried, convicted, and transported to New South Wales. With her family gone, she becomes despondent. Life holds no meaning for her, and The ocean waves look inviting.

Captain Guy Manning is a frustrated and injured redcoat soldier returning to Sydney to take up a new assignment. He notices Martha trying to jump overboard and rescues her. How do two cats bring them together?

A convict ship is no place for romance, and she's far too young anyway, isn't she?

Can Guy save her and forge a life together for them? What connections does he have to try and save her siblings? Why is marmalade important for their future?

Paperback ISBN 9781923097933   eISBN9781923097285

A NaNoWriMo 2023 book winner

October 2025

A 100-year, six-part Australian Colonial series

The Lockleys of Parramatta 1800-1900

Hands upon the Anvil

A blacksmith's life and love are more than work

Parramatta 1830s

Eddie Lockley's parents were transported for their crimes. Can a steadfast lad rise above his origins and guide others to succeed in a land of opportunity?
Ten-year-old Eddie longs to help his mum and dad. Living in a convict town with his family, the keen youngster has been working with the local blacksmith since his sixth birthday. But when a lieutenant doesn't stop abusing his older brother, the young boy yearns for the day when he can stand up and end the torment. Though he's thrilled when his mentor offers to send him off to learn his letters, Eddie fears he won't be around to watch his sibling's back. But as he takes on the biggest adventure of his life, the brave believer soon discovers God is looking out for everyone he loves. Does this young man in the making have what it takes to change everything for the better?

ISBN 9780994578235   Ebook ISBN 978-0-9945782-5-9   Hardcover 9798496177368

Released 2021

https://amazon.com/dp/0994578237   https://amazon.com/dp/B08TB51L19

Out Where The Brolgas Dance

Gold is found, and so is love

Parramatta 1840s

How can a question change so many people?

It's the 1840s, and discoveries across the Blue Mountains continue. Major Mitchell's new road is complete, and towns are planned and being built. Abundant land is available for those who want it.
William "Wills" Lockley, 18, has laid a solid foundation for a respectable career as a blacksmith, but the Lockley lust for adventure flows deeply within his veins. He dreads the monotony of work at the blacksmith's forge and yearns for adventure in a new frontier. Wills meets six Englishmen (*Coping with what is now known as PTSD*) who have the means to make his dreams come true. What they discover changes the Colony and their lives forever. Gold fever ensues. In the West, Wills has to deal with an uncertain romance. Does she even want him?

ISBN 9780994578242 Ebook ISBN 978-0-9945782-6-6 Hardcover ISBN 9798755445504
LP ISBN 9781923097155

Released 2021

https://amazon.com/dp/0994578245   https://amazon.com/dp/B08T6NS3XX

Diamonds in the Dirt

Diamonds, love and money… but there is much more to life.

Parramatta 1850s

Luke Lockley, the youngest Lockley son, has completed University, and his life has no direction. No job, no money, and no love. Desperately alone, he prays for guidance. How can Luke trust that God has a plan for him if he can't even find a job? He does the only thing he can … he prays. Within a week, life has changed … oh, how it has changed as his brother Wills turns up with a suggestion. Would Luke be interested in joining the expedition with John Evans? **Reverend William Clarke** needs assistance on a Government Mineral Survey. The challenge, adventure and finds are life-changing for many. However, it gives Luke meaning, purpose and direction. The condition of his heart problems also takes a turn. Can he walk away?

ISBN:9780994578273 Ebook ISBN: 978-0-9945782-8-0 Hard cover ISBN 979-8788011141

Released 2022

https://amazon.com/dp/099457827X   https://amazon.com/dp/B09NH1MLXZ

The Earl's Shadow

Who or what is the 'shadow'? How does it affect so many?

<u>Parramatta 1860s</u>

Charles Lockley is the Earl of Coxheath. He spent his youth as a convict in Parramatta and had no idea he was an Earl. He had minimal education and few social skills. His eldest son, **Charlie,** is no different.

Now faced with his own mortality, Charles has to work out how to live the remainder of his life after a near-death experience. He is called to step way out of his comfort zone in London. His action will change the world for many. The echoes from the past still haunt Charlie. London is calling the family, and they can't postpone the trip. How does the Cobb and Co. coach driver **Jim Leslie** fit in? And precisely what is *'The Earl's Shadow'* that he speaks about? What happens if the 'Shadow' is gone?

ISBN: 9780645110708 Ebook ISBN 978-0-9945782-9-7
Released June 2022
https://amazon.com/dp/0645110701   https://amazon.com/dp/B0B158SKSK

Once a Jolly Swagman

An old black Billy Can contain the secrets of an incredible life

An Australian Historical Novel

Set in Parramatta 1870s and Kent, UK

Rick Lockley, battling his family's expectations, runs away to find himself. **Jack**, a jolly swagman, takes him under his care. Even after years together, Rick knows little about the old man.

On his death, Jack leaves Rick his precious billy can; the contents reveal Jack's identity. Stunned, Rick must travel to England to finalise Jack's wishes. There, he uncovers Jack's life of love, betrayal and a link to his own family. Rick also discovers there is much more to learn about this enigmatic man.

ISBN 9780645110753   Ebook ISBN 978-0-6451107-6-0
Released Sept 2022
https://amazon.com/dp/0645110752   https://amazon.com/dp/B0B5JN1WCV

Jonty's Journey

Gems, Love, Artists and a Golden Lion

<u>Australia and South Africa 1880-1902</u>

Sydney Jeweller Jonty Evans' passion for gems takes him to Africa at a volatile time. He finds the diamonds he wants and is given a lion cub. Jonty is all but kidnapped. His experiences in the Transvaal plunge him into questioning everything he knows of life. Soon, nightmares haunt him. (Now known as PTSD.)

On return home, he nearly messes up his love life with **Lottie** before it even starts, and he struggles to settle. Lottie's father, **Luke** Lockley from Parramatta, takes him in hand and points him to someone who can help.

Jonty is then recalled to Africa as a liaison and reconnects with his lion, Chimbu, when he saves the life of his security detail. His life journey introduces him to the most amazing Heidelberg artists, politicians, poets, rebels, and the scapegoat soldier Harry Breaker Morant. Can Jonty bury the past and regain the peace he's lost?

ISBN 9780645110777 HC ISBN 9781923097124   Ebook ISBN: 978-0-6451107-9-1
Released Feb 2023
https://amazon.com/dp/0645110779   https://amazon.com/dp/B0BLJ7ND1Q

Australian Colonial Trilogy 1840s

By Sheila Hunter

Co-Winner of 1999 NSW Senior Citizen of the Year, In the Year of the Senior Citizen

Mattie

Coming of Age in Convict Australia

Twelve-year-old London street urchin **Mattie Paul** is convicted of petty theft and sentenced to seven years of transportation to the penal colony of Port Jackson, NSW. Peg, another female convict, takes Mattie under her wing and gives her a chance to make something of her life by teaching her to read. Mattie seizes every opportunity that comes her way. Though life is not particularly kind to her, she battles through earning her freedom, marrying and becoming a mother in her homeland. On this journey, she encounters bushrangers, is widowed, and becomes an entrepreneur in the Bathurst goldfields. She mixes with escaped convicts, but her spirit is indomitable, and she becomes a pillar and much-loved treasure of her adopted community. Mattie may be a fictional character, but her experiences are only too real and invest us in immersing ourselves in the lives of those remarkable women who helped to make Australia what it is today. *(Mattie's story continues in The Lockleys of Parramatta - bk 2+)*

ISBN 9781503252370 & ebook AISN BOOTTEDBTO

(The story continues in The Earl's Shadow & Once a Jolly Swagman)
Released 2015
https://amazon.com/dp/150325237X   https://amazon.com/dp/B00TTEDBT0

Ricky

A boy in Colonial Australia

Ricky English and his mother immigrated from England to join his father in the new Colony of Sydney. Upon arrival, there was no sign of his father. Ricky's mum uses the tiny amount of money they brought to get lodgings in a run-down building. Things go from bad to worse when his mother dies; he is thrown out of the rooms, and the caretakers confiscate all their possessions.

Ricky lives on the streets of Sydney Town as a street waif. Ricky finds safe places to sleep and befriends freed convicts who can help him survive. One day, he encounters a lost child and helps reunite her with her family. These people try to help him, but he insists on doing things his way because of his stubbornness. However, he has found a mentor and confidante. The story follows him through his life. He survives and turns his life around, helping others along the way. **(The Story continues in Jonty's Journey)**

Paperback ISBN 9780994578211   Kindle ASIN: B00MLYN6IG
Released 2014
https://amazon.com/dp/1500770574   https://amazon.com/dp/B00MLYN6IG

The Heather to The Hawkesbury

Four Scottish families brave a new life in a strange land.

Mary Macdonald and husband **Murd** and family; her brother **Fergus** MacKenzie; sister-in-law **Caro** MacLeod; cousin **Alex** Fraser and all their families who have had to emigrate from the Isle of Skye during the "Clearances."

The story follows the four families from Scotland on the ship out to the NSW colony in the 1850s. Mary does not cope with the changes and losses that occur in the first months in the colony. The other women in the family rely on her, and she nearly crumbles. The families struggle together through accidents, losses, trials, floods, and hard work and forge a strong bond with their new country. Trials, tribulations and triumphs see the four families make a firm mark in their new homeland. The immigrants from Scotland helped make Australia what it is today.

ISBN 978994578228   ebook AISN B01A21JYWQ   Large Print ISBN1533473641
Available on Amazon/Kindle & Large Print
Released 2016
https://amazon.com/dp/1503251438   https://amazon.com/dp/B01A21JYWQ

Sara's Author Bio

Sheila Hunter and Sara Powter were a passionate mother-and-daughter team of amateur genealogists. While working together on their family tree, Sheila and Sara made many captivating discoveries. The greatest of these was finding four convicts, and these four had very different perspectives. They were sent to Australia from 1792 to 1814 during the height of Convict transportation. Before her *passing* in 2002, Sheila adapted some of these histories into enchanting stories, her Australian Colonial Trilogy. Sara later had these published. A fourth she left unfinished, and this inspired her to finish it. However, before she did, **The Lockleys of Parramatta** were created. The first two in the series were completed before she completed 'Dancing to **Her Own Tune'** for her mother. (*Sheila wrote the first 30k words*)

Vividly living through the Colonial Era, these books delve further into the theme of overcoming adversity in Colonial Australia and how it developed, the demise of the Convict system and the discovery of mineral wealth.

Sara intricately weaves accurate archival data and a charming narrative to create a series of tales of faith, love, loss, and redemption.

And so, two hundred years after her family arrived in Australia, Sara continues the Australian Colonial stories started in **Lockleys of Parramatta,** followed by the **Unlikely Convict Ladies** Trilogy. **The Hunter to Macquarie Collection** and **The Convict Birthstain Collection** are all stand-alone novels. More Historical Fiction books are to follow… as they are already in the editors' queue.

See Sara's web page to keep up to date with more stories.
With an online store available for a signed copy of Sara's books.
www.sarapowter.com.au   (Australian Postage only)

Feel free to email me at
saragpowter@gmail.com
(Australian Postage only)

Feel free to email me at
saragpowter@gmail.com

Amazon Aus QR

BOOK BUB https://partners.bookbub.com/authors/6273615/edit

FACEBOOK https://www.facebook.com/profile.php?id=100063887262514

FREE Newsletter signup
https://preview.mailerlite.io/preview/41388/
sites/77987646202184961/wCAAcK

www.ingramcontent.com/pod-product-compliance
Lightning Source LLC
Chambersburg PA
CBHW031612240626
47153CB00002B/733